IN HONOR BOUND

Gerald Seymour

IN HONOR
BOUND

W · W · NORTON & COMPANY

NEW YORK   LONDON

Permission to quote from Rudyard Kipling's poems 'Gunga Din', 'The Young British Soldier',
and 'Arithmetic on the Frontier' is gratefully acknowledged to The National Trust and
Methuen Limited.

Library of Congress Cataloging in Publication Data
Seymour, Gerald.
    In honor bound.
    I. Title.
PR6069.E73416   1984   823'.914   83–25513

ISBN 0-393-01859-8

W. W. Norton & Company, Inc., 500 Fifth Avenue, New York, N.Y. 10110
W. W. Norton & Company Ltd., 37 Great Russell Street, London WC1B 3NU

1 2 3 4 5 6 7 8 9 0

To Gillian, Nicholas and James

The author gratefully acknowledges help from many sources in the researching of this novel. Every character in it, however, is purely fictional, for all that the context of it is a grim and daily reality for the people of Afghanistan.

IN HONOR BOUND

1

They had been coming back for four days.

Four crippling, painful days of tramping out a stride across the knife rock of the mountains. Brutal days because the pace was set by a guide who moved as if he were ignorant of the bitter sharp of the stone and the scree as they climbed, then descended, then climbed again. When they moved by day there was the ferocious heat of the sun. And when they travelled by night there were bruising falls and the stumbles and the cutting of the rock on their shins and knees and hands and elbows.

Going had been easier. The outward journey had been in a caravan of a hundred fighting men, and in the midst of a mule train column. The going had been the time of anticipation. Joey Dickens was not an athlete, he was not especially strong, but as Royal Air Force technicians (Maintenance) went, he was tough and fit. The pace of the outward journey had not been difficult for any of them, because the mules had been loaded down with food and weapons and ammunition and Joey Dickens and Charlie and Eddie had kept up with them without discomfort.

Now it was the coming back for Joey Dickens and for the two men who had sought him out in the pub a few miles from the helicopter station of Culdrose. Charlie and Eddie, in tailored suits and monogrammed shirts and wide knotted ties, had come to Cornwall because Joey Dickens had written in answer to a box number advertisement in an aviation weekly magazine. Over their pints, Charlie and Eddie had made Joey Dickens an offer, and because he was screaming under the burdens of a wife and two small ones and a terraced house on the Abbey National and furniture on the never-never he had accepted the offer of employment for the time of his summer leave.

In that first week of the year in a pub in the Cornish countryside, Charlie and Eddie had told of going into the wilderness of Afghanistan to carry out the mechanisms and electronic entrails of downed Soviet helicopters. All a little drunk, all a little noisy, and past eleven, and while the publican swept the cigarette stubs and dirt and plastic crisp and nut packets into heaps, Joey Dickens had clasped Charlie's hand and Eddie's hand and pledged his company. There was an envelope containing a thousand pounds in tenners that had slid from the inside pocket of Charlie's jacket to the hip pocket of Joey Dickens' jeans, there was the swift silk patter from Eddie that the valleys of Afghanistan were littered with Soviet hardware that fetched a colossal price, if it could only be lugged back out to the Pakistan border . . . Joey Dickens in the late hours had been quite captivated with the romance of digging into the guts of a Russian whirly . . .

Charlie said that he was just a businessman, and Eddie said that he was just a bottle washer. We can get there, they had both said, and we can get back, and we can find a client who'll pay through the nose, but they had to have someone with them who knew about the business end of Soviet helicopters, and they reckoned that Joey Dickens fitted the bill. It ought to be the paying off of the mortgage and the buying outright of the furniture. Charlie had said that he had a little company, and Eddie had said that Charlie had all the friends he needed for the disposal of the merchandise, and Charlie had said that he was in touch with a Brigadier in London, and Eddie muttered about under the counter, and Charlie had said that it was a piece of cake, and Eddie had said that all they were short of was a chappie who knew the guts of a whirly.

8

Nine weeks later, Charlie had brought Joey Dickens an airline ticket, return, to Islamabad/Rawalpindi.

It had taken them six days to reach the ravine. Joey Dickens had never seen such country and, to a young man from the flatlands of Lincolnshire, the ravine was something else. The ravine was a mighty fissure of the rock, and down at the base greyness and hard to see because of the camouflage paint was the broken fuselage of an Mi-24 helicopter. Close to the helicopter shell were white scrapes on the rock and black scorch squares. Joey Dickens recognised the signs of high explosive bombs and napalm canisters that had been dropped into the ravine to destroy what remained of the helicopter, but which had failed to do their work.

They parted from the caravan, left their guide on the path and edged their way down a steep gully to the floor of the ravine. The waiting in Pakistan for a helicopter carcase to be identified, and located, was forgotten. Joey's difficulties of communicating with the flash Charlie and the small talk Eddie were obliterated. The worst job had been the first: disentangling the bloated and grotesque-grown body of the pilot. Even in the cooler depth of the ravine the stench was suffocating. Joey had been violently, shudderingly sick and Eddie made a litter from a door panel and carried the body out of sight before he picked its pockets. And then, for half a day, armed with a screwdriver and a wrench and a set of spanners, Joey had worked at the in-flight computer and the radar and the guidance systems. Each item he took from the helicopter he annotated in a jotting book.

They had climbed with their loads to the top of the ravine.

They had seen the guide who sat in the shade of a rock fall waiting for them, and they had seen that on the mule that had been left for them were now fastened two wicker litters. They had seen the men who were pale from wounds who lay on the

9

litters, and the protest had died in Charlie's mouth, and the guide had pointed to the ground and scratched the shape of a butterfly's wings, and Joey Dickens had known that two men had detonated the butterfly shaped anti-personnel mines that were scattered from the sky.

In their own back packs, Joey Dickens and Charlie and Eddie would carry the working parts of the Mi-24 helicopter.

That evening, on the bivouac beside the goat path, the diarrhoea snapped in the stomach of Joey Dickens. He had taken the pills, but he had ignored the food.

Two days back from the ravine, and the lack of food and the work of the pills had finally clamped to a halt the movement in his belly. But two days of walking in the terrible heat without the sustenance of food had drained away his strength.

Each succeeding day was harder.

On the fifth day the speed of the little group was increasing, one of the wounded men had his leg severed above the knee, and the other had his intestines bound into the ripped stomach wall with old cloth and, unless they hurried, the men would die. Charlie and Eddie were friends and could lift each other with their talk and their laughter. Sometimes before they rested Joey Dickens was a long way behind, and his feet were an agony of blisters.

Across the southern slopes of the Hindu Kush, a group does not slow for a straggler.

His boots gnawed at his heels and toes, his muscles ached, his belly ground in sweet pain, his breath gasped in the rarefied altitude. The glare of the sun beat into his eyes from the rock surface as he followed the group up the shallow file of a dried river bed. Sometimes he heard the banter of Charlie and Eddie, sometimes he heard the curse of the guide and the welt of a stick on the mule's back, sometimes he heard the cry of a maimed man as the pain lurched in his

10

body, sometimes he heard only the leaden scrape of his own boots.

He did not hear the helicopters.

He wondered why he had come. And he thought of the terraced house that was five miles from the base at Culdrose, and he thought of the pinched feet of his elder girl that would have stayed pinched for another month . . .

If he had stopped, if he had stood completely still, then he might have heard the engines of the helicopters.

Joey Dickens was three hundred yards behind the others. The straps of his pack bit down into his shoulders. Christ, if he'd known he was going to have to carry the stuff he wouldn't have been so bleeding keen to strip it out of the whirly. He glanced from his footfall to his wrist watch. In twenty minutes they would stop for water. The stops were regular, when they stopped he would catch up. And by nightfall, by the creeping of the dusk across the mountains' sides they would be across the frontier. This would be a dream, a time of delirium. Within moments of crossing that undrawn frontier, a cairn of stones, it would all have been a bad dream. Past the cairn, into Pakistan, six hours in a taxi to Dean's in Peshawar, a day of hotel baths and hotel food, and four hours in a taxi to Rawalpindi, and thirteen hours in the London Tristar, and then scarcely a dream.

He had to say that he had never met a man like Charlie. A bull of a man was Charlie and, when he charged, the fences broke. He'd made that little spook in Peshawar jump to it on the home shipment for Charlie's Brigadier. The guy didn't like it, but, by God, he'd do it. And even if Charlie was ten years older than Joey Dickens then he could still walk faster. He wondered what he would tell his wife. Down in the Gulf somewhere he'd said, and she'd looked at him as if he was off with a woman to Torquay and not dared make the challenge. Christ, her bloody eyes would be out on stops when he came back without a roll on his stomach and with the black bulge of his bank account. When he was back, in the solid comfort of the front bedroom, he might tell her about Charlie.

He had to shade his eyes to see the group in front. He blinked. The right heel blister was the worst . . . bastard. He wiped the sweat that ran from his forehead down into his eyes. He saw the guide run from the mule he had been leading. He saw Charlie and Eddie scramble away from the river bed towards the surrounding rocks.

Joey Dickens did not understand.

Just the ache in his head, the pinch of pain in his stomach, and the hurt in his feet. He did not understand what he watched and what he saw.

There was a rumble behind him, the light throb of a coming drummer.

The mule walked on, the rope dangling from its head collar, same pace, same destination. The man with the shattered leg rose up from his litter on the flank of the mule. He gestured into the brightness of the sky behind Joey Dickens. The man who was wounded screamed in his fear and the words reached Joey Dickens, but he did not know the Pushtu language.

He spun, and looked up. The ache and the pain fled.

They were a pair.

Two helicopters for Corporal Dickens to stare up at. An RAF maintenance technician, and he was watching the dive descent of two battle cruiser helicopters. He saw the break-up of camouflage paint; he saw the serial number on the belly; he saw the tinted glass bulbs that masked the gunner and the pilot; he saw the nose machine gun meandering for an aim; he saw the rocket pod clusters; he saw the mark of the red star. He began to run; he pounded after the mule; and the skin ripped off his heel blisters. There was a patter by his feet, and dust sprinkling up from the track, and the whine of a ricochet, and the snap of fractured rock, and the shrieks of

12

the men who were wounded and lying on the mule's litters, and the crash as the first rocket exploded.

There were no trees. There were no bushes. There were no sheltering rock crevices. He ran.

A few yards, and his breath was weeping in his throat when the spray of machine gun bullets trapped him, imprisoned him. The rocks around were wet, red and soft with his intestines.

The machine gun bullets cut the body of Joey Dickens into pieces. The bullet path moved forward to punch into the laden mule, into the men who were already wounded, into Charlie and Eddie who had found no hiding place, into the low huddled figure of the guide.

The helicopters hammered the still air, quartering the sides of the valley then rose again for the high empty skies.

In the evening, after darkness had curtained the river bed, some tribesmen who were making their way to the Pakistan border found the bodies of their countrymen and the mule and the three white foreigners. They piled the bodies together and placed over a shallow scuffed grave a heap of stones to keep off the birds of prey.

They had taken the back packs from Charlie and Eddie and Joey Dickens and tipped away the weighty equipment, so that one man could comfortably carry all three packs.

They would take them to the bungalow office of the American consul in Peshawar and would be rewarded with dollars.

The mule's body they left across the path.

It had been a small luncheon party, in an upper room of the United States Embassy in Mayfair's Grosvenor Square, to introduce the Director of the Central Intelligence Agency who was making a rare visit to London. The guest of honour was Her Majesty's Secretary of State for Foreign Affairs, and the two were now alone at the table.

13

'Foreign Secretary, there's a thing I've been waiting for this opportunity to discuss with you, and it's for your ears only,' the Director said.

'Tell me.'

'Afghanistan is *our* problem. We wouldn't mess on your territory in Zimbabwe . . . Afghanistan's ours.'

'I am afraid I don't know what you can be referring to, Director.'

'Look, we're private, we're colleagues, and we share what we get, but what you've started doing in Afghanistan is off the park. We'd prefer you to put the brake on it, a hard brake.'

'I said, I don't know what you're talking about.'

'Three weeks ago you had three men shot up when on their way out with aircraft parts, helicopter parts. We know what they had because among the possessions of one of them was an inventory. We had something in the works to get the same stuff, we had to abort after your people messed up. Just do us a favour, will you, and stick to interrogating Afghans when they're on Rest and Recuperation back in Peshawar.'

'I find your attitude quite offensive,' said the Foreign Secretary, 'and I repeat: I have no knowledge of this matter.'

'Your people need a lot from us, more than we need from you . . . I'll tell you something, the Mi-24 Hind helicopter is the best the Soviets have. When it comes down they blow it to pieces. This one was more or less intact because the terrain prevented their bombers getting in to destroy it. While we were putting our thing together, to go get it properly, your people went in and botched it.'

'That is offensive and unwarranted.'

The Director smiled, bland and cold.

'I'm concerned that, in the future, professional work isn't hampered by the bungling of British amateurs. Of course, if you would have me believe that you know nothing of teams of

14

incompetent Englishmen tramping around the edges of the Soviet Union, well, with some reluctance I'll believe it. Just this once.'

The Ambassador had crossed to them. Within a moment the smiles were wide, the handshakes crisp.

An hour after returning to Foreign and Commonwealth Office, his vexation undiminished, the Foreign Secretary waved to an arm chair the Deputy Under Secretary who headed the Secret Intelligence Service. The Foreign Secretary briskly retailed the American complaint.

'Not our bailiwick, I'm afraid, sir . . .' The Deputy Under Secretary was a pillar of calm in the storm. 'We're clean, and that's what I told our cousin two days ago. I said that if they wanted to stamp on this sort of thing that he should take advantage of today's lunch. If you'll forgive me, sir, I would stress that my people in Pakistan are interested in detailed and expert analysis of the military and political situation appertaining to the Soviet presence in Afghanistan and the resistance with which their occupation is confronted. Put bluntly, sir, I don't regard the collection of ironmongery as my service's priority. These three mercenaries were in touch with Army Intelligence, and I gather they had an understanding with a Brigadier Fotheringay for payment if they delivered. Against our better judgement, we had agreed to ship their stuff home. That was the limit of our involvement.'

Next he welcomed into his office the First Secretary who headed the Afghanistan desk at FCO. He offered him a drink that was politely declined. The First Secretary glanced openly at his watch as if one train home had been missed.

They talked for an hour.

'The military position is, in summary . . .?' The Foreign Secretary stretched at his desk.

'Quite satisfactory for the Soviet forces inside Afghanistan. Since they don't have a public opinion problem, their

15

casualties are acceptable. The *mujahidin* – that's what we call
the dissidents, the Resistance forces – can cope fairly well
with the Soviet and Afghan Army tanks, artillery, all the
ground force elements. If that was all there was to it, then
we'd have stalemate. It's the helicopters that make the
difference. You will recall, sir, that it is the policy of Her
Majesty's government, and Washington's policy, that
ground-to-air missiles should not be supplied to the *mujahidin*. The local chaps can't touch the helicopters. The
helicopters are the decisive element. Given time, and this is
our assessment, the helicopters will be the foundation of
Soviet victory over the Resistance.'

'Is there a special helicopter?'

'There's one, the gunship. It's the Mi-24 . . . It's the best
they have, perhaps the best anyone has.'

'What do we know about it? How much of it is worth
finding out more about?'

'I'm not a military man but, as I understand it, the D and
E versions are in Afghanistan, those are the latest . . .
They're very much worth finding out more about. Anyone
who builds helicopters would be more than grateful for
information about this chappie!'

The wife of the Foreign Secretary had gone to church. He'd
told her to make his apologies to the rector. His detective let
the Brigadier into the house. The couple who kept house for
them in London and in Herefordshire always took Sundays
off. At weekends the detective was more of a butler than a
bodyguard.

He didn't know a great deal about the man who was
ushered into his study. Only that he was Henry Fotheringay
(known as Fo'am to only a very few), that he held the serving
rank of Brigadier, and that he headed that department of the
Ministry of Defence that specialised in acquiring the details
of Soviet weapons systems. A tall sort of cove, very straight in

16

the back, and with a fidgeting tick in his hands. It was early in the day, but the Foreign Secretary poured two thin sherries.

They talked.

'You'll forgive me for saying this, Foreign Secretary, but we find it extremely hard to work alongside SIS. On this particular case . . . a fellow comes to see me, says he's going into Afghanistan, offers me first option on any hardware he brings out, for a fee. I don't mess about, I tell him he's on. Down I go to SIS, and they don't want to know. The attitude is: if we haven't thought of it, it's not worth thinking. The most I can get from them is that they'll bag the stuff once it's in Pakistan. They seem to think they're the best and the brightest because they're all Oxbridge. I didn't get the chance to go to University, I was fighting with the Commonwealth Brigade in Korea . . .'

The Foreign Secretary nodded sympathetically.

'I'd like to hear about the Mi-24.'

'We call it Hind . . . it's big and powerful and quite naughty. The tribesmen in Afghanistan can't cope with it. It's the one thing that scares the hell out of them. The D and E versions of Hind, the most advanced, are deployed there, but they're also littered across every Frontal Aviation base in the Warsaw Pact. We'd love to have our hands on one; we'd love a camera round one. We'd love the paperwork for the inside.'

'What shoots it down?'

'Occasionally the Afghans get one with conventional ground fire, once in a green moon. A ground-to-air missile would give it a bit of a fright.'

'And the Americans?'

'The Americans, in my experience, believe either that they have everything or, failing that, then they can buy it. They haven't much of a file on Hind, which peeves them.'

'If we possessed that information?'

'We'd be happy to share it, at a price. I'm sure we'd find a price, and a high one.'

17

'I'd like that.'

The Brigadier glanced up sharply.

'This isn't meant to be an impertinence, but do you know what you're getting into, sir? Do you know how deep the water gets? You'd have to snaffle one for yourself, you couldn't sit around banking on the locals getting one with their fire power.'

'I'd like to be in a seller's market,' the Foreign Secretary said easily.

The Brigadier had gone long before the Foreign Secretary's wife returned with a long, impassioned complaint about the sermon.

The following Sunday, the Foreign Secretary was once more absent from his place in the front right hand pew of the village's small Norman church.

Again he entertained the Brigadier.

'We've done nicely on the missile, sir.'

'Tell me.'

'American, and we can cover the tracks quite beautifully . . .'

The Brigadier grinned, they shared a moment of mischief.

'. . . Found the works down at the School of Infantry in Wiltshire. I've requisitioned it. The paperwork says it's for evaluation in case the Provisionals get their hands on the system in Northern Ireland; and there's nothing that says Uncle Sam needs it back. If there was a risk of it blasting us out of the Irish skies, then we'd have to know the capabilities. And if those buggers were to get their hands on ground-to-air missiles it would only be through the States. The cover's going to work rather well, actually.'

'What about the personnel?'

'I've taken in tow a fellow who used to be with us. Made it to Major, I think, before he was passed over, he's an old hand in that part of the world, in FCO now, quite used to muddy jobs . . . I hope you'll excuse me, but I need your ink on this, sort of a requisition paper for him . . .'

The Foreign Secretary had signed it, and the Brigadier had pocketed it, before a bell rang in the Foreign Secretary's mind. The clever bastard had picked a man from the Foreign Secretary's own stable, and had the authorisation for it. The Foreign Secretary breathed deep, smiled again.

'He'd be the organiser, the fix-it fellow. We need an instructor, I'm looking down in the Gulf for him. There's a fair few running around Muscat and Oman, but that's just a detail.'

'You'll require SIS co-operation.'

'I might require it, but I won't get it. Put it this way, we'll by-pass SIS if you want this to happen. If you don't want it to happen, then we can involve them, up to their bloody throats.'

The Foreign Secretary fancied he walked on ice. He remembered the rudeness of the man in the private dining room at the American Embassy.

'I want it to happen very much,' he said distantly.

'You'd best leave it to me, sir,' said the Brigadier affably. 'That way it will happen, happen well and satisfactorily.'

The Foreign Secretary heard the crunch of his wife's car on the gravel drive.

'Thank you, Brigadier Fotheringay. I'm much obliged.'

He had climbed two thousand feet from the valley floor to the summit of the escarpment in a few minutes over four hours. He was breathing heavily, and the weight of the loaded Bergen pack dug down into the small of his back. The sun had soared into a blue hazed sky, and the wind blew warm suffocating air that dried out his throat, and made him crave for water. He would resist the craving, because the route march he was tasked to make would take him five more days,

19

and he had no more water than that which he carried, and on the roof of the mountains he would find no more water.

His ankle was sore. Not cracked but sore from the landing after the parachute descent in the High Altitude Low Opening fashion. He knew of no man who would not admit to a knotted cold stomach at the prospect of a HALO free fall and late rip-cord jump. Bad enough to jump from the Skyvan with only the moonlight to show the rock ground hurtling up to meet you, bloody daft when you were free falling and counting 'one pineapple', 'two pineapple', all the way to fifteen of the lousy, sweet, messy, bloody fruits.

He had a fondness for these mountains between the beaches of Muscat and the northern extremity of Oman, the Empty Quarter. Not a love of these mountains, but an affection. It was a soldier's place, a man's place. It was a place of raw survival. If he was grateful for anything in this life, and if he were he seldom made his feelings known, then he would have thanked the distant War House in Whitehall for decreeing that men of the 22nd Regiment of the Special Air Service could still take their recreation in these magnificent hills.

When he had rested, he stood and eased the load of the Bergen and crooked the Armalite rifle over his lower arm before setting off westwards. And the sun coming behind him blasted his shadow into his path.

A turban hid his hair, and baggy trousers covered his legs, but his boots and his smock and the big pack and the high velocity rifle identified him as a serving soldier of the British army.

There were no casual watchers on the peak of the escarpment. Had there been, had they watched his departure from the rock lip where he had regained his breath, then they would soon have lost sight of him. It was within the skills of this man to blend into the upper lands around him.

He was Captain Crispin.

2

'You're late.'

'I wasn't driving,' Barney Crispin said.

He looked past the tall, gaunt, wire-thin man who had met him, shaken his hand at the entrance to the Terminal building.

He *was* late. For five hours he had sat at Dofar waiting for the connection that would complete the long, hot sleepless journey from Muscat to Rawalpindi. He was in no great humour and he didn't need a stranger telling him he was late.

Yesterday morning was the first he'd known of it. The Colonel would like to see Captain Crispin. Before lunch? No, Sir, not before lunch . . . Right away, Sir. The orderly had saluted, Barney had grunted, tucked his shirt into his shorts, and ambled away across the sand compound to the Colonel's office. There were only a few of them now, the British officers who trained and 'advised' the armed forces of Muscat and Oman. The Colonel wore no badges of rank, no flashes. Five minutes of conversation. Something out of the ordinary, something from London, a particular request for Captain Crispin. So, the afternoon flight to Dhofar, the small hours flight to Rawalpindi. Pack for a few weeks, no letters home as to where you're going. The passport flipped across the Colonel's table gave Technical Representative as his profession. Might he ask what he would be doing in Rawalpindi? Yes, he might ask, but no, he wouldn't be told, couldn't be told because the Colonel didn't know. Better just get on with it, hadn't he, better get himself packed. Not a lot of time to spare. The Colonel had wished him good hunting, yes, very good hunting and we'll expect you when we see you. Oh to be young, eh? Handshake across the desk. Salute at the door. Goodluck. Goodbye.

Barnaby Crispin had been ten years in the regular army, and seven of them in the 22nd Regiment, Special Air Service. Those ten years had given him a type of patience, he could wait a few more hours to be told why it was thought necessary to pitch him out of a quiet billet in Muscat.

He disliked the name of Barnaby, and called himself Barney. He was 5 foot eleven. His hair was blond with a tinge of redness when the sun caught it. He was fit, solid, muscled. He walked with an easy stride, rolling on the balls of his feet. He spoke with the accent of the south of England, usually cursorily as if words were running-away bath water and were useless things. Not an easy man to read, and a difficult man to ignore.

Now Barney Crispin stood at the entrance to the Customs and Immigration hall and took in the chaos around him. Men with suitcases straining against their string bindings, women bent down with the burden of London department stores' soft furnishings, kiddies in long-trousered grey suits and bright frocks holding tin toys and howling. All around him, pushing him, shoving him, elbowing him, and he didn't even know why he was in Rawalpindi.

'I wasn't blaming you, I just said you were late,' Howard Rossiter said.

'I didn't say you were blaming me, I just said I wasn't driving.'

Rossiter decided there was little point in pretending a good humour. He had been out of his bed at first light to meet the flight. He had sat about for five hours, occasionally sipping warm orange juice, never once finding anyone capable of giving him an accurate arrival time.

He gazed into the face of the younger man. All the same

these SAS men, arrogant and conceited because they're a bloody élite. This one didn't look any different. But he had to work with this one, so he mustered a thin puddle of a smile.

There was a pain behind his temple. He'd been with some pathetic businessman the night before, all piss and wind and money success talk, but the creature had brought a quart of Chivas Regal into Pakistan, and Rossiter hadn't taken a drink for the previous ten days. All right for a business creature to run the Customs gauntlet, not all right for anyone in Rossiter's line. Crap on Islamisation, they'd agreed. About the only bloody thing they had agreed upon. Crap on dry countries. God knew how much they'd drunk while the creature spelled out the triumphs of his line of commerce and seemed to think Rossiter should be interested. But he wasn't, not one atom. Foreign and Commonwealth Office career man, that was Howard Rossiter. Not a diplomat, a diplomat was too grand for Howard Rossiter. He was an official of FCO, a road sweeper for the Foreign and Commonwealth Office. Something to be done that's not Intelligence and that's not Embassy or High Commission, then wheel out old Rossiter because he's a good sort of chap who gets on with things, a good sort of chap who'll get his hands dirty and hasn't the clout to whine if the work's a bit messy.

He would be fifty the next year. His grey, cut-short hair was thinning. His suit was too weighty for Pakistan in August, but his ranking did not run to Overseas Dress Allowance. He was pale and he was sweating. He thought he loathed the place they had sent him to, he thought he had loathed it from the moment he had stepped off the plane from Heathrow with the family row still clamouring in his mind. Should a sixteen-year-old girl be at a drinks party until three o'clock in the morning? That had started it. Somewhere along the way his wife had declared her imperative need of a new refrigerator. Could he leave a cheque? No, alas, he could not. What a bloody way to leave home. No kiss on the

23

cheek, not from his wife, not from his daughter, not from his son still in bed, just a slammed bloody door and a smirk on the face of the cab driver who had heard most of it from the pavement. The row still rankled.

Getting himself out through the Customs areas and onto the apron to meet the Tristar passengers had been his one hard earned victory of the day. He'd given the officious little fart in Customs uniform a part of his mind, and that had been joyous. It was twenty-five years since Rossiter had been in Pakistan and, God, how the place had changed, and nothing for the better that he'd noticed.

He pulled back his concentration. Again the smile.

'I'm Howard Rossiter, I'm usually called Ross.'

'Pleased to meet you, Mr Rossiter. I'm Barney Crispin.'

'You didn't bring a bottle, did you?'

'No.'

'We'd better get your bag.'

Barney Crispin's bag was one of the last onto the conveyor belt.

It didn't matter to him. He yawned a couple of times and stood with his legs firm and apart and his arms casually folded and waited, and quietly enjoyed the impatience of Rossiter hovering behind him. They'd been fast enough through Passport Control and when they'd left the Immigration area a little man in uniform had snapped a salute to Rossiter as though he were the bloody Viceroy, and that had curled a smile at Barney's mouth.

The heat didn't bother him. It was his second tour to Muscat and Oman that had been interrupted. The sun didn't burn him, just leathered his face and his arms, and he could absorb the scents and smells and odours of the East.

The canvas grip bag was collected.

Rossiter shouldered his way through the hawking taxi cab drivers outside the terminal, as if he were a man for whom a

24

limousine and chauffeur waited. Barney followed. When he was not required to lead, he was happy enough to follow. Through the noise, through the bodies, through the shouting. Coming home in a way, a sort of home, a home that had once been in his family's history. His grandfather had been here, married his grandmother here, his father had been born in some fly-blown cantonment up the road in Raj days. There had been photographs in a drawer in England, old, dog-eared and sepia. His grandfather had died here, further up the road. That made it a sort of homecoming, somewhere that his family had trod before.

It was not a limousine but a paint-scraped land-rover.

'You'll be dying to know what it's all about. I'm sorry, you'll have to wait till we get to the hotel.'

Barney raised his eyebrows. He didn't join in the game. He gave no hint of disappointment. Rossiter would be suffering because he couldn't yet play the big briefing man. Barney threw his bag into the open back of the land-rover.

There was hazard enough on the road without distracting the driver with small talk. They weaved amongst the curtains of white-robed cyclists. They stuttered over the no-give-way cross roads. They swerved onto the verge to avoid the lorries blundering down the crown. Rossiter was hunched over the wheel, grinding his gears, intent on the traffic as if engaged in combat. They had turned off the main road after half an hour. Now they were flanked by rich green undergrowth and by the white-walled bungalows of Islamabad's diplomatic community. The blue jacaranda blooms were failing on the trees. Quite pretty, Barney thought. Not a bloody flower in sight in Muscat, and no rain to grow them. Just the sun and the wind and the sun and the mountains.

'They didn't tell you anything?'

'Nothing.'

'So you haven't been asked whether you want the job?'

'I don't expect to be asked,' Barney said.

25

'Well, it's a bit out of the ordinary, but not at all hair-raising. In fact I expect you will think it's pretty straightforward.' Barney didn't prompt him and Rossiter volunteered no more, so they drove to the hotel in silence.

Barney knocked on the door.

'Come.' Muffled and peremptory, like he was a bloody headmaster. But, of course, Barney had to wait for Rossiter to remember that the door couldn't be opened except by himself. He was laughing when he went into the room and Rossiter looked at him with irritation.

'I've ordered some coffee.'

'Good.'

'Please sit down, Barney.'

Barney sat down. He was close to the window and near to him was a table with a briefcase on it. He clasped his hands, rested his chin on them. He waited. Rossiter ignored him, paced until the soft tap at the door. Rossiter let in the waiter, signed the chit with a flourish, took the tray to the table, heard the door close behind his back.

'Milk?'

'No.'

'Sugar?'

'No.'

Rossiter poured thin black coffee, pushed the cup and saucer towards Barney. Rossiter was walking again, head up, as if counting flies on the ceiling, drawing his thoughts together. Abruptly he stopped, turned and faced Barney from the centre of the room. Barney stared back at him.

'This is to be a highly secure operation . . .'

Barney inclined his head. God, what crap.

'. . . Would you read this, please?'

From an inside pocket of his jacket, Rossiter took an envelope, passed it to Barney. Barney opened it. Ministry of Defence paper, a Brigadier's signature. Captain Barnaby

26

Crispin was to work while in Pakistan under the direction of Mr Howard Rossiter, FCO. Barney tore up the envelope and the letter and flaked the pieces into the table's ashtray and set light to them.

Rossiter coughed, poised himself, rose twice on the balls of his feet, and started to speak.

'. . . Through the helicopter, the Soviets have achieved a quite critical area of superiority over the *mujahidin*. The helicopter in question is the Mi-24, armoured undercarriage, armoured cockpit, big bastard . . . They're virtually invulnerable, they soak up the small arms fire, ignore it, spit at it. They're hard, the Afghan tribesmen, but the Mi-24 makes them run, makes them shit themselves. Another couple of years of the helicopters and there's the prospect of the *mujahidin* losing serious effectiveness. We don't want that. We like it the way it is at the moment, we like a dozen Soviet divisions getting bitten, we like the Soviets getting kicked around the Third World scene for aggression against a small country. We think the chaps up in the hills need a small shot in the arm, and we have the opportunity to provide it.'

We're arriving, Barney thought, slowly but finally. His eyes never left Rossiter's face.

'We're going to blow out a helicopter, Barney, or two, or three . . . I don't know how many. Just as they're flying along, nice and safe, nice and happy, we'll give them a bloody great shock up the arse, up the exhaust. I'd like to think we'd be there to see it when it happens. But, that's too much. I'm the fixer, you're the instructor, but we don't get onto the field. We're strictly on the bench. I find the people we work with, you train them, and off they go over the border and do their stuff. We don't cross the border, Barney, under any circumstances, but with my organisation and your expertise, they go across the border, all the way up the backside of an Mi-24.'

27

Rossiter stopped. He saw the astonishment spreading on Barney's face, a cloud over sunlight. He plunged on.

'So, we're on a double bonus. We've never had a decent look at the modern Mi-24, and that's going to be rectified. I'm not suggesting they load the bloody thing's wreckage on a mule train and bring it over to us, but they'll have cameras, they'll rifle all the paperwork inside, and they'll be briefed on which bits of the electronics we want hand-carried. You can't quite believe it, can you?'

'I didn't know they had the balls,' Barney said.

'They can be quite bullish when they set their minds to it, our masters.'

'What's the missile?'

'Redeye, American . . .'

'It's British and American policy not to supply missiles.'

'Redeye goes to Israel. Israel shipped into Iran when they were scrapping with Iraq. Iran is a conduit for the *mujahidin* . . . there'll be Israeli markings on the kit underneath the last coat of paint, the top coat markings will be Iranian. Pretty?'

'Very pretty, and you've been here a month?'

'Finding the men who'll fire Redeye, whom you'll train.'

'You've found them?'

Rossiter looked away from Barney, looked out through the window. 'I think so . . . it's not easy. Had to be people that we could be reasonably certain wouldn't blab to the world what they had.'

'And you have these men?'

'I said that I'd found them, but that's my problem. Your job is to train them.' An edge in Rossiter's voice.

'I'll train them, Mr Rossiter . . . if you've found them. How many missiles?'

Rossiter had not turned back to Barney. His answer came quickly, off hand.

'Twelve.'

'Twelve . . .' Barney echoed the figure in derision.

'That's what I've got coming in.'

'And what's twelve going to change?'

'Who said it had to change anything? It gets us an Mi-24, it gets us a hundred photographs, it gets us the manuals, it gets us target acquisition and locking sensors, low speed data sensor, IFF antenna, Doppler radar, you want the rest? And if we drop a few of them, think of the morale, what it'll do for the *mujahidin* in their caves, up in their mountains.'

'Twelve,' spoken softly by Barney, spoken to himself.

'You're not required to express an opinion.'

Barney smiled coolly. 'You won't hear an opinion from me, Mr Rossiter.'

'You can call me Ross, I've told you that.'

'I'd like a Redeye manual, it's a long time since I've seen one.'

'You trained on it in Germany. I read it in your file.'

'Oh, yes? Did the file go into the disappearance of the FCO chap on the jaunt in Libya or not? Well, it wouldn't want to upset you, would it, Mr Rossiter?'

'I'll tell you what it does say, Barney. It says "He's a cold bugger". Someone's Commanding Officer wrote that in. Those very words.' The twitch of a smirk on his face.

'Have you a Redeye manual?'

'Your bedtime reading.' Rossiter took the bruised, handled manual from his briefcase, gave it to Barney.

'And the Pakistan government?'

'If they heard anything we'd be out in five minutes.'

'British High Commission?'

'The resident spook's bringing in the hardware. He won't know what's in the package.' Rossiter came close to Barney. 'I hope we can work well together,' he said gruffly.

'I hope so.'

'I gather your grandfather was in Afghanistan.'

'He died there.'

'I read that.'

'He died after they'd put his eyes out, cut his testicles off. It took a bayonet charge by a whole platoon to get his body back. He's buried there.'

'I didn't know.'

'Third Afghan War, 1919. Why should you have known?' There was a smile at Barney's mouth, a smile without humour. 'Do you like poetry?'

'I don't know a lot . . .'

'Try this . . .

"When you're wounded and left on Afghanistan's plains,
And the women come out to cut up what remains,
Jest roll to your rifle and blow out your brains
An' go to your Gawd like a soldier . . ."'

Barney looked Rossiter full in the face, blue gimlet eyes piercing into the discomfort of the older man.

'He was too badly wounded to turn his own weapon on himself, but they heard him screaming before they went in with the bayonet to get his body back. I don't suppose that was on the file . . . I'll see you at dinner, Mr Rossiter.'

'I told you to call me Ross.'

But the door was already closed behind him.

3

Rossiter was better with the sleep behind him, almost human and almost interesting to Barney.

'Look at it this way, Barney, from the point of view of the opposition. There are men like you, your age, your expertise, who command flights of Mi-24s, one flight or two flights, and you're going to let them know there's a different game being played, Redeye's game. For three years and more those bastards have been steaming up and down soaking up the small arms fire like it's a gnat's bite . . . and suddenly, out of bloody nothing, there's a sodding great ball of fire and Ivan's in a dive, and he's yelling and next thing he knows he's dead. They've had it very easy, those bastards, chopping up villages from five hundred feet. They're going to sweat a bit now, and they won't be so bloody happy saddling up in the mornings. Think what that's going to do to the hairies on the ground, too. Going to be bloody shouting and singing, aren't they, the hairies?'

Barney chewed at his toast, spoke through the mouth-ful.

'I want detail on the Hind.'

'I've got all that.'

'I want maps and photographs of inside, where it'll be used.'

'I have that too.'

'I'll want to feel the ground a bit.'

'It's the same this side as their's, that's fine.'

'That's all I need for the moment, but I want it before we meet the group.'

'We'll clear out of this dump then, get ourselves off to Peshawar.'

'Peshawar's how far?'

'Three hours' drive, half a day in our tractor. Peshawar's where the main refugee concentrations are and the base camps of the Resistance, last substantial town before the frontier.'

'My father was born there. Are you going to wear that suit, Mr Rossiter?'

'Why not?'

'Just that you're going to be rather hot.'

Barney stood up, walked away from the table, left Rossiter to pay.

Rossiter sat stock still for a moment. Was the man laughing at him? Or just Rossiter's fancy? He got up from the table and his knee caught against the edge. The table shook and his coffee spilled on the white cloth. He caught up with Barney, in the passageway by the boutique.

'It's going to be good, Barney.'

'Of course.' Barney was smiling, and the light rippled in his eyes.

'Really good, I mean.'

'Or we wouldn't be here.'

Barney loosened Rossiter's grip on his shirt and made for his room. Rossiter went back to the coffee shop to pay their bill.

They drove west out of Islamabad at a steady trundle with taxis and cars and lorries chorusing their protest behind them. Rossiter confined himself to shouted insults when he was cut up by passing vehicles, otherwise was silent.

Beside him Barney sat with his fingers clamped on a typed Hind treatment to protect it from the gusting draughts spinning through the side windows. When Rossiter spared him a glance he saw only a forehead furrowed in concentration beneath the waves of falling fair hair. They'd said in London that the man would be good, said he was serious and not a bloody cowboy. He was hellish short on human relations, but they hadn't said that.

Barney read. Hare, then Hound, and ultimately Hip begat Hind. Hind version A introduced to the 16th Tactical Air Army in East Germany in 1974. Exceeded expectations as a battlefield helicopter. Big bugger, loaded total weight of ten tons, 56 feet main rotor diameter. Powerful bugger, two 1500-shp Isotov TV-2 turboshafts. Barney scanned the diagrams that showed the extent of the titanium armour plating guarding the gunner's and the pilot's cockpits and the engines, fuel tanks, gear box, hydraulics and electrical systems. Maximum ground speed and maximum altitude, 200 mph and 18,000 feet. Armaments: 32 × 57mm S5 rockets and Swatter or Spiral guided missiles and traversable four-barrelled 12.7mm machine gun with drums of 1000 armour-piercing or HE incendiary rounds. But in the design of the Hind there was no infra-red signature suppression. The engine exhausts that are the target for a homing ground-to-air missile were considered ill-positioned by the Western evaluation. Safe against everything but the Redeye family. Barney drew quick strokes across the diagrams to measure for himself pilot and gunner visibility. He calculated speeds of descent and rates of climb. Finally he read that the defensive powers of the Hind lay in its own attacking and counter-attacking capacity. Anyone firing at a Hind had better be sure of knocking it right out. Anything less than a fatal blow would invite a lethal counter-punch.

Barney stuffed the file back into Rossiter's briefcase.

'It's a rather good weapon.'

' "Rather good" is a bit of an understatement,' Rossiter said drily.

'And in the European theatre, it looks after our tanks.'

33

'Our tanks, and our helicopters that are looking after their tanks.'

'Even with a Redeye it's not just straightforward.'

'What's not straightforward?'

'You don't just aim Redeye into the sky when there's a helicopter above and blast away. There's a bit more to it.'

'You're going to teach the hairies that little bit more,' said Rossiter sharply.

'I'm going to try to teach them.'

'You're *going* to teach them. That's what you're here for.'

'There are decoy flares that draw off a missile. There are all sorts of procedures. The pilots will be trained for European conditions, they'll know their anti-missile flying.'

'You'll tell the hairies all that.'

'I'm saying it won't be easy,' Barney said quietly.

'I didn't say it would be easy.'

At Attock they crossed the spread of the Indus river, at Nowshera they passed the camps of the Pakistan tank brigades. Rossiter took the new road, half completed and bone shaking, driving into a storm of dust from the lorry in front.

First as a pencil line, then as a crayon stripe, Barney saw the mountains that are west of Peshawar. They lay like a distant wall stretching right and left until they blurred into the haze. Behind them was Afghanistan.

The father of Barney's father had made this journey. More than sixty years before he had come by train with his battalion and travelled on the line that still ran beside the new road, and seen those mountains, and seen the buffalo beside the tracks, and seen the baked mud walls of the villages, and seen the women dive from sight, and seen the children run beside the carriages as they now ran beside the loaded lorries. His father's mother had come this way, and returned, returned with a baby and without a husband.

They had reached Peshawar.

They passed the towering sloped ramparts of brick that

34

walled the Bala Hissar fort, they nudged into a confusion of scooter taxis and horse carts and brightly painted buses and laden-down lorries. Rossiter's finger was perpetually on the horn button, his face a furious scarlet as he took issue with one obstacle after the other.

'Where are we going?' Barney asked.

'I've hired a bungalow. Chappie from one of the refugee charities, gone home on leave. It's out of the way.'

At last Rossiter swung the land-rover off the main road, onto a dirt strip. They drove between small bungalows and took one turning and then another.

'It's not quite Eaton Place for the charity people,' Rossiter said from the side of his mouth.

He had to talk, Barney recognised that, and the older man craved for an answer. It would have been simple for Barney to engage in small talk, price of beer, bloody awful government, Pakistan going to the knackers, anything. It wasn't his way.

Barney gazed out at the bungalow as Rossiter braked. There was a small concreted yard in lieu of a garage and beyond it a squat building behind a raised verandah. Half hidden was a brickbox for a servant near to the kitchen door. There were untidy flower beds around the verandah from which the bougainvillea reached up to the tired white plaster walls.

'What do you think of it?'

'Fine,' Barney said.

'What would you do if I kicked you in the arse?'

'I'd break the bones in your arm,' Barney said.

'Just wondering if you were alive, that's all.' Rossiter laughed, loud and bleating.

Barney carried the bags into the bungalow. Rossiter muttered something about the cook having gone back to his village for the charity man's leave, that they'd have to fend for themselves, and took for himself the bedroom with the air

35

conditioning. Barney was next door, an iron-framed bed, a wardrobe that didn't shut because the doors had warped. He stamped on a darting cockroach, sliming the tile floor. The water came hesitantly from a cold tap at the basin, he gathered enough in his cupped hands to wash the dust out of his face.

Rossiter stood in the doorway.

'What's for the rest of today?'

'We take delivery tonight, but there's something I'd like you to see first. It's a short drive, won't take long.' Something of a grin on Rossiter's face.

Fifteen minutes in the land-rover.

They stopped outside a compound and walked through the open gates, between the high walls. From a central flagpole flew the red cross on white. A European nurse in snow white floated across the compound dirt, as if blind to the surroundings. She saw Rossiter and inclined her head in a formal greeting. A slope-shouldered orderly, grey-bearded, sad of face, manoeuvred a wheelchair down a wooden ramp, the man in the wheelchair sneezed but could not lift his hand to wipe away the mess. There were two huts inside the compound, long and low and single storied. Barney knew what was required of him. He walked to the wide central door of the nearest hut, paused to allow his eyes to assimilate the grey interior. He counted fifteen beds for paraplegic and quadriplegic patients. He saw the head clamps that kept the skull completely still, he saw the beds of others tilted so that their bodies would be moved and the bed sores would be less acute. They were all men, in both of the huts. Every one with passive eyes, the same dropped mouths of help-lessness. He willed himself to walk past each bed, past each wheelchair, and for each man he tried to smile some comfort.

He walked out into the sunlight, into the live world. He strode to face Rossiter.

'Very clever,' Barney hissed.

'I thought there was a chance that you didn't quite understand what it was all about,' Rossiter said affably. 'The helicopters did most of them. Spinal lesions caused by rocket shrapnel, or by being under buildings that the gunships have knocked down. Pretty grim thought, isn't it, if the only treatment is days away on the back of a mule. Only a few get here, they're the ones done near the border. Bringing you here was my way of kicking your arse without getting my arm broken.'

After dark, after an awful meal out of tins organised by Rossiter, they drove out of Peshawar on the Kohat road.

There was no street lighting. Animals and people loomed late from the blackness into the glare of the land-rover's headlights. Rossiter was quiet, but his face was satisfied as if he had won something of a victory at the International Red Cross rehabilitation clinic, and taken pleasure from the success. Barney tried to put the sights behind him, could not. Impossible to ignore, the paralysed bodies and the devastated features of the men who had come from the war across the mountains. A moon was creeping up, a thin sickle that threw only a small light on the fields and homes that lay below the causeway road. From the darkness, from the few pinprick lights, there was a bubble of noise, of voices, of animal sounds, of running water in the canal dykes, of chanting songs on the radios.

They drove for nearly an hour until they came to a junction where Rossiter pulled off the road and bumped the land-rover over the dirt before switching off the engine and the lights. The night was around them, and the mosquitoes. Barney waited for Rossiter to speak, Rossiter kept his peace. Sometimes the lights of an oncoming truck lit the interior of the land-rover's cab and then Barney could see the anticipation rise on Rossiter's face, and then fade with the vehicle's passing.

37

It was a Japanese pick-up truck that finally groped into position beside the land-rover.

A man stepped down from the cabin. Quite young, Barney's age, dressed in the white man's uniform of knee socks, pressed shorts, and an open-neck shirt festooned with pockets.

'He thinks it's radio stuff, thinks you're a communications wizard, thinks we're setting up a listening post,' Rossiter whispered.

The truck's lights were shut down, Barney heard a door closed carefully. There was the shadow of a face at Rossiter's window.

'You can give me a hand, old chap. Christ knows what you've got in there, weighs half a bloody ton, you'll be able to hear them picking their noses in Kabul with that lot. Bloody near did my back in getting it on the truck. You can get it off.' The sharp, clear accent of a south of England private education. Barney wondered how they chose him. There had been spooks in Muscat, confident and supercilious blighters who revelled in their mystique.

Rossiter shone a torch beam out through his window and onto a wooden crate that was roped down in the back of the truck. The beam found stencilled printing, and Barney leaned across to read the letters. BRITISH HIGH COMMISSION ISLAMABAD PERSONAL FURNISHINGS   FRAGILE.

'Went through Karachi customs like a dream.'

'Thanks,' Rossiter said.

'For nothing. What's going to happen to it afterwards?'

'It'll be disposed of, not your worry.'

'I don't worry easily, friend. If you two shift yourselves we'll get it into the back of your's.'

Barney and Rossiter stepped down from the land-rover. Together they lifted the crate from the truck and edged it across the tail board of the land-rover. The sides of the square

38

crate were a little more than four feet across. Barney had taken the strain, Rossiter a grunting second fiddle.

'No need to make a fuss, I did it on my own,' the spook said.

'Thanks,' Rossiter said without kindness.

'You'll go a bit softly, won't you?'

'Depends what you mean by softly.'

'You're out from London, you may not know the local scene that well. If you're going to be sitting on a mountain top with a damn great wireless then the Pakkies won't be that pleased. If they find you, there'll be a fair old fuss. I've a useful piece of co-operation going on here . . .'

'Why don't you just piss off?' Rossiter said.

'I've a fair idea of what's going on over there without your having to sit on a mountain – playing with a radio.'

'Piss off, will you, and don't tell me how to run my show.'

'I'm just telling you: people out from London are just a bloody nuisance.'

'Goodnight . . .' Rossiter turned to climb back into the land-rover. 'When you're a very big boy you may just get to learn what's going on, perhaps.'

Barney grinned in the darkness. He heard the angry intake of breath from the spook. He eased himself into his seat, and Rossiter was away, turning noisily before Barney had the door closed.

'An object lesson in tact and discretion, Mr Rossiter.'

'Arrogant little shit.'

Rossiter laughed. When a car passed them, heading for Kohat, Barney saw that Rossiter was still grinning broadly to himself.

They backed the land-rover up to the verandah steps and carried the crate into Barney's room before they turned on any of the lights. Rossiter almost at once said he was going to bed. Barney drew the cotton curtains. He took a heavy knife from his kit, and began to prise away the nails that fastened

39

the crate. The boards creaked as he dragged them up. Barney was no weapons buff. He had come across them in his time, but not in the Regiment. Weapons were no more or less than a tool of Barney's trade. He could not have said why Redeye was different to him from every firearm he had handled. He saw the slim symmetrical shapes of the top layer of the tubes that protected the missiles and that were wrapped in greased waterproof paper, each holding one missile and the battery coolant unit. Separate and wedged to the side of the crate with polystyrene filler shapes was the launch tube grip stock and optical sight. When he had looked down for a few seconds at the wrapped tubes and the launch mechanism he felt a sense of the ridiculous, and he shook himself as if to get rid of a hallucination, and then lifted back the crate boards. He shut away the Persian lettering that had overstamped the Hebrew script, and banged with his clenched fist down onto the wood so that the nails slid again into the sockets.

He slept long and well that night.

'He says that the *mujahidin* have learned to be cautious of foreigners who come with offers of help . . .' said the boy who played the part of interpreter.

Rossiter sighed. 'You must explain that the help we are going to offer is very positive.'

Rossiter eased back on the low plastic coated settee. Barney sat beside him, eyes alert, unmoving. They heard the boy speak, then the reply.

The boy turned to Rossiter. 'He says the leader of your country has been here, and the great men of America, and of Germany and France, and the princes of Saudi. They have all offered their help, they have all promised their support. They all tell us that we are fighting for freedom, they all tell us of our courage and that we are heroes. He says that they do not want to be told of their courage, and that they are heroes, they want the help that has been promised . . .'

40

It was four hours since Rossiter and Barney had driven to the refugee camp outside Peshawar. They had walked between the open sewers, they had gone amongst the lines of tents with their surrounds of mud walls, they had come to the prefabricated home of a leader. Now they sat on a settee and around them the shadowed room was crowded with men. Fighting men, hawk-eyed and sharp-nosed and long-fingered and heavy-bearded men. Some stood, some sat on the floor. Only their leader had another chair. Four hours, and God knows how many of the tiny cups of sweet tea Barney had dutifully drunk. He was used to it, that was the way it happened in Muscat. He almost felt sorry for Rossiter. Rossiter in his bloody suit, as if he were a District Commissioner come to sort out a problem with a bagful of beads. He'd learn. A part of the plan had emerged during the drive to the camp. Rossiter had found a group, yes. But the group had not actually been propositioned. No, that was going too fast. He'd found a group that fought, that didn't just talk about fighting, that's what Rossiter had said. But Redeye, Redeye was far in the future. Redeye hadn't been talked about. And Rossiter's status was not yet established. So, they'd talked for four hours and the way it was going they'd talk another four bloody hours. Barney was settled, comfortable on the settee, and could watch the closed faces of the fighting men, and wonder if those who had killed his grandfather had looked in any way different.

'I have come to talk to the leader about real help, tell him that.' Rossiter snapped his instruction to the boy. Barney's hand flickered to Rossiter's sleeve. Steady, old thing, there's no hurry.

Again the exchange of words between the leader and the boy.

'He says,' the boy chattered out the answer. 'He says he has no need of blankets or food for his people. He says that each time the *mujahidin* have asked for real help, for the

41

work they have to do, then the help has been refused them.'

Barney's hand tightened on Rossiter's sleeve, 'Ask him what is the real help that he needs.'

Rossiter flashed him a glance of annoyance. It was the first interruption.

'All the world knows what is the help that is needed,' the boy replied pertly and without reference to the leader. 'Help is needed to fight the helicopter . . .'

The boy broke off, translated for the old man with the white beard and the narrow spectacles and white cotton trousers and the embroidered waistcoat against whose legs he sat. There was a growl of agreement from the shadow recesses of the room, then a scatter of voices. The boy looked from face to face, absorbing the talk. The boy clapped his hands for quiet.

'They say that from the time the first foreigners came offering to help us, we have asked for aid in fighting against the helicopters. The helicopter is armoured, protected, against it we have rifles. They say, what can a rifle do against armour plating? They say the helicopter massacres them because they are not given the help they have asked for. They say that if the foreigners cared for their freedom then they would be given the weapons to destroy the helicopters.'

Rossiter looked into Barney's face. Barney raised a finger slightly, the gesture that Rossiter should not speak.

'I say again, what is the real help that is needed?'

The boy translated, the voices rose in reply.

The boy held up his hand for their silence. Cheeky little sod, Barney thought, but he can be cheeky when he's pretty and has smooth cheeks and when his back rests against the knees of the leader.

'They want the missile, the missile that will destroy the helicopter.'

'What is the missile you want that will shoot down the helicopter?'

42

'We have asked the Americans for Redeye, we have asked the Egyptians for SAM 7, we have asked the British for Blowpipe. We know what is available, we are not just peasants off the fields, we know the names of the missiles, we can read . . .' the boy catapulted his answer to Barney without pause for translation.

'Which is the best?'

'Redeye,' the boy chimed in instant answer.

Rossiter leaned over close to Barney. 'Where in God's name are you going?'

Barney clipped back. 'I thought we'd better get on with what you should have done last week.'

'Watch yourself . . .' Rossiter whispered and flushed.

Barney smiled sweetly at Rossiter. All the eyes in the room were on him. The eyes of the fighting men. He saw a helicopter, he saw the burst of exploding flame, he saw the eyes and the faces of these men as they inched from cover to cover, from rock to rock, across the floor of a valley, inched toward the survivors of a helicopter crash. He wiped the sweat from his face.

'I'm going to clear them all out,' Barney said. 'All except the boy and the old man.'

An hour later they stepped out into the rich afternoon sunlight.

A bargain had been struck.

The leader of a tribal fighting group of the Afghan *mujahidin* and a boy of seventeen years who had learned his English at a Lycée in Kabul and an official of the Foreign and Commonwealth Office and a captain of the 22nd Regiment of the Special Air Service had all shaken hands on a deal.

'You did well,' Rossiter said hoarsely when they were in the land-rover.

4

Long before, Barney knew the proverb of the Tajik people of the north of Afghanistan which said: 'Trust a snake before a harlot, and a harlot before a Pathan.' The men he would train to fire the Redeye missile were southerners, Pathans.

He had not brought the weapon system the first morning. He would bring that later. First he would take stock of the men he had to teach. They went out on the Jamrud road, to the first foothills at the approach to the Khyber. Barney had said six men only. There were fourteen. Barney had said that only the young and the fit, the true fighters, should come. The beards of four men were white with age. They drove in a rusty Volkswagen van, pressed together, smelling and scenting together, hawking and spitting together, the sun not up two hours and the heat suffocating.

In the front, beside the driver, was the boy who made the translations.

The road took them past the big refugee camps. Two and a half million displaced persons from Afghanistan living in tents or in mud homes they had built for themselves. Three and a half million of their livestock grazing on land at the fringes of the camps, sheep and goats and cattle. And they believed that one day they would go home, which is why they sat patiently before their tents or the mud brick homes and waited for victory. One day . . . Barney had never before seen refugee camps, there was something unreal about these camps, something that happened only to other people. He wondered if he could ever have been a refugee, if he could have sat with a pipe and a cup of sweet tea waiting for a victory to be won far away against ten divisions of the Soviet army.

Barney leaned forward against the crush of men in the back of the van, he tapped with his finger on the boy's shoulder.

'What is your name?'

'I am Gul Bahdur, what is yours?'

'I am Barney. Gul Bahdur, why are there so many in these camps, what was the one weight they could carry no longer?'

'Some foreigners say it is because they have free food here. This is a lie, Mr Barney. It is the attacks from the air.

'Tell me.'

'The helicopters attack the villages. The helicopters have bombs and rockets, there is no defence against the helicopters.'

'Always the helicopters.'

'Before the Soviets came to Afghanistan, these men did not know fear. It was not possible to make a Pathan afraid, but the Pathan is afraid of the helicopter, do you understand me?'

'I understand you.'

'Mr Barney, you are a soldier?'

'A sort of soldier.'

'Would you not be afraid of the helicopter?'

'I understand you.'

'If you are truthful, if you accept that you too would have fear, then you will know why we have left our homes.'

'I said I understood.'

Barney lapsed back to silence.

The road was full, noisy, slow moving. They headed towards the mountain line.

'Mr Barney . . .'

'Yes.'

'Have you ever fought against the Soviets?'

'No.'

'Would you like to?'

Barney grinned. 'You have no right to ask me that question, and I won't answer it.'

The boy turned full face to Barney, a wide happy smile. He seemed younger than his seventeen years, little more than a child. The boy boasted as a child will. 'I have fought against the Soviets.'

'How many did you kill?' Barney asked lightly.

'More than a hundred.'

Barney was laughing. 'And how many did you wound?'

The boy shook his head and the dark hair flopped across his brow. 'None were wounded.'

Barney said quietly, 'And how many did you capture?'

'None were captured.'

They drove off the road and away parallel to the mountain line, along a shallow valley, and soon were lost from the sight of the traffic. Where the van stopped there were scattered scrub trees, with foliage sufficient to throw down patches of shade. The men spilled from the doors of the van and hurried to find a place where there was shelter from the sun. Barney was last from the back of the van. He walked slowly towards the trees, squinting his eyes, gazing deep into the emptiness around him. There was a silence here, a silence of the wind ruffling against rock and sand and bush and hillside. They sat and they watched and they waited for him, these men who did not wound or capture Soviets but who killed them.

'You'll translate for me, Gul Bahdur,' Barney said brusquely.

'Of course.'

'And exactly. You don't add and you don't take away.'

'What else?' The boy's smile was rampant.

'And don't give me any bloody cheek.'

The cheerfulness was stripped from the boy's face. He

46

was a chastised child. His eyes dropped. 'What you say to me I will tell to them.'

Barney talked to the men under the trees about Redeye.

They knew the workings of the Kalashnikov and the AK-47 and the Lee Enfield and the Heckler and Koch rifles. They were familiar with the Soviet RPG-7 rocket launcher. They could lay a mine. They could site an ambush. Patiently Barney talked them into a world that was new and which might be bewildering. Gently he spoke to men from one of the most unsophisticated regions of the earth, to men who could not read and who could not write.

Each morning for a week the Volkswagen van brought them to the same place, and each morning Barney edged forward in his exposition and detail. He was never interrupted, he was never asked a question. The eyes never closed, the heads never turned away from him. In the middle of each morning the boy brewed tea over a gas camping stove, and then the men would talk and fool and ignore Barney. Ignore him until the tea was drunk.

By the end of that week Barney talked of a portable, short range missile to be used against low flying aircraft or helicopters. He spoke of a missile with flip-out cruciform tail fins. He led them into a two stage solid propulsion unit with short boost and longer sustain. He explained a guidance system of passive infra-red homing. Scratching with a sharpened stick in the dirt he drew the missile to scale. Jabbing with his finger he pointed to a rock that he judged to be a mile away and then said that his missile would cover the distance to the rock in the time that it took him to count four seconds.

The next day was Friday. On the Friday he would not meet them. He told them that when they next came to the place he would bring with him the Redeye so that they could feel and hold the weapon, and then he would speak of the technique of firing and the science of target acquisition.

At the end of that week, as the men trooped back to the

47

van, Barney found that the boy had fallen into step beside him.

'What do they say?' Barney gestured towards the men ahead of him.

'They say that if it helps them shoot down a helicopter that this torture will have been worthwhile.'

'You little bugger . . .' Barney swiped at the boy. 'You are going to go with them?'

'Perhaps I will be the only one who knows how it works.'

'You could get the shit kicked out of you,' Barney was laughing.

The boy looked up into Barney's face, questioning and intent. 'It works, Mr Barney, your Redeye?'

'The pride of General Dynamics, California, young man. Yes, it works.'

'How's it turning out?'

'It could be all right.'

Rossiter leaned against the open door, watching Barney swilling his face in the basin.

'I'd have thought that after a week you'd have a decent idea.'

'They'll probably get a helicopter.'

'You're none too bloody sure.'

Barney straightened, the water fell from his face. 'I said it could be all right. I said they'd probably get one.'

'You're a grudging sod.'

Barney turned to Rossiter. 'You want to know why it's only all right and why it's only probably?'

'You tell me,' Rossiter said grimly.

'You found the wrong people, Mr Rossiter.'

'What does that mean?'

'It means that the men you found are pig ignorant. They don't know how a car works let alone a supersonic heat-seeker.'

48

'And where would I have found a Cambridge physicist?'

'Inside . . . inside, half the leadership is defected Afghan army officers. Inside there are bright kids out of school, kids from the university, kids from the cadet college. They're what we should have had.'

'Precisely why we haven't got them, because they're inside and we're outside. And we cut our bloody cloth to the circumstances . . . And you've a whole week more to get them to the start line. Stop bloody whining.'

'You asked me and I told you . . . but if we get a helicopter, and it's not burned out on impact, and you've some pretty pictures for your pocket, and some electronics for your suitcase, then everything's rosy . . .' Barney dived his face again into the basin, sluicing away the sand grime.

'Just one helicopter will do me very well,' Rossiter said with emphasis. He turned away, then paused, pivoting back towards Barney. 'By the by, I heard of a party weekend after next, managed an invitation.'

'I wouldn't have thought we'd be waving ourselves round Peshawar society.'

'Anyone ever tell you what a miserable creep you are, Crispin?'

'We're supposed to . . .'

'One of the Red Cross girls,' Rossiter snapped. 'Of course, you don't have to come. I'm stuck here, you know. Stuck here like a bloody plain-faced virgin. You're out every day, I'm here. And don't you lecture me about security. I was organising bloody security when you were still wetting your bed. I also made Major, which it seems you've forgotten.'

Barney towelled the water off his face and shoulders. Rossiter watched him. Barney slipped into a clean shirt, walked to the door, didn't hesitate, and Rossiter made way for him. Barney went through the living room, out through the front door and onto the verandah, then off towards the land-rover.

49

'Where are you going?'

'Out.'

'Can I come?'

Barney heard the desperation in Rossiter's voice, heard the pleading.

'No. You're too old for where I'm going, like you said.'

Barney heard the door of the bungalow slam shut. When he turned to look he could not see Rossiter.

It was early afternoon.

Barney drove west, through Jamrud, past the turn off where he went each morning in the Volkswagen, onwards and upwards off the plain and into the Khyber. The road climbed, snaked, in curve patterns around the bleak greyness of the mountains. Always above him, always on the highest ground, were the old British picquet forts, square-based towers now roofless and weather scarred. Alongside the road was the railway, reaching onto viaducts, diving into tunnels. He saw valleys with thin streams far below and village clusters and handkerchiefs of green cultivation. He saw the barracks of the modern Pakistan army, and the dragon's teeth of tank traps, and anti-aircraft guns aimed loftily to the west and the Afghanistan border. Clear of the Khyber he came to the township of Landi Kotal, and where the road narrowed into a gorge between steep cut rock faces, Barney pulled onto the gravel shoulder. Set in the rock and painted in vivid greens and whites and reds were the emblems of the old British regiments that had served their tours in this far border country. The Gordons, the Royal Sussex, the Essex Regiment, the First Battalion 22nd Cheshires. Barney shook his head, slowly, happily, as if he heard a lament of pipes, and a church parade hymn, and the cry of a bugle, and the shout of a drill sergeant. His grandfather would have been here . . . would have come through the gorge on his way to a battlefield in Afghanistan. He felt a bond with this man, younger than himself, who had come through the Khyber on a fighting

50

mission more than half a century before. He felt the touch of family.

He locked the land-rover, bent to tighten his boot laces, and climbed away from the road first up a steep gully, then onto a sharp-backed, fish's spine ridge. He climbed easily, fluently. His breathing was calm and relaxed as he stretched his stride away from the road and out into the wilderness. Beneath him was the town of Landi Kotal with its pimples of minaret towers and flat cement roofs and spiralling wood smoke columns. He turned his back on the town, setting himself instead to absorb the mountain sides. He saw caves that were dark in shadow and crevices never penetrated by the sunlight. He saw boulders behind which one or two men might hide. The exhilaration stayed with him, was his companion. He studied the ground of rock and scree and boulder, searching for imagined firing points for Redeye, hunting for the escape routes for the group once they had fired Redeye and brought down on themselves the counter-attackers of the surviving helicopters. It was why he had come to this place, to learn the feel of the mountain sides, that he might better achieve the destruction of the Mi-24.

He climbed to a summit and sat gazing out over a great distance into Afghanistan.

It was dark when he returned to the bungalow. Without calling Rossiter he went into his own bedroom. He lifted the loosened boards of the crate top and stared down at the slim shapes of the wrapped missile tubes. Rossiter started to hum in the next door room, to tell Barney that he was awake, perhaps it was an invitation for Barney to come and talk to him.

Barney closed down the boards of the crate, undressed, and climbed into bed.

He sat cross-legged in the sun with the boy beside him.
Gathered in front of him in the shade were the men.

51

He wore jeans and a long-tailed shirt of green cotton outside his belt, and the flat peakless cap of the Nuristan region covered his fair hair. Flies crawled on his face and were ignored. Close to his feet, in separate parts lay a launch tube holding a single missile and the control unit of Redeye.

Barney talked quietly into Gul Bahdur's ear, pausing every half sentence for the boy's translation. Since he had brought the missile to the valley, the interest of his audience had quickened.

'You have to stand still to fire. So you have to expose yourself. If you hurry, then Redeye misses. When you fire there's smoke and then the flash as the main rocket ignites. It's two stages, booster first and then main rocket . . . if you stand still the main rocket firing can't hurt you, it ignites more than 20 feet from you, so you're safe. It's difficult to judge distances in the air but if the helicopter looks to you very high or very far away across the valley, then don't fire. The best range is between 600 yards and 1800 yards, less than that and the guidance system may not have time, more than that and the rocket loses strength. We go through the drill again . . .'

Barney fastened the missile tube to the launch unit, swift, trained movements. He eased Redeye onto his shoulder, peered through the cross-wire sight.

'You hear the helicopter coming, when you actually see it you have to stand, you track the helicopter through the sight, you fasten on the engine exhaust . . .'

His right eye was up against the back marker of the sight, his vision wavered across the hillsides and came to rest on a hovering hawk. He tracked the hawk, lingering with its flight.

'You switch on the battery coolant. You take your time and don't hurry. The heat of the engine exhaust talks to the guidance system – you have to listen for the buzzer that tells you Redeye has found the target of the engine exhaust – and when the buzzer is at its peak then you fire. If you've done

52

everything I've told you, then the missile is locked on the engine exhaust and that helicopter's dead . . .'

The sight fell from the hawk's flight, traversed back over the far hillside, over the stones of the river bed at the base of the valley to where a stork bird stood. Barney passed Redeye towards the clutch of hands that stretched out to receive it.

'Remember, it can curve a bit and bend a little, but it's not an acrobat. It flies faster than the helicopter flies. You fire it after the helicopter, not into its path, and you don't fire straight up, not in the day. You remember that, don't you?'

He paused. No point in continuing now that they had their hands on the launcher. He remembered the general weapons instructors at Sandhurst military academy ten years before, and the specialised weapons instructors in Hereford. One and all they'd have been tipping towards coronaries if they'd had this lot for cadets. Redeye was tugged from one set of hands to another. One tribesman wriggled on his haunches a few feet from the group so that he could savour in greater isolation the feel of the launcher on his shoulder before it was wrenched from him.

'Do they understand the camera?' Barney said to the boy.

'Of course.'

'And they know what they have to try to bring me back?'

The boy rifled in the breast pocket of his shirt, produced a new notebook.

'Underneath the gunner's seat, behind armoured doors, is the fixed pod containing stabilised optics for target acquisition and tracking. Beside that is the radio command guidance antenna . . .' The boy read carefully from the notebook. 'Above the gunner's position is the low speed air data sensor, that you want as well. From inside the cockpit of the pilot you want photographs of all the dials . . .'

'Do you have to read it?'

'I know it by heart,' the boy said.

'If you didn't have a notebook could you remember it?'

53

'I know everything you have said . . .'

Barney snatched the notebook from Gul Bahdur's hand. He read the clear copper plate writing. He flipped the pages, then tore out all those that covered the shopping list of the helicopter's instrumentation. He ripped the paper to small pieces, scattered them on the ground.

'Why did you do that?' Shrill anger from the boy.

'In case you're captured, that's why.'

Barney stood up, his face was twisted away from the boy. He started to walk, a lizard that was sand-coloured and perfect in camouflage scrabbled clear of his feet. The boy caught up with him and, like a father, Barney put his arm around Gul Bahdur's shoulder.

'When are you going?'

'Tomorrow.'

'And you will be gone . . .?'

'A week, not more. Only into Paktia province, across the border. There are many helicopters in Paktia.'

'You go carefully,' Barney said.

The boy looked up into Barney's face. 'We are fighting the *jihad*, that is the holy war. What have I to fear? If I die in the *jihad*, what have I lost?'

'I just said you were to go carefully.'

'If I die I am a martyr.'

'If you are captured you are a disaster.'

Barney walked on towards the Volkswagen. The boy followed him, and after him the men, and amongst them and hidden from Barney's sight was the Redeye missile.

Barney came up the bungalow steps. From the verandah he could hear Rossiter singing . . . 'And did those feet in ancient time, walk upon England's mountains' . . . supported by the echo chamber of the bathroom.

All the way back to the bungalow the doubt had eaten at him. Barney sat at the table in the living room, he was dirty

54

and dusty strewn, and he listened to the singing and the splashing of water, and the hiss of the under arm spray.

Rossiter came out of the bathroom, he had a towel round his waist, and was buttoning a clean white shirt over his chest. Barney felt the filth in his hair and the warm wetness and the chafe of his trousers at his groin. Barney's head dropped into his hands. He closed his eyes. He felt a great tiredness. He heard the suck of exasperation from Rossiter.

'You're not coming?'

'Coming to what?'

'Don't play the bloody ass, to the party.'

'I told you what I thought about us chucking ourselves around town.'

'Your funeral . . . for me, I'm going to be bright and busy and in good time for the festivities. You want the sackcloth, laddie, your problem . . .' Rossiter was moving to the door of his bedroom. 'And get the stuff ready, please, Barney. As soon as I'm decent, we'll drop Mr Redeye off at the camp. After that if you want to sit here like a bleeding abbot . . .' and was gone.

'They're not ready to go,' Barney said quietly.

'. . . If you want to sit here on your bum and play with yourself . . .'

'I said, *they're not ready to go.*'

Rossiter reappeared. He seemed to play the senior officer, the man who had the Brigadier's letter of introduction, and his uniform was an unbuttoned shirt and a damp towel.

'The schedule gave you a fortnight, and that's what you've had.'

'I didn't draw up the schedule, and I'm telling you that they're not ready.'

Rossiter smiled coldly. 'You're telling me that in two weeks you've failed to prepare them, that it?'

'I'm not on a bloody promotion course, Rossiter, and I

don't have to and I won't take that shit. I'm telling you that they're not good enough.'

Perhaps Rossiter thought the towel would fall. He grasped the knot tightly.

'What do you want me to do, Barney?'

'I want a stop put on it, I want another week. I told you before, this isn't an easy weapon. If I had British infantry kiddies, I'd want more than a fortnight.'

'Don't give them all the missiles at one go. Keep some back.'

'Where does that get us?'

Rossiter sighed. 'It gets us that if this crowd screw up, then we find someone else to have another go.'

Barney flared up out of his chair. 'Very bloody bright, and wrong for two reasons. Wrong because if they screw up they'll lose the launcher of which we have one, so nobody gets a second chance. And second, because if they screw up they're all dead.'

'I'll think about it,' Rossiter said, and disappeared into his bedroom.

'There's nothing to think about. I've told you they're not ready.'

'I'll think about it.'

'How long are you going to think about it?'

'I am going to a party. Your bloody doubts, nor your bloody wild horses, will not keep me from that party. While I am at that party I will think about it. When I come back I will have made my decision. Got it, Barney, my decision . . .'

Barney stormed out of the front door, heard it slam behind him and then fly open. He was opening the door of the land-rover when he heard the shout from Rossiter's bedroom.

'I need the bloody transport tonight. You know I need it.'

Barney turned the key in the ignition. 'Get yourself a

taxi,' Barney said to himself. Rossiter couldn't have heard, because the engine had coughed to life.

He drove west towards the foothills of the mountains that were the frontier with Afghanistan. When the dark steep shadows crowded close to the road, he had parked and locked the land-rover on the hard shoulder.

He sat, alone with his thoughts and his doubt, on a smoothed rock.

It was just a job, the training of an Afghan resistance group to shoot down a Soviet helicopter with a man portable surface-to-air missile. But a job should always be done well. That was his own training. And these bastards weren't ready.

The stars glimmered down at him, down at him and down at the high wilderness of Afghanistan where the helicopters flew and where a group would be badly savaged if they went before Barney Crispin was satisfied that they were ready.

There was just enough reflection from the apples and pears painting above the bookshelf in the living room for Howard Rossiter to comb his hair. He had the problem of all balding men who seek to cut a dash, to comb back and to hell with it, to comb forward and pretend. He was buggered if he knew what to do about Crispin's whining.

He heard the sharp rap at the front door. He felt a shiver, ridiculous, but he felt it.

He went to the front door. Through the glass he could see the young man standing under the verandah light. Slim, European, familiar in a vague way.

Rossiter opened the front door.

'Yes?'

'Can I come in?'

'Who are you?'

'You don't remember me? . . . I brought you a crate. You've a short memory.'

Rossiter remembered the messenger boy from the High

57

Commission in Islamabad. Complacent little prig. It was the drawling, satisfied voice he recognized.

'I've come to mark your card.'

'So mark it,' Rossiter said crisply.

'Easy, sir . . .' The 'sir' was a sneer. 'I've just flogged up from Islamabad. My name's Davies, I've come to mark it before you drop us all in the shit, which is what you seem to be trying to do.'

'Have your say, Mr Davies, then please go away.'

The spook was in no hurry. He walked easily round the room, stopped with his back to the opened door of Barney's room. Confident, relaxed, amusing himself. He wore slacks and a short-sleeved shirt.

'What did you say your name was?'

'I didn't say what my name was,' Rossiter said.

'I've come to tell you that you're attracting attention.'

Rossiter felt the draught in his stomach. 'Who's been asking?'

'Security in Islamabad . . who you are, what you're doing here?'

'What's been your answer?'

'Not easy to answer when we're in the dark . . . that you're something to do with the charities. As yet Security hasn't shifted itself sufficiently to find out more, why you're spending time with one of the groups, as yet . . .'

'If I was into the charities then I'd be meeting groups.'

'The people you're with, I'm told, aren't the ones who'd be interested in blankets and sacks of grain. Anyway there's a setup for charities and you've ignored it. You're making a bit of a ripple. And it's a crap group.'

Rossiter's lips were close set, pinched. He spoke with a whistle between his teeth, and he was late for picking the woman up, for phoning his taxi. 'You'd better tell me.'

'I thought you knew all the answers . . . The ones who *do* the fighting are round Kabul, round Kandahar, round Jalala-

58

bad, round where the Soviets are. The ones who *talk* about the fighting are round Peshawar. You're with the talkers. If the best you could find was them, then you're pretty useless. You wanted to be told.'

'We have a high level government clearance.'

'If you hadn't had, I'd have seen to it that you were out on your necks by now.'

'How long do we have?'

'Perhaps a week . . . I've said I'll check you out with the charities in London . . . not for your bloody sakes I'm doing it. I got a packet of fall-out last time we had idiots here and nothing more to send home than those back packs in a cardboard box courtesy of the Yanks.'

'We'll be quiet for a week, after that we're on our bikes,' Rossiter was trying to smile and failing.

Davies returned a warm and winning smile. 'What's the real game, what's the radio for?'

'I was just going out when you came.'

The smile slipped from Davies' face. Quickly he turned, twisted, went fast into Barney's bedroom. Before Rossiter had reacted, the spook had found the manual that was under Barney's pillow. Rossiter tried to shake it from him, and was shrugged away. He stood by the door, panting.

'It's a fucking manual for missiles . . .' the spook whispered in wonderment. 'Ground-to-air fucking missiles.'

Rossiter went back into the living room.

'You have to forget what you saw.'

The spook was breathing heavily, he followed Rossiter. 'I'll tell you something. The weapons that come through Pakistan are controlled. There's not a drought and there's not a flood. There's just enough to keep it going. Too little and the war ends, too much and the war escalates into Pakistan. That's the understanding and it suits everybody.'

Rossiter had regained his composure. 'Don't give me that

59

rubbish. If ground-to-air missiles suit your government, then they suit you.'

'What comic strip did they dig you out from?'

'Just run along like a good lad and keep your friends in Islamabad stalled for a week while you wait for verification of us from the charities . . .' Rossiter managed a smile now, an ice smile. 'That would be the best thing you could do.'

The spook, Davies, on the payroll of the Secret Intelligence Service and running the Islamabad desk while his chief was on long leave and who was nominally a Second Secretary (Consular/Visas) at the High Commission, walked out of the living room and into the night without a word.

Rossiter heard the start of a car's engine. As soon as it was gone he slapped his hands together to control his trembling. Rossiter knew what he would do. First he went to his bedroom and stripped off the blanket from his bed, then took more blankets from the top shelf of the wardrobe. Inside Barney's bedroom he manhandled the crate from under the iron frame and lifted off the crate top. He wrapped four missiles in the blankets, and hid with them the launch control unit and the loaded Polaroid camera and the spare film cassettes and a carton of flash bulbs.

The sweat dripped and ran on his body, he could not control the trembling. When he was asked over the telephone for the destination of the taxi he required, he gave first the Peshawar address of the group's camp and second the street of the International Red Cross compound.

Three hours before dawn the Volkswagen van started out for the town of Parachinar in the blunt salient of Pakistan territory jutting into Afghanistan and eighty miles from Peshawar. Against the leather sandals of the men, spread on the floor, were four Redeye missiles in their protective casing and launch unit, and Howard Rossiter's blankets. Gul Bahdur sat beside the driver, nestled close to his shoulder,

60

the Polaroid hanging around his neck, and recited silently the
words that he had memorised.

'Underneath the gunner's seat, behind armoured
doors . . .'

Over the holed, winding road it was a six hours' drive to
Parachinar, where they would eat and then sleep. Later they
would drive for another hour and then leave the van and
collect the small arms that were not carried in the refugee
camps, and start the climb to the Kurram Pass.

'Beside that is the radio command guidance antenna.
Above the gunner's position . . .'

Soon the boy was asleep, cuddled by the warmth and
motion of the van.

In an hour it would be light.

Barney left the land-rover in the road, walked briskly
towards the darkened bungalow. He felt no tiredness. He felt
as if he had been resurrected by the commune under the
stars. He wondered if Rossiter would now agree with good
grace to give him the extra week, and he thought how he
would use it and how he would insist on organising the group
to be certain that only one man had the responsibility of firing
Redeye.

He let himself into the living room. He went silently
towards his room. He heard a woman's giggle, and a deeper
laugh, and a whisper for quiet, and the metalled heaving of a
bed.

Lying on the sheet of his own army neat bed was the
Redeye manual. He saw the tip of the crate protruding
beyond the bed side. He bent, scraped it out, lifted the
loosened lid, and counted the four launch tubes and the
launch control mechanism gone. Quietly, in fury, he opened
the cupboard drawer to find the Polaroid and the spare
cassettes and the flash bulbs gone too. He swept out through
his door. He threw open the door into Rossiter's room. His

61

finger found the light switch, snapped it down. Rossiter sat on the side of his bed, his eyes blinked at the ceiling light and then in hatred at Barney. He was naked save for one sock. Sitting across his waist, naked too, with her legs wrapped hard at his hips, with her arms around his neck, was a woman who was dark haired and plump and red skinned and sweating.

'Fuck you, Crispin,' Rossiter shouted.

The woman screamed.

'Get that cow out of here,' Barney said.

A sob gathered force in Rossiter's throat. 'You bastard . . .'

The woman whimpered, buried her face in Rossiter's chest.

'Get her out,' Barney said.

Now Barney turned away. The woman was crying. She slid off Rossiter, twisted him, hurt him. She stumbled across the tiles to retrieve her scattered clothes and ran past Barney into the living room.

With his heel Barney kicked the door shut behind him.

'You treacherous little behind-the-back bastard.'

'You came in here to tell me that?'

'You hadn't the nerve to tell me to my face.'

Fear on Rossiter's face, wide and staring eyes under the thin tangle of his hair. He tugged the single sheet on his bed across his lap.

'You weren't here, you don't know what happened.'

'What's happened is that you've sent a rubbish group away when they're not ready.'

'I didn't have a week.'

'They needed that week.'

'They needed it, they couldn't have it. The spook came. Security in Islamabad are interested in us. We're on our way in a week, a week's how long the bloody cover can stretch.'

Barney felt hideously ashamed, soiled.

'You weren't here, where in God's name were you? If we'd waited a week we'd have had to go home without any group going at all.' Rossiter rolled onto his side on the bed. He was pathetic. His white stomach flopped close to the outline of his drawn up knees, the hanging light glistened the skin on the crown of his head. He was weeping.

'That's the best woman I've known in years. A nurse, a kind sweet woman. You think I get that at home . . .?'

The front door slammed. There was a clatter of heels on the wood planks of the verandah.

'The spook came here?'

'It'll keep until the morning,' Rossiter said bitterly, and his cheeks were wet. 'I've a lady to take home . . . It's only one helicopter we need. We're not joining their bloody war.'

Barney went back to his room, undressed, and fell on his bed.

5

When he had left the Officers' Quarters for the staff briefing he had unfastened the leather holster flap, tested that the lanyard was secured to the handle of the weapon. It was standing orders that officers in uniform should be armed when walking out in Kabul, Pyotr Medev thought the order was of particular relevance to those such as himself who were unfamiliar with the capital city, who were occasional visitors from the out of town divisional commands. Once a week the MilPol had the job of scraping some idiot out of a blood-stained gutter, in uniform or civilian clothes. One of his own corporals had gone that way.

He had noted the cluster of Soviet civilians in front of him, men and women, slacks and open shirts and pretty floral frocks, meandering past the small stores. He had noted the four man patrol that was behind him. He was sandwiched and safe as he walked.

He had turned into the bazaar that bulged with the smells and sounds of this high-table city. Men cried from their shop fronts for custom, youths carried on their turbaned heads the wide trays of meats and cakes, children skipped between the donkeys and the horses that showed their lined rib cages. But no one barged into the path of a Soviet officer wearing the uniform of Frontal Aviation and the shoulder insignia of Major. They wafted around him as though he did not exist.

They were animals. They were dirty, filthy, ignorant and cruel.

He didn't give a shit for the animals. He shouted that in his mind.

As Medev walked he checked again that the civilians were in front of him, that the patrol was behind. A careful man would return to his home at the end of a year.

There was a small, sharp grin at Medev's mouth, triggered by the thought of home, mingled with the thought of why he was now in the bazaar where the high-sided buildings shut out the high sun. Home was five weeks away, home was a woman that he sometimes loved and a small boy that he perpetually adored, but he walked in the bazaar to buy a trinket of jewellery for a married girl, bored and entertaining, and living in the Mikroyan residential sector for Soviets in Kabul. Visiting the wife of a Ukrainian agronomist on his journeys to staff briefings in Kabul roused in Medev the same excitements as piloting the Mi-24 gunship.

A child ran from a sack-draped doorway and pulled a blind man from his path. Medev had been far away. He had not seen the blind man with the yellowed socket eyes.

When he was past the blind man and the boy, Medev heard the gurgle of gathered spit in the boy's mouth, heard it smack on the street dirt behind him. He did not turn.

He lifted his wide-brimmed cap, smoothed down his short sandy hair, felt the perspiration settle on the back of his hand.

A dog hustled across the street, moving fast and low on emaciated legs, clutching raw meat in its jaws. A thrown stone hit the rear legs, spinning it, collapsing it. A man sprinted forward, billowing clothes, a shout of fury, a stick raised. The dog was beaten. It yelped, it howled under the blows, but it would not release the meat. The blows rained on the dog's spine. If a man would do that to his own dog how would he thrash a Soviet?

The nightmare of the pilot was that the helicopter should plummet down towards the dry river bed of a valley, and that the pilot should live . . . It was the nightmare that was always with him, with him in each waking moment, harboured in each sleeping hour. Even when he walked to find a

65

brooch of lapis lazuli to take to the woman who was married to an agronomist.

He could see the bright shirts and dress materials of the civilians in front. He looked behind and saw the patrol.

He was thirty years old. For eleven years he had flown helicopters. He had served two tours in the forward squadron bases in the DDR with the Mi-24A. He was a graduate of the Cadet Academy of Moscow, he had passed through the Staff College of Frontal Aviation at Kiev. He was qualified as an instructor on the Mi-24D. He was a member of the Communist Party of the Union of Soviet Socialist Republics. He was of the élite, he was of the chosen ones. He was a professional serviceman. At the airbase at Jalalabad in Nangarhar province he commanded two flights, each of four Mi-24D helicopters. Each month he came to Kabul for 36 hours of intensive debriefing by the staff officers of the Taj Beg palace, headquarters of the Soviet High Command.

He stopped beside a table of jewellery.

Behind an opened doorway, deep in the recesses of the shop, men were squatting at their work, shapes in shadow, only the sounds of their tool-work clear. Hanging from the arch of the doorway were old curved swords and a musket that was called a jezail. Close to an old man with the whitened beard and the tight-wrapped turban who sat behind the table were hookah vessels of brilliant blue glaze. The old man sat on a rich carpet square. The Soviet officer loomed above him. Medev pointed to a lapis brooch. Without speaking the old man counted out the price of the brooch with his fingers. Medev knew the game. From his hip pocket he took a wad of Afghan notes. Medev's turn to count, notes to the value of a half of the sum that the old man had indicated. Medev picked up the brooch, dropped the notes on the table, walked away. He heard the protest croak of the old man.

Animals, weren't they? And right that they should be treated like bastard animals.

He went on his way. She would have prepared some food and after that he would have two hours only before he must collect his transport and get himself to the airport's military side for the flight back to Jalalabad.

The faint bleating of the mule had attracted them.

They stood, half a dozen men, on the narrow path high above the floor of the valley. They stood and looked over the edge to the miniaturised rocks and smoothed boulders below the rock wall. On such a path, so insecure, it was not hard to believe that the two laden mules could have stumbled and fallen. They were two hundred feet above the pain-filled cry of the animal in which some small portion of life remained.

One man stood apart from the group. He wore the same clothes as they did, the fustian trousers, the baggy grey shirt with the tails loose to his knees, the wound turban of blue on his head, but he was apart. There were boots not sandals on his feet, old and worn but still serviceable. His beard and moustache were a cropped grey stubble as if once a week he abandoned the attempt to grow a full length of hair and shaved himself with a blunted razor. He was taller, his eyeline fully three inches higher than the men with him. Across his chest were two ammunition belts swathed diagonally, and cradled in the elbow of his right arm was a Kalashnikov assault rifle, two magazines strapped head to toe.

The man took no part in the debate on the crying mule.

When he wiped a fly from his nose he used his left arm and the motion drew back his sleeve and revealed a metal claw in the place of his left hand. The claw was flecked with ochre rust set as a rash in the black paint.

On the back of each of these men was a coarse webbing pack, and thrusting from the top of each pack were clustered tail fins of mortar shells. In the pack of the man who stood apart were three 88mm mortar shells, shiny and bright with

67

the new Cyrillic lettering of Soviet ordnance. He seemed to carry no food and no spare clothing. With the smooth surface of the curve of the claw he rubbed gently against the weathered skin of his nose, wrinkled skin because he was not a young man.

The men were gathering for an ambush on the convoy that came every two weeks from Kabul to replenish the supplies of the Afghan Army garrison at Gardez in Paktia province. When such an attack was prepared by the Resistance, when there was the need for a force of more than two hundred *mujahidin* then the word would spread as a whisper of wind through the villages, and the men would gather at a given point. It was not for two hundred fighting men to remain in concentration for any but the briefest time, the helicopters dictated that. When the call came, the whisper, the men collected. As soon as the attack was completed they went their separate ways. These half dozen would reach their rendezvous that evening. They had little time now to spare.

One man aimed a stone down the cliff precipice and missed the head of the live mule and struck it in the stomach and the mule gave out a shrill scream, and the man laughed.

Another man waved Maxie Schumack forward, made a gesture of shooting. They liked to watch him fire his Kalashnikov. It always amused them to see the way he clamped the shoulder stock of the rifle hard into his right shoulder and rested the barrel on his outstretched and crippled left arm. When the echo of the single shot died in the valley there was only silence. They had no time to recover the loads on the mules' backs. They set off along the path, Schumack a little behind.

He was apart from these men, yet with them. He had found the relationship that he desired. Apart but accepted. He asked for nothing more.

Pyotr Medev wondered what in exact terms was the work of an agronomist. He sat in his long underpants at the table of the small living room listening to Ilya singing from the kitchen.

He was drinking from the neck of a beer bottle when she came out from the kitchen. She had tied a towel round her waist, and her tanned breasts hung towards the towel's knot, her hair still sweat-streaked from their love-making hung to her shoulders. What *did* an agronomist do? What could make it worthwhile to be down in Kandahar grubbing in the dirt beside a stinking irrigation channel, when this creature was abandoned back home? And Ilya was nuzzling her cheek against his ear, and the breasts and the nipples were playing patterns on his back, and there was a salad plate with sliced sausage in front of him, and another beer bottle on the table. He drank his beer, he picked at his sausage. She reached for his underpants, and tugged the elastic of the waist band. He groaned through a mouthful of meat, tomato dribbled from the side of his mouth. Medev sighed. The breasts, large and soft and warm and sweated, covered his mouth now, and he nibbled and felt her hand going down over him. He turned his head, extricated himself, drank from the bottle, ate from the plate, then spluttered at the sensation won by the painted nails of her fingers. Sometimes he wished she would say something, she never seemed to think it necessary. As if she could cope with signs, signs and the heavy bloody breathing.

It wasn't as if he was doing the agronomist any harm. He wouldn't have wanted to hurt the poor bastard. She'd have to play the good actress when winter came, when he made it back from Kandahar. She'd been taught things by Pyotr Medev, things that a good Georgian girl should stay ignorant of. She'd be explaining all night if she wheeled out her new tricks when he came back from Kandahar. It was three months since Medev had met Ilya, a spring afternoon at the Kargha Lake where an officer could swim in some safety, and find himself a nurse from Kabul's military hospital if he was lucky. Three months and three visits later. They hadn't wasted time. And who had time to waste? Not a bored woman in the Mikroyan residential complex while her husband was digging a ditch in Kandahar. Not an officer who commanded the pilots who flew the convoy escorts, who had to bring the big birds down through the cones of rifle and machine gun fire . . . Shit, and the armour was thick and good on the belly of the big bird . . . and if it wasn't they'd all have been home months ago in the body bags what was left of them, in the body bags and not feeling those bloody nails down in his crotch.

She wriggled on his knee so that the towel knot loosened. She was going to be the sweet death of the poor agronomist when he came back from Kandahar. Better stay put, old friend. Stick to the irrigation ditch, keep the good cold water up to your thighs.

And it wasn't as though he was being unfaithful to the woman back in Moscow.

Not really unfaithful, though the nails worked at him and teased him and the towel fell further, because she wouldn't have an idea, his wife in Moscow, of flying the big bird, Mi-24D, in combat up the long Afghan valleys, over the high Afghan mountains. Safe enough up there, up in the azure, up in the cloud, the evil waited at ground level. Only took a lucky hit or a fuel pipe blockage or a stress fracture that Maintenance hadn't caught, and he'd be down into that evil that was the ground. He'd shoot himself, he wouldn't stand about and wait, he'd shoot . . . Shit, and he was with a woman, a woman with hungry breasts and wide hips, a woman into whom he could drive himself and bury himself.

He cleared the food from his throat, he swigged the dregs from the beer bottle. He stood up, he picked Ilya high off the floor and her legs circled his waist so that he could carry her better, and she laughed out loud and he managed a smile, and carried her to the bedroom. For a month he could savour her. A memory for a month. He had no photograph of her, because if he carried it in his flying suit and was killed and his body recovered, then the picture would travel with his watch and his wallet back to Moscow. If he had left a photograph of her in his quarters in Jalalabad and failed to return from a mission, then the picture with his other possessions would slip into the plastic sack to go to his wife and his son. And that was why when he took her to bed he never closed his eyes, never ever, because if his eyes were open then he would remember her better when he flew over the mountains and valleys, above the convoys, through the rifle fire.

The bed shook and creaked and heaved as the Major made a play at loving the agronomist's wife.

Four days out on the trail from the salient of Parachinar, the group of Hizbi-i-Islami *mujahidin* with whom Mia Fiori travelled had stopped at this village for food and sleep. But she was a nurse so she was taken at once to the house of the mullah, and was shown the wounded. She spoke only a few words of the dialect of the Pathan tribespeople – but enough to communicate the basics of information.

Her destination was the Panjshir valley, eight or nine days and nights march ahead. The *mujahidin* who escorted her would allow her to spend this one night caring for the wounded they found in the village. She had little influence over these people. It would have been different if the doctor had travelled with her, but a sudden stomach infection had put the doctor to bed in Peshawar and dictated that she travel alone with the Hizbi-i-Islami. Mia Fiori had work that had to be done in the Panjshir and she had determined to make the journey. In this village, through the hours of darkness, she could accomplish her best at cleaning and cauterising the wounds, she could feed into these wracked bodies a little of

71

the morphine that she carried in her back pack, and then when the dawn came she must walk away from them to the next village.

There had been fourteen in the group, she was told. Eight were dead already. Five more lay on the makeshift bedding that had been spread across the swept concrete floor of the mullah's house. A boy cowered in the black shadow against a windowless wall of dry stone, hunched in a blanket, protecting something hidden. Already there was the stink of infection from the opened bowel wounds, from the embedded shrapnel, from the protruding bone splinters. She was not a surgeon, she was a nurse. She did not have the skills of surgery, nor the equipment.

On her knees she moved amongst the wounded five, dabbing with lint cloth. When she looked up and into the faces of the watching tribesmen she was met with only cold stares. As if they read her despair and wondered why she bothered. Death in the *jihad* was martyrdom, why then prolong a hopeless life? To win them a little comfort, she exhausted that small stock of morphine.

She had long hair, dark and curled in ringlets and falling over her ears. She had deep wind-tanned cheeks. She had the strong nose of a fighter, and the chin of a combatant. Something of the hawk in her face, something too of the lion. A small bosom that would go unnoticed under a grey cheesecloth blouse. Long and rangy legs, loose moving in the full skirt that when she stood would cover her ankles. Grey socks rolled low on her ankles and heavy duty walking sandals.

Mia was not concerned about her appearance. The passing of the first bloom of her youth was a matter of supreme indifference to her. Appearance had not helped her as a teenager living in the tower flats of Rome's Via Nomentana, nor when she trained in nursing at the Policlinico, nor when she married the club-foot French medical student who was misshapen and whom she loved, nor when he had qualified and they married and he had piled their old Renault into an unlit parked lorry, nor when she had buried him. Appearance was an irrelevance when she had taken a job as a ward nurse in a public hospital close to St Germain. On a bright spring morning, without a comb in her hair and without cosmetics on her face, she had walked into the back street office at Aide Médicale Internationale and said matter-of-factly that she had her summer leave to fill. She had spent the previous summer with a doctor and another nurse in the Panjshir. She had spent the long Paris winter fretting again for her leave and the chance to return. A long winter of dreaming of a sort of homecoming, and on the floor of the mullah's house was the reality of the homecoming.

She stood up, and shrugged. The men gazed back at her without emotion.

Of course she knew of the *jihad*. All last summer the creed of the holy war and sacrifice had been belted into her by the fighters. Mia was a survivor. She sighed, and cleaned her hands on a cloth. The kerosene threw waving shadows through the room, flickered in the eyes of the men, flashed on their teeth. There were the soft, patient sob groans of the wounded for whom she knew there was no hope. She saw the boy in the corner, against the far wall from the doorway. He was wrapped in a blanket of fine bright colours and his knees made a tent of the blanket and were drawn up against his chest, and he shivered in shock, and there was dark congealed blood on his forehead.

She came close to him, knelt in front of him, seemed to shield him from the scene of dying men.

'Parla l'italiano . . . l'inglese?'

'English, I speak English'. A little whispered voice.

'I can speak in English. My name is Mia. What is your name?'

'I am Gul Bahdur.'

73

'You were with these men?' She gestured behind her.
'How long ago?'

'Four days ago, the helicopters came . . . I have to go
back to Peshawar.'

'When you are ready you can go back. First you must
rest.'

'I have to go back to Peshawar.' The boy was crying. He
struggled against the tears and failed.

'When you are ready.'

Mia wiped at the tears on the soft brown cheeks of the
boy. She held his chin in her hand to steady the trembling and
peered at the head wound.

'It is nothing,' the boy said.

'It is your only wound?'

'It is nothing, I am here to wait for my companions to
come with me.'

She felt the boy draw back from her as she dabbed at the
wound. She looked into his eyes, into his youth.

'Why do you have to go back to Peshawar, Gul Bahdur?'

'I have to.'

Mia pulled back the blanket, catching the boy by surprise.
She saw the Redeye missile launcher, the light of the
kerosene lamp winked on the wires of the sighting. It was
something she had not seen before. She dropped the blanket,
concealed it.

'You have to take that back?'

The boy did not reply.

She reached into her back pack, took out a bandage and
wrapped it fast and tight on the boy's forehead. His eyes
glowed beneath the white of the bandage, his hair peeped
above the binding. She knotted the ties, then stood up. She
went back towards the five men on the floor, looked down on
them, shrugged again. The gesture was understood, and the
despair in her face.

Only in the Panjshir were the nurses and doctors who

74

came from Paris accorded a genuine welcome. In the Panj-shir the resistance had achieved a liberated zone. In that valley the doctors and nurses were honoured.

Away in the high desert lands of the Hazaras a French doctor had been forced to quit when the village people he sought to help would not feed him because their mullah had branded him an unbeliever. But whether they were welcomed, or whether they were shunned, the small medical teams with their trifling supplies of French-donated drugs and antiseptics, lived and worked in the knowledge that their efforts were pitifully small.

And there were dangers. After the principal guerrilla commanders, the Soviets put the doctors and nurses on the top of the list for death or capture. Eight years in a Kabul gaol had been the sentence handed down to a young French doctor trapped in a surrounded village. Perhaps they all felt a sense of adventure, the doctors and the nurses, when they went to the offices of AMI to offer their services. But the spirit of adventure died fast inside Afghanistan. The first sight of a foot blown away by a butterfly anti-personnel, the first sight of a body disembowelled by the rocket's splinters, the first sight of the lemon-sized exit wound of a high explosive bullet, all of those extinguished the spirit of adventure. And for Mia Fiori it was a daily sorrow when she must move on, away from men that she could not help.

She had nursed in tragic, miserable public wards in Paris, and she had learned to hide her feelings well. Harder here, bitterly hard.

An hour later Mia left the village, a tall and long-striding figure in the middle of the column of weapon-laden men of the Hizbi-i-Islami *mujahidin*, and was swallowed in the pale dusk light.

The sun cascaded in gold over far mountains to the west as the helicopter wound along the thread of the Kabul river.

75

They flew high, more than a thousand metres, safe from ground level small arms fire.

Medev had waited nearly two hours at the officers' transportation shed at the military side of Kabul's airport before the helicopter was ready to fly. He was in lacklustre humour, always the same when he was leaving Ilya, going back to Jalalabad. He could smell the scent of her body on his skin, he thought he could feel the taste again of her tongue in his mouth. A Colonel sat beside him in the hold of the Mi-4 troop carrier, beneath the pilot's cockpit. Behind the Colonel and Medev sat six conscripts of Mechanised Infantry. The Colonel offered Medev a slug of vodka from a hip flask. The conversation was desultory above the engine noise. Soon after take off, the sun slipped from sight. It was a journey of an hour, going fast enough as Medev brooded on the agronomist's wife and five more weeks to be served in Afghanistan. One more visit to Kabul. One more afternoon with Ilya. Then the long flight on the Aeroflot back to Moscow, and Medev's back turned once and for all on this shitty place. Everyone believed in their own war, didn't they? It wasn't said out loud, but he supposed the Americans must have believed in their Vietnam. And the British in the South Atlantic, they would have believed in their war, although that was the reimposition of the colonialist regime. And the Israelis in the Lebanon. Medev believed in the war of Afghanistan, just wished most of the time that another bugger was there to fight it for him.

And he thought they were winning. Bloody slow, but they were winning. He had studied Vietnam. Sometimes he thought of the awfulness of fighting a war, Vietnam or Afghanistan, when you knew you were not winning. At least they were winning in Afghanistan. The helicopters were decisive, his helicopters, his Mi-24s.

'You're in helicopters?'

'I have a squadron of gunships, two flights,' Medev replied.

'Do they use them for Intelligence?' The Colonel grinned.

'We fly free fire reconnaissance.'

'No . . . no . . . Intelligence had a trick in Herat where I was before, using the helicopters.'

'We can be given assignments by Intelligence, if there is something particular.'

The Colonel looked at Medev as if unsure whether the Major beside him was play-acting dumb or merely stupid.

'Herat is difficult, close to the Iran border, they have the Khomeini disease there. It takes a rare power of persuasion to make the bandits talk under interrogation. Anything normal and they spit in your face. There was a helicopter squadron in Herat that co-operated in a most successful scheme for Intelligence.'

'What did they manage in Herat?' Medev felt the slow descent towards the Jalalabad navigation lights.

'They'd get hold of three of the bastards and put them in the back of a gunship and fly them up to a thousand metres. They'd throw the first one out, no questions, throw him out and let the others hear his squeal as he went out through the hatch. Sometimes the second isn't too sure if it's for real, if he has a doubt, he goes. The third always talks, that's what we found in Herat.'

Medev coughed. The vomit had risen in his throat. He swallowed hard, and wiped saliva from his lips with the sleeve of his tunic.

'I don't think we've tried that in Jalalabad.'

The helicopter landed, bounced on its four wheels, settled.

He heard the whine dissolve as the engines were cut. He unclipped his seat harness, waited for the door to be opened.

He saw the perimeter lights of the Jalalabad airbase, and under the lights were the hoops of close coiled barbed wire.

The squadron's Adjutant, Captain Rostov, met him on the tarmac.

The Colonel had an entourage waiting, salutes and clicking boot heels. Medev had Rostov. A fat little creep. Not a flier, wouldn't know how to turn the engine, but good with the paperwork.

Medev shouldered his overnight grip and walked briskly past the Colonel's party. Away to his right, inside sand bag revetments was the line of Mi-24 helicopters that he commanded. Ahead of him were the lights of the Administration building of his squadron and the living quarters of his crews. Rostov followed, scurrying to keep up.

'What's happened?'

'Since you've been away?' Rostov sniggered. 'Hasn't been quiet.'

Medev punched the Captain's arm, punched it hard.

'You want the scandal first? Two Mig-25s came in this morning, testing the runway length or something, ground crew got at them. They have alcohol in the coolant and braking system of the Twenty-Five. Ground crew were caught draining off the alcohol . . .'

'I don't believe it.' A gasp of astonishment from Medev.

'Truly, draining off the alcohol, one was already pissed, three in the MilPol cells. That's the scandal . . . The flight's back from Gardez . . . Alexei took it down you remember for a week, they're back and boasting their bloody tongues off. They hit a group four days ago, and they broke up an ambush this morning but the other lorries made it through, they reckon they really crapped on the ambush. Funny thing I heard about the hit four days ago, they reckon a rocket was fired at them . . .'

Medev had been listening quietly, happy to let Rostov chatter as they made their way to Administration. Now he turned his head sharply.

'What did he see?'

'If he'd seen anything he might have known what it was. Middle of the day, saw some movement, he was last in the flight, flash on the ground and didn't see what was fired, only the flash. Nothing hit him. He reckoned it was an RPG-7, that was the best he could do. Desperate, aren't they, if they're firing anti-tank rockets at helicopters?'

Medev knew the RPG-7. Effective range against a tank was 300 metres maximum. No guidance system, wasted against a helicopter. 'Couldn't be anything else.'

'Whatever it was, Alexei got them, blasted the arses off them.'

'He didn't go down?'

'Zapped them and got the hell out.'

'Couldn't be anything else because they don't have missiles.' They parted at Medev's door.

The image of his wife filled his mind, hurting him and blaming him. He never slept well when he came back from Kabul . . . in five weeks time he could forget the whole bastard place.

He looked from the window of his small room. He saw the blazing line of the perimeter's lights and a speeding patrol jeep and a sentry with a dog. He drew the curtains and started to undress. He saw the photograph of his wife and his son.

Five more weeks.

6

Rossiter leaned across the table at lunchtime, a meal of tinned spaghetti hoops and toast, held his chin in his hands and took the deep gulp of breath to prepare himself for a rehearsed speech.

'It's bloody stupid, Barney. It's imbecile, it's not even professional.'

'I know that, Mr Rossiter.'

'It's the way we go on at home. I don't want to bring my bloody home to Peshawar.'

'I'm sorry, Mr Rossiter.'

Barney had seen the weight drift off Rossiter's face, seen his back straighten in relief.

Barney wondered when he had last apologized to a grown man, he didn't think he could remember. There might have been times when he had used a tactical apology to extricate himself from a difficulty. He doubted if since he had become an adult he had ever apologised with a wide and open face to another man. It was not his way.

'That's big of you, Barney, I appreciate that.' Rossiter kneaded his hands nervously. 'Won't you call me Ross.'

And Barney had smiled, and picked up the plates and gone to the kitchen with them. Barney had apologised, but Rossiter had first stamped down on the ice. Perhaps the fool who might have chosen the wrong group, who might have waved himself round small-town Peshawar, who lived in a world of white men that was dead thirty years ago, perhaps Rossiter was the brave man.

On that morning after the echoing clatter of the woman's

heels as she fled over the verandah, had filled the bungalow, Barney had been first to the shower, and when he had dressed he had circumspectly dismantled the wooden packing crate in his bedroom and made a pile of the boards by the window and a heap of the remaining eight Redeye missiles on his bed. The boards he buried low under the woodpile that climbed against the outside kitchen wall ready for the winter. The missiles he laid in a pit dug from the hard ground of the vegetable patch behind the bungalow, and after they were hidden he covered the newly turned earth with the spread of tomato and pumpkin fronds that he had uprooted.

For the next six days there was a truce. There was slowly and painfully a coming together.

They waited for news of the group.

Day and night the waiting, and the whine of the mosquitoes, and the scuffle of the lizards, and the lowing of distant traffic horns, and Rossiter finding any excuse to get himself away from the bungalow, and Barney sitting in his chair by the window of the living room and staring out over the verandah, and waiting. Some evenings Barney would still be in the chair in the darkened room with a closed book on his knee when Rossiter came back from wherever he went with his woman, some evenings he would stumble past Barney's chair, and go to his room with an unanswered greeting.

Sometimes, in the still evenings when he was alone, Barney tossed his memories back to family, to old photographs. He could make a vague picture of his mother, dead when he was seven. It had been many years before he had discovered the circumstances of her death. A seven-year-old hadn't been told that his Mummy was in another man's car. Wasn't suitable for a seven-year-old to know that. The picture of his father was clearer. A man who had lost his verve and his way when his son was seven years old. The picture of his father was always of an old man with a sadness alive in his eyes, a man marked down for tragedy, and he'd found it as surely as if he'd been searching. Barney had been nineteen, a cadet at the Military Academy, escaping from something he wasn't certain existed. In the autumn, and he hadn't been home for four months, and his father had gone to collect a pension form from a Post Office. Barney's father confronting a man with a sawn-off shot gun. Anyone else would have lain on the floor. Gone in with his knees and his elbows, that's what they'd said at the Coroner's court and at the trial, before the front of his head ended on the ceiling of the Post Office. When your mother dies in another man's car, when your father dies protecting Post Office money that would have been replaced three hours later, then relationships tend to get stunted, that's what Barney thought. Barney Crispin's next-of-kin was listed on the Regiment's file as his Colonel. There had to be a name, so it was the Colonel's name.

They were eight days into the waiting vigil. Late afternoon. Barney sitting by the window. Rossiter was behind him in the living room, grunting and whistling in his teeth as he attacked the week-old crossword in the *Daily Telegraph*.

'What's "He might be said to help the car go on board, but not principally", eight and five?'

Barney didn't answer, Rossiter wouldn't expect him to.

Barney watched the boy come through the open gates into the garden.

He knew immediately that it was Gul Bahdur. The sight of the boy was disaster. Gul Bahdur sidled up the driveway, hesitated and looked at the land-rover as if to check the authenticity of the bungalow. The bandage on his head was yellow from dust, his flapping trousers and his long shirt and the blanket gathered over his shoulder were grimed in the same colour. Barney saw the stumble of tiredness as Gul Bahdur stepped up onto the verandah, and rose swiftly from his chair.

'Eight and five, I haven't an idea,' murmured Rossiter.

Barney went to the door, swung it open, and helped the boy step inside.

'Mr Davies, I do not have to remind you of the position taken by my government in relation to aid and assistance supplied to the Afghan Resistance movement . . .'

'You don't have to remind me, Colonel.'

'We have always drawn the line at any form of foreign intervention.'

'I know that, sir.'

'It is our public attitude, it is also our private attitude.'

Davies from the High Commission shared a sofa in the lobby of the Islamabad Holiday Inn with a Colonel of Internal Security. The Colonel wore a dark suit, a London shirt sewn with his initials and a silk tie. Martial Law had been kind to him, popping him from conventional armoured corps staff job into the shadowed heights of Security and Counter-Subversion. Davies found it hard to keep his eyes away from the man's face. It was the way the Colonel continually rolled the tips of his moustache that attracted the spook. But this man with his precise English accent was power. Davies, the spook, must show respect for such power.

'Your government has been totally consistent in its attitude, Colonel.'

'We believe that foreign intervention in the Afghanistan war poses a dangerous threat to the interests of Pakistan.'

'Understandably.'

'We have discouraged any form of mercenary involvement in Afghanistan by foreigners operating from inside our territory.'

'Successfully discouraged it, if I may say so, sir.'

'Mr Davies, these two men in Peshawar . . .'

'I've had the telegram back, from Refugee Action . . .' Davies reached into the breast pocket of his safari shirt. 'I was going to bring it to . . .'

The face of the Colonel was very close to the spook's. Davies could see the sheen of the wax that bound together the moustache hairs. The Colonel's voice was very quiet, a whisper in Davies' ear, his pupils uncomfortably close and dark.

'They are not mercenaries, Mr Davies. If they had been mercenaries then your Secret Intelligence Service would not have been concerned with providing them the hasty cover of charity works.'

The spook squirmed. 'Refugee Action confirm from London . . .'

'Don't be silly, Mr Davies.' The Colonel's voice dropped further. The spook leaned forward to hear him better. 'They should go home.'

'What do you mean, sir?'

'I think it is clear, to me it is clear. I am not saying you are lying, I am suggesting you are merely a carrier of telegrams. Get them out immediately before I am obliged to look into the objective of their mission.'

Davies leaned back on the sofa, considered whether to continue with the fabrication.

'If they are not gone, and immediately, it will be seen as a grave provocation, Mr Davies, to my government.'

'I understand, sir.'

'Just get them out.'

'Yes, sir.'

'Would you like me to have the telegram you were about to give me?'

'I don't think that's necessary, sir,' the spook said bleakly.

The boy reached under the blanket that was wrapped around his upper body and took the missile's sighting and launch control mechanism from its hiding place. He swayed on his feet, a birch in light wind, as he held out the equipment to Barney, and lifted from under his shirt the Polaroid camera.

'What happened? In God's name what happened?' The piping voice of Rossiter.

'Sit down, Gul Bahdur,' Barney said gently. He guided the boy to his own chair.

'What the bloody hell happened?'

'Have you eaten anything?'

The boy looked from the face of Rossiter that rippled in anxiety to the calm of Barney's. He found a haven with Barney, his arms dropped loose into his lap, his neck bent, his chin fell to his chest.

'Will somebody tell me what happened?' Rossiter shrill and frightened.

'You should have something to eat, Gul Bahdur.'

The boy shook his head.

'I've some coke, would you like that?'

Again the boy shook his head, and his eyes closed for a moment and seemed to open only with effort.

'Hey, kiddie, did you get another hundred? Did you kill another hundred Soviets?' Barney said softly, with the smile of a friend.

'It's been a shambles, hasn't it?' Rossiter shouted.

Barney turned, as if reluctantly, away from the boy towards Rossiter. His voice was low. 'Will you be quiet, Mr Rossiter, please . . . How bad, Gul Bahdur?'

The boy was shaking, as if in pain.

'Awful?'

The boy did not have to answer. Barney squatted in front of him and looked into his eyes.

'Worse than awful?'

The boy nodded.

'Tell me.'

Rossiter pulled his chair across the room, scraping the legs on the tiles, and sat over it back to front. Barney crouched close to the boy so that he would be Gul Bahdur's target.

'Two days after we had crossed from Parachinar we were on a path over a valley, we were near to the village of Sazi. We were fourteen men and four mules. There had been a great argument amongst the older men as to where we should go to find the helicopter for the Redeye. Only two of the men knew this path. Because so few men knew it, they were all frightened when they heard a helicopter. If all the men had known the path they would not have been so frightened, we all heard the helicopter, but we could not see it, it was on the far side of the mountain. Some wanted to go back, some wanted to go forward. We were in the open on this path, it was very narrow, if the helicopter had seen us then we would all have been killed. There were two mules roped together at the front, and two mules at the back. The men were pulling at the harnesses of the front mules, pulling the harnesses two ways. One man fell. The path there was not wider than a man's stride. He was hanging to the harness of a mule. He pulled the mule from the path. His weight and that of the mule, that was enough to pull over the second that was roped. They fell all the way to the valley. Do you understand me, Barney? . . . On the back of the second mule we had tied two Redeyes . . .'

'Bloody shambles,' Rossiter sighed.

Barney bit at his lip. 'The other two, Gul Bahdur, tell me.'

'We went from Paktia into Logar province. There is a river that runs south from Kabul through the town of Baraki, they told us in a village that the helicopters often use that river as a marker when they are flying to Gardez or Ghazni. We thought that we could find a helicopter there. We had walked for a day and a half and then we found the river, we came upon it by surprise because this was not a place we were familiar with, we are all from the north of Logar, you understand me, Barney? . . . There was a helicopter, flying fast, very low over the river, almost beneath us. The men

86

were arguing about who should fire the Redeye. One man had the launch part and he took the missile tube from another man's back. He showed his knife to get the missile tube from the other man's back. I think we were not ready to know what you told us, Barney . . . I tried to tell them, Barney . . . They would not listen. The Redeye was fired after the helicopter, it went one hundred metres, it exploded in the ground, the helicopter was more than a thousand metres away . . .'

'What time of the day was it?' Barney asked without anger.

'In the afternoon.'

'Geothermal heat from the ground,' Barney said quietly.

'You told us that, I tried to shout it to them. They would not listen.'

'Pig stupid bastards.' A whine from Rossiter.

'I'm not blaming you, Gul Bahdur.'

'I told them. I promise that I told them.'

'It is very difficult to hit a low flying aircraft, I know that.'

'And the fourth missile, how did you screw that?' The sneer from Rossiter.

'Tell me, Gul Bahdur.'

'All that night there was an argument as to who should fire the last missile. There were three men who said they were the best. By the morning it was decided that the man who was the brother of the wife of our leader in Peshawar, that he should be the man. He is not a young man . . . He would fire it. In the morning we walked north towards Agha valley. It is very dangerous there because they know the people feed the *mujahidin* from their crops. We were near to the village when we heard the helicopters. There were four, two and two. I think he remembered what you had said, the man who had the Redeye, he remembered that you had said we should not fire at the first of the helicopters. As the last went overhead, he fired . . .'

87

'Overhead?' Barney closed his eyes, no longer prepared to disguise his anguish. 'When the sun was overhead?'

'The Redeye went for the sun . . . you told us that is what would happen.'

'It missed?'

'It went for the sun, it exploded very high.'

The voice of the boy tailed away. The silence suffocated the room. There was a tear at the boy's eye.

Rossiter's chair scraped the quiet. He stood up.

'You all need bloody kicking, each last one of you bastards.'

The boy stared into Rossiter's shadowed face.

'The helicopter was aware of something, perhaps he saw the flash of the missile. Everyone was standing up to see better the hitting of the helicopter. We were seen. The helicopters came with rockets and machine guns. Eight were killed there, in the open. We were all in the open. Five more were wounded. I don't know how I lived, why I was saved. When the helicopters had gone I went to the village, and the people came and carried back to the mullah's house those who still lived, and buried those who had died. There was a nurse, a European, who came through the village, she could not help them. I am the only one who lived, Barney.'

'Easy, boy . . .' Barney's hand settled on Gul Bahdur's shoulder.

'For four days I was alone, until I came to Parachinar. I did not stop for sleep or to eat.'

'Thank you.'

The boy was sobbing, tears gurgling in his throat and snuffling in his nose. Barney picked him up and carried him into his room and laid him on the bed and drew the curtain tight and left the boy in the darkness and shut the door behind him.

'That's the end,' Rossiter said. 'Whether you were right, whether I was right.'

Barney stared back at him.

'I'm not asking you, I'm telling you. That's the end. They've wrecked it. Do you laugh or do you cry, Barney bloody Crispin?'

Barney gazed out through the window. From the verandah's light he watched a fly thrash in a spider's web amongst the leaves of a creeper on the outside wall.

Rossiter was pacing, hand behind his back and hunched. 'It's the finish. All that work and for nothing. It's pathetic.'

'What are you going to do, Mr Rossiter?'

'I'm going to drive myself to Islamabad; I'm going to avail myself of secure communications at the High Commission; I'm going to call London; I'm going to tell them it's down the drain. Have you a better idea?'

'You're in charge, Mr Rossiter,' Barney said crisply. 'You'll do what you think best.'

'That's not helpful.' A flash of uncertainty from Rossiter.

'I'm not being helpful nor unhelpful. You're in charge.'

Rossiter showed his pique, found the land-rover keys. He went to the verandah door.

'It's not that either of us is to blame, Barney. It just didn't work out.'

'Not to blame for failing to bring down a Hind, or not to blame for sending thirteen men to their deaths?'

'That's bloody ridiculous.'

Barney walked to the kitchen. Rossiter heard the chink of a metal spoon in the coffee jar. He heard the spout of water running into the kettle. He heard the match strike.

Rossiter slammed the door shut behind him.

The Brigadier rang the front door bell of the St James's flat of the Foreign Secretary at three o'clock in the morning.

The door eased open to the length of a security chain. The Brigadier held his ID card at the gap, though he could see no one. In a few moments the chain was unhooked and the door opened. The detective was shirt-sleeved, there was a revolver poking from the waistband of his trousers and a radio hanging from a strap looped over his shoulder. All a bit melodramatic, the Brigadier thought.

'Fotheringay . . . I have to see the Foreign Secretary.'

The detective pulled a face. He left the Brigadier standing in the hallway and lighting a cigarette. He went to a telephone to wake the man he guarded.

'Freddie, can we have some coffee . . . in the drawing room.'

The Foreign Secretary came down the stairs and led the way into the heavily curtained room. He switched on a fierce ceiling light, waved for the Brigadier to sit down.

'You have my attention.'

'Afghanistan, sir.'

'The Redeye business?'

'It's collapsed.'

The Foreign Secretary tugged at a tangle of his hair, pursed his lips. A kettle whistled, muffled, behind closed doors.

'We'll wait until the coffee's ready or would you prefer tea? No? Please smoke, Brigadier.'

The Brigadier blushed. The Foreign Secretary passed him an ashtray.

The detective carried in a tray. A jug of coffee and hot milk.

He left them.

'How has it collapsed?'

'Lack of discretion by our people, the Pakistan security authorities want them out. We'd stalled on that for the last week, run up a yarn about Refugee Action to give the mission a chance. That's exhausted now.'

'You gave the mission a chance?'

'Our instructor had two weeks with a group preparing them to use Redeye. The group went into Afghanistan nine days ago, fourteen of them. They bungled it. They lost two missiles, they fired two more ineffectively. Thirteen of the fourteen died. That's how it collapsed.'

'And why are you here now?'

'To clear with you that we extricate our personnel as soon as possible. Dispose of the equipment that remains and get out. Lunchtime flight to Delhi, something like that, before the Pakistanis start hollering.'

'What are the alternatives?'

'There are no alternatives, sir.'

The Foreign Secretary played with the tassel of his dressing gown cord, quite furiously. He had not touched his coffee.

'You promised me.'

'I beg your pardon, sir?'

'You promised you were going to give me the workings of a Soviet gunship helicopter.'

'I promised that you would have our best effort.'

'And you've fouled it.'

'It's not an exact science,' said the Brigadier. 'Nothing exact about downing a sophisticated helicopter when you've got a savage on the trigger with two weeks coaching behind him.'

'Did I tell you what the Americans said to me, the provocation I was under that led me to bring you in? And now you're calling it off before we've even begun.'

The Brigadier bridled. He stubbed out his cigarette.

'I'm calling nothing off, you're calling it off. You authorised an intelligence-gathering mission. You started it and now you have to end it, sir.'

There was a light smile on the Foreign Secretary's face, the smile of the disillusioned. He said nothing.

The Brigadier fidgeted in his seat. He wanted to be out, in his own bed.

'I'll send the signal then, for them to get out soonest.'

91

The Foreign Secretary said, 'The man you sent to Pakistan, the Special Air Service instructor, he couldn't go and get the helicopter himself, could he?'

'A British serving officer, inside Afghanistan, with a heat-seeker missile? Preposterous and out of the question. I'm sorry, sir, I've been in Intelligence fifteen years, what you learn in fifteen years is to accept a fact. The fact is that you win a few and you lose a lot. That's the way it is, whether you're playing against the Soviets or the cousins. Another thing you learn, sir, you don't throw good after bad, when it's bad you cut and quit.'

'Well, Brigadier. I am very disappointed. I am sad beyond means at thirteen pointless deaths, but I am bitterly disappointed at the failure of your mission. Send your signal and see at least if you can end the affair without any more of a mess. Freddie,' he hardly raised his voice, but the door opened, 'please show the Brigadier out when he has finished his coffee. If you'll excuse me, Brigadier, I'll go back to bed. Goodnight to you.'

Barney came into his bedroom carrying the missiles cradled across his outstretched arms. He laid them on the rug beside the bed. The boy was sleeping, on his back, mouth open, half covered by the blanket.

Beside the missiles Barney started a small pile. A bottle of penicillin tablets, a packet of three morphine-loaded syringes, a packet of salt tablets, a bottle of glucose sweets, aspirin and dysentery and diarrhoea pills. All he had rifled from the Refugee Action surgery cupboard. Onto the pile he put the hard bar of soap that would last, and then his thick socks.

Other than that his eyes were open, the boy gave no sign of having woken.

Barney undressed. His face was set, grim masked, without expression, shadowed by the light squeezing through the half opened door. He replaced his short sleeved shirt and his jeans with the dress of a Pathan tribesman. He climbed into the wide waisted trousers of rough cotton, pulled tight the waist string. He slipped the long shirt over his head. Then the heavy woollen socks. He was lacing his boots when the boy spoke.

'You are going home, Barney?'

'No.'

'Where are you going?'

'Walking, Gul Bahdur.'

'Where I have been?'

'Tell me about the helicopter attack.'

The boy twisted off his back, lay on his side with his hand holding up his head. Barney threaded the laces through the eyes of the boots.

'After we had fired the missile? After that? First the helicopter we had fired against turned fast away. Then it circled us, going very quickly, as it searched for us. Then it came at us. They began with the rockets. I think four rockets at a time, then when it was very close there was the machine gun, the big machine gun, the big machine gun at the front. It came over us once and when it had gone by then it turned and stayed a little way from us. Then there were more rockets, and all the time the machine gun. Each time one of the men tried to run he was caught by the machine gun. You couldn't even fire at it, every time you fired, the machine gun came after you. When it came the last time it came so low that I could see the gunner in the front and the pilot behind. I could see their *faces*, Barney. And all the time the other helicopters circled high above us. They watched to see that we had all been killed. I could see their faces, then the helicopters went away. It was not a very long time, the attack.'

'Why did you carry back the launcher?'

'I think you know why,' the boy whispered.

'You tell me why you brought back the launcher.'

93

'Without the launcher the Redeye cannot be fired.'

'Who is to fire the missile?'

'We cannot.'

'Who is to fire the missile?' The harsh grate in Barney's question.

'You, Barney.'

The first grey of dawn nudged at the material of the curtains. Barney watched the boy's face, saw the mixed paints of caution and confusion merge into understanding and then excitement. The boy leaped from the bed and flung his arms round Barney and hugged him and kissed him on the cheeks. Gently, Barney loosed the boy's hands, set him back on the bed.

'We have to go this morning.'

'Together we are going?'

'You have to be my ears and my eyes, Gul Bahdur.'

The boy bubbled with his words. 'If we go very soon, to the Red Cross hospital, then we will catch the ambulance that runs each morning to Parachinar. The ambulance will take us. It is always possible to go in the ambulance, straight through the blocks of the Pakistan Guides . . .'

Barney shovelled the bottles and packets and clothes into his back pack.

He heard the land-rover scrape the gravel of the drive. He heard the engine switched off, then the footsteps over the verandah.

'We're moving out, Barney, soon as we can,' Rossiter called from the living room. 'Taking the Delhi flight . . .'

Rossiter was standing in the doorway.

'What in Christ's name are you doing, bloody fancy dress?'

Rossiter peered in the half light at the back pack and the pile of missiles.

'Where the hell are you going?'

Rossiter clapped his hands, as if that were a way to escape

94

an aberration. He spoke with slow schoolmaster's emphasis.

'We're called home. Home, Barney. It is an order.'

Barney smiled. 'You'll think of something to tell them, Mr Rossiter.'

Rossiter was white faced, eyes roving, nervous. 'You'll crucify yourself. They'll have your bloody guts for it. Don't be so bloody stupid. It's your whole bloody career . . . It's against the bloody orders, Barney.'

'You'll think of something to tell them, you're good at that.'

'You'd be on your own.'

'That way's best.'

Barney was tying the missile tubes together, making two bound bundles.

'I have eight Redeyes, I have one helicopter to get, then I'll come out. There's a month before the weather turns . . .'

'It's against an explicit order . . .'

'A month is long enough.'

'Don't you understand . . .?' Rossiter gripped at Barney's arm, was shrugged off.

'What I understand is that something was started that hasn't been finished.'

'Barney, listen to me . . . I may be out of my fucking mind.' Rossiter went, furiously, to his room and slammed the door. Ten minutes later Barney was finished packing. Gul Bahdur had said nothing at all. And then Rossiter reappeared, a fool, a crass old fool . . . 'I'm going to go to Chitral. You know where Chitral is? I'm going to lie up there and wait for you.'

'You don't have to . . .'

'Don't bloody interrupt me, and don't put motives into me . . . so you have some back up, so there's someone to pull you out of the shit when you come back . . . On Shahi Bazaar in Chitral is the Dreamland Hotel, I didn't give it the bloody name . . . Any message, any messenger goes to the Dream-

95

land, reception, name of Howard . . . You have to have some back up, Barney, because they're going to crucify you for this.'

'Thank you, Mr Rossiter.'

'I don't know why I'm doing this. I must be out of my mind. They'll skin us . . .'

'You'll think of something to tell them. Would you take us down to the Red Cross hospital, Mr Rossiter?'

'Us? Are you taking that child back? Oh, my God. I am out of my mind.' Rossiter murmured and walked outside to the land-rover.

7

The would-be conquerors have come many times to Afghanistan.

The armies of Alexander, the hordes of Genghis Khan, the legions of Tamerlane all thrust into the deserts and mountains and crop lands of this region. All butchered and devastated and burned, all built cities and temples in their own image, all failed. Time destroys the man who would seek to impose his will over the Pathans and Uzbeks and Tajiks and Hazaras. His cities are buried in the sands, his temple's stones have made walls for the farmers' fields. The troops of Victoria, of Imperial Britain, came twice with their baggage trains and their servants and met disaster, won a brief victory, and then retreated again.

In 1919 Britain tried for the last time to impose its authority over the tribespeople of Afghanistan and the rulers of Kabul, they brought artillery and aircraft and the machine gunners who had been the widow-makers of the French and Belgian trenches, and when they returned to their homes they had won nothing.

Some lessons are not easily learned.

In late December 1979, Soviet advisers to the puppet government took over the airfields at Begram and Kabul, preparatory to the landing of a flying column of transport aircraft that would be spearheaded by the élite paratroop units of the Red army. The 4th and 105th Airborne Divisions are the cat's cream of the Soviet fighting machine, the best paid and the best equipped and the best trained. In the wake of the paratroops came the divisions of Mechanical Infantry

97

with their tanks and armoured personnel carriers, and above them flew the fighter bombers and the gunship helicopters of Frontal Aviation. The Kremlin had decreed that a 'sympathetic' government should not be toppled by an Islamic fundamentalist rabble.

Four years later. For the man at war, four years is a life time, four years is very often a death time. Four years later, when the general drives through the streets of Kabul from his Residence to High Command HQ, his car is lined with armour-plated steel and his windows reinforced to protect him from the assassin's gun. When the convoy drives from Kabul to Jalalabad it is studded with T-64 tanks and BTR-50 troop carriers. Four years later, the air crew and maintenance crew of an Mi-24 squadron are still working round the clock to maintain the critical air supremacy. They are not fighting the North Atlantic Treaty Organisation forces, not the marines who are the veterans of Da Nang, not the paratroopers who crushed their opposition at Goose Green. Their enemy is a man who cannot read a tactics manual.

Bitter lessons being learned by the armed forces of the Soviet Union four years after invasion day. Each week the body bags are loaded on the transport aircraft. Each day the wounded are strapped down in the hulls of the Antonov transports for the journey to Tashkent and Dushanbe and the intensive care wards and the rehabilitation hospitals. Killed and maimed in Afghanistan because the scriptures of history had not been learned.

Barney Crispin could have told them. Kipling had taught Barney Crispin the lesson learned a century before the Soviets came.

> A scrimmage in a Border Station –
> A canter down some dark defile –
> Two thousand pounds of education
> Drops to a ten-rupee jezail –

The Crammer's boast, the Squadron's pride,
Shot like a rabbit in a ride!

The photograph of his grandfather was Barney's text book.

At first the ambulance driver had refused to take Barney and the boy to the Parachinar salient. The spitting voices of Gul Bahdur and the driver had washed over Barney as he sat in the land-rover beside the downcast Rossiter. Barney had finally opened his door and walked to the driver and put 500 rupees of bank notes into his hand and seen the hand close. Barney lifted the back packs and the two blanket-wrapped bundles into the ambulance and laid them on the floor between the two raised stretchers. Barney went to Rossiter's door, shook his hand through the window.

'Drop me in it, Mr Rossiter, doesn't matter how deep.' A mischievous grin on Barney's face.

'Let me tell you one last time that you're a fool . . .'

'I'm not listening, Mr Rossiter.'

'The Dreamland Hotel, then.'

'The Dreamland Hotel on Shahi Bazaar in Chitral. I won't forget.'

'Your entire bloody career . . .'

'And yours, Mr Rossiter.'

'A few bits of helicopter aren't worth it.'

'You're entitled to your opinon, Mr Rossiter.'

'Is it the bits of helicopters, or is it the thirteen men I sent?'

The boy was tugging at Barney's sleeve. Rossiter had closed his eyes, dropped his head down onto the steering wheel.

Barney walked away, didn't turn, climbed into the back of the ambulance after Gul Bahdur.

It was difficult to see through the dark glass windows of the ambulance. Darra and Kohat and Thal were invisible, identified only because the ambulance slowed in their traffic,

99

and the noise of voices and vehicles seeped into the scrubbed interior where Barney and the boy lay on opposite stretchers. Slow progress, poor roads, sometimes the siren wail when they were brought to a complete halt. Once when they stopped Barney thought he heard the sharp authority voices of the military, but the delay was trifling, and Barney was soon asleep again. An ambulance has a magical run through a road block. They drove for six hours without pulling off the road for food or drink or refuelling.

At Parachinar, Barney saw nothing of the long, dust-billowing street of the frontier town. Gul Bahdur told him that he must keep his head low, that he should not be seen through the grey glass however faintly. They were a long time negotiating that street, through the bleat of goats and the whine of sheep, their smells reaching into the ambulance. Beyond the town the pace of the ambulance quickened and the road was rougher. Barney and the boy rolled on their stretchers.

Those last miles, that last hour in the ambulance, Barney was wide awake.

Concentrating and considering.

He didn't have a gun. He had no language. He had no large scale map. He had no contact other than the seventeen-year-old boy opposite him. He had no plan and he was going to war.

What had Rossiter said? Didn't know whether to laugh or cry . . .

Men made poor decisions under the influence of emotion. In the Regiment's world, emotion was a perverse word. But uncontrolled emotion had put Barney Crispin into the back of an ambulance running west of Parachinar towards the border. He had worked for two weeks with fourteen men to train them to shoot down an Mi-24. Thirteen were dead, the Mi-24 might as well have wiped Barney's face with the back of a fist. That's a good culture for breeding emotion. That and the boy with a bandaged head, in shock, walking for four days to return the launcher. He expected it of Barney. And, remoter though, was the mission's first aim. Bring back the bits. But what's this? Someone hurt? Pakistan intelligence a little cross? Oh dear, end of the party. Better get young Crispin and old Rossiter onto the next plane home. Don't mind the bits, fellows. Must keep the slate clean. Christ Almighty.

The ambulance stopped. The back door opened, bright mid-afternoon sunlight bathed them.

The ambulance had parked beside a wood-built shelter with a roof of corrugated iron. The road behind them had been dirt, it went no further. In front was a failing path stretching to the mountains ahead. The engine of the ambulance was switched off, the noise in the air was of wind and emptiness and of the call of a circling crow. Barney lifted the back packs and the missile bundles out of the ambulance. He breathed in the air that was dry and clean and hot.

'We have to move on from here,' Gul Bahdur said.

'How far?'

'This is where the ambulance waits for the casualties from inside, sometimes the wounded come in the early morning, but if they are near to death then they will be brought across the frontier in daylight and the ambulance will take them in the evening. In the early morning and the evening the Pakistan army is often here, the Guides. It is here that they find how the war is going inside, they talk to the fighters here and go with them to the *chai-khanas* in Parachinar, and take tea with them. If you are here and the Guides find you . . .'

Barney grinned. Great start that would be, locked in the Guard House of a Guides barracks, while the shit spiralled and the telegrams flew.

'Learn one thing, boy, when I ask a question I want an answer, not a speech. How far do we have to go?'

'A thousand metres, out of sight of this place.'

101

On the selection course for the Regiment, on training exercises in the Brecon hills and on Exmoor, Barney had walked for ten or twelve or fourteen hours with a weight equivalent to his back pack and the launch mechanism and a bundle of four Redeye missiles.

'And then?'

'When it is dark we go through the Kurram Pass. They do not try to seal the border, the Soviets and the Afghan army . . .'

'Just the answers, Gul Bahdur.'

The boy's head dropped. He turned away, sulking.

'We're going to need a mule,' Barney said.

A defiant reply. 'I can carry my share.'

'I said that we need a mule.'

'I said I can carry my share.'

Barney stood in front of the boy. The driver of the ambulance lounged against the engine bonnet, watching them. Barney towered over the boy.

'Another lesson, Gul Bahdur. When I say we will have a mule, we will have a mule. When I say you cannot carry the bundle, it is because you cannot carry it.'

The boy struggled to return Barney's gaze. He was exhausted, he had not slept in the ambulance. Gul Bahdur swayed on his feet.

'Why should I listen to you?'

'Because you came back to fetch me.'

'Why should I go with you?'

'Because you have to be with me if you are to kill another hundred Soviets.'

Barney was laughing. The boy's face broke, images all together of dislike and pride and exhaustion and happiness. The boy rocked in his happiness.

'In the evenings, when the caravans come together, perhaps it is possible to buy a mule. You have the money, Barney?'

Barney tapped his chest, the leather purse hanging under his shirt from a strap around his neck. 'I have the money. Perhaps when we are inside we'll buy a tank and save our feet.'

Another gurgle of Gul Bahdur's laughter. They looped their arms through the straps of the back packs. Barney lifted up one bundle and rested it on Gul Bahdur's shoulder and saw the boy slip under the weight, and recover. He took the second bundle. They walked along the stone and sand of the path, watched all the way by the driver of the ambulance. Twice Barney stopped him before they came to a small bluff cliff, and when they were past it they were gone from the sight of the ambulance driver. Barney went a hundred yards further, then climbed away from the path over wind-smoothed rocks. He laid down his bundle, took off his pack, went to help the failing boy. Barney flopped down between the rocks and was hidden from the path. The boy sat cross-legged near to him. Barney lay on his back in the sunshine of the late afternoon, he tilted his cap over his eyes.

'When you've found a mule that I can buy, wake me.'

Barney slept, on the slopes leading to the Kurram Pass.

Schumack sat straight-backed in the mouth of the cave. The air around him was cool, clean. The cave was high in the hills, above the scrub line that reached up a little from the floor of the valley below. Four men slept in the recess of the cave behind him, snoring and grunting, noisy shites. There would have been six, but the ambush of the previous week had taken two. Crazy men, they'd been, Schumack reckoned, standing up clear of the rock cover to fire their rifles at an armoured car and shouting some fool message about Allah and *jihad*, that kind of crap, inviting the machine gunner to waste them and he'd obliged. They did things, these hill men, that gave Schumack the shakes. Their excitement at close quarters combat was enough to make a one-time Marine

Corps sergeant senile. Perhaps he loved them for it. He couldn't despise them for it. Their arses getting blasted not his. If he didn't love them, he supposed, then Schumack would not have been sitting in the cave looking down on the pin prick lights of the Jalalabad airbase. When they asked his advice, he gave it. If they didn't ask, then he stayed silent. He went his own way in combat, used his training. Sometimes they watched him and afterwards copied him. More often, in combat, they forgot everything.

Schumack had found the war he wanted. Sometimes he thought it was the best war he could have found. It was not easy for a one-handed man, to find himself a war. Schumack was good with the mortar, good with the DShK 12.7mm machine gun that had been captured off the Afghan army in the spring with a tripod mount, and learned to be good in Da Nang and Hué and Khe Sanh, when he had cudgelled the conscript cropheads into believing they could stay alive. There were other phantom medal ribbons that might have decorated his chest, up to the time he had flown to the Desert One rendezvous in the sand plains of Iran with the Delta team, before the abort amongst the flames of crashed helicopters and Charlie One Thirties. He had left behind a mangled hand at Desert One, sliced away by molten aluminium, but he didn't live in the past. The present and the future concerned Schumack. The present was sitting on his bum in a cave a long way from Jalalabad. The future was the war of the *mujahidin* against the Soviets. He had killed three Soviets in the last ambush, he knew that, he'd seen them fall when they spilled from the truck that was disabled. When he had first come to Afghanistan he had counted the Soviets he'd killed. He didn't count any more.

He hadn't kept a body count since he had been alone. When he had first come he had been with Chuck and Paddy and Carlo. He hadn't meant to join up, just happened because they were all in Peshawar together, and two of them had been there longer than him, and Carlo came the week after, and they could all feed from each other. Chuck said the hairies would pay for Airborne and Marine experience, and Paddy said that the Yank spooks would pay for merchandise and photographs, and Carlo said it was decently far from the state of Oregon where there was a warrant on a shelf. Maxie wouldn't call them buddies, but at first there had been a kind of a union, as good as most marriages. That was back fifteen months. Chuck had found that the hairies wouldn't pay, and he'd walked out on them, and they heard a month later that he'd put his big fat foot on a butterfly, and what the HE had started the gangrene had finished. And Paddy had stood up in an ambush because all the hairies were standing up. And Carlo had tried to wet his wick, because in Oregon that was no big deal, and before the sun was up her father had opened his throat for the ants to have a drink.

So now he had no one with whom to keep score. Sometimes when he was lonely, and it wasn't very often, he would wonder if there was a Soviet out there behind the lamps of a base camp who would ever count Maxie Schumack on his score sheet. He'd make the bastard sweat for it.

Mia Fiori lay on the cement floor of the village school, in her sleeping bag, with her head resting on her back pack. Sometimes she would be taken away by the women to the rooms used by the elderly and teenage girls. In this village she had been given the long-unused office of the schoolmaster.

The schoolmaster had been sent to the village from Kabul in the summer of 1979. A week after he had taken charge, his throat had been cut because he came from the ruling Parcham faction of the Afghanistan Communist Party and he had spent four years at a College in Samarkand, and because it was said by the men who murdered him that he was no longer a believer in the faith of Islam.

There was a gaping hole in the roof. A helicopter's rocket

had given her this window to the night skies. She had been in the village two days. Her guides said that a Soviet attack had started on the Panjshir and that it was too dangerous for her to go further forward.

How long would she be here?

She might be in the village for another day, or another week. The guides looked away when she had said she was as capable as any man of climbing the mountain routes into the Panjshir. She hated wasted time. When she was idle then the memory of her husband was alive. Because she had loved him, she hated to remember him. In her sleeping bag on the floor of the schoolmaster's office, her blouse and skirt folded and placed under the back pack, the loneliness washed around her. Two French doctors and a nurse waited for her in the Panjshir, she could laugh and work with them, and she was separated from them by a mountain range and by a regiment of Soviet troops. She heard the voices of the guides in the school's only classroom. Where in their priorities lay the needs of a nurse who must rush to the Panjshir and spend a month's leave in a field hospital before returning to a Paris clinic for the long winter?

Perhaps in the morning word would come that the column could go forward.

Outside the window above her head a man urinated, long and noisily, and spat on the ground when he had finished.

Barney woke.

It was dark and cold, a chill was on his skin.

He heard the strike of iron shoes on the stones.

He felt the soreness in his back from the rock on which he had slept. He heard the faint curse of the boy and a faster movement of the shoes stamping down on the ground for a sure foothold.

The shapes of the boy and of a mule against the sky were silhouetted. The boy tugged the mule after him, straining to

106

drag it from the path and over the rocks to where Barney lay. A second mule came behind, roped to the first.

'Barney.' A quiet call in the night.

'I'm here, Gul Bahdur.'

'I brought two mules.'

Barney heard the sighs of the animals' breath, and the scrape of slipping feet. He sat up. He could smell the mules and the scent of dry fodder and the odour of old excrement.

'You stole the mules?'

'I did not.' Defiance from the boy.

'If you have two mules, if you have no money, then you must have stolen them.' Barney yawned, rubbed his eyes.

'I paid for the mules.'

'With what?' Barney wondered why he argued. They had the mules. If the kid had nicked them, what did it matter?

'With your money, Barney,' the boy said proudly.

Barney's hand went inside his shirt to the leather pouch. He pulled it open, held it close to his eyes. The pouch was empty.

'You took it off me?' A sharp anger in Barney's voice.

'I had to pay for the mules.'

'You cheeky bugger.' Whispered astonishment from Barney. 'While I was asleep . . .?'

Barney stood up. He felt the boy's hand pull at his arm, he felt a roll of bank notes slide into his fist. He put the money back into his pouch.

'I wouldn't have thought it possible,' Barney said.

The boy chuckled. 'I could have taken your boots if I had wanted.'

Barney swiped at him with his fist, the boy swayed away, Barney felt his fingers brush against the boy's shirt.

'What was the point of waking you?' the boy said coldly. 'You could not have bargained for the mules. Without an introduction you could not even have gone into the camp

107

where I went to get the mules. You can fire Redeye, Barney, what else can you do? Without me you are blind.'

'When do we go?'

'There is a long caravan that will be here in an hour. They are going into Paktia and then across the Helmand river to the Hazaras, they take ammunition and food to the Hazaras. I have arranged that we can start our journey with them.'

'And then?'

'You have to decide where you want to go.'

'Where the valleys are steep, where there have been rock falls, where there are trees at the bottom of the valleys, where the valleys are disputed.'

'How far inside will you go?' the boy asked.

'As far as is necessary. I want a valley where the helicopters fly each day, every day of the week. I want a valley which they cannot ignore, into which they must come.'

'To shoot down one helicopter, to take your photographs and your pieces of that helicopter, you do not need to walk to a disputed valley.'

'I have told you the valley I want, a disputed valley.'

'It will take ten days to find that valley.'

'Then we walk for ten days.'

'Can you walk for ten days, Barney?'

'You'll know it, the next time when I hit you.'

Two hours later the column came winding up the hillside path. Barney heard the drumming footfall of the approach of the animals and the chink and rustle of their harnesses. As ghosts the men and beasts went past. He saw the weapons and the ammunition crates. A long, crawling column, and soon Barney and the boy had merged with the chain. A little before midnight they reached the high point of the Kurram Pass, and then the path fell and ran down into Afghanistan.

8

They walked in silence and around them floated the column of men and animals. There was little noise. Only the scrape of leather on mule skin, the spitting of phlegm, the soft Pushtun whisper. Most of the walking hours there was a thin cloud lacing the near full moon. A light wash of silver settled on them.

The men walked with a long flowing step, gliding their sandalled feet onto the roughness of stone and rock. Barney listened for the panting exertion that would tell him these men felt the pace of their march, but these were mountain men, they could walk for twenty hours in a day, they could walk for seven days in a week. They went straight backed, they moved with their heads held high. These men danced on the track while Barney's step was awkward and without grace.

The darkness was brushed with grey before the thin dawn light crawled onto the landscape. First the individual stones under his marching boots, then the curl of the path in front of him, then the dull brown blanket draped on the body of the man in front, then the raw opened sores on the flanks of the mule that this man led, then the line of mules and men that reached as far as the path's curl, then a valley beyond escarpments and lesser hills, then the blur of tree foliage, then the shadow of far distant cultivated fields.

With the coming of the day the pace of the column quickened. Barney wondered whether this was from fear of aerial surveillance, or simply the grumble of empty stomachs and the demands of tiredness. Barney looked up the line ahead to see if there was one man who walked separately from the others and kept his head cocked to the small winds for the sounds of helicopter's flight. Barney saw no man who walked separately. They were noisier now, and faster in their descent, as if there was a relief at the return to their familiar places from the refugee camps.

Their war, their battlefield. If he walked in their column he must abide by their rules. If Barney had been a helicopter pilot, and seen this ant-paced column, he would have wet himself with excitement. Their war, their battlefield, their rules. His eyes scanned the top ridges of the hills, his ears groped for the rattle of rotor blades. He heard nothing and he saw nothing.

Beside a river bed of stones was a village, a smear of dun brown amongst the green surround.

They came down off the open slopes and hit the tree line and Barney saw figs hanging ripe in the branches and further on the track there were peaches in an orchard, and the sun was shaven from the back of his head by the leaves' shade. The mules tried to stop and graze between the trees and were dragged on.

When they were close to the village they skirted a blackened crater. They walked on a raised path between two irrigation channels and came to a place where rockets had breached the channels, spilled the waters, dried them. Barney felt the tightness crawling on his skin. The village was a cluster of earthbrick compounds with the walls smeared with more earth as if to make a plaster covering. Barney saw the brick work where rocket fire and cannon shells had gouged away the smooth mud skin. The homes were small fortresses, each an individual refuge, with narrow doors of heavy planked wood. Over one building at the far end of the village was a rough crenellated tower, the mullah's mosque. A desperate scent of poverty and of filth. Small children in the bright clothes that made a nonsense of the dust dirt in which they

110

lived ran to greet the column. A knot of men, young and old, had gathered at the point where the path came from the orchards and fields to the outer line of the village.

The boy hurried to Barney's elbow.

'They are strangers, these people, to the ones we have come with . . . We have to be patient.' Gul Bahdur made the explanation with awkwardness, as if the tribal divisions of his nation were a personal responsibility.

'What happens?' Barney asked.

'They talk a bit, they flatter a lot. There is a protocol . . .' The boy shrugged. 'The village is often used by the Resistance caravans, that is why it is often bombed.'

The column broke from its line and took sanctuary under the trees. The mules hacked at the thin grass and weed growing from the dry earth. At the entrance to the village, men from the column and men from this small community negotiated their credentials.

'How long will they be?'

'They will be as long as it takes them to discuss what has to be discussed.'

Now that the column was halted, now that the sunlight was full on the trees, now that Barney could be seen, he became the object of detached interest. Coffee eyes watched him and followed his movements.

'Will we sleep here?'

'Probably it is best that we sleep here, but we go no further with these people. They are going to the west, we are going to the north or the east.'

'Will they give us food?'

'The Pathan has pride in the hospitality of his home. He will share what food he has . . . You have walked all night, Barney, why now do you want to hurry?'

Why indeed? Barney Crispin had flouted an order. He had ripped to shreds a whole career, broken the chain to the superiors he had obeyed in every waking moment of his army

111

service. So why hurry? Nothing to go back to, unless every-thing he did from now on was well done, thoughtfully done, done without haste.

The man who led the column embraced the mullah of this village. The protocol was completed. The men of the column rose from their squatting rest under the peach trees. The mules were hobbled. Barney saw the boy tie the back ankles of their two animals together and then loop the rope around the base of a tree.

Barney walked carefully alongside a ditch that ran the length of the central aisle of the village. The stream of the ditch was the colour of polished jade, a green shine of oil. Because he was hungry, Barney thought he might be sick. The smell of the ditch caught in his throat. Still the men of the village stared hard and distantly at Barney.

Some of the roofs of the buildings carried the marks of a rocket strike, torn holes, scorched woodwork.

The walls were pocked by cannon fire, but not pierced. From the slope of the walls Barney could sense their thick-ness at the base, a width sufficient to absorb the strike of a helicopter's machine gun fire. Be against the base of a mud wall if you have to take cover.

They sat on the floor of a darkened room. The *nan* bread was already cooked, for the villagers had been watching the advance of the column down the hillside for a long time. The men who were heading for Hazarajat were dispersed amongst several huts. The light around Barney was faint, filtered through one small window with a cracked pane, and the half opened door. The *nan* was passed to Barney on a plate of beaten metal. He broke the pieces, dipped them singly into the central ironware pot of meat juice. He had been so hungry that he had not looked for the boy, had not seen that the boy had not come into the hut with him. On the earth floor behind them the men had laid their personal weapons. There were Soviet made Kalashnikovs, and old

112

bolt-actioned Lee Enfields manufactured for the British Imperial army half a century before, a single Heckler and Koch rifle from Germany.

He heard shouting outside, a dispute, an argument.

Barney ate wheat bread, and then scooped with his fingers at a bowl of rice that had been drenched with a bitter orange juice.

Again he heard the shouting, something shrill and desperate.

No man spoke to Barney. Between their mouthfuls, between their feeding they watched him.

A child gave a small china cup for tea to each man who sat on the floor.

Barney heard the shout, and knew then that it was Gul Bahdur who cried for help.

As if with a single movement he was onto his feet, his knee buffeting the shoulder of the man beside him, spilling his food into the floor. He was out of the house and into the bright sunshine. The compound walls engulfed him, he spun on his heel and heard Gul Bahdur cry in pain. Barney sprinted along the ditch, out of the village.

He saw the crowd under the trees. None of the men around the boy, and around the boy's mules, knew of Barney's approach. He flung himself into the group of men, eight or nine men. A fist was raised, smashed down into the boy's face. Hands were pulling at the sacking cover hiding the missile tubes. A terrible anger in Barney. The boy flailed with his arms to try to pull back the man who had the most secure hold on the sacking, and fell.

Barney took hold of the shirt collar of the man who had struck Gul Bahdur and threw him away so that he stumbled back into the mass of the watchers. His arm swung up, the hard edge of his fist chopped down onto the shoulder of the man who tried to pull clear the sacking.

One instant of quiet. Then the scream of the man who had

113

been hit, and the shout of the man who had been thrown clear, and the whimper from the ground of Gul Bahdur.

The boy pulled himself up from the ground and stood behind Barney. The men gave them room, but had formed a half circle.

Barney saw the flash of a steel blade.

He heard the rattle of a weapon cocking.

A few feet of open ground separated the men and the knife and the gun from Barney and the boy. The eyes, Barney stared always into the eyes, raking from one to another to another. Brown and chestnut eyes spilling their hatred. Barney felt the boy's hands clinging to the clothes on his back, felt the fear tremble in the boy's fingers.

He never let go of the eyes. He stood his full height. He opened his arms wide and clear to his hips. He unclenched his fists, exposed the whiteness of the palms of his hands. Empty arms, empty hands.

A fly crawled on Barney's nose, searching at the rim of his nostrils.

He was without a weapon. There was a loaded and cocked rifle pointing at him, and the double-edged blade of a knife, and enough men to tear his throat from his shoulders and his eyes from their sockets.

He heard the moan of the man he had hit, he heard the chatter of Gul Bahdur's teeth.

More men had come from the compounds, those who lived in the village and the Hazaras from the column.

The mullah was amongst them, brown-cloaked, black-bearded, a tight white turban strip on his head. A man whispered in the mullah's ear.

Barney stock still, and the rifle still aimed at him, and the knife still poised to thrust at him. He stared them back. The mullah shouted at Barney.

'He is telling us to go . . .' the boy whispered from behind Barney's back.

114

The mullah pointed away from the village, his voice was a tirade.

'He says we are to go. He says because we have received the hospitality of this village we are not to be harmed. He says that the men of this village do not kill those who have received hospitality at the same hand . . . We have to go, Barney.'

Slowly, deliberately, Barney turned his back on the crescent of men. He felt the tickle in his spine, exposed to the rifle and the knife. Barney rearranged the sacking cover over the missile tubes.

'Untie the mules,' Barney said, a brittle crack in his voice.

The boy bent down and unfastened the ropes at their ankles and then untied the knot at the base of the peach tree.

Barney held tight to the bridle of the leading mule, the boy was behind him. Still the eyes on them, and the silence of the watchers.

Barney walked forward straight to the centre of the crescent.

The men parted. They formed an aisle for Barney and his mule, and for Gul Bahdur and his mule. The sweat dribbled on Barney's forehead, ran from his neck down the length of his shirt.

A man spat a wet, sticky mess onto Barney's cheek. Barney did not turn to him. They had made a narrow path and Barney brushed against the man who held the rifle, forced the barrel back. If he stopped they would kill him and the boy, if he ran they would kill him and the boy. He reckoned the mullah's protection was thin armour. The right speed was the slow speed.

They passed out of the tunnel of men. Barney felt his knees weaken, sighed in a great pant of breath.

They walked around the edge of the village and the boy came level with Barney and showed the track they should take, away along a valley and towards climbing hills.

115

An idiot ran alongside them, trying to stand in front of Barney and his eyes were wide apart and wide-opened and there was a dribble in his mouth and old scar marks on his face. The idiot was grey-haired, grey-bearded, and he seemed to dance in front of Barney.

Gul Bahdur picked up a stone and threw it with savage force at the idiot's stomach, and there was a yelp, and Barney heard the sounds of a retreating footfall.

'Tell me, Gul Bahdur.'

'They knew we carried weapons, they would have wanted to take them for themselves. They could not have used the Redeye, but they did not know what we carried. They saw that we had weapons. It is not easy for them to find weapons . . .'

'Why did they not kill us?'

'I told you the words of the mullah. You had eaten with them . . . We are not savages, Barney.'

'No, Gul Bahdur,' Barney said gravely.

'You are laughing at me, Barney.'

'I've just found very little to laugh at. Is it safe to go on, in daylight?'

'You want to go back and sleep in the mullah's bed?'

And they both laughed, out loud, raucous and relieved.

Their laughter carried across a spinach field, across an irrigation channel to the outer compounds of the village where the men stood and watched the going of the European and the boy and the mules that carried weapons. They wondered why a man who had been close to death should laugh for all the world to hear him. Near to the men a group of children joined hands and danced around the idiot and avoided his kicking feet and jeered at him. The men watched the European and the boy until they were small, hazy shapes with their mules, far up the valley.

Later the children would throw pebbles from the river bed at the idiot, and he too would leave the village.

116

Sharp squalls of dust wind blew through the morning in Peshawar. The winds caught at the dust, picked it and tossed it from the unwatered beds of the bungalow's garden. And with the dust were pieces of paper in eddies above the driveway where Rossiter had previously parked the land-rover.

The front door of the bungalow crashed shut, then swung back again. Inside the bungalow was devastation. The Colonel of Security had planned to arrive before the departure of those gentlemen of the charities. He had believed that his arrival at the bungalow as they were making their final preparations for departure would have confused them sufficiently for him to discover the true nature of their activity in North West Frontier Province. Stripping shelves, tipping out the cupboards, ripping open the roof space had been his retaliation at finding the bungalow empty.

But there had been rewards. In the garden, in the base of a burned out bonfire, underneath scorched foliage, he had found charred pages from a manual for the use of the American Redeye ground-to-air missile.

These remnants lay in a cellophane packet on the back seat of the Colonel's car, now being driven hard back towards Islamabad.

They had left the first river bed valley and climbed beyond the tree line and onto a scree of loose stones, over a bare and grey brown hillside. A moon surface of sliding feet and razor fine rock. They dragged the mules after them, braying in anger because they had not been adequately rested in the village and had not been watered and had been allowed only a short time for grazing under the peach trees. The sun burned down on them.

To Barney it was lunacy to be climbing an open hillside in the brightness of daylight. If the helicopters came, the boy seemed to say, then it was willed. Against all of Barney's training, against all that he had taken as a second nature, he climbed to the summit of the range.

They were out of sight of the village, that was enough for the re-establishment of the disciplines.

Beyond the lip of the topmost summit they rested. From now he would dictate the method of movement. No crest outline, always a mountain shape behind them. They would rest for ten minutes in each hour, rest regardless. He told the boy what would happen, braced for a dispute, and the boy seemed indifferent.

Beneath them were a series of lower hill tops. Beyond and below the hill tops, hazed and vague, was a dark strip placed against their path.

Barney squinted, peered forward. He had no binoculars, and he had no weapon, and he had no map.

'It is the Kabul river,' Gul Bahdur said.

Barney nodded. His hand shielded his eyes.

'We have to cross that river, Barney. Beyond the river are the mountains and the valleys that you want for Redeye.'

'How long to the river?'

'Three days, perhaps.' The boy sat close to Barney. 'When you reach the valleys, what will you do?'

'Damage a few helicopters, Gul Bahdur,' Barney said.

The boy heard the lightness in the words and their emptiness. He looked quickly at Barney, and there was a bleakness in Barney's face that discouraged a reply. The boy stood and went to the bridle of his mule, and waited.

They came down the hillside, sometimes slipping, sometimes relying on the sure grip of the mules to hold them.

Barney's forehead was lined from a private pain. The flies buzzed at his face, the water ran on his body, the sun burned at his neck.

What was the shelf life of Redeye? Ten years? Who has asked how many years this consignment of Redeye had lain on the shelf? Anyone? Good enough for the hairies, and

118

some of them should work. Barney in his briefings had skated over the small matter that Redeye was now out of service with the US, replaced by Stinger. Don't give them the bad news, Barney. Give them the good news, the news that Redeye is supreme. No reason to tell them that Stinger's better, or that Britain's Blowpipe is better. Or that you're not certain what happens to the infra-red seeker optics stored in an atmosphere of dry nitrogen all those years. Don't tell them any of that or they might not be so keen to have their arses shot off.

Barney jerked at the rope tied to the bridle of his mule.

'It's not a wonder weapon, Redeye. It's good but it doesn't work bloody miracles,' Barney said.

The boy did not answer. His eyes were cast down. The hillsides dropped away in front of them.

In the late afternoon Rossiter drove into Chitral. He had been at the wheel of the land-rover for thirteen hours, stopping only once for fuel. His head ached, his shoulders were knotted in tiredness, he felt filthy all over his body.

He came into town past the polo field on his left and the cargo jeep station on his right, up the main street of white washed cement and dun brown brick, over the fast-flowing river, past the mosque, past the Dreamland Hotel, past the Tourist Lodge, past the land-rovers and the Toyota trucks, past the oak and juniper trees. Through the town he forked off from the main road.

Chitral lies eighteen miles by crow's flight from Afghanistan across the first tower-high mountains of the Hindu Kush. He had thought through the long hours of his journey where he would stay. It was the end of summer, the time when the holiday bungalows of the Islamabad diplomats and the Rawalpindi autocracy would be abandoned for the winter. He would find a remote bungalow, with a back door window that could be broken. Howard Rossiter's friends – not many

119

of them but there were some – would not have believed that he could be considering both house-breaking *and* deliberate mutiny to the department of the Foreign and Commonwealth Office that employed him. They would, those few friends, have been astonished to learn that Howard Rossiter had sung at the top of his voice and until he was hoarse, much of the way between Peshawar and Chitral. He held the independent Pakistan in contempt. He held the Islamised Pakistan, ruled in recent years by Martial Law, in total contempt.

He had cheerfully calculated that it would take the authorities many hours to circulate a description of himself and details of his land-rover to the police posts around Peshawar.

He didn't doubt that he was through whatever feeble net was now being cast for him.

It was cold on the hillside. Barney shivered. The boy was close against him having crawled under Barney's blanket. The village was a thousand feet below them, and three miles in the distance. Once the sunlight, falling fast and crimson behind them, had glinted on the white paint of the mosque minaret. Once the sunlight had snatched at the perspex glass of the helicopter's cockpit.

That was the helicopter that flew lowest, drifting over the flat roof tops, hunting out the targets. When the rockets were fired, then the skies around the helicopter seemed darkened to a blackness by the brilliance of the flame flashes. From their vantage point, Barney and the boy could hear the impact of the rockets and the chatter of the forward machine gun sited below the pilot's canopy. Above the low-flying helicopter was its mate, circling and suspicious, another eye for the partner.

Barney watched in fascination. He did not think of the villagers who might be on the floors of their homes, nor the *mujahidin* who might be running for firing positions between

120

the dry brick compounds, nor of the beasts that would be stampeding in their corrals of thorn hedge. Barney watched the movement of the helicopters, and learned. Barney recognised in this attack the standard procedure. One helicopter low, one high above in support. A fire had started on the edge of the village. Grey smoke spinning from the grey landscape into the grey skies.

Beside Barney the boy wept. Behind them and underneath an overhang of rock, the mules stamped their hooves and strained against the tethering ropes and the drone of the helicopter engines and the explosions.

'Why do you do nothing?' The boy said the words over and over.

When the darkness had settled onto the village, the helicopters climbed and turned. The fire in the village blazed. The engine noises sidled away.

Barney stood up.

'We'll sleep here.'

'Were you frightened to attack the helicopters?' The boy spat the words at Barney.

Barney caught the collar of Gul Bahdur's shirt, gripped it, seemed to lift the boy.

'Take me to the mountains and valleys north of Jalalabad. That's where our work is. Not here.'

A secretary from Chancery sat opposite the spook, across his dining room table, the candlelight flickering her lipstick and the perspiration sheen of her shoulders.

It had taken him weeks of nagging persuasion to get her to dinner at his apartment. There was a bottle of French wine beside the candle, diplomats' privilege over the prohibition legislation. He'd served soup (albeit from a tin), the mutton chops were under the kitchen grill, and some quite passable potatoes and carrots were steaming on the rings, and there was ice cream in the fridge and cheese on the sideboard. She

121

hadn't said much, and he didn't know yet whether the evening would be successful.

He heard the knock at the door, repeated before he was out of the chair. He smiled weakly at the girl, and cursed to himself.

He opened the door.

The Colonel of Security swept through the hallway, past him, into the room. He held a cellophane bag in his hand.

'The lady should go to the kitchen.'

'I beg your pardon . . .' Not said bravely.

'Please put her at once out of this room.'

The girl ran to the kitchen, the door slammed behind her.

'This is an intolerable intrusion . . .'

The Colonel threw the cellophane bag onto the table.

'Your friends from Refugee Action, Mr Davies, why would they have needed the manual of the Redeye missile? Tell me that.'

The spook closed his eyes.

'I told you to get them out of the country.'

'They'll have gone by now.'

'That is one more lie, one more to the many you have told me.'

The Colonel reached to the table and retrieved the cellophane bag.

'I would not drink too much tonight, Mr Davies. You will need a clear head when you compose your cyphers to London.'

Davies watched him leave through the door he had never closed, heard the engine of a car start, heard the car purr away into the night. The secretary stood in the kitchen doorway and saw the spook's head sinking and saw his fist beat down onto the tablecloth beside his nose.

9

Pyotr Medev had made the mess the meeting place of the young pilots. It was where they relaxed, where they fooled when there was no flying in the morning, where talk of tactics and detail were banned.

There were arm chairs around the walls and the centre of the room was taken by a long wood table, well polished, at which thirty officers could be seated. More arm chairs were in a horseshoe around the stove. The Frontal Aviation transport and fighter-bomber squadrons at Jalalabad had their own quarters, and there was another much larger complex across the runway for the offices and accommodation of the 201st Motor Rifle Division. Eight Nine Two of Frontal Aviation was a compact squadron, an entity of its own. It was under strength, two flights instead of four, but Medev believed it to be as efficient as any in the country. He was proud of his officers, proud of their qualities.

All the pilots but two were there, and the Maintenance Officer and the Stores Officer, and Rostov. The gunners, of course, were not officers, they had separate quarters. This was the room for the fliers, of the young and the élite. Sometimes they made Medev feel an old man with their horseplay. He believed he loved them all, even when they were drunk and daft. They were like children to him, his family.

Pyotr Medev had not lost a single young man under his command in Afghanistan. Other squadrons of Frontal Aviation had taken casualties. The big troop carriers, the Mi-8s, they took losses, they were not as armour-protected as the

123

Mi-24s. If there were no casualties, no helicopter losses, at the end of his twelve months, then that indeed would be a triumph for Medev.

The orderly saw Medev when he was not more than a dozen feet into the mess and hurried forward with Georgian brandy in a small glass. Medev thought he kept the glass filled and ready in the kitchen for the squadron commander's entrance. He liked that, and the cheerful greeting from the orderly. And he liked also the way that the fliers snapped up from the chairs on his entrance, so that he could wave them down again, and make something of it.

If they were busy, Medev thought, they would have little time to reflect. If they had little time to reflect then they would have less time to doubt. Doubt was the prerogative of Pyotr Medev. Doubt amongst the fliers was unthinkable.

Carrying a tray with two bowls of soup, the orderly passed him again. Medev turned, saw the two pilots who had come into the mess after him. They smiled, dropped their heads in a gesture of respect. Meals were kept back for those on late flying duties. Medev had eaten earlier at Divisional HQ, but he took a chair and sat opposite the pilots. They would talk and he would listen and ask a few questions, but listen. That was his way with the young fliers.

'Wasn't easy to find, not in that light, not with the references they gave us . . . we found it all right, but the map co-ordinates were wrong, that ought to be sorted out . . .'

Medev waved his hand, enough about the maps.

'I went down, Alexei stayed up. I used the rockets first. I took the target of a large compound in the village centre . . . that's where the bastards usually are, that's where they'd entertain their bastard guests, right? . . . then I put the machine gun into them. I didn't get any munition explosions, just one fire, probably cattle fodder. We took some ground fire on the third pass, some under-carriage hits.'

'It was the right village?' Medev asked.

'It was the village we were sent to.'

'I'm sure it was the village we were sent to . . . the Intelligence report for the tasking said that a European with weapons would be in that village. If a European was coming to the village with munitions then I have to believe the village would be waiting for him, there would be men who would defend the village waiting for him.'

'Perhaps Intelligence gave us wrong information.'

'I cannot believe Intelligence gave us incorrect information.'

Medev grinned, pulled a face. The fliers would make light of a dusk mission. Medev knew the problems. Thermal updraughts after the heat of the day, the swirling winds of the late afternoon that made contour flying hazardous, the difficulties of night navigation back down to Jalalabad from the mountains. He wouldn't tolerate Intelligence messing with his fliers.

'They told us at the briefing that this man and his mules would reach the village in the late afternoon, that was why we had to attack late . . . perhaps he had not reached the village.'

'Perhaps not,' Medev said.

'Are there really Europeans out there, Major Medev?'

'How could Europeans help these shits? Wouldn't they know what they're really like, Major?'

'I don't know,' Medev said softly. 'To your first question and to your second question, I don't know.'

'There was one fat bastard, he ran from the houses, I followed him at 40 metres up. My bloody gunner wouldn't fire, it was like a fox chase, he ran till he dropped. When he'd dropped my gunner punctured him . . . he must have run 200 metres. My bloody gunner says he likes to let them run, says it's good for their health.' The pilot, Alexei, was spilling soup from his spoon as he laughed.

Medev left them to their meal. He muttered his congrat-

125

ulations and headed for his room. He had a letter from his wife to read, but the letter competed in his thoughts with the confusions caused by an Intelligence assessment that reported a European with munitions heading for a village south of Jalalabad.

They buried the martyr early in the morning.

The ground was too hard for the village men to scrape out more than a shallow hole. The cannon from the helicopter had decapitated the man, and they laid his head in the space between his knees and then made a high pile of stones over his body as protection against the vultures, and set amongst the stones a stick with a white strip of cloth tied to it as indication that he had fallen in battle.

Schumack stood a little aside from the men who had carried the body from the village and who had listened to the few words of the mullah. He had stood with his head bowed, but he had not intruded on the burial. Close to him had crouched an idiot, a strange shrunken creature with a wide grin and gap-toothed smile and torn clothes and scars on his face. He had not seen the idiot before the attack by the helicopters. Perhaps he had come in the night and slept under a field wall of stone. There was little charity in the villages for idiots. Feed the fittest, because the fittest were the fighters. An idiot would roam from village to village, and get scraps of food if he was fortunate.

The man they buried had been the last of Schumack's companions. They had been together but they had only had the basics of a common language. If a man wanted to run out of a house where he was safe and protected by mud brick walls and stand upright in a compound yard to get a better aim at a strafing helicopter, that was his business. Since Chuck and Paddy and Carlo had gone he would never walk out from this war . . . but, shit, he wouldn't make it easy for them, not as easy as standing in the open with an AK against a big bird.

Slung on his shoulder were two rifles. His own Kalashnikov and that of the man now buried.

If they were to follow the airstrike of the previous evening then the Mi-8 helicopters would come to the village with the Soviet troops mid-morning. That was their pattern, and they were a methodical people.

As the last stones were piled on the grave cairn, Schumack left the village. He was alone when he strode away down the goat path, his pack on his back, his blanket hanging on his shoulders, his right hand taking the weight of the rifles' straps, his left hand that was a claw hanging loose against his hip. They had given him some bread, they had filled his water canteen. He left for the emptiness of the high slopes, for the places where the wild flowers grew in their blues and yellows in the rock fissures. Always when he was alone he aimed to climb above the flight path of the helicopters. If Schumack hated one thing in his life it was the helicopters of Frontal Aviation.

By the time Schumack was out of earshot of the village they were already repairing the damaged roofs and slapping wet mud onto the cannon holes in the walls. No man watched him go, only a few children, and the idiot.

He would drift like a feather in the winds. The feather would fall, and Schumack would find a group that would permit this itinerant warrior to attach himself to their column or to their fighting base. He was an uncomplicated man. He could endure the boredom of the weeks between combat because time meant little to him. He asked for food, for water, and for ammunition for the two strapped magazines of his Kalashnikov. Because he asked for so little he did not go short. He had walked for two hours when he saw them.

Ahead of him and above him. A dust puff on the scree alerted him, a tiny inconsistency in the shape of the upper hillside.

He took from his back pack a one-eyed spy glass. He

127

rested the glass on his damaged left arm and with his right hand fiddled with the focus.

Two men, two mules.

A man taller than the other and more solidly built. A man who walked in short chopped strides. No stranger could walk like an Afghan.

He turned off the path. He found a way through the tree line, through the scrub line and out onto the scree, a way that would bring him to the same height but behind them.

It was raining. It always rained in London in late August. Dripping streets, slippery pavements, traffic snarled. Rain doubled the time of the journey to Whitehall and FCO. The detective varied his route these days. Sometimes he came via the Mall, sometimes by Birdcage Walk, sometimes round by Victoria Street. Pretty pointless, the Foreign Secretary thought, because he always ended up at the Foreign and Commonwealth Office back door, the trusty Ambassador's entrance.

His Personal Private Secretary made a point of meeting him just inside the doorway.

'Good morning, Minister . . .'

Down the corridors and past the portraits – he'd be there himself soon, Heaven help him, hung for posterity, picking their way along the Eastern carpets.

'Quite a quiet day for you, Minister.'

'We went through my day last night. I know what I have today.'

'Not everything, you don't, sir. Brigadier Fotheringay is camping outside your office. Says he has to see you. I've told him you're busy, but . . .'

'I'll see him immediately,' the Foreign Secretary said.

'You have a number of other appointments, sir.'

'Immediately, I said, and put everything else on hold.'

'What advisers will you want to sit in?'

'I'll deal with this alone, Clive.'

In the next fifteen minutes the Foreign Secretary would drink half a dozen cups of black coffee. The Brigadier's cup remained untouched and grew cold.

'A specific instruction was sent to this man Rossiter in Peshawar, an instruction stating unequivocally that he should at once leave Pakistan, plus the instructor, and return via New Delhi to the United Kingdom, and you are telling me that your instruction was communicated to Rossiter, and that so far as you can discover that instruction, that order, Godammit, has been ignored? I find that incredible. And to cap it all, your best intelligence is that these two men, two men whom it took Pakistan's chaps ten minutes to smoke out, have simply disappeared.'

'That is correct, sir.'

'And what is your explanation?'

'My explanation, sir?'

'I am entitled to ask for an explanation.'

'I don't have one. Other than that an order has been ignored, there is no explanation.'

'Could they have gone . . .'

'Not Rossiter, he's too old.'

'Could the instructor have gone?'

'Into Afghanistan, he could have.' The Brigadier sighed. 'It has to be a possibility, and a very ugly one. The repercussions, if he's caught, hardly bear thinking about.'

'What would he have gone into Afghanistan *for*?' the Foreign Secretary asked.

'To shoot down a bloody helicopter, what else?' The Brigadier's voice was shrill. 'To strip the thing.'

'He'd be a brave young man, Brigadier.'

'I'll have him strung up by his thumbs when I get him back. I'll break him, smash him . . .'

'And Rossiter?'

'Rossiter's a low grade, second-rate nobody. He was hand

129

picked for this sort of thing. He's never made an original move nor had an original thought in his life.'

'I see. What about the instructor? Has he ever given way to an original thought, I wonder. Who is he?'

'Captain Crispin of the SAS.'

'If Captain Crispin has entered Afghanistan, and if the Soviets were to capture him there, then the implications would indeed be quite horrifying. Bad enough if the Pakistanis were to find him. But if that's the journey he's embarked on, then I have to say that I am rather taken with him. A gutsy young man.'

'He wasn't asked to be gutsy, Foreign Secretary. He was given his instructions and expected to obey them.'

'Quite so, Brigadier. But as you keep saying, you win some, you lose some. Little did I suspect how prophetic you would be. Tell me this: if he has gone into Afghanistan, just how likely is he to succeed, provide us with Hind's innards?'

'A total stranger to the country, not speaking the local tongue, one chance in a thousand, and a better than even chance of getting himself killed or captured.'

'Well, that's a pretty prospect, Brigadier. If you can come up with any fresh disasters, you'll keep me posted, will you?'

'That's not quite fair,' the Brigadier said and let himself thankfully out of the room.

He was a foreigner and he was a soldier.

Schumack found over the next three hours as he tracked the man and the boy and the two mules that he could have set his watch on the minutes they spent resting each and every hour, on the hour. A trained man would rest for a few minutes in each hour.

Much of the time Schumack could not see them as they hugged the curved hillsides. He estimated that he was a mile behind them. He had closed his speed to their pace. Schumack, Marine Corps Sergeant, knew a soldier's trail when it was laid in front of him. He wondered when he should close with the foreigner, perhaps at dusk. He'd considered whether the foreigner could be a Soviet surveillance officer, but dismissed the thought.

'He's a Maxie Schumack,' he said aloud to himself. 'He's the same as Maxie Schumack, fighting man, come to kick Soviet ass like Maxie Schumack does. Not a white bum Soviet. Too dangerous for the shites to be walking the hills, love their balls too much to go walking.'

The sun beat down on him, played tricks with his eyes, and twice he retrieved the spy glass from his pack and searched the backgrounds of rough rock wall and low scrub trees for the men and their mules, and could not see them. But there was always the track of the hooves for him to follow, the outline of small sandals, and the imprint of a soldier's boots.

'What in Christ's name is the mother doing here?'

'There are many problems associated with flying in Laghman province.'

'I would remind you, Major, there are problems for all of us when we operate in Laghman.'

'The problems of helicopters are acute in the high ranges.'

'Acute but not insurmountable. I am sure your fliers are quite capable of meeting our requirements.'

The Colonel General flicked his pen irritably back and forth on his table. Major Medev sat opposite him.

'My fliers are the best.'

'Be realistic, Medev. We are all concerned with equipment losses, we are all concerned with casualties. You have no greater right to concern than a major of infantry, of artillery, of armour. It is dangerous for the Mi-24 to fly in the valleys north of here. It is dangerous for the infantry in their personnel carriers, for the artillery in their bivouacs, for the tanks on the river bed roads. I cannot send the infantry and the artillery and the armour into the mountains of Laghman, if first I have to tell their officers that their colleagues from Frontal Aviation believe it is too dangerous to fly above those valleys. You understand me, Medev?'

The flush burned on Medev's skin. He had allowed himself to be out-manoeuvred, then scolded. Perhaps he was too close to his men, perhaps he cared too much for the magic of the clean casualty sheet.

'I was merely making the point that at altitude . . .'

'The point is made . . . Now, the resupply of the bandits reaches a peak before the first snows close the upper mountain passes in Laghman. They have two, three weeks to bring their materials from Pakistan. I have a direct order from the Taj Beg to frustrate the transhipment of those supplies.'

'They are taken through the high passes, at the maximum altitude of the helicopter.'

'I know where they are taken, Major.'

'In the high passes we have grave difficulties with turbulence in the airstream, and the thermal effects can be dramatic, a helicopter can be sucked up . . .'

'Each time I make a statement, Major, you interrupt me. This is not a conversation, it is a briefing. If you feel that your pilots, under your leadership, do not have the necessary confidence . . .'

'Forgive me, Colonel General. There will be no failings from my squadron.'

'How long does your tour have to run?'

Medev hesitated. 'I think a month, something like four weeks.'

'I imagine you know to the day how long you have to serve here. I think each man in Afghanistan, each man of a hundred thousand knows exactly how many days he has to serve. You are not alone. But I give you some advice. You have had an excellent tour. Do not spoil that in the remaining four weeks you are with us. You understand my advice?'

'And I thank you for it, Colonel General.'

'You won't fail me, Major Medev.'

'There is no possibility of failure, Colonel General.'

'I am gratified. Your own commander would have given you these instructions if he had not been in Kabul. They are cleared with him, of course. Your helicopters should be grounded for the next forty-eight hours for extensive maintenance, after that there may not be the chance. You'll be flying the arses off them. There will be an airborne battalion on stand by, three hours . . . that's all.'

Medev saluted, and turned for the door.

He walked out into the brightness of the afternoon. The light bounced at him from the runway. A fighter bomber roared away, smoke and flame belching from the engine exhausts, then waddled into the sky weighed down by the bombs and rockets clinging to the belly and wing pods. The taste of burned fuel settled on his tongue. He spat onto the concrete. In a neat line on the far side of the runway from Division's headquarters were his helicopters, safe behind their sand bag revetments and wire. The Colonel General knew nothing of flying in the high mountain valleys of Laghman, knew nothing of a helicopter straining for altitude at 4000 metres, surrounded by mountain cliffs. Impossible to exercise the control needed for contour flying at that altitude. What did the Colonel General know? The Colonel General knew nothing.

Each day Mia asked the same question.

'When do I go forward?'

Each day she hunted down the leaders of the column.

'I am supposed to be in Panjshir, not in southern Laghman. If there is fighting in Panjshir then that is where I should be. If there is fighting then there will be people who are hurt, if they are hurt then they need my help.'

133

Each day she pleaded. Each day she achieved nothing, beyond the promise that news would come soon giving permission for her to go forward.

'You don't care about the casualties, not about the children, not about the women, you don't care what happens to the children and the women. All you care about is your own fucking martyrdom.'

Each day they smiled at her, because when she was angry and her French was fast gabbled then none of them could understand her.

In the afternoon, each day, she climbed the hillside above the village and sat under an old rooted tree and picked herself flowers and sometimes made a chain of them and watched the children who shouted at the goats and the sheep flocks, and wondered why there was a war, and where there was a war. Sometimes she would unbutton her blouse and feel the sun against her skin and cry aloud in her frustration that the war was outside her reach.

It was more than an hour since he had last seen them. The first shadows were falling and heaving the great cataracts of grey onto the rock surface. He was sweating, and when he had walked all day it was usual for the stump of his left arm to be rich agony and the straps of the claw to work weals into his skin. And his feet hurt, boots filled with grit because the soles were adrift from the toe cap. Bloody Soviet boots. Each time he had himself a Soviet and a chance to get to the body he always looked first to see if the bastard was size 10. Each eight weeks he needed a Soviet stiff, size 10.

One more corner, one more outcrop around which the tracks of the men and the mules disappeared. He was noisier now. The lightness of his tread had gone hours earlier.

He turned the corner, he could see the tracks' line stretching ahead of him, falling towards the lights of Jalalabad. He didn't want to go down to the river plain. He wanted

134

to stay high, but the tracks led down, so Schumack followed.

'Where are you going?'

The voice boomed out. A big voice, a voice of command. The words in English.

Startled, Schumack spun, and ducked.

'I said, where are you going?'

The man was sitting easily on a rock a dozen feet above the path.

'Who are you?' Schumack said.

'Let's start with who you are.'

Schumack gazed up into the fair stubbled face, saw the camouflage smears on the cheeks. He saw that the man was not armed.

'Schumack, Maxie Schumack.'

'You're far from home, Mr Schumack. I'm Barney Crispin.'

'You're not adjacent yourself, Mr Crispin.'

'What's your business?'

'Same as yours, I fancy.'

'Why are you following me?'

Schumack watched as the man slid down from the rock, landed on the track, slapped the dirt from his blanket.

'I was lonely.'

'That's a piss poor answer.'

'And a piss poor question. What's on the mules?'

'Go whistle, Schumack.'

Barney turned away, set off briskly down the track. From a distance Schumack started again to trail him.

10

Behind them in the cave the mules stamped. The boy was hunched with his head low on his chest. The pile of fibreglass missile tubes made a back for Barney to lean against.

He had lit no fire, he preferred to be swathed in his blanket. He was no longer with a column of *mujahidin*. He was his own master. His own rules did not allow for a fire. The hunger racked him, but he was a trained soldier. He wondered how the boy could sustain himself without food and water. In the morning they would have to come down from the hills to the plains of the Kabul river to find food and water.

The pebble landed in the entrance of the cave, rolled and came to rest against Barney's boots. When he was in the field he would never remove his boots, not even to sleep, if sleep were possible on the floor of the cave with the hunger in his stomach. He had loosened the laces, that was a concession. It was the third pebble.

Barney heard the voice close to the cave's mouth. A voice shredded with impatience.

'You haven't eaten, Barney Crispin. All day you haven't eaten. If a man has no food then he cannot be on his own.'

'Be careful,' the boy whispered.

'I will be careful, Gul Badhur,' Barney said. 'But we have no food . . .'

He heard the voice call again.

'A man isn't a crapping island, Crispin.'

'What food have you?'

'Some bread, some dried fruit.'

136

The shadow crossed the mouth of the cave. The moon was lost for a moment as the shadow crossed it. There were the sounds of a man moving on knees and elbows over the dry ground.

'You don't hurry yourself, making up your mind you're hungry.'

Barney heard a hand searching in the darkness, felt fingers touch his boots, reach to his socks. He stretched out in the blackness, took the hand in his fist.

'Thank you,' Barney said. The boy had moved back into the cave and sensed his nervousness at the intrusion. Now he edged forward. They ate fast, eagerly.

Barney pulled his blanket over his knees to catch crumbs of bread. Dry, hard bread, but satisfying for all that. And after that were the raisins that he could gulp down, and beside him the boy ate his share in silence.

'I'll ask a question, it's "yes" or "no" for an answer. If it's "yes" then we talk about it, if it's "no" the questions finish. Is Maxie Schumack a freelancer?'

'He's a freelancer.'

'Tell me.'

His stomach warbled on the food and Barney settled himself back against the missile tubes.

'I was born Maximilian Herbert Schumack, Christ knows where they took the names from, and they're dead so I can't ask. I was born in New York City, fifty-two years ago. There's not much to show for it, where I was born, it's a car park and garage now. So, I'm an old bird, what we call a clover fucker. I took a Greyhound to Bragg when I was seventeen and enlisted. I went up and I went down. I had stripes, I was busted. First place I kept my stripes was Da Nang. Shitty place, shitty bars, shitty expensive girls. My first trip to 'Nam, we hadn't much time for bars and whores, and I'd been fifteen years in the Corps and I was a veteran, and I'd never had a shot fired at me before. To stay alive with the

137

god-awful kids they gave me I stayed clear of the bars and the whores. I didn't get clap and I didn't get my arse shot off. You're a fighting man, you know what it was in 'Nam, and you don't need the fucking *New York Times* war stories from me. Next time I went back was Khe Sanh. They say the Corps doesn't dig. My platoon dug at Khe Sanh. I stood over the bastards till they'd dug. And dug. Didn't do a lot of fighting, just sat in holes with the rain pissing down plus the incoming. Had a bit of time to think there, and I reckoned I'd cracked it. Sam's got himself in a heap of shit here, I reckoned. Weren't many to say Sergeant Schumack got it wrong. I took my platoon out of Khe Sanh with one KIA and three WIA. That was good. Sam gave me a medal, said I was a credit to the fucking Corps. I went back one last time. On the roof of the Embassy chucking slants off the Hueys, that the fat cats wanted for a ride out to the fleet. Sam was deep in the shit by then, up to his ears. Didn't take me to tell Sam that. We'd been seen off by the fucking gooks. I did some time at home after Saigon went, and I got another medal, not that any bastards Stateside wanted to know. On Stateside they reckoned that Sergeant Schumack and half a million others had lost Sam his little war. The old shits, who'd never walked the paddies with the incoming, they reckoned we'd lost a war we should have won. Most didn't but I stayed in. Nowhere to quit to. I burned a bit and I boiled and I stayed in the Corps. I got Kabul in '78, Embassy marine guard. Piss awful place, on the front desk in full dress, spit polish boots and the medal ribbons. And then we lost the Ambassador, "Spike" Dubs. Great guy. Some shite-arses lifted him between the Residence and the Embassy. Sam screwed again. The Soviets, the advisers in the fucking ministry there, told the Afghans what to do, they crapped on all we told them. They busted in where he was holed up and played a shooting gallery. "Spike" Dubs died. Sam couldn't help him. I was brought home. Another Stateside garrison town for a super fucking veteran. Then the mothers took our Embassy in Teheran, crapping all over Sam, like everyone was, like it became a habit. They put a force together, a Marine Corps force, and Schumack was on the team. Eight times we were due to go and bust that place open, and seven times Sam hadn't the balls, rubbing his fucking hands together and wondering what the civvie casualties would be. Who gave a fart what they'd be? The eighth time we went. I don't have to tell you what happened, Mr Crispin, the whole bloody world knows what happened. Sam fouled up. I tell you this, the 'Nam wounded my faith in Sam, Kabul butchered it, and Desert One buried it. I quit. Too late but I quit. I took the money and I holed out. I went up to Canada and I bummed. I was putting canoes in the water for smart arse kids, and clearing up their fucking garbage. To the kids I was like something from under a stone. Last year I bought a ticket, I paid a one-way airfare to Pakistan. I lost my hand at Desert One for Sam. They said they'd keep me in, as an Instructor or a drill pig, but Sam's all shit. Sam's no longer my place. I took a bus ride to Peshawar, and I walked in here a fortnight later. I'm here for keeps, Mr Crispin. I'm staying like we never used to. I'm staying here, and no bastard in the Pentagon tells me I'm aborting. I'm happy as a pig in mud. You understand me?'

'I understand you,' Barney said.

'I talk too much.'

'You don't have a lot of chance to talk.'

'Here? I've shit all chance to talk . . . My turn, same question, yes or no. Are you a freelancer?'

'No.'

'That means . . .'

'That means there are no more questions.'

'What's the load on the mules?'

'No more questions.'

Schumack persisted. 'I had a glass on you. You didn't tie the sacking too well. It's tubes you're carrying.'

139

'As you said, you talk too much.'

'Tubes is mortars, but you don't carry on two mules a load of mortar bombs that's worth a damn. Tubes could be anti-tank, but they've all they want of those from the Soviets and the Afghan army. Tubes could be ground-to-air . . .'

Barney could smell Schumack close to him, he could make out the dim shape in front of him.

'Ground-to-air would be rich, Mr Crispin.'

Barney heard the boy wriggle nearer to him, heard the tension of his breathing.

'I tell you straight, you won't have any idea what it's like to be under the helicopters and have no way of hurting the bastards. What makes these guys in the hills crap themselves? The helicopter. What makes Maxie Schumack wet himself? The helicopter. To see a ground-to-air knock the pigs out of the sky, I'd laugh myself sick.'

Barney said nothing.

'I'm going north in the morning,' Schumack said. 'Which way are you going?'

'North,' Barney said.

'Across the river?'

'Into Laghman, north to the mountains.'

'I've something you're short of, Mr Crispin.'

Barney put out his hand. His fingers brushed the smooth wood of a rifle stock, felt the cold metal of a curved magazine and the sharpness of the foresight. He took the Kalashnikov in his hand. He was a man who had been naked and was now clothed. His hands ran the length of the barrel, flickered over the working parts, found the cocking lever and the Safety catch.

'There's two more magazines for you.'

'Thank you. You've given us food, you've given me a weapon. I've nothing to give you.'

'You've plenty.' Schumack laughed. 'You'll give me the

happiest moment of my life. You'll hear me cry laughing when you blast a helicopter mother.'

His laughter bubbled in the quiet of the cave and Barney managed a smile and, sitting apart from the two men, Gul Bahdur could not understand their enjoyment of the moment.

In the morning they came down to a village.

The two men and the mules stayed back from the mud brick buildings marooned in the cultivated fields. There was no chance of a secret approach to the village, the dogs howled a warning of their coming. The boy went forward.

Barney and Schumack said little to each other as they waited. They had not spoken when Barney had loaded the mules at the cave's mouth, and Schumack had not pressed forward to see the markings on the tubes. Between such men understanding came fast. When they had started out Schumack had led, not because he tried to assume control, but because it was better that a man not leading a mule be on point a hundred metres ahead.

The boy returned with a bucket of brackish water for the mules, and with bread for the men.

After they had left the village they were all the time descending, following the shepherds' paths that headed for the ribbon of villages beside the river. The boy had pointed out to Barney the grey and white scar of Jalalabad cut into the green beside the river. The line they took would bring them to the river some eight or nine miles short of the town.

As they walked, there was no scent of war. Finches darting in the scrub bushes, butterflies hovering on their path, the far away chime of a goat's bell. Mid morning, a high sun, small shadows under their feet, and Gul Bahdur had come level with Barney's shoulder.

The boy looked into Barney's face.

'Why do you give yourself to this man?'

Barney blinked back at the boy. 'What do you mean?'

'He is of no use to you.'

'Who is of use to me?'

'The *mujahidin*, my people, they are of use to you. This man is unimportant to you. Without the *mujahidin*, the fighters of the Resistance, you can do nothing.'

'That is true.'

'When we climb into the mountains of Laghman you will meet the real fighting people of the *mujahidin*, not the people in Peshawar who play at the fighting, you will meet the real warriors of the Revolution.'

'What are you telling me?'

'I am warning you that the fighters in Laghman will be careful of you. Do not expect them to fall on their knees just because you bring them eight Redeyes.'

'I know that.'

'You are a foreigner and an unbeliever. To some of the fighters you will seem like an adventurer, to others you will be an exploiter. You must win the respect of the fighters.'

'And Schumack?'

'It is good that he has fed us, and it is good that he has armed you, but he cannot help you to win the respect of the fighters. Do you know why you must have the respect of the fighters, Barney?'

'You're going to tell me, Gul Bahdur.'

Gul Bahdur ploughed on, ignoring the interruption.

'When you fire the Redeye and you kill a helicopter, then the Soviets will bomb the nearest village. When you kill another helicopter then they will bomb another village. For each helicopter, another village. The men whose respect you must win are the men from those villages. Because of your Redeye the bombs will fall on their families, their homes, their animals.'

'I know that.'

'That man cannot help you to win the respect you must have . . . You are not angry with me for saying this?'

142

The boy looked keenly up at Barney. Barney slapped his hand onto Gul Bahdur's shoulder. There was relief on the boy's face.

'Barney, you are going to kill one helicopter, take the pieces from it, then go?'

'Yes.'

'Barney, why did you bring eight Redeyes, for one helicopter?'

Barney walked on without replying. They were dropping down over the hill slopes towards the Kabul river.

Abruptly the mule that Gul Bahdur led came to a stop.

The boy pulled at the rope attached to the bridle, the mule eased its weight back and braced its rear legs against the pressure. The boy tugged hard, viciously, and the mule was immovable. Its eyes were fierce, obstinate in their refusal. Barney had halted, turned to watch. He saw the way the mule had taken the strain from its front right leg as if to shelter the hoof. The boy picked up a handful of stones and started to throw them at the rear legs of the mule. The teeth were bared at the boy, but the mule moved neither forward nor back. Barney whistled twice, sharp and clear, and ahead of them Schumack stopped on the track. Barney felt their vulnerability. The boy slapped the haunches of the mule with his fist, but the animal would not move. Barney cursed. He gave the rope of his own mule to the boy and bent to examine the right fore-leg of the animal. The hoof flashed in a kick close to his head.

'It'll be a stone,' Schumack said from behind him. 'It'll be tender. Let it rest a bit, then we'll get it out.'

Barney looked up into the clear blue of the skies. He saw a hawk circling, up in the wind swirls. The hawk gave him the thought of the helicopter. A dozen yards from the path there was a shallow cliff and a slight rock overhang and a tree grew against the cliff. He led the way to this shelter.

Schumack said, 'If we rest him half an hour he'll calm, we can handle him after that.'

143

Together they urged the mule off the path. Barney sank down, closed his eyes, pulled his cap down over his forehead. He heard the whirr of the flies close to his skin, felt the brush of the legs around his mouth. It was a drowsy warm heat without the breezes of the upper hillsides. Barney's head was nodding. Schumack lay full length on his back, perhaps asleep, perhaps awake, unmoving.

It was the boy who heard the footfall. His hand caught at Barney's arm. Schumack had seen the boy's movement, sat upright with his rifle held across his thighs.

The footsteps came fast, the figure came into Barney's view. Barney remembered the idiot with the shambling limbs and the spittle smile and the wide eyes. Now the same clothes and the same features, but a fast and wary stride and the head bent low to follow the mule trail and a heavy pack on his back. The man stopped where the mules' hoofmarks had left the path. His head spun to seek the answer. He saw the tethered mules beside the cliff face, he saw Barney and Schumack and the boy. A cracked sound broke from his throat, anger and astonishment and fear. For a second he was rooted, then he turned and started to run back up the path the way that he had come.

Schumack was cat fast. Off the ground, onto the path, the left arm raised as a bridge for the rifle barrel, the snap of the Safety, the aim, the single shot.

The man who had played an idiot fell, sledge-hammered, in full stride – smashed down onto the dirt path.

The shot blitzed the quiet from the trees.

In the pack they found a Soviet army radio transmitter. Schumack put his heel into it. Sewn into an inner pocket and close to the bloodied exit wound, they found a Parcham faction Youth cadre card. Schumack ripped it to small pieces. The pack was earth dirty as if it had been buried. A chill recognition for Barney that the idiot had seen him, a European, had followed him, would have reported that he would

144

reach a certain village, would have broadcast his knowledge. He remembered the vantage point from which he had watched the attack on the village, and the tears of the boy. His estimated time of arrival in that village had dictated the hour of the strike. Schumack spoke of the idiot . . . Barney sucked the air into his lungs. And, Christ . . . Schumack had been fast, faster than himself.

Barney and Schumack held the mule. The boy lifted its front right leg, gouged with a knife, a sharp edged flint stone fell to the path.

They set off on the path again.

After a few hundred yards the boy, without explanation, gave Barney his mule's rope and skipped back along the track.

Within five minutes he was again at Barney's side.

'When the Soviets find the body of their traitor, they will have something to think of.'

Barney caught at the shirt of the boy. 'You horrible little bastard. Don't ever do that again, not when you're with me.'

'You do not own our war, Captain Barney,' the boy shouted back, and pulled himself free of Barney's grip. 'You do not own us because you have eight Redeyes.'

Further up the track Schumack had stopped, listened. He called back, 'Oh boy, *Captain* Crispin, eh? And his Redeyes. Redeye, Jesus, that went out with the Ark . . . Only eight, shit . . .'

Schumack spat on the ground, shook his head, started to walk again.

Twice during the flight the pilot of the helicopter had complained to his Jalalabad control that he was unable to make contact with the ground signal. Twice he had complained that the search was impossible if he could not be guided onto his target. He was careful. One helicopter only had been assigned. They should have flown in pairs, that was the

145

standard procedure, but the excuse had been given that all of the squadron's machines were to undergo extensive servicing maintenance, that an exception would be made of one Mi-24. He had the wavelength open, for more than an hour, tuned for the message that would tell him where his quarry could be found. He flew over villages, over orchards, over the small cultivated fields that were outlined by irrigation ditches. Without the ground transmission it was hopeless, wasted time and wasted fuel. The second time he had spoken to Jalalabad control they had patched him through to his squadron commander. Major Medev was adamant, Intelligence swore that the source was good.

The helicopter drifted above the flat roofs of the village homes, above the minaret towers, above the goats, above the women who had been taking in the summer's second harvest and who now ran in their full skirts to the compounds.

Because they had been ordered to fly at 400 metres, the gunner in the nose bubble of the Mi-24 was able to see the wheel and the hover of the first vultures. Specks in a clear sky, falling fast, then hovering, then dropping down amongst the sparse trees on the last slopes before the river plain. Through his mouthpiece radio, the gunner alerted the pilot.

What else to look at?

The helicopter settled high over a track, clearly visible between the trees. The gunner could see the birds below, in a clutch quarrelling over a bundle of blanket. The pilot disobeyed his standard procedures, he eased the helicopter down towards the tree tops. The vultures scattered. Hovering just above the path the gunner saw the smashed radio set. Close to it was a man on his back. The gunner saw the trousers at the man's knees, the raw blood mess in the man's groin, the bulge of blood at the man's mouth. The gunner retched, across his knees, his boots, onto the floor space between his feet. The pilot radioed again to Jalalabad control, and the dust driven up from the path by the rotor blades

146

settled back onto the flies and later the vultures made a feast of the bloodied corpse of a man who had chosen to collaborate.

They waded and swam the Kabul river at dusk.

Low water with summer near spent, and the autumn rains not yet falling on the low ground, and the winter snows not yet cascading onto the mountains of the Hindu Kush that lay as a grim barrier ahead. The mules were fearful of the water, had to be bullied into the centre stream depths, coaxed into a frantic swimming stroke. The river bed mud oozed into Barney's boots, and when they came to the rocks on the north side, on the Laghman side, his grip slipped under water and twice he was ducked to his nostrils.

They had seen a helicopter once, quartering the far bank and the villages to the south, and then turning to the east and Jalalabad. The boy had said that the river could not be crossed at this place at any time other than late summer. Only when the water was at its lowest could the crossing be attempted, and all the bridges were guarded by Afghan army units. If it had been earlier in the year they would have had to trek away to the west, towards Kabul.

On the Laghman side of the river they came to an orchard of apple trees, and stripped off their clothes and wrung the dark water from them, and lay on the cool grass. When Barney went to help Schumack get the water from his shirt and trousers, he was waved brusquely away. The boy dressed first, crawled into his sodden shirt and trousers in the last light of the day to walk to the village whose lights they could see, to beg for food.

After the boy had gone, after the light wind had caught coldly at Barney's skin, he stood to take his clothes down from the branches where they were hooked alongside the ripening apples.

'You did well, Maxie.'

147

'If you don't do well, you're dead.'

'I'd never thought we could be tracked, hadn't thought of it.'

'The Soviets aren't playing games. They play hard, if it's dirty why should they give a shit?'

'You have to be dirty to win, right?'

'Up to your arse in shit to win.'

'I had a grandfather here, he died here. In 1919. Third Afghan War. His hands would have been pretty clean.'

'And he didn't win. Where did he die?'

'A place called Dakka.'

'Near the border, about forty miles from here.' There was an edge in Schumack's voice as if to stifle any sentiment. 'I hope he died well, your grandfather.'

'They'd made a camp at Dakka. Six infantry battalions, artillery, even some cavalry – that dates it – they were out on flat ground, no shade, not a lot of water. The Afghans had the high ground, had guns there. Usual British answer, send in the infantry to get the guns. They used the old county regiments from England, Somerset Light Infantry and North Staffs, exhausted before they even started because they'd legged it from the garrisons in India. They went up the hillsides with bayonets fixed. They cleared the guns but too late for my grandfather. When I was a boy I read some of my grandmother's papers, some nasty things were done to him. I don't know whether my grandfather died well, I'm pretty sure he died screaming.'

'Not an easy place to die well in, Afghanistan,' Schumack said.

The boy was coming through the trees. Before he reached them they could smell the fresh baked bread that was wrapped in muslin cloth.

For two days Barney and the boy and Schumack and the two mules plodded north from the plains of the Kabul river up

148

into the dry brown hills, on towards the grey mountain sides of Laghman.

Remote, barren countryside. Small villages set close against escarpments for protection against the winter's weather. Handkerchief fields that had been scraped for stones and that were withered for lack of water. Lonely shepherds who sat away from the tracks and who watched their passing without greeting. An exhausting, dangerous countryside, devoid of hospitality. Once Schumack had shown Barney a butterfly anti-personnel innocent on the path in its camouflage brown paint, scattered from the sky. And when they were past the range of its effectiveness he had detonated it with a single shot.

They needed to eat, they needed to sleep well, they needed shelter from the growing winds that flew into their faces from the wastes of the Hindu Kush.

Barney would sniff with his nostrils up into those winds and seem to sense that this was the place he had come to find. When they stopped, the regular five minutes in each hour, Barney would stand straight and gaze forward at the mountains and slip off his cap and let the wind into his hair. His place, the killing ground for the helicopters. But he must eat and he must sleep, and his body was filthy, and the lice had started to work over his skin, and his beard was an uncomfortable stubble.

The second night they sought out a village, walked in the late afternoon up the stamped earth path towards the tight corral of houses with the dogs raucous around them and snapping at their legs and running from the kicks of the mules. The men who watched their approach were armed. Barney saw the Kalashnikovs and the Lee Enfields and one rifle that he recognized from pictures he had seen as the SVD Dragunov, the standard Soviet sniper weapon. Men with cold faces.

He felt the nervousness of the boy.

149

'These are not the people of Peshawar . . .'

'We have to eat, we have to sleep. I know these are the fighting men.'

The boy went forward. Barney and Schumack stood back, holding the bridles of the mules. Fifty metres in front of them the boy spoke to a man who wore a close bound turban of blue upon his head, with a night-dark beard uncut and hanging against his chest, and a Soviet assault rifle loose in his hand. No smile, no welcome. The boy talking fast and the man listening.

'It's all down to the boy,' Schumack said from the side of his mouth.

'Yes.'

'If he says the wrong thing they could chop us and take the mules.'

'Just shut up, Maxie.'

'So as you know.'

'I know,' Barney said tightly. His finger was on the Safety of his Kalashnikov, his eyes never left Gul Bahdur's back.

The man shrugged, assumed indifference, gestured back over his shoulder into the village.

The boy turned to Barney, his face alive with relief. Barney felt the tremble in his knees. They walked into the village. There were rocket craters, there were shrapnel scars, there were the pattern lines on the walls of machine gun fire, and there were roof beams rising jagged and charred from the buildings.

They went up the steps of a once white washed concrete-faced building with a flat roof.

'They are going into the mountains tomorrow,' Gul Bahdur said. 'They are of the Hizbi-i-Islami group. Their leader is one day and a half's walk away. It is what you wanted, Barney?'

'It is.'

After dark they sat on the floor of the house that had once

150

been a school. A dozen men and Barney and Schumack, under a paraffin lamp hanging from a ceiling hook. While they sat, while they drank tea, the loads from the mules were carried in and placed under the supervision of Gul Bahdur against the far wall. At the sight of the uncovered missile tubes Schumack screwed his face up to stare at Barney, and Barney looked through him. Later they were given goat bones to chew. There was bread. There was a gummy rice that stuck behind Barney's teeth. By the door were heaped the weapons of the *mujahidin*. He was amongst the world's most feared guerrilla force. He felt a desperate elation.

A girl stood in the doorway.

Barney shook his head, unbelieving.

'I am Mia Fiori . . .'

He heard the words, the soft-accented English of the Mediterranean. He rose to make her welcome. Schumack didn't move.

'I am a nurse with Aide Médicale Internationale . . .'

He saw the dark ringlets of her hair, and the buttoned blouse, and the long skirt that was gathered at her waist and fell free to her ankles.

'They say you are going north in the morning . . . Will you take me with you, take me where I can be of use . . .?'

He watched the shimmer of the skin of her cheeks, and the way she held her hands and clasped and unclasped her fingers.

To Barney she was beautiful, a mirage in this place. He shook his head.

'These people won't take me. To them I am only a woman.'

All the room watched Barney.

'My name is Crispin. I'm a collector of strays.' Gul Bahdur flashed him a look of pure hatred and Schumack waved once to her with his iron claw, grinning. 'I'll take you, but it will be early that we leave.'

151

11

The valley was slightly more than thirty miles long, gouged as a deep ditch, running north to south. In places it was as narrow as five hundred metres, at its widest point little more than two thousand. The sides of the valley alternated between cliff precipices and more gradual slopes, but from any place on the floor of the valley the flanking walls seemed to rise high and intimidating. A water course ran the length of the valley, but it was dry, waiting for the rains and the first snow fall. Winding amongst the boulders and stones of the river bed was a track that would be suitable only for a four-wheel-drive lorry or jeep, or for a tank. Where the valley was widest there had lived until quite recently whole village communities. Now they were gone. They had herded together their sheep and their goats and their mules, and they had trekked over the mountains to Pakistan. The villages they had left abandoned had been bombed, rocketed, devastated. The fields were now caked in stringy dried yellow grass. The valley was a place of ghosts. Into the side walls ran small valleys, fissures in the granite rock, water drains for the change of season that would bring the melted snow down from the high peaks. These small valleys, these fissures, gave access from the valley floor to the upland pastures where the herds were grazed in summer. But the herds had gone, and the shepherds. The flowers remained, growing as weeds in the field squares, sprouting ochre and red and blue where once there had been vetch and lentil and pumpkin plants.

The valley had formerly been prosperous. It lies across a nomads' and caravanners' trail from Pakistan's northern mountains towards the Panjshir of Afghanistan. The trail comes down into the middle of the valley, crosses between three villages and then climbs again westwards. If the valley is not open to the traveller then he must resign himself to the minimum of another week's walking at altitude to skirt this trusted route. It is a trail trodden with history. The great Alexander brought his army from Europe along this path, through this valley, perhaps the first of the bands of fighting men to find this by-pass of the mountain peaks. In this area the people carry the stamp of those former armies, now they are called Nuristanis, before that they were the Kafiristanis — the strangers, known for their pale skins and their fair hair and their blue eyes and their old ways of animism worship. They are a world set apart from the tribespeople of the Pathans and the Uzbeks and the Tajiks and the Hazaras, and they live now in the refugee camps in Pakistan.

The war has fallen with its full ferocity on these villages under the high cliff walls. Along this trail the *mujahidin* carry their munitions and weapons before the winter halts the resupply of the mountain fighters, and in the valley's villages they rest and take shelter. The bombers and the helicopter gunships stampeded the people of these villages into exile.

The morning after they had arrived at the southern entrance to the valley, Schumack had gone.

They had shaken hands with a certain formality that was a part of neither of them, and the American had muttered something about joining up with a group further into the mountains to the west. He had gone early and blended away with half a dozen men who were laden down by the weight of mortar bombs and the ammunitions belts for a DShK 12.7mm machine gun.

The girl went with Schumack because he was going in the direction of the Panjshir. Perhaps he would reach the Panjshir, perhaps not. He would take her towards Panjshir. The girl had thanked Barney as if he was responsible for her moving towards her goal, and she had headed off walking easily at Schumack's side.

Barney felt a sort of loneliness when they had gone, winding away along the river bed and then becoming ant creatures as they started to climb into a side valley. The girl had been with him for two days, the American for five. He thought of them as friends, and they had gone as casually as if they would surely meet before the day's end and, or as if, for their part, they had nothing to share with him or his life.

The camp was a collection of tents pegged out under trees a quarter of a mile from the nearest empty village. Eight tents, all sand-brown and carrying the stencilled markings of Afghan Army and Soviet equipment. Captured weapons, captured ammunition, captured tents. After Schumack and the girl had gone, Barney went back to the tent that he had shared with them and Gul Bahdur. He looked down at where she had slept, separated from himself and Maxie Schumack by the boy whose back had been to her as if she might eat him in the darkness. He saw the place on the rug where her curled body had been.

The boy read him. He had opened the tent flap and pulled a face at Barney.

'The Chief will talk to you.'

A quick grin from Barney. The meeting that was the make or the break.

He followed Gul Bahdur out of the tent.

His name was Ahmad Khan. He was the leader of the *mujahidin* in the valley. He was his own master and he acknowledged no superior. The Hizbi-i-Islami Central Committee in Peshawar exercised a fragile hold on his activities provided that weapon and ammunition were supplied to him above what he took from his enemy. In his territory his authority was undisputed.

He was not from these mountains. He was a man of the city, from Kabul. He was twenty-five years old. Barney found

154

a slight, spare man with moustache, with full lips and a jutting clean-shaven chin. He wore a black turban, wound loosely and with the end hanging like a tail on his shoulder. His dress was a grey check sports jacket without front buttons, torn at the right elbow, cotton jeans, a pair of jogging shoes bright blue and white. He sat on the ground a little way from the tents and alone.

Barney came to him, sat cross-legged in front of him.

'I speak English, I was taught English at the Lycée Istiqual in Kabul. Later I worked with an Englishman, an engineer. Before I came here I had begun to be a schoolmaster. My English is good?'

'Excellent,' Barney said. He waved Gul Bahdur away, saw the boy hesitate and then drift back from them, out of ear shot and disappointed.

'Who are you?' The eyes were unwavering.

'I am Barney Crispin . . .'

'And who is Barney Crispin? His name tells me nothing.'

He had known since Parachinar that the question would be asked, but he had never been clear what would be his answer. The eyes stared into him.

'I am British.'

'Who pays you?' A soft singing voice that demanded an answer.

'I am Barney Crispin, I am British, and I have the weapons to shoot down eight helicopters.'

'You were sent here by the government of Britain?'

Barney offered no reply.

'Why does the government of Britain wish to help us shoot down eight helicopters?'

Barney gazed into his face, saw the clear lines of white teeth, saw the flies that haloed his head.

'You do not have to know, I do not have to know. If you allow me to stay, then the helicopters will have their power over your valley destroyed. At the moment the helicopters

155

are safe from you. With the missiles that I have, the safety of
the helicopters is ended. Why I am here is not important to
you.'

'I decide what is important to me.'

Barney recognised the twist of anger.

'What is important to you is that I destroy eight helicopters, that I change the pattern for flying of all the helicopters
that come to this valley.'

'What is important to me, I decide that. Why should I not
take your missiles and send you away?'

'Because you are not trained to use the missile. You might
hit one, if you were lucky, you are not competent to hit eight.
That is why you won't send me away.'

'What is the missile?'

'It is the American Redeye missile. It is satisfactory but
not modern. If the missiles have not been destroyed by the
journey here, if there is no malfunction, then the missile is
effective.'

'What is the principle of the missile?'

'Heat-seeker, it targets onto the engine exhaust vent. Do
you understand that?'

'I was trained to be a schoolmaster. I am not ignorant.'

'It is necessary to pick with great care the moment of
firing.'

'Eight helicopters only?'

'How many have you shot down this year?'

It was Ahmad Khan's turn to peer into Barney's face, and
not reply.

'Not even one?'

The drone of the flies, the flutter of a single bird, the
tumble fall of a distant stone on the valley's walls.

'If you have not shot down one helicopter how can you
refuse the opportunity to shoot down eight helicopters?'

'You guarantee eight?'

'I guarantee my best efforts, eight times.'

'Can the helicopter avoid the missile?'

'If the pilot is cleverer than I am, then he has that chance. If he is not cleverer his helicopter is dead. You want to know what is in it for me? I want the opportunity to strip the first helicopter, not for its weapons, for its electronics. That is all that I ask in exchange for the opportunity to travel with you.'

'I tell you what I think . . . You are a military trained man, you are sent here by your government . . .'

'That's not the point . . .'

'Hear me out.' A blaze in the eyes.

'The little of the truth you have told me is that you wish to strip the first helicopter that is not destroyed on crashing. Not all of the truth is that you say you will stay until you have fired eight missiles. I believe you at the first, I do not believe you at the second. If you are a soldier then you will have an order, when you have achieved that order you will run away with your prize.'

'You have my promise.'

'Why should I value your promise? You come to kill a helicopter, to take its working parts. The knowledge will not help me, nor my people. That knowledge is for you, for your own people.'

'You can have my word, my hand.'

'Last year from a village north of here a helicopter was shot down, from above, perhaps it was a lucky shot, the Soviets came the next day with their airborne troops. They caught a dozen of the men of the village, they chained them together, they put petrol over them, they set fire to them.'

'Try me,' Barney said, as if he had not heard.

'What do I have to do, to try you?'

'You have to bring the helicopters to your valley.'

A snort of derision from Ahmad Khan. 'The helicopters come. I do not have to bring them. When the *mujahidin* are in the high valleys the helicopters cannot reach them, but the

157

mujahidin must come down into my valley, and when the helicopters come they do not come at my bidding.'

'I tell you this, Ahmad Khan, before the snow falls, if you will trust me, the helicopters will not fly with impunity to this valley.'

'We have been fighting for four years. We shall fight on here after you have gone. In our struggle for liberation you mean nothing to us.'

'A helicopter destroyed is more than you have managed.'

'You take a freedom with me.' A flaring anger, loud at his mouth, bright in his eyes. 'We did not ask you to come here. We do not need the sacrifices that the help you offer will demand of us.'

'That is the talk of an obstinate man,' Barney said.

Ahmad Khan stiffened his back straight. His hand clasped at something through the thickness of his jacket, perhaps a pistol, perhaps a knife. Barney felt a strange confidence.

'You dare to call me obstinate?' Ahmad Khan spat the question at Barney.

'If you send me away then I call you an obstinate fool.'

'To us you are an unbeliever. You do not have the faith of Islam, you have no commitment to our freedom. You seek only to help yourself.'

'In helping myself I help you,' Barney said evenly. 'How often do the helicopters come?'

'Every two days, every three days, every day, it changes, but I do not want your help.'

'What do you do when the helicopters come?'

'We hide,' Ahmad Khan shouted.

'I can destroy them for you,' Barney shouted back.

'I fight my own war.'

'From the back of caves?'

Ahmad Khan hissed his surprise. 'You take a chance with me, Englishman.'

158

'You take a chance with the lives of the men that follow you. To be obstinate is to throw away the lives of your men.'

Barney saw the hand loosen from whatever was concealed under Ahmad Khan's coat. Ahmad Khan stood, rising with an easy grace from the squat. Suddenly he smiled, the sweet smile of dismissal.

'I do not know why you are here, and I do not want you.'

'It is for you to decide.'

'I have decided.'

Barney did not argue. He shrugged.

'You can take some food, then you should go back to Pakistan.'

'I thank you for the food, but I will not go back to Pakistan.'

'You go where?'

'I will go ten miles up your valley, perhaps you will see the smoke from the first helicopter.'

Barney looked up at the young guerrilla commander and saw his puzzlement. He felt no hostility towards him. There was an openness about the man that he admired. Barney had not been open. He had not spoken of the age of Redeye, he had not fairly detailed the limitations of targeting onto the engine exhaust vents. He had not mentioned the potential damage to the electronics from the long overland journey on the backs of the mules. He had not described the evasion techniques available to the pilots of an Mi-24. He had not said that he would leave when the instrumentation was strapped on the mules' backs. He had played an arrogant game, not an honest game. But he had lost nothing, and everything. He stood up.

'How many men do you have?' Barney asked.

'What is it to you?'

'How many men?'

'More than fifty,' a scent of pride from Ahmad Khan. 'In the side valleys there are more.'

159

'And the valley is important?'

'You know the valley is a route used by the Resistance.'

'If they were to come with tanks and armoured cars . . .'

'I have machine guns, I have anti-tank rockets.'

'Be ready for them, but they will not have the helicopters.' Barney smiled carelessly. He held out his hand, took Ahmad Khan's, gripped it.

'Why are you here, Englishman?'

'I think we will meet again.'

Barney walked away, over to the boy. He saw the apprehension in Gul Bahdur's face. He told the boy that the leader had said that they should take food from the camp, and asked the boy to collect it. Barney went back to the tent beside which the two mules were tethered and grazing. In the dimness of the tent interior he bent over the piled parts of the Redeye missile kit. He had made a promise, he had given his word. He thought of Rossiter who had torpedoed his FCO career. He thought of the boy with the bloodied head who had walked back to the frontier with the launcher. He thought of thirteen men who were dead. He thought of a village that he had seen under attack from the hovering helicopters. He thought of a schoolmaster and the fierce pride that had taken him from the city to the valley shadows. Lastly he thought of an old man who was his father who had scuffled with a gunman without thought for his own safety. They were clear, sharp, painful thoughts.

Barney stowed the missiles onto the backs of the mules and lashed tight the ropes.

It was mid morning when they left the camp, Barney holding the bridle close to the jaw of the mule and the boy a few paces behind him. More than a hundred yards along the track stood Ahmad Khan. Barney looked straight ahead, said nothing as he passed Ahmad Khan, who stared over his head, ignored his going. There was the clipping tread of the

160

mules, the stamp of Barney's boots, the shuffle of the boy's sandals. A great hush over the valley, a great quiet and emptiness that was not moved by the steady pace of Barney and the boy and the two mules.

Once clear of the camp, Barney's eyes roved across the valley floor and the bouldered river bed and the uncultivated fields and the fruit trees that were overgrown, unpruned from the previous year. Over the jagged shapes of the rock falls at the base of the cliff walls. Up onto the steep, smoothed slopes where only the hardiest of scrub bushes had taken root. Out into the fissure valleys that groped away to the sides. Towards the mountain peaks that were distant, pale in the sunshine, deceptively close.

He was hunting for cover, for advantage, for a firing position.

The map was sheeted with a cellophane cover, and marked with chinagraph symbols that positioned Soviet and Afghan Army garrisons and suspected bandit concentrations.

They were crowded into the room, eight pilots for eight Mi-24s. They would fly the following morning, return for their machines to be refuelled, go up again in the afternoon hours. They would fly in four pairs on different patrol routes, and the pattern would be repeated after refuelling. The helicopters were capable of covering great distances, they would quarter many of the deep valleys and rifts of Laghman province during the two patrols.

They were young, early twenties, they wore the common uniform of close cropped hair, tanned faces, keen and aware eyes. Since he had taken command of Eight Nine Two he had not lost one of them. He had earned their trust.

Two helicopters to prowl the wide Kunar river valley from its fork with the Kabul river and upstream to Asadabad.

Two helicopters to trace the river between Qarqai and Ali Shang to the west.

161

Two helicopters to take their start point at Mehtarlam and then follow the road track north towards Manduwal.

Two helicopters to operate in the vacuum wilderness between Mehtarlam and Mahmud-e Eraqi, the wilderness designated as patrol area Delta.

He stabbed with his pointer at the contour lines of the map. The squadron had been there before, into area Delta. Medev grimaced. There existed in Delta only deep valleys and cliff escarpments and friendless mountains. None of his fliers wanted Delta.

Medev caught the eye of one of the young men who would fly an Mi-24 into area Delta in the morning, the pilot Nikolai. He had been into area Delta before, he was reliable, he was careful. Area Delta was in their tasking. Area Delta must be covered. A silence had fallen on the briefing room, the pilots waited on him. Silence was an infectious disease at the briefings. They were good pilots, those going into area Delta, as good as he had. They hated area Delta for its wildness, lack of friendly force base camps, for its weather, for the problems of rescue pick-ups.

'It will be search and destroy, what you search out you destroy. I suggest a ground speed of 70 kph. Met report for tomorrow is clear visibility, no cloud, winds strong to severe with a possibility of 50 klick gusts. That's all.'

There were seldom questions. He tried to be exhaustive in his handling of all matters that might prove of concern to his fliers. He did not encourage his fliers to ask questions for the sake of hearing their own voices. There was the shuffling of feet, the scraping of chair legs. Medev smiled warmly, saved an additional warmth for the pilot, Nikolai, who would lead in the morning into area Delta.

Just when the light was failing, Barney found the place.

They had travelled five hours since leaving the camp. He

had been restless, pushing himself forward, unwilling to talk with the boy. Now he had found the place.

He estimated that the width of the valley floor was a thousand yards. To the north and the south were villages. Between the villages and on either side of the river bed were orchards still with the summer's leaf canopy. At their lowest point the valley walls sloped gradually into the tree line, and above the trees on one side were scrub bushes of thorn and then heavy boulders that a millennium before had crashed from the upper rock face.

Standing now amongst those rocks he looked across the valley to the cave entrance opposite him. Near to the mouth of the cave, a lateral slit, he could see the movements of the boy who worked to collect dried grass and small branches for the fire that would be lit in the cave the next morning.

He was satisfied. Barney came down over the rocks, dropped through the cracks and gullies and into the twilight of the orchard where the mules were hobbled.

Before the light had gone, by the time that the boy had returned from collecting the materials for the fire, Barney had assembled the Redeye missile.

12

They had eaten when the first of the sun broke over the western lip of the valley's roof above the rock crack where they had slept. They were both shivering from the cold dew damp. Barney had stamped and banged his arms across his chest as the boy unwrapped the *nan* bread he had carried from the camp. Below them but close and hidden under the trees were the mules moving noisily on the hobbling ropes.

The boy was quiet, quieter than at any time since he had carried the launcher into the bungalow at Peshawar. Barney remembered the talk of killing a hundred Soviets. None of the crap and bubble from the boy now, and no cheek. This was real, on the valley's wall and above the valley's floor, the time for boasting past. When they had first woken, the boy had gone a few yards from Barney and sunk down to his knees and elbows in prayer; he had not prayed before, not when it had just been the two of them together. Gul Bahdur was to go into combat in the company of a foreigner, he was to fight alongside an unbeliever, he was to stand back to back with a man who could not speak his first language. Barney understood why the boy was quiet, why he had ripped at the food and not cared to gather the crumbs.

A bird came, a finch of brilliant yellow feathers, and hopped and skipped near to them and revelled in the unexpected feast.

Barney saw the freedom of the bird when it fled from him and perched out of reach on a branch before diving back with courage reassembled to the ground beside him.

He wondered whether he could lure it into his hand.

The bread was finished. The grey light was spreading down the far wall of the valley. The Redeye missile, launch tube attached to the launch mechanism, rested on a rock beside Barney. Time for the boy to go.

The boy knew. There was fear in his face that he could not hide.

'If you fire at the helicopter and you do not kill it . . .'

'I will kill it, Gul Bahdur.'

'You can promise you will kill it?'

'Watch me, Gul Bahdur.'

The boy smiled back, thinly, without certainty, and was gone, down into the first line of the trees in the orchard.

Barney started to climb up the west side of the valley. He took with him a second tube.

He hoped if the helicopters came that day that they would come early, before the sun straddled the centre of the valley in the white midday heat. He hoped that the simple lure he had baited for the helicopter would draw it to within his firing range. He hoped the helicopters would be cruising gently as a dragonfly in flight . . . Cut the bloody hoping, Barney.

He reached a rock boulder, lichen covered, and balanced some one hundred and fifty feet above the orchard's trees. The boulder was fifteen feet high, twenty feet from front to back and, behind it, and accentuating the precariousness of its grip on the slope, was a narrow gully wide enough for a man to pass. It was a firing position. Whether the helicopters came from the north or from the south he would have the cover of the boulder until they had passed. Barney set down the missile and the spare tube. He took his one handkerchief from his pocket and ripped a tear in it with his teeth, and then pulled it to narrow shreds with his hands and screwed up two pieces and plugged them in his ears, and was satisfied, and took them out and laid them on the stone beside the missile. Next he loaded the battery system into the body of the launch unit.

The sunlight was clearing the haze of early morning, sharpening the greens of the valley floor, and the greys and brown tints of the valley walls. He could see more than two miles each way down the valley.

Across the valley a spiral of smoke drifted up from the dark entrance of the cave that was below the height at which Barney now sat. He saw the boy bend over the fire at the mouth of the cave, and a further billow of smoke as green wood replaced the kindling of dried branches.

Remember that at all times the missile must see the engine exhaust vent that is set port and starboard on the upper side fuselage, behind the pilot, below the rotor blade transmission.

Remember that the engine exhaust is the only target for Redeye.

Remember the helicopter must be in steady flight for all of the missile's journey time.

Remember to aim forward, to aim high.

Barney looked down as the sun winked on the transparent disc at the forward end of the launch tube, and behind the disc onto the infra-red seeker optics and sensor element.

The time for waiting.

And as he watched the rise of the smoke from the cave slit he thought of the instruction he had given to the thirteen men who had died with the Redeye. No bloody way they could have mastered the principle of 'fire and forget' ground-to-air missiles, launcher acquisition electronics, the azimuth angle of target aiming. And because they were dead, Barney Crispin now crouched beside the boulder and strained with his ears for the sound of a helicopter in the valley.

The smoke from the cave crept up the rock face.

He crouched down beside the boulder, his shoulders covered by the blanket, his hand close to the Redeye launcher. And waited.

166

They would fly in formation from the Jalalabad base and when they were north of the Kabul river they would split to their pairs and their assigned patrol sectors.

Medev bent his body away from the thrash of the rotor blades as the engines were readied for take off. Rostov was sunk behind the Major, using his body shamelessly as a wind break. Some of the ground crew had come to stand in the sunshine and watch the departure of the heavy-laden gunships. A deafening howl of engine power, a film of scampering dry dust that slitted Medev's eyes. Through the haze of the storm he could see the rocket pods on the stumpy down-slung wings. Ugly beasts, and they always brought a grim smile to Medev's face. Ugly as sin. Sand and green-brown broken camouflage on the bodies of the beasts, and underneath a grey paint hull. Two bulging domes forward of tinted bullet proof glass for the gunner and pilot. Above the pilots' canopies were the gaping circular intake orifices for the TV-2-117 Isotov powerhouse engines. Ugly as shit, and he loved them. Loved their clumsy stamping roll as they shuddered on their wheels, weighed down by a carcase of armour plate, a stomach sack of fuel, fists and teeth of machine guns and rocket pods. The helicopters, in line, lifted off. The grit flew at Medev's face. He watched them climb above the dust storm, then saw the noses dip as they turned towards the perimeter fence, towards the foothills beyond the Kabul river. He watched until they were specks in the azure sky, and until he could no longer see them.

Medev spun on his heel. He walked to Operations, the shed in which were the radio sets that would attempt constant communication with the patrolling helicopters. Other than when the patrols were masked by a mountain mass, usually when deep in the hinterland valleys, contact would be a free flow.

Two helicopters to follow the Kunar river valley north east to Asadabad. Two helicopters to trace the river bed between Qarqai and Ali Shang to the north west. Two helicopters to skim the ground traversing the mountain passes from Mehtarlam to Manduwal. Two helicopters over the wastes of area Delta. The quiet slipped again to the apron. Those who had watched the departure of the eight Mi-24s went back to their desks and their maintenance hangars.

Barney saw the boy heap more wood and leaves onto the fire. In a moment the smoke soared again, and above the cave it was caught by the wind and blown out across the valley and spread as a milk skim above the trees and above the dry river bed.

He looked at his watch. He wondered if they would come that morning, or in the afternoon, or the following day. If they were to come that morning then they would come soon. And, if they came, would he have the opportunity to fire? The first shot must be a killing shot. Better not to fire, if the first shot was not certain to kill.

He heard the rustle of a dragonfly's wings, but he was too far from water.

He heard the drone of a searching bee, but there were no flowers on the rock slope close to him.

Slowly, deliberately, Barney stood up. His head was back, pricking at the wind to identify the source of the rustle and the drone. The noise welled in the air around him.

He heard the approach of the helicopters. He waited motionless to identify the direction of the advance as the sounds grew in his ears.

He bent and picked up the cloth wads that he had made for his ears. His ears could no longer help him, the helicopters were coming from the north. He stuffed the shreds of cloth into his ears, pressing them hard. He took the Redeye, lifted it lightly onto his shoulder, and ducked through the gap behind the boulder to cover himself from the approach of the helicopters. There would be very little time when the helicopters came, thirty seconds, he thought, not more. Thirty seconds to engage the battery coolant, sight the Redeye, find the target, fire. And through all the sighting and the finding and the firing he must have a clean view for the missile head of the hot metal of the engine exhaust vent. Not a view of the nose, not a view of the underbelly, not a view of the sloped wing set into the fuselage behind and below the engine's vent.

The first helicopter he saw was lower than he had expected, meandering over the dried-out river bed, as a shark will that is in shallow water, ebbing and varying its tack. He hugged close to the boulder. The helicopter hovered five hundred metres from Barney, five hundred metres from the smoke that drifted from the cave slit.

Barney's thumb slipped over the battery switch beside his ear. They always flew in pairs, he could hear but not see the second helicopter, above and behind, masked from Barney's view by the boulder, close enough to pierce the ear wads. To kill the first helicopter was to kill himself. To destroy the lower helicopter was to invite the retaliation of the escort above, all-seeing the moment the missile was launched. You wait, Barney, you wait and you don't fire.

The second helicopter was above him, more frantic and busy than its lower partner, faster and higher, manoeuvring because its work was that of a watchman.

The smoke was as blood in the water to a shark.

The lower helicopter dipped to face the cave. There was a tumult of rocket fire, the crash of smoke and stone and shrapnel. There would be tribesmen in the cave, helpless fools who had lit a fire. The second helicopter came down, level with Barney, and made a fast run south to north up the valley before banking sharply and turning. Barney had seen the pilot's face, jutting from the front of his flying cap. He had seen the gunner in the forward turret.

Again there was the bellow of the rockets exploding around the cave's mouth.

169

The second helicopter came past Barney. It was the escort, the sentry, the one that should have been flying high as guard, the one that now came to join the game of rocketing the arse-shits who were fool enough to have lit a fire in the cave in which they rested.

The second helicopter swung back again up the valley, level with Barney's eyeline, without caution. The lower helicopter presented its tail rotor to him. He heard the crack of machine gun fire aimed at the cave.

He took a great gulp of air into his lungs. The launcher was steady on his shoulder, held firm with the right hand, manipulated with the left. Right thumb on the battery coolant switch. The second helicopter flew back across Barney's line of sight. Right thumb down. He could see the yawning hole of the engine exhaust vent above the wing, below the swirl of the rotor circle. Through the crossed wires of the sight he watched the second helicopter, watched the engine exhaust vent. No more trembling, only a great calmness. The launcher was vibrating, homing and the howl of the buzzer was in his ears. His right index finger slowly squeezed the trigger stick. Aim ahead, aim for elevation.

Fire.

Go, you bastard. Go.

The missile limped from the launcher. Strangely slow and pathetic, the first movement. Then the flash, the blast. Twenty feet in front of Barney, the main ignition. The heat snapped into his face. A fire ball streaking across the valley's space, in pursuit of the second helicopter.

Barney heard the impact, the thunder of collision, and saw the sheet of flame and the lifting, slow motion, of shrapnel metal.

He bent to lift the spare missile tube, and ran down the hillside with the wind stripping his hair, towards the cover of the trees.

Neither man had a warning, however brief, of the catastrophe speeding towards them. At the short range of eight hundred metres and because the helicopter was utilising no anti-missile procedures, the effect of the impact of the high explosive war head was fatal. By the time that the pilot had recovered from the pile-hammer blow above and behind him, his helicopter was careering towards the stone of the river bed. The pilot heard the scream of his gunner as the helicopter fell nose first. At that height the pilot did not have the chance to flutter down on the free run of his rotors. Loaded with fuel and ammunition, weighing close to nine tons, the big machine's plummet ended in a scraping collapse of metal on rock in the river bed.

Then the fire.

The helicopter that had been firing into the cave, its tail facing the launch position of Redeye, veered hard to starboard in answer to the single shouted exclamation of a brother pilot. He scudded fast along the valley floor, down with the loose and rounded stones, using his skill to extricate himself from danger while the gunner, craning back, yelled over the internal radio a description of their burning partner.

From the depths of the valley the pilot could not report to the Jalalabad operations room. He climbed for altitude, for safety, for vision, for communication.

Below him, climbing more slowly, was the dense column of oil black smoke.

He could not know what their reaction would be.

He was under the cover of the trees. He lay in the lee of a rock that stood half a dozen feet high between the trunks of the orchard trees. He discarded the used missile tube, looked down at the Hebrew and Parsee stencil stamps on the fibreglass tube. He loaded the second missile. He doubted he would fire, he would not look for a second opportunity, not while the blood was still hot in him, not while his chest still

171

heaved in elation at the kill, but he would be ready. The mules were hobbled a dozen yards from him, tight against two trees that had grown up against each other and provided a double thickness of leaf roof. The boy was across the river from him, separated by the open ground of the river bed.

Between gaps in the foliage, he could see the smoke streaming up against the sky, and he heard the report of exploding ammunition, and his nostrils filled with the smell of ignited aviation fuel.

He could not know what their reaction would be. Whether the undamaged helicopter would stay on station, whether a force of infantry would be flown in to sweep that part of the valley, whether an air strike by fighter bombers would be called down. It was morning, and he needed darkness before he could move again in real safety with his mules, before he could call the boy back from across the river bed.

Barney took the cloth wads from his ears. There was a new depth of sounds, from the ammunition, from the beat of the helicopter's engines above him. The elation had been fast coming, it slipped away now, a discarded skin. He believed he had killed two men. Minutes before he could have stood on his feet, screamed his triumph, waved a clenched fist salute above his head. The exhilaration, a passing luxury, was spat from his mind.

The voice of Pyotr Medev as he spoke into the microphone in Jalalabad Operations was quiet and detached. The voice was a fraud.

In answer to Medev, winning through the static and crackle of an intermittent radio transmission, was the voice of the pilot now hovering high over the valley 80 kilometres away to the north.

'Are there survivors? Over . . .'

'Not that we have seen. I repeat, there has been a fire and

172

explosions. The fire was total. There is no movement around the helicopter, over . . .'

'Is there a possibility of survivors? Over . . .'

'No possibility, over . . .'

'After the fire is there any chance the bandits can salvage anything? Over . . .'

'The helicopter is destroyed, over . . .'

'Tell me again: you did not see Nikolai go down? Was it ground fire or a malfunction? Over . . .'

'I saw nothing, repeat, nothing. My gunner believes he heard an explosion, but Nikolai was out of our vision at that time. My gunner was hammering a cave. My gunner says there was an explosion, he thinks, then there was a shout from Nikolai, garbled. My gunner thinks he saw them just as they went in. He says he thinks they were already making smoke. He cannot be sure, it was very fast. Nikolai was flying low, over . . .'

Medev's lips were pursed in resignation. 'How low? Over . . .'

'Forty, fifty metres. They were behind me, over . . .'

Nikolai should have been high above, not down on his arse near the floor of the valley. Medev shook his head.

'And there is no possibility of survivors? Over . . .'

'The fire is still burning, there is no possibility.'

'Return to base, over, out.'

The static snapped off, the transmission was completed. Medev put down the microphone. There was a silence in the Operations Room. He looked up at the operations wall map, into the wilderness of area Delta unmarked by roads or the red squares of towns. When he reached up on his toes he could make the chinagraph mark, a black cross, at the co-ordinates where the helicopter had crashed. It was the first helicopter he had lost, they were the first crew he had lost. He felt sick in his stomach. Perhaps there had been an explosion, perhaps the helicopter had been making smoke before it

173

came down. There was sufficient uncertainty for him to know that an accident investigation team must be flown into that valley in area Delta. For an accident investigation team to land there, he needed infantry to be lifted in to secure a perimeter around them. If Mi-8s were to go into the valley then the gunships would have to be above them. A bloody shambles . . . a military operation on some scale was called for. Medev strode out of Operations and headed away in the sunshine for Divisional headquarters.

If there had been an explosion before the crash, if there had been smoke before impact, then the Mi-24 was in all probability the victim of ground fire. Medev had to know.

The helicopter had gone.

Barney lay for half an hour in the shelter place after the engine drone had left the valley. He lay in the silence that is the world of small foraging birds, and of the first leaves falling. He lay close to the peace of field flowers. There were no more explosions from the fuel tanks and ammunition of the helicopter. He lay in the silence and the peace of the orchard.

Then, abruptly, Barney moved.

He would not wait for darkness, he would move out.

He hurried down towards the river bed, paused at the tree line and called the boy's name.

The boy came quickly, breaking from cover, fleet and light-footed.

Barney saw him coming, walked back to the mules. He had untied the animals and was already heading north, up the valley, when the panting boy reached him.

'It was marvellous, Barney, magnificent.'

Barney didn't look back at him, just tossed back the bridle rope of a mule.

'I saw it happen, Barney, I watched you fire Redeye . . .'

Barney lengthened his stride, dragging his mule along after him through the trees.

174

'You are pleased, Barney, it is what you wanted?'

Barney came to the edge of the orchard. His face furrowed in concentration. Half a mile of open field and rock to cover and then another orchard in front of him that was laid out beside the shell of a village. The helicopter was behind them. Barney started to trot forward, short chopped steps. He heard the wheeze of the boy's breath and the stamp of the mules' hooves.

They came to the tree line of the far orchard, crossed it, by-passed the village of broken mud-brick homes and free swinging doors and untended graves. On across more open ground where the valley narrowed, and they took a rough trail at the angle of the cliff wall, where the sun could not touch them.

Once they passed a shepherd who sat surrounded by his herd of goats that had found a feeding place in a small field from which, before the evacuation of the valley, he would have been chased. The shepherd watched them, gave no sign of interest.

Where the valley was narrow, where the trees were close set, where there was cover, and where the smoke from the helicopter could no longer be seen, Barney stopped. He tied his mule, flopped down, closed his eyes and waited for the boy.

'Will you kill another helicopter?'

'I have seven more missiles,' Barney said.

'Seven more helicopters . . .?'

The boy roped his mule to an apple tree's root and took some bread from his pack and broke it into two portions.

'It was wasted,' Barney said flatly. 'The moment the fire caught, it was wasted.'

'Is that all you care for? After what we suffer from the helicopters all you care for are the mechanisms?'

First the gunship helicopters strafed the empty villages on either side of the burned out skeleton fuselage, then the Mi-8 carried in the infantry.

While the investigation officers worked, the gunships clattered overhead.

Medev was there.

It was rare for Medev to be away from the Operations Room at Jalalabad, but then he had not lost a helicopter before. He had insisted, the Frontal Aviation commander had relented. Medev could prowl the rocks and boulders of the river bed and walk amongst the fragments of the crashed Mi-24. He had seen a trooper vomit as a charred and black-bodied corpse, unrecognisable as the man who had eaten breakfast beside Medev that morning, was taken from the upper cockpit. He had seen what seemed to be three burned logs removed from the nose cockpit and zipped into a white plastic bodybag. He had seen the investigators climb carefully up to the starboard engine exhaust vent. He had seen them scribbling notes, he had seen the flash of the camera lights.

Later a green brown fibreglass tube was brought from the tree line to the investigators.

Later a place was found fifty metres up the valley's side where the ground beside a large boulder rock had been scorched by a fire flash.

Medev did not quiz the investigators for a preliminary finding. He would hear their conclusions that evening, before the planning of the next day's patrols.

They were gone, back to Jalalabad, by the late afternoon, and on their way home a shepherd, taking no cover, was machine gunned to death.

13

The accident investigation officer was a thorough young man. He was not in awe of his audience – the Frontal Aviation commander, the Colonel of Intelligence, a divisional army staff officer, and Major Medev – and they heard him through without interruption.

'An Mi-24 was downed in area Delta after receiving a direct hit in the proximity of the engine exhaust from an infra-red guided ground-to-air missile. The missile was fired from an elevated position at the side of the valley at a lateral trajectory from a range of eight hundred metres. We discovered a launch tube for an American manufactured Redeye missile, sometimes given the designation FIM-43A. The markings on the missile tube tell us it was nine years old, that it was issued to the Israeli Defence Force, and then transferred to the Iranian army. We found the tracks of one man and two mules . . .'

'The tracks of one man?' Medev said. 'Tell me of those tracks.'

'They were boot marks, they have been photographed, but I do not yet have the prints. A large boot with a heavy gripping tread.'

'The bandits wear sandals, or shoes, not climbing boots.'

'Not my concern, Major Medev. I merely report the type of boot that was worn at the place where the tube was found.'

'We wear boots, a European wears boots,' the Colonel of Intelligence said. 'We have to be careful not to leap to conclusions, but the Afghan does not generally wear boots.'

177

'We are dealing with a ground-to-air missile, not a foot-wear problem,' said the staff officer.

The Colonel of Intelligence said, 'Five days ago, perhaps a week, we received information that a European and a local national and two mules were crossing Nangarhar province coming north towards the Kabul river and Laghman . . .'

'You acted on that information?' enquired the staff officer.

'We were able to trace the path of these persons for some days. The trail was lost as we were in the process of an airborne interception. I am correct, Major Medev?'

'The interception was aborted. The final directions close to the river did not materialise,' Medev said quietly.

'Unfortunate,' the staff officer said.

'More unfortunate for our comrade who operated the ground radio. He was shot; he was castrated; his testicles were left for his lunch.'

The staff officer said nothing.

The Frontal Aviation commander leaned forward over his desk, his finger pointed at Medev. 'When the helicopters fly in pairs, one should cover the other. Evidently this did not happen?'

'A fire was lit in a cave, possibly the fire was a trap. The pilot paid with his life, and with the life of his gunner, for ignoring his orders.'

'It is important that your pilots fully understand their procedures,' the Frontal Aviation commander stiffly divorced himself from the responsibility.

'Eight Nine Two has two bodies to send home, I think our pilots have been reminded of their procedures.' Medev looked each man in the face. 'If we have a European in area Delta, if we have a man who will lay a trap to kill one helicopter, then I ask what is to be our response?'

'You find the bastard, that's my suggestion,' said the staff officer. 'Find him and kill him.'

The Frontal Aviation commander said, 'I will send a preliminary report to Kabul this evening. Find this man tomorrow, Major Medev, and I can send a further report to Kabul.'

'It will not be straightforward, sir. Area Delta is . . .'

'Aggressive flying will make it straightforward, Major Medev.'

It was the end of the meeting.

As the light failed, they had left the resting place, moved on, gone north. The valley floor was a gentle gradient, but the slightest of slopes over the rough ground was hard on the leg muscles, aching on the lungs.

The sinking sun was behind them. Barney walked into his moving shadow. He felt the tiredness. He felt the dirt on his body. He felt the lice-bite sores chafing under his arms. He felt a weakness, a looseness, in his stomach. And no bed tonight, no shelter from the evening wind. He wondered how long the boy could sustain the route marching and the lack of warm food. Barney stopped.

'Gul Bahdur . . .'

The shout echoed in the valley, came back to him from the rock faces.

'. . . By first light tomorrow we have to be on top of the valley, where is the place to climb?'

The answering voice, weak and failing in the winds. 'You cannot climb in the dark.'

'Where is the place to climb?'

The boy was staggering closer to Barney, slipping on the rocks, tears nearly suppressed. 'You cannot climb in the dark, in the day you can climb a side valley. You can see the side valley as well as I can, ahead.'

'If I can climb in the dark, so can you.'

'Not in the dark, Barney.'

Barney watched the boy, watched his spirit driving him

179

closer, watched his courage. He stumbled, he grazed his knee, he squeezed his eyes, he clung to the mules' bridle ropes. Barney set down the Redeye launcher, sat beside it, waited for the boy to reach him. They could only climb to the summits by using the side valleys. He wanted to taunt the boy, to tease more strength into his slight body. He thought he had succeeded. Only by the inventive use of their stamina would they live.

There were no trees here that had survived the last winter. There was a fallen, bark-peeled bough beside the river bed where it had been left by the spring's floods. Barney led a mule to the bough and roped it to the dead wood. He unloaded the two missiles and his back pack from the mule. From the pack he took trousers, the only pair other than the ones that he wore, and a shirt, and without asking he took the turban from the boy's head.

'What are you doing, Barney?' the boy asked, a small tired voice.

'I have to trick them for each firing to succeed. With the fire we tricked them. With this too, perhaps.'

He took small stones and stuffed them into the legs of the trousers and into the waist, filled the trousers. He laid the shirt above the trousers and found more stones for the body of the shirt and for the arms. The trousers and the shirt were half masked by a rock, but would be visible from the air. He took a stone that was the size of a ripened melon and put the boy's turban on it and placed it against the neck of the shirt.

Together they loaded the two missile tubes and the pack onto the other mule's back. They tramped off into the grey shadow light towards the place where the side valley dropped onto the valley's floor. The boy looked back, he saw the tethered mule and saw the half hidden shape of a man who slept beside the mule.

It had taken Barney and the boy three and a half hours to reach the roof of the valley.

180

Without the mule it would not have been possible. A dull, stubborn animal but even when blindfolded by darkness the animal uncannily found a secure foothold. They had clung alternately to the rope, to the bridle, to the packs and missile tubes, to the mule's tail. Their shins were raw from the rocks they had blundered against. High over the valley the winds whipped their clothes and chilled them. The last five hundred metres he half-carried the boy, held his arm crooked through his own.

The side valley wavered in no clear course, darting right and left over what in the spring would be torrent courses. No lights shining in the mountains, no sounds other than the scrape of their own feet and the mule's hooves straining for grip, and the stones that were dislodged and tumbled away under them. Higher on the climb there was a murmur of light from the crescent moon, thinly washed, so that Barney could see the shape in front of him of the mule's head, and could see the outline beside him of the boy's body. Hours since they had eaten, more hours since they had slept the sort of sleep he needed.

They came to the summit, they reached an upland plain. The stars were around them. The wind pinioned their clothes against their bodies and there was no respite from it. The mule would go no further.

The mule had taken them to the upper reach of the side valley and would go no further. Barney discovered a shallow gully, discovered it by falling headlong into it, and his momentum carried the boy in after him, and the mule bleated at the sudden dragging on its bridle. He hobbled the mule with difficulty and tied the rope to his ankle. They drew their blankets around them, and lay snuggled in the gully.

'Barney . . .'

'We have to sleep, Gul Bahdur.'

'When you go home, when you have fired the eight Redeyes, who will you tell of this time?'

181

'No one.'

'There is somebody?'

'There won't be anybody.'

'There has to be someone, you will tell of this to someone.'

'No one. I have to go to sleep . . .'

'You have a woman at home?'

'No.'

'Who do you do this for, Barney?'

He dragged the blanket tighter over his head.

'Who for, Barney?'

'Is it important, Gul Bahdur?'

'What I do is for my people, for my country. What you do is not for your people, not for your country's sake. It is not for money?'

'Not for money.' He smiled to himself.

'Who for, Barney?'

'Look, boy, when the helicopters come tomorrow, and they will come tomorrow, when they come if I am asleep then I am dead, if I am dead you are dead too . . .'

'I am not afraid to die.'

'I am not a warrior of God, I am not a potential martyr of the Resistance. I'm not going to die here. I'm not going to die because some little bastard won't let me sleep.'

'A cheeky little bastard, Barney?'

'A little bastard with about one minute to live if he doesn't shut up and sleep.'

'Why is there no woman at home to whom you will be able to tell this?'

'It didn't happen.'

'Why not?'

'There was nothing to give a woman,' Barney said quietly.

'There is yourself.'

'No woman would want the things I know of. I know how to break a man's neck with the edge of my hand. I know how

182

to lie in bracken and watch the back door of a farmhouse for three days without moving, in my own country. I know how to walk twenty miles with sixty pounds on my back and then take an assault course. I know how to put down mortar fire so that six have gone before the first lands. I know how to administer morphine and fit a saline drip when a man's in shock with his guts in the mud. I have nothing to give a woman, not any woman that I have met.'

'Did you try?'

'Go to sleep, boy.'

'What do we do in the morning?'

'I tell you, and then you don't talk any more.'

'I won't talk any more.'

Barney rolled on his back. He smelt the stench of his own body, he felt the dirt in his feet. He was canopied by the stars. His voice was a whisper.

'They will sweep the valley tomorrow. They must come back to the valley because they have been challenged. They have to find and remove the missile. They will try to fly in a formation that will flush us out. They will accept that one of their helicopters will always be vulnerable, but they will reckon I won't fire on the low flying bird and give my position. One helicopter will fly high, above the roof of the valley, probably to the rear of all the others. That helicopter, the high fly bird, is mine for tomorrow. That helicopter cannot be seen by those that fly in front and below. In the morning we have to find a hiding place for the mule and for you, and somewhere that I can reach quickly after I have fired. The helicopters will come from the south because that is the direction of Jalalabad. I want to be a mile or so further south than the mule we've left. I want to be behind the highest flying helicopter when they find the mule . . . That's the plan.'

Barney heard the rhythmic snores of the boy.

Even in the gully, the cold of the night wind tugged at his blanket, ate at his bones.

In the first grey sheen of morning the *mujahidin* knelt in prayer.

A ragged gathering of old and young, educated and illiterate, from the cities and from the villages. They knelt on their hands and elbows and squashed their foreheads into the dirt in the centre of their camp. They were in two rows, straight lines, and in front of each man was his weapon, close to his hand even when he was in obeisance to far away Mecca. Alone, out in front of his men, was Ahmad Khan with the loaded Kalashnikov beside his thighs. He led the men militarily and spiritually. He called now in the high pitched singing voice of prayer to the God of Islam. He called for victory, he cried for revenge. He called for the destruction of the Soviet occupation army, he cried for the expulsion of that army from his country. His prayer united the old and the young who followed him. He was devout. He was traditionalist. Islam had fashioned Ahmad Khan over the anvil, beaten steel into his leadership.

He had heard in the night that a helicopter had been shot down further north from his camp. The still smoking burnt wreck of a helicopter had been seen.

At that first light, Ahmad Khan and his men broke camp, folded away their tents and packed their few belongings.

With the shadows still long they began the trek away from the river bed and the trees and the scrub and the lower boulder falls of the valley. If a helicopter had been destroyed the previous day, then the Soviets would return in force the following morning, that Ahmad Khan knew. There were times when he was prepared to stand and fight, and there were times when he believed in survival under the cover of the side valleys. He had learned a long lesson at the hands of the helicopters, he fought them only when there was no escape.

Everything that they owned, they carried on their backs.

He was neither pleased nor resentful at the downing of

184

the helicopter. He felt no especial pleasure that a helicopter had been destroyed and the crew killed. The destruction was a fact. Later, as he climbed, he pondered on his meeting with the foreigner. He recalled the stubble on the foreigner's face and the pale skin beneath and the strength of the white-palmed hand that had taken his. He had set himself at a distance from the foreigner with the eight Redeye missiles. But the distance was not a great one. Already because of the presence of the foreigner in his valley he had broken his camp and was moving his fighting men to higher and safer ground.

The foreigner with the Redeye would be further north in the valley. Ahmad Khan controlled this valley, secured it against ground attack, protected it for the *mujahidin* convoys that wound across the mountains from Pakistan to the liberated Panjshir. But because a foreigner had come to his valley with a missile launcher, his control over this valley was diminished.

In practice that control exercised by Ahmad Khan over the valley and the fighting men who operated there and the few civilians who existed there was complete. No man who followed him had cause to challenge his leadership. In the way that a man might develop the talent of an engineer or a mathematician, Ahmad Khan had mastered the fine art of guerrilla warfare. He was followed because he was the best, he was good enough at his self-appointed role for the Military Governor of Laghman province to have offered a reward on his head, dead or alive, of 10,000 Afghanis. He was respected enough for no man who walked with him to have dared, or tried, to earn that reward.

Beside him was a man who wore the scarlet waistcoat that might have come from the costume of a dancing boy who entertained the caravan travellers with acrobatics, and a man who limped because a Soviet bullet had nicked the tendon behind his knee-cap. He was the leader, but he listened to the men who were closest to him, heard out their grumbling at his

185

treatment of the foreigner who had come with the missiles. He heard the criticism, but he rejected it.

Barney lay on his stomach.

Below him, as if a sharpened chisel had made the cut, was the valley floor, a full four thousand feet beneath. The green of trees, the mottle of the scrub, the grey white strip of the river bed. When he squinted his eyes he could see the tethered mule, and once he thought he could hear a braying cry for there was no shade on its back, no water for its throat.

The poem came to him, the poem of a man who had known and watched the soldiers who had lived in their Frontier Province barracks, who had fought in these mountains.

'I shan't forgit the night
When I dropped be'ind the fight
With a bullet where my belt-plate should a' been.
I was chokin' mad with thirst,
An' the man that spied me first
Was our good old grinnin', gruntin' Gunga Din.
'E lifted up my 'ead,
An' he plugged me where I bled,
An' 'e guv me 'arf-a-pint o' water green.
It was crawlin' and it stunk,
But of all the drinks I've drunk
I'm gratefullest to one from Gunga Din . . .'

Kipling, bless him, had been here with his pen, with his compassion for the fighting men of these mountains, foreign and native.

'You are not going to be hit by a bullet,' the boy said fiercely from behind Barney.

'No, I am not going to be hit by a bullet, Gul Bahdur.'

'Why do you talk about it, if you are not going to be hit?'

'It's about the friends that you find,' Barney was smiling. 'It's about the people that you find who will help you, Gul

186

Bahdur. It gives you a strength when you find such people, when you had not expected to find them.'

'But you will not be hit.' The boy was desperate for his assurance.

Barney laughed. 'They will not hit me, I promise you.'

The boy had looked away. His face was set, frightened.

Barney said, 'You see the mule. The mule is the trap for the helicopters. The flight line of the highest helicopter, the one that watches all the others, will be up here, up at the height that I am. He is the guard for as many as they send, that one is mine.'

'You have an arrogance,' the boy said.

'If I had no arrogance I would not be here.' Barney cuffed the boy gently. Without the boy he was nothing, and without the boy's confidence he was helpless.

'You've hidden the mule?' The boy nodded, distracted. 'Go back to the mule.'

Barney saw him hurry over the rough open ground, saw him drop down into a gully a hundred yards away, saw him rise, again running now, then disappear finally.

He checked the Redeye launcher. He had checked it three times that morning.

The pilot, Alexei, saw the tethered mule, whooped in excitement into his radio, hovered his helicopter a dozen metres above the river bed, and shouted for his gunner to engage the sleeping figure beside the mule with machine gun fire.

The pilot, Sergei, held his position five hundred metres above and five hundred metres behind.

The pilot, Vladdy, was a thousand metres above the valley floor, a thousand metres further south from the helicopter now blasting the screaming mule and the shape beside the low rock.

The pilot, Viktor, watched through the blue tint of his cockpit dome. He flew level with the top of the valley's walls.

187

He slackened his speed, felt the wind gusts heave at the bulk of his machine's fuselage. He was a good flier, had graduated from the Academy with commendations, but a good flier could do little to hold a stable station in these bastard winds and ceiling altitude. The helicopter dropped, fell in a pocket, was restrained as if by an elastic string. He felt the tightening of the belts that strapped him to his flying seat.

He saw that the fall had taken him below the top rim of the valley walls. He nudged his stick, edged the bird closer to the shelter of the cliffs. Far away below him Alexei darted low over the ground, difficult to detect because of the broken camouflage markings.

Viktor knew nothing of the attack on his helicopter before the thundering impact of the Redeye warhead down through the rotor blades and into the fuselage casing above him. Because the missile, on its downward flight at supersonic speed, had first sheared through one of the five rotor blades, lopping it clear, the pilot's possibility of feathering down onto the river bed was lost.

The pilot and his gunner died as they struck the ground, in the scattering wreckage of the Mi-24, before the flame spread.

The sun was not yet high over area Delta as the black billowing smoke soared up from the valley's floor.

14

He had run with all the strength and speed and power of his body across a hundred metres of open ground and then into the first gully, diving from sight as his mind made images of the helicopters' pilots surging out of the valley depths in their search for the source of the fire that had destroyed their friend. Once in the gully he had splayed out his blanket, tucked two corners under the tight straps of his back pack, between the straps and his shoulders, manoeuvred the blanket out over his body, and began to crawl away. Sometimes the fast leopard crawl of his training, sometimes the wary snail crawl.

He reached the boy. The boy had done what was asked of him. The mule was tied front legs and back legs, had been toppled over and lay on its side under the shelter of a lip overhang of rock. The boy's weight lay across the upper legs of the mule. The back of the mule, with the baggage still fastened, was in the depth of the rock shelter. The boy, too, was covered by the rock overhang. Barney lay beside the boy, also across the legs of the mule. He pulled up his blanket so that it covered his head. No chance yet to reload the Redeye launcher.

They must weather the storm that would break around them. If luck smiled they would survive. If luck turned away they would be machine gunned, rocketed, and wrenched apart by bullets and shrapnel.

It seemed to Barney that the helicopters quartered the ground at the roof of the valley. Dividing, quartering, co-ordinating, searching. Above their heads was a continuous thunder rumble, of the engines of the hunting gunships. Above their heads was the bone rattle of the machine gun fire.

To Barney they seemed to winkle every crevice, gouging into each cranny. And then they were above them, hammering blasts first, then the earth-shaking terror of shells hurtling into the gully, prising and ricochetting the rocks around them, deafening, terrifying. Their rock lip protection seemed to dissolve in a splattering mess of stone chips. Into the earth and stone beyond his head and his feet, howling, splintering, flinging rock debris. When the boy screamed in his fear, Barney flung his arm over the slight shoulders and pressed him down further onto the warm, thrashing legs of the mule. Biting into Barney's stomach was the shape of the missile launcher. And then a terrible silence. The silence of the deaf, until very slowly it came to Barney that the attack had moved on, but that there were still helicopters cutting the sky. Gradually his hearing came back. There would have been a target for him if he had been able to discard the spent tube, if he had been able to take another loaded tube from the baggage pack, if he had the room to load the new tube and fasten in place the battery coolant equipment. But he had no room, no time, and to have exposed himself now would have been to wave an idiot's farewell. He whispered to the boy, daft to whisper because he could have shouted against the distant thump of the rotors, he whispered to the boy what words of comfort he could find. He whispered that the helicopters hoped to break their nerve, to make them run. The wind whistled and preyed around their hiding place and sung amongst the rock crests above them. Difficult for the pilots to stay stable, difficult for them to search the rock and stone and shadow beneath them. When the helicopters were close, he was quiet. When they chased other spectres, a thousand, two thousand metres away, then he whispered his encouragement to the boy.

190

And then there was only the wind. The helicopters had gone.

They stayed under the rock lip more than an hour after the engine sounds had filtered away.

He exchanged the darkness of the blanket's cover for the brightness of the midday sun. He stretched himself. They left the mule and crawled to the edge of the valley wall, they peered down into the middle day haze. Barney could see the spread-out wreckage of the helicopter. He stared down, he bit at his lip, his hand was tight on the bridle rope of the mule. He saw the pall of smoke hanging over the wreckage, sucked up the tunnel of the valley's walls, and the licking of the fire. A second time and nothing to retrieve. He detached the used tube from the launcher. He threw it far out into the void beyond the cliff face. He watched it fall, heard it scraping and sliding away beneath him.

The boy untied the legs of the mule and hung to the bridle rope as the animal kicked and lunged and felt its freedom and lifted its head and shouted its call. There seemed a cleanness on the mountain side, a purified and scrubbed down hygiene from the air around Barney's face. He drank it, gulped at its goodness.

He thought they had won. He thought they had won a second time.

'Where do you want to go, Barney?'

'I don't know.'

'You have to tell me, otherwise how can I lead you?'

'Away from here.'

'There is a village at the top of the valley, I think there are people still there.'

'Would they let us sleep in the village?'

'Perhaps they would let us.'

'I have to sleep, Gul Bahdur, somewhere I have to sleep.'

The wind was in his face, buffeting his cheeks, watering his eyes. The wind dragged at his clothes as they went north.

191

Barney walked alone with the missile resting across his shoulder, and the boy and the mule were away behind him.

He had butchered two helicopters, and six more Redeye missiles remained to be fired. And from two butchered helicopters he had retrieved nothing.

'. . . You are not recruits, you are not cadets. You are trained, you are supposed to be the best,' Medev shouted.

They stood their ground. Their eyes beamed back at him. Before the crash of Viktor's helicopter they would have fidgeted in embarrassment at their squadron commander's onslaught. Before the crash of the second helicopter they might have averted their gaze from his. Not now. They stared him out. Their refusal to ride away from his attack fuelled the Major's aggression.

'You were given instructions that a child could have followed, and you allow yourselves to be picked off, sniped out, wiped and not one of you can locate the source of a missile firing. There is a great flash, you know. There's flash, there's smoke, there's movement. And you saw nothing. I tell you what I think... I think you're good enough to fly against tribesmen with rifles when you're safe inside an armoured plane, and any shit can do that. I tell you what else I think. I think your attitude to flying against skillful opposition is inadequate.'

Medev had regained control of his voice, an icy quiet. 'What do you think, gentlemen? Do you think you are inadequate?'

'We flew as we were instructed,' said the pilot, Vladdy.

'We were given a formation, we maintained it,' said Sergei.

'When I found the mule . . .' said Alexei.

'When you found the trap, when you sprung it . . .' snarled Medev. 'Yesterday the fire was a trap, today the mule

192

was a trap . . . When Viktor was hit he was flying below the level of the valley top, why?'

'Viktor is not here,' Vladdy said sharply.

'Flying below the level of the valley top, so that his upper fuselage was exposed. So was the hot metal of the engine exhaust vent.'

'A man who is not here to answer for his error, not here because he is dead, should not be criticised in front of his comrades,' said Alexei.

'You want niceties? You want to go home to your parents in bodybags all swaddled in niceties? You want that? You want me to tell you how superior you are? You, who have been tricked, twice by one man?'

'If there is one man, perhaps there are two . . .' said Vladdy.

'Ah, there might be two?' said Medev. 'I tell you, if there were two, two men with Redeyes, then it would not be one helicopter only each day. Not the way you fly . . . You want to tell me about air currents, about camouflage cover on the ground, you want to tell me that one man can pick the moment of his attack, I tell you . . . listen hard to me . . . I tell you, I knew about air currents and turbulence and about camouflage cover and about surprise advantage when the rest of you still needed your mothers to wipe your arses. The way you fly, if there was more than one man with missiles, the whole patrol would be destroyed. You understand me, there is just one man who is disputing with me the territory of a valley in area Delta. Because of one man there are two of our friends out there on the floor of that bastard valley. You tell me they are dead, and I believe you, you tell me they could not have survived the landing, and I believe you. They will be lying there this afternoon, this evening, this night. Perhaps the bandits will come to these bodies in the evening, in the night. That is why I shout at you. If you think about your friends who lie in that valley tonight then you will understand

193

why I lecture you on the disciplines of formation and procedure.'

'We should go and get them,' blurted the pilot, Sergei.

'We should, and it is forbidden. It is tradition that we get our bodies back, but I have to pay a price for the failure of Viktor to stay in the formation given him. The price is the breaking of tradition. It is something for you to think of, gentlemen.'

Medev turned away from them. Behind his back he heard the door open, he heard the slide of the pilots' boots away into the corridor. The room was refilling. The cypher clerks, the signals men, and Rostov. He gazed up at the map, up at the contour whirls of the mountains and the sharp drawn line of the valley astride area Delta. One man, one bastard man only, and his fist hammered into the palm of his hand.

It was a gamble, it was a chance, he had no option but to play the table.

The money, the close furl of bank notes, blurred between Rossiter's fingers and the Night Manager's hand. It was dark in the alleyway at the side of the Dreamland Hotel. A moment of mind-bending risk, and Rossiter was vaguely surprised that he was not in tears of laughter. He knew how to treat these people, they could *always* be bought. If the Night Manager was compromised, then the gamble that no report would be filed at the Police Station in Chitral was justified. A necessary hazard, the buying of the bastard. It would probably be a boy who would come, an Afghan boy. And Rossiter would each evening be in the shadow of the alleyway to hear of the boy's arrival. The Night Manager leered in the half-light at Rossiter. Rossiter grimaced at him, shook his hand as if they were equals. There was a bloody laugh . . .

Rossiter wore slacks and a white shirt that was open at the neck, and a light pullover. He had grown a thin beard at his chin and around his throat. The suit was discarded, and he believed with the touching faith of all fugitives that he had altered his appearance beyond recognition. Rossiter stifled the impulse to wipe his hand on the seat of his trousers. Afterwards, when he was alone.

He had not hurried to make the liaison with the Night Manager. Three nights he had loitered in the darkness outside the old, paint-stripped façade and watched the faces of those working the evening shift behind the front desk. He learned from what he saw through the glass doorway, that was his training, it was the sort of occupation that commended itself to Rossiter. He could judge a man like the Night Manager, he had no doubt of that; he was well practised in judging the type of man that he could buy.

From what he believed to be a successful transaction with the Night Manager, Howard Rossiter went shopping. He moved quickly into an open-fronted store, to scoop up tins and the last of the day's bread, and a packet of imported tea, and a jar of coffee. He paid smartly, standing impatiently over the man who added the item's costs, and faded into the night.

He walked away from the central street lights of Chitral, off up the side road to the remote bungalow he had made his home. Turbaned and robed men floated past him on the dimly lit road. There were the smells of the *chai-khana* houses where the old men sat with their ankles hidden under their haunches and sipped their sweet green tea. There were the scents of the cooking spices. There was the barking of the dogs. There was the yelp of a cyclo-taxi horn. He held the paper bag against his body, thought of the supper he could manufacture from it, pulled a long and droll smile. He had made a judgement. His judgement told him that a hill community such as Chitral was not a place for police informers. If he was discreet he could survive in this place for three or four weeks. The Night Manager of the Dreamland was the first man with whom he had taken the risk of conversation

195

since he had driven into Chitral. He had found his bungalow, he had broken a window, made his entry, he had set up his base. He had forced the garage door and hidden the land-rover. He had emerged from his refuge only at dusk. Of course it could not last, not for ever. It could last three or four weeks, and after that, stuff it . . . As he stumbled between the pot holes, left the *chai-khanas* and the eating houses and the shanty homes behind him, he was happier than he could remember. Howard Rossiter was returning to his operational headquarters. The source of that dream sense of happiness was the scale of the outrage that he had inflicted upon his employers and his family. Sod them. By now he would have been posted as 'missing' . . . A man from FCO never went 'missing' without permission. His family would know that he had disappeared in Pakistan. His happiness was knowing that for once they'd be scratching their bums in FCO, wondering what in Christ's name old Rossiter was up to. Happiness was knowing that his woman, Pearl, and those bloody awful children would be crouched on the front room settee with the bloody telly turned down and wringing their hands and wondering where the hell the old dog's body had lost himself.

He climbed easily over the wooden gate that blocked off the winding drive up to the bungalow from the side road. It would be a rotten supper. He hadn't trusted himself to light the stove. Supper would be cold and eaten in the light of one shaded candle. His bed was a mattress on the kitchen floor, he would be on it by eight, nothing else to do . . . but it was worth it. Worth it just to think of FCO, and Pearl and the children on the front room sofa.

The kitchen door opened easily. He slid into the shadow, into his safe house. He laid his paper bag on the table. He wondered where Barney Crispin would sleep that night, what he would eat. A funny bugger, that Barney. Once he could have killed Barney, always he could have accepted his friendship. He thought about Barney in those distant mountains.

For the second day they kept to the high grounds above the valley.

It was a land of desolation, of beauty, of their feet falling on the small petal violet and white flowers, of limitless cloudless skies, of staggering views far into a fantasy land of summits and crags.

Once the boy whistled from behind Barney, and Barney froze and turned and looked to the boy who pointed away with his arm to a rock escarpment near to their trail, and after a hesitation of identification Barney saw the creature.

A snow leopard, a cat of infinite and still majesty, astride a rock.

Barney had passed it, not noticed it. The cat would have watched his coming, his going. Alone, self-sufficient. The ears of the cat flicked back, flattened on the sleekness of its head. It rose in an easy lithe movement and was gone. Barney looked for it beyond the escarpment, but didn't see it again. The cat had brought a smile to his face, he waved his thanks to the boy and trudged on.

He was a wild sight, a sore sight. He was filthy, he smelled the smell of his own body, the hair under his cap was matted and tight, his trousers were torn from the times he had run and tumbled for cover amongst sharp stones.

They would not reach the village at the top of the valley that night.

They would sleep once more in the open, they would find a fissure to drop into. The food had been husbanded but was not finished. They would sleep again on the roof of the valley, shivering, coughing, enduring.

When they stopped, when the boy had caught up with him, Barney cupped the palms of his hands together and told the boy to pour water from his bottle into his hands, and he let the mule drink. Twice the boy filled the bowl of his hands, and he felt the rough mouth of the beast and the slurping tongue against his fingers. Afterwards Barney patted the neck of the mule. He called the mule Maggie. He thought the mule had a Maggie personality. He could mutter sweet things into Maggie's long soft ears. For what it had gone through the mule deserved a name. Maggie had been half-starved, denied water, tied under a rock and strafed. Maggie deserved better than they could give her.

'Tomorrow we will reach the village.'

'Why have the people stayed, Gul Bahdur, in this one village?'

'It is in a gorge at the furthest top of the valley. The valley sides are very close. It is said that it is difficult for the planes to make their attacks, they cannot easily approach. I think they have machine guns there, they used to have machine guns. The Soviets cannot attack every village in Afghanistan . . .'

'Which group is there?'

'The village is used by the men who follow Ahmad Khan, your friend . . .' The boy could still manage a darting grin at Barney. 'It is Hizbi-i-Islami. It is not important inside Afghanistan to which group the fighters belong. It is important in Peshawar, not here. What is important here is the killing of Soviets.'

'Bravely spoken, Gul Bahdur,' Barney said drily. 'When the Resistance has won they will make you the Minister for Propaganda.'

'What should be more important than killing Soviets?'

'For you, nothing.'

'And for you, Barney?'

'It is not your concern what is important to me.'

The boy wriggled closer to Barney. In the half-light his face was near to Barney's, keen and questioning.

'Why did you come, Barney?'

'It is not your concern why I came.'

'I have the right to know.'

'No rights.'

'Will you tell me? The truth.'

198

'Talk about something else, Gul Bahdur,' Barney said softly.

'Why do you hide?'

Barney laughed.

The boy persisted. 'You said there was no woman you could tell of this to, when you returned.'

'I said that, yes.'

'Your mother?'

'She was killed a long time ago.' Barney's voice was far away, as remote as the presence of the snow leopard on the escarpment.

'Your father?'

'He's dead. He was shot. There's a man in prison at home, the man who shot him. My father was trying to stop this man robbing something. That's all that happened.'

'I'm sorry.'

'Why should you be sorry? It's not your concern.'

'You have no brother or sister?'

'There are no brothers, no sisters. There is no one, Gul Bahdur.'

'Is that why you came, Barney, because there is no one?'

Just doing a job, and it seemed a feeble reason for sitting in a rock crack cuddled with a heat-seeker. Better not to look for explanations, better to pray that the next big bird doesn't catch fire on impact, and better to be out and away before the explanations as to what Barney Crispin, Captain, was doing in Afghanistan became too feeble.

'There's no one gives a damn, Gul Bahdur . . .'

The boy moved away. Barney watched him turn his back, wrap himself into his blanket and settle onto the hardness of the rock.

15

At their northern end, the valley's walls made a plunging ravine. Save for the torrent slides in the side valleys the walls were all but vertical and at the foot separated by a few hundred yards of flat ground on either side of the river bed. For much of the day, the floor of the valley at this point lay in shadow.

On large scale maps, the village of Atinam was marked as a black speck inserted between the two coils of contour lines at the valley's extremity. Only on large scale maps. It was too small a community to have exercised any but the most exact of cartographers. With the coming of the fourth year of the war, Atinam was the only inhabited village in an otherwise depopulated valley. Before the Soviet invasion, the valley had been home for some thousands of Nuristanis. Many of them now lived in the camps for refugees across the border. But the villagers of Atinam had stood their ground.

The village that was defensible and often defended when the grandfather of Barney Crispin was still a swaddled baby was equally defensible against the incursion of the bomber and the helicopter close to a century of years later.

The village of Atinam lay as a barrier across the floor of the valley, dominated by the cliff walls. It sprawled from the base of those walls inwards to the river bed bisecting the valley with a bridge of rope and planks linking the halves. The homes of Atinam were not built from the mud bricks found further south in the valley but were constructed from dry stone walls by craftsmen who had their skills handed down from generations past. Some of the houses were of a single storey, more were of two floors and built with the lack of shape and pattern found in an uncompleted game of dominoes. On the right side of the river bed, where the eye witness faced north, was the tower of Atinam's mosque. The mosque was the one building that had been made with concrete, and though the whitewash was now flaking and dirty, it remained the beacon point of the village.

Below the village and on lower ground to the south were fields. Small, mean fields, but sufficient in the past for two maize crops in the summer and for the growing of a few hardy species of vegetables. Some of the fields were now scorched by the flaming petrol jelly dropped from the bombers, some were dried out at this late time of summer because the irrigation water courses had been damaged by the high explosive dumped from the bombers. But a bare sustenance could be drawn from the land for the villagers and fighters. Below the fields, a few hundred yards south of the core of the village, were the mulberry trees with their white and sweet fruit clusters dangling between the rich green of leaf foliage, and these also gave sustenance. And scattered amongst the wild mulberries were walnut trees, the forbidden fruit that should not be picked by the boy passing with the goat herd, nor by the girl who took washing to the river pool, because to do so would offend the rigorous laws of husbandry that were the bedrock of the community's survival. And below the mulberry trees and the walnut trees were the thin grazing grounds for the livestock that provided the white cheese that was staple to the villagers' diet.

There were juniper flowers close to the village, and violets, and sometimes the dropping orbs of the sunflower, and wild roses that were pink and ragged.

The village of Atinam might, in other years, have been a place of peace and beauty.

In the fourth year of the war, Atinam was a fortress.

Whereas other villages in the valley had proved open to

201

the bomber and helicopter attacks, Atinam's position forced
the Sukhois and Mi-24s to fly a low gauntlet up the valley,
between the steep cliffs, drop their loads and at once soar
upwards to escape impalement on the rock faces. This made
for skilful, difficult flying, flying that was frequently ineffec-
tive. In the valley walls were caves, some shallow, some
deep, providing safe fire positions for the fighters. To reach
their target the aircraft must fly through cones of defensive
fire, through machine gun fire, through automatic rifle fire.
The task was relished neither by the pilots nor by their
superiors who were accountable for losses of men and material. After a fashion the village survived.

The men of Atinam recognised a vague allegiance to the
Hizbi-i-Islami group in Peshawar, but the man with direct
and daily control over their military operations was the
stranger schoolteacher from Kabul, Ahmad Khan. The word
of Ahmad Khan was the law of the village. He organised the
military defences of Atinam, and the training in tactics and
weapons, and the teaching of propaganda to the young, and
the supply of food. He had taken reponsibility for the defence
of Atinam. Atinam had become the jewel in Ahmad Khan's
valley.

Maxie Schumack sat amongst the men who formed a
horseshoe around the instructor.

In his pantaloon trousers, in his long-tailed shirt and with
the blanket draped on his shoulders, he merged with the men
about him. Only the features of his head were different. He
had gone to the pool in the early morning and scraped
savagely at his face with the old razor that he had carried
since he had first come to Afghanistan. He had washed his
short-cut hair and combed and quiffed what there was over
his scalp. White and grey hair if he had bothered to look in a
mirror, and he hadn't. No space for a mirror in Schumack's
back pack. If he had looked in a mirror he might have wondered what an old bastard like himself was doing in Laghman

province, messing in a village, listening to a lesson in the use of the Soviet-made RPG-7. If he had looked in a mirror he would have seen the wrinkle lines at his mouth, the crow's claws at his eyes, the skin high on his forehead where the hair had long gone. He did not understand much of what was said, a few words had stuck with him in the months inside Afghanistan, but not enough to know whether he could have done better. It was clear that this was the stop line. Why should he care? One village was like another village. One place to fight was like another place to fight. He watched the instructor. The rocket anti-tank grenade was a great weapon for the valley, played bloody hell with the Soviets when they came lumbering up the track with their T-62 tanks and their armoured personnels. Made them think . . . scares them shitless, more like. Later, perhaps, he would be asked to contribute, but not before he had proved himself to these men. Nothing bothered him in that. There would be fighting here. All of the village knew there would be fighting, because all the villagers talked of was the story of two helicopters downed in the valley. They were dealing with the sighting, Schumack tried to hold his mind on the instructor. Goddam difficult, the sighting. First round usually missed, and that was smoke and a back blast flame, and it was 14 seconds for a good man to fire a second round. He tried to hold his mind on the instructor, and the stump ached. If his mind was not on the instructor, not on the sighting mechanism of the RPG-7, then his mind was on the woman. Shit, that was a disaster, the woman was a bastard disaster. Shouldn't have been like that, not a bastard disaster.

That afternoon Mia took her first clinic in the village.

She had no medicines, she had only the advice she could offer through translated French passed on by a girl who had drifted to the village the previous summer from Jalalabad. When she had come to this village, when she had seen the tailing away at the north end of the ravine, she had known that she had reached the end of her journey. There had been talk of movement by a Soviet airborne regiment in the mountains between northern Laghman and Panjshir; there had been talk of a new offensive of Soviet armour and aircraft into Panjshir. She knew only that she could go no further than the village that was called Atinam. It was a small thing to her, it was something, that she could identify the ailments. She found some dysentery. She found the coughed-up blood of tuberculosis. She found the rash of measles. She found gangrene in a young girl's arm from a shrapnel wound. At first the men did not come. Their women came and their children. The men waited outside the door fearful that this woman would touch them. She found the psychiatric cases, the numbed young faces of those who turned inside themselves to eliminate the fear of the screaming bombers. She worked swiftly, dismissing her patients with sharp matter-of-fact advice that was handed on to them by the girl from Jalalabad. Of course when she wiped her hands after each examination she seemed to wash those hands of the case history.

She was washing her hands after the last of the patients had gone, she had asked for boiled water and they had given her warm water, when she heard the shouting of children outside. Through the opened door she saw the children running down the track alongside the river bed, and pointing. She saw the American go past the doorway, not looking at her, and she thought she might be sick from the memory of the awfulness. Mia walked out into the open air.

Through the mulberry trees approaching the village was the Englishman and his guide and one mule. Walking slowly, some way apart.

The boy had talked them into Atinam.

Barney had sat on a stone at the edge of the village and the boy had gone forward.

The whole village was there, lined in a pressing half circle

204

behind the man who had broken off from his instruction of the RPG-7, listening as the boy made the request for hospitality and shelter. Once he turned and pointed with his finger towards Barney and then showed with the gestures of his hands the motion of a falling helicopter. Barney thought that the boy would have no need to explain their credentials. The village would know. He saw Schumack in the ranks of the listeners, saw him take no side in the discussion around the boy.

Gul Bahdur turned, waved imperiously for Barney to come forward. Cheeky sod, Barney grinned. He tilted his head, acknowledged the boy, and came forward. The children watched him, and there were women standing in the doorways of the houses and not running from view as the Pathan women of Paktia would have done, and old men, and the fighters. All watching Barney because this was the man who fired the missile that had destroyed two helicopters.

They made an aisle for him, the children, the women, the old men and the fighters, they stepped from his path as he followed Gul Bahdur and the mule into the village. He passed Schumack, winked at him. He passed Mia, and blushed and smiled, and she looked away from him and cut her eyes to the ground.

The fire was of dried goat dung.

The small flames gave a little warmth to Barney's hands and arms and body. The fire was set amongst bricks in the centre of the room and the smoke rose to a hole in the ceiling, He had washed, he had eaten *nan* and a crumbling white cheese and a scrape of goat's meat on a bone. He sat on a floor rug and Schumack was opposite him, across the fire from him. They had been left alone by the village men and Barney didn't know where the boy had gone; probably he had found somewhere to sleep where he could talk first of the crashing helicopters and then gossip chat into the night.

205

Barney had eaten with Schumack. The woman could have eaten with them but had said she was not hungry. She was in a room off the main chamber where the fire was lit.

Schumack, amused and playing the older man, said, 'We heard that Ahmad Khan booted you out. News chases you faster than the Revenue in this valley. We heard about the helicopters, they were back this morning collecting the bodies. How many Redeyes for two helicopters?'

'Two,' said Barney, looking into the flame flicker.

'Good thinking or bad flying?'

'We lit a fire in a cave for the first. We tethered a mule for the second . . .'

'Bright thinking, Captain Crispin. You have six missiles left. And you've showed up here . . .?'

'To rest up, eat and sleep a bit.'

'When are you going to fire again?'

'When the chance arises, when else?'

'You want some help?'

'Yes,' Barney said simply.

'What sort of help?'

'Twice I've been able to take the rear bird, once from low down, once from the top of the valley. It can't be as easy again. I need fire support.'

'Someone to take the pressure off your arse when you're running, when you've fired.'

'Something like that.'

'We've two DShKs in the village, twelve seven millimetre. It's a hell of a rate of fire they put down, don't hit much, but the tracer puts the shits up the fliers. If they were in support of you . . .'

'That would be good,' Barney said.

'Ahmad Khan's supposed to be here tomorrow. He flits about, they say he's sometimes here when he's expected. You should talk to him.'

'He might not care to talk.'

206

'You've two helicopters, he'll talk to you.'

The fire's light played in the brightness of Barney's eyes.

'You want some ideas when you sit down with Ahmad Khan. He's a sharp guy, if he gets involved with you then he has to know he's going to win. Time for sleep . . .'

Barney leaned forward to whip loose the laces of his boots. Past the fire Schumack lay on his back. Barney felt the cold, felt it deep in him because of his tiredness. He wrapped the blanket close round his body, made a pillow for himself with his pack. Against the wall he could see the pile of the missiles. He flopped back, closed his eyes.

Through the inner door he heard the woman's cough.

Barney saw her image. Barney felt her skin. Barney touched her hair, twined his fingers in the black ringlets. Barney's arms were loose around the neck of the woman.

Again the hacking cough.

'The bitch'll keep going all night,' Schumack growled.

Barney twitched, the pinching of a nerve. He remembered how she had stood at the side of the path as he had entered Atinam.

'She's like a tiger, Barney. I screwed her last night . . . wrong, she screwed me, humped the balls off me . . . She came in here, lifted her skirt, dropped down on me. I was piss all use to her. Not a fucking word she said, like an animal, like a tigress. She screwed me, she dropped her skirt, she took off. Not a fucking word. I'm not much good, but she made me think I was worse. Just looked through me in the morning like I didn't exist . . .'

'Shut up, Maxie,' Barney whispered.

He heard the cough, heard it choking in a slender throat.

'Bitch, all last night she coughed.'

'Shut up,' Barney whispered, louder.

The bodies made up the last cargo to be loaded onto the transport aircraft.

207

Not just the Killed in Actions of Eight Nine Two. There was also the corpse of an infantry trooper who had shown his colleagues how not to fool with an RG-42 HE grenade. There were two Frontal Aviation bomber ground crew conscripts whose mutilated bodies would make a good example for the Education Officer when he preached the dangers of sneaking to the Jalalabad bazaar for hashish.

All of Major Pyotr Medev's fliers were in a crisp line on the tarmac and behind them were the non-commisioned gunners, and behind them the maintenance crews. No bands, no speeches. An impromptu farewell without organised ceremonial. Not even a flag to cover the tin coffins in which the bodybags were laid. Medev had reckoned that the sight would do his pilots no harm, might concentrate their minds. He stood in front of his pilots, but too far back to be able to read the cardboard tags on the coffin handles. He did not know when the pilot, Viktor, went up the ramp of the transport. Sometimes the bodies went all the way home to the families . . . as long as the casualties were low then the bodies went home, that's what was said.

The last coffin was carried forward. Medev snapped, as if in afterthought, to a parade ground salute; behind him the pilots, the gunners and maintenance crews followed suit.

The ramp creaked up and closed on the tin coffins. Medev heard the quiet crying of a pilot behind him. Nothing wrong in that.

He made a sharp left turn. The small parade spluttered away in broken rank. The engines of the aircraft were turning.

He found Rostov in Operations. He would plead the excuse of overseeing the radio and communications. That he hadn't been on the apron was enough to burn at Medev.

'The whole squadron's up tomorrow, including the replacement flier.'

'Where to?' Rostov said easily, as if in the previous few minutes he had not stood and looked from the window.

'Where the Hell do you think?' Medev flared. 'That shite valley in Delta. We're to hit everything, wherever the bastards are . . . villages, caves, everything. They may have thought themselves smart to have some fuck pig foreigner walking their valley with a Redeye. When the airstrikes have finished with them they'll know how smart they were.'

Rostov shrugged. 'There are no decoy flares on the base. I've requisitioned Kabul for them, I don't know how long they'll be in coming.'

'After tomorrow we won't need decoy flares.'

Medev strode out.

Barney and Ahmad Khan walked away from the village, beyond the fields and into the groves of mulberry and walnut.

They sat in the shade. It was colder that late afternoon. The sun was already beyond the valley wall. Barney's blanket was on his back with the corners gathered at his chest. He had slept, he had eaten, he had washed again and rinsed an old foulness from his mouth. He was fresh. The chill meant the end of the summer. The coming of winter meant snow on the high passes that were the trail to Pakistan.

Ahmad Khan spat the last of the mulberry fruit from his mouth, wiped his lips with the sleeve of his jacket.

'In the years they have been here, the Soviets have learned the pattern of our weather, and of our movement of weapons and ammunition. They know that through this valley we transport much of what we will need when the winter comes. So, they will try to prevent the caravans coming through the valley, of course . . .' A slow, serious smile from Ahmad Khan. 'And now you have come here with your missile and you have made me a problem.'

Barney gazed into the deep mahogany of his eyes.

'Because of the missile launcher, will the Soviets counter-attack with such force that the route for the caravans is blocked; or because of the launcher will the skies be empty of

209

Soviet helicopters? This is my problem, to know which is the truth.'

'You have to find that truth for yourself, Ahmad Khan.'

'You will not tell me that your missile will destroy the helicopters when they come?'

Barney spoke softly. 'There are two helicopters in the valley. Before I came there were none.'

'You will not claim that without your missile we cannot hold the valley?'

'I make no claim. You alone can decide.'

'And what do you want in Atinam?'

'The opportunity to kill helicopters.'

'Will the missile protect us, or will it bring upon us a retribution we cannot survive? You make another problem for me.'

'For you to answer.'

'What will you do when you have exhausted your missiles?'

'Go back to my home.' His head jerked up to face Ahmad Khan. 'When I have fired them, there is nothing more I can do here.'

'Most men would tell me of their commitment to the Afghan Resistance . . .'

'I am not most men.'

'If I do not help you, what will you do?'

'Go back down the valley, and fire the missiles until I have a helicopter I can strip,' Barney said.

'And if I expel you from the valley?'

'Then you give life to the helicopters.'

There was spittle in Ahmad Khan's mouth as he laughed, a grating laugh. Their hands met, gripped and held. There was not friendship. Only a contract, an understanding.

They talked until it was dark, and on after the shadows had vanished in the night fall. They planned the battle. They talked of the siting of two DShK machine guns that could fire eighty rounds a minute, of ball and tracer. They talked of the concentration of automatic rifle fire.

As they walked back to the village, Ahmad Khan took Barney's hand. It was without embarrassment, without affectation. 'I asked a question which you did not answer. Will the missile protect us or will it bring disaster?'

'Wait till the helicopters come,' Barney said. 'And listen to them scream.'

'And after you have brought down one helicopter that is not destroyed, you will leave us?'

'You won't be crying when I do.'

Late into the night Barney sat with Schumack. Behind the closed inner door there was the woman. Barney had not spoken to her that evening. She had gone to her cell of a room before he had finished the meal he had taken with Ahmad Khan and his lieutenants. More refinements now for the defence of the village, more specific positioning for the heavy machine guns. Schumack had much to offer, a bedrock of experience that reached far beyond Barney's. Once Gul Bahdur came to the door of their house and peered in and saw the American and the Englishman close to the fire and bent over a diagram, and closed the door without sound and went away, and Barney had not seen the unhappiness on the boy's face, the child who believes his friendship has been usurped.

'I'll be beside you when they come,' Schumack said, and yawned. 'Without me you'll get your arse kicked.'

'Probably,' Barney said.

For an hour the man who wore the red waistcoat and the man who had the limp from the bullet scar behind his knee-cap were huddled on either side of Ahmad Khan and in front of the slow guttering fire.

He was a stranger, he was an unbeliever, he was an adventurer, a foreigner who offered nothing to the long-term defence of the valley. He was the parasite on the sheep's neck. The American was different, the American asked for only bread and bullets and the American was the known enemy of the Soviets. The woman was different because she gave her help to the children and the women, and if there were to be a battle she would treat the wounded amongst the fighters. The foreigner, they set apart from the American and the woman.

'He has no feeling for the struggle of the Resistance, only for the mission that is his own.'

'You cannot know whether his missile will protect us, or devastate us.'

Ahmad Khan heard them through. The man in the red waistcoat and the man with the limp were allowed their say until their argument had run its course. They lapsed to silence. When Ahmad Khan gave his decision they would not dispute it.

'He said there were two killed helicopters in the valley, when before there had been none. He said that when the helicopters came back to the valley that I would hear their screams . . . He will stay.'

Barney washed in the pool below the bridge as the sun sidled on the rim of the valley's west wall. He had slept well. He had heaved his shirt off his shoulders and knelt beside the ice cold water to cup the wetness over his body, over his face, over his hair. The cockerel, the pride of the village, had wakened him. The water dripped from his hair, ran round his ears, fell from his face, dribbled on his chest. The pool ripples fled away from him as he scooped and scooped again at the water. His chest was white except for the patches of the scarlet lice sores. He was a disciplined man and had not scratched them. Bloody near impossible to ignore them.

There was a great beauty in the stillness of that morning, the haze of the sun between the jagged upper crags of the

212

rock face, the droplets of water in the first frosts of autumn, the shadows drawn out amongst the trees.

'Will you fight today, with your missile?'

Barney started up, the water tumbling from his hands. She stood on the path above the pool. She carried a handful of clothing. She wore the blouse of yesterday, unbuttoned at the throat, and the long sweeping skirt that flicked at the buckles of her sandals. She pushed the hair from across her eyes. There was a mockery in her question, there was the tease that fighting was the game of boys not yet grown to adulthood.

'If the helicopters come, yes.'

'You have come across the world to find a place to fight?' A half-laughing voice, a face that showed no amusement.

'As you have come, half across the world.'

'I came to help people, not to interfere . . .'

'Perhaps they'll pin a medal on you, when you go home,' Barney said.

She came past him, down to the water. At the edge of the pool she dropped the clothing she had brought. A brassiere, a pair of sparse pants, woollen socks. She hitched up her skirt and squatted and started to scrub with her hands at the garments.

In the air, whispering high above the valley, was the sound of an aircraft engine.

'I have no medicines, I have nothing.'

'I know that.'

It was not possible for Barney to believe what Schumack had told him. Not a woman of this loveliness. Not a woman who squatted beside the river pool at dawn and washed her clothes, and whose long free hair tumbled over her cheeks.

'There is nothing I can do for those who are hurt in your fight.'

'I know that.'

213

'I have no morphine, I have no steriliser, I have no disinfectant.'

'You should cut some dressings.' Barney could barely recognise the coldness in his voice.

She smiled him a pale smile.

'It is just that you fighting men should know of the havoc for those who have to clear up after you.'

He heard the whine approach of a slow-moving aircraft.

'I am sorry about your medicines, truly sorry.'

She snorted as a reply, she flung back her head and her hair waved away onto her neck. He saw her swan throat, he saw the flash of white teeth and coral soft lips. Away to the south he saw an aircraft. A biplane, single-engined, a silhouette clear against the upper cirrus haze.

'Your sorrow will not help the people who are wounded in the fighting, the fighting you have travelled a long road to provoke.'

Barney threw his shirt back over his head. 'I can't say more than I'm sorry.'

'You have come to shoot down one helicopter so that you can take home the parts.'

'Yes.'

'For these people your missile is a disaster, and when you have made the disaster you will not be here to gather up the bloody parts.'

Barney was stung. 'I don't make a habit of bleeding my principles round the place.'

'You're a spy,' she spat the words. 'You are dirtied . . .'

'You're not a spy? You don't talk with your bloody consul when you get to Peshawar? You don't get debriefed? You don't talk to Aerospatiale and Dassault about every Soviet aircraft that goes over your bloody little head?'

'I said you were dirtied, you are filthied. You cannot believe anyone has a motive above yours. You cannot believe in anyone who does not creep behind the coat of their government . . .'

'You should cut some bandages.' He hated himself.

He tried to see into her eyes, to win some softening. She twisted her head away from him. He saw the cherry flush on her cheeks.

He walked away. Gul Bahdur was running breathless to meet him.

Above was an Antonov Colt. It was the aircraft that Frontal Aviation used for high level reconnaissance. The aircraft from which the cameras pinpointed the targets for the strike aircraft and the gunships. Gul Bahdur had caught Barney's arm, was hurrying him back to the village, chattering at him. Barney turned once. The woman still squatted at the side of the pool. When the reconnaissance aircraft came over early in the morning then the aerial bombardment would follow. Night on day, certainty.

The Antonov Colt had roused the village. There were men running with rifles in their hands, others pulling behind them the wheeled frames of the two DShK machine guns. There were mothers screaming for the children to begin the climb to the caves in the valley walls.

Barney and Schumack and the boy, between them, carried the launcher and the five spare missile tubes towards the position that had been agreed south of the village, beyond the fields and the groves of mulberry and walnut.

They passed Mia on the path. She was cartwheeling her arm, as if to dry the brassiere and the pants and the woollen socks in the cool air.

16

Three pairs of Sukhoi SU-24 all weather interdiction/strike bombers had been sent from the sprawl of the Begram airbase outside Kabul.

Codenamed 'Fencer' by the NATO planners, the SU-24 is the pride of the Soviet air capability in Afghanistan, and is as familiar in the blue skies above the Hindu Kush mountains as the wheeling kites and buzzards.

From altitude, from beyond the reach of the small arms and machine gun defences, they deliver with the casualness of a newspaper boy's dawn drop the 500 kg and 1000 kg bombs that are slung beneath the wing pylons and hard points of the lower fuselage. The SU-24 has an awesome record. A maximum speed of 2120 kilometres per hour. A combat radius of 1100 kilometres on the hi-lo-hi flying profile. They carry an armament of 5700 kgs. But the maximum speeds of the SU-24 are irrelevant in the circumstances of Afghanistan. There is no aerial combat here. There are no hostile interceptor fighters, there are no batteries of radar-guided missiles against which the technology of the Sukhoi's inbuilt defences can be pitted. No harm can come to the kites and buzzards that circle over the valleys, and no harm either to the SU-24s that swoop down from the upper turbulence to run in over their given targets.

Anything that moved in the valley was designated as a target. The abandoned villages in the central part of the valley were smashed. The rockets arrowed with laser controlled aim towards the mouths of the caves, setting up in the recesses the shock waves that would pierce the ear drums and

216

blast the air from the lungs of men who hid there. No counter strike was possible. The bombers owned the skies, owned the floor of the valley. Along the length of this gouged-out cut in the mountains, men and women and children huddled in the protection they had chosen when they had first seen the speck of the Antonov at dawn, huddled and shivered and prayed to their God of Islam.

A creeping carpet of bombs fell on the valley floor. The carpet roll was kicked out at the southern end of the valley and spread towards the northern fastness of the valley, towards the village of Atinam.

In their briefings at Begram, the two-man crews who would sit cramped beside each other in the Sukhois had been told to husband sufficient of their bombs and rockets to strike a devastating and unnerving blow at the village.

As the carpet strayed north along the valley towards the village of Atinam, so the white heat flares spilled from the bombers, flaming in vigour as they fell. If a missile had been fired then the flares would have diverted the warhead away from the hot metal of the tail engine exhausts.

No missile was fired.

There was no ground fire from the *mujahidin* of Ahmad Khan who had taken to the caves and the natural camouflage of the valley's walls, and to the gullies and ravines of the side valleys. There was no response to the shattering thunder bellow of the bombs exploding in the valley.

From the skies the bombers fell upon the village of Atinam.

They swept down in a blast that smashed across the valley, was trapped by the valley sides and echoed and echoed up the cliff walls.

The bombs dropped from under the wings and fuselages of the Sukhois. Graceful pellets as they arced away from the aircraft, falling casually at first while the bombers above them surged upwards for altitude. Growing in lethal size as they

217

fell. No longer pellets as they struck the ground, as the detonation flashed, as the smoke dust ripped into the air above the fields and the mulberry trees and the homes of Atinam.

Falling slower than the bombs were the flares that drifted down in their brilliance to spend themselves in a flaming beauty amongst the houses and the irrigation canals and the orchards.

On his stomach, from the entrance of a cave, Barney Crispin watched the airstrike.

Schumack was beside him, and crouched over his back and peering across his shoulders was the boy, Gul Bahdur.

The village was no simple target for the Sukhois' pilots.

They were reluctant to come low into the valley. Their line of attack was not a tree-skimming, house-hopping flight close to the fields and the path and the river bed. They flew high where they could not be taken by automatic rifle and machine gun fire. Sometimes they hit the homes, more often the big bombs whistled down with a cat's screech short of the village into the fields and the orchards.

In the cave's mouth the blast of the explosions sung in Barney's ears. He had never before been under aerial bombardment. Simulated stuff, of course he had been through that. But never this . . . And he was safe, away from the village. He was safe while the women and children of Atinam cowered in caves that were nearer their homes, and they could see their homes and their food stores burning, and they could hear the screams of their animals under the orchard trees. Mia would be closer to the bombs, she would be with the people that she could help. He thought that Gul Bahdur was pounding his back but he could hear nothing.

He saw an explosion amongst the trees. He saw goats scatter away, those that had not been caught by the winging shrapnel. He wondered where Gul Bahdur had tethered Maggie. And he heard through the bomb blasts the voice of

Mia Fiori beside the river pool; he saw the skin of her neck; he heard the light tread of her feet; he saw the gentleness of her fingers.

'You are a coward, if you won't fire . . . a coward . . . you should have stayed with your own people.'

Gul Bahdur's hysterical screaming spilled onto Barney.

'Not against the planes, Gul Bahdur.'

'You are frightened of the planes.'

'I can't kill them, not like the helicopters.'

'Shut your silly little face, kiddie,' Schumack said.

'It will be different when the helicopters come, I promise you.'

'You are a coward, you are frightened . . .' Gul Bahdur sneered.

'Shut up, kiddie.' Cold anger from Schumack.

Barney turned away from the valley and faced the boy.

'Do you see those flares? They would divert the Redeye system. They are too fast for us. If we fire the Redeye and we hit, that is a victory. If we fire and we miss, that is a defeat. We want only to win, Gul Bahdur. Wait till the helicopters come.'

'Watch your bastard mouth till then, kiddie,' Schumack said. With his claw he scratched at Barney's shoulder. 'I don't know what you said to Ahmad Khan, I've never known the hairies hold their fire like this. They've given you a chance. For them not to fire on attacking aircraft is like telling a man in the desert not to drink. It's the hardest thing in their lives. They've given you a chance. You'd better take that chance.'

'You think the helicopters will come?'

'Bet your ass,' Schumack said.

The Colonel of Intelligence dropped the blown-up photograph onto Medev's desk, slapped down on top of it a heavy magnifying glass. Rostov craned over Medev's shoulder.

Medev found a woman walking, a trembling image under

the wavering glass. Something white held above her head. He gazed at it. His eyes squinted, his brow furrowed at his inability to see the significance of the image. Rostov leaned further forward, his breath on Medev's neck.

A grin broke over Rostov.

'It's a bra . . . we have discovered there is a woman who wears a white bra in area Delta. Excellent.'

'Past her on the path.' The Colonel of Intelligence flicked his fingers irritably. 'Further down the path.'

Medev found three figures walking on the clear line of a track beside a river bed. His hand was trembling, the image jumped before his eyes. The one who walked ahead of the other two caught his attention. There was an outlined smear on the man's shoulder. Instinct told him it was a man with a missile launcher. He traversed to the other two figures behind, they could be carrying replacement tubes or mortar tubes or RPG-7 tubes. But the man who walked in front carried a missile launcher. He knew it, he would have sworn to it.

'Your man,' the Colonel of Intelligence said with satisfaction.

Rostov could not see the image on which Medev focused. 'What woman would wear a bra in that valley?'

Medev did not look at him. 'Try a European woman, try a nurse . . .'

He spoke from the side of his mouth as if unwilling to break away even for an instant from the figure who walked with the missile launcher balanced on his shoulder. His man, his enemy. The man who had downed two helicopters, filled four bodybags.

'Where is this path?'

'The village of Atinam, north end of the valley, this morning. The Antonov's camera.'

'Would we be permitted to fly the whole squadron against the village, only against the village?'

'It is not my decision. For myself, with the launcher identified, I would recommend that the village is destroyed.'

Medev pushed the photograph and the magnifying glass away across his desk. He seemed to shake himself, then bit briefly at his lower lip as if the pain could somehow sharpen him.

'All the crews on "Ready", I want an immediate briefing.'

Rostov hurried from the office.

'And there was no firing at the aircraft when they attacked Atinam?'

'None,' the sombre reply from the Colonel of Intelligence.

'Why should they not fire on the aircraft, however futile that would be?'

'Because they play a game with you, and the game has continued too long. It is time that the game was finished.'

Medev walked to the window. He stared out at the line of Mi-24 gunship helicopters.

'Each time he thinks in terms of a trap, a trap to draw me in,' Medev mused. But he could not stay away from the valley, not when Photo Reconnaissance showed him a man walking with a missile launcher on his shoulder. His pilots must fly. Trap or no trap.

The pilot, Sergei, was twenty-two years old.

A little past one o'clock in the afternoon he lifted off the tarmac at Jalalabad, took the Mi-24 sluggishly up in company with his pair, the helicopter of Alexei.

He was consumed at that time with a sense of anger. He had asked at the briefing when all the pilots had been present, in front of them all, why they had not been issued with the anti-missile flares that could be fired from the helicopter. He had been told that the flares had been requested from Kabul, that they had not yet arrived. He had asked whether the fixed wings flying earlier over the valley had been equipped with

221

decoy flares. He had been told that flares were standard for the SU-24 aircraft and not for the Mi-24 helicopter. Medev had barked at him that what could be done was being done, that if he thought he was better able to breathe some fire up Kabul's arse then he could try himself to get the flares from Central Equipment Depot.

Such was the anger of the pilot, Sergei, that he had given no consideration to the possibility of his death on that September afternoon.

They flew in pairs, as always, and at staggered heights into area Delta.

Above the valley was the Antonov spotter that would circle high over the village of Atinam and maintain a constant radio relay link between the helicopter pilots when they dived low for their attack and Jalalabad Operations.

At twenty-two years old, the pilot, Sergei, was already highly qualified in the technique of helicopter flying, was regarded as of outstanding officer material. In his tour of duty he had twice been commended for the quality of his flying at low level in support of ambushed military convoys.

Over area Delta, over the entrance to the valley, his temper had abated to a sharp irritability as he ordered his gunner to test fire the nose canopy machine guns. He could not hear the blast from the depressed barrels but through the tinted glass he could see the bright flashes and feel the rocking on the momentum of the helicopter.

From all the pilots who flew fast and on full power along the valley from south to north, he had been selected, marked down.

Four kilometres short of the village of Atinam they had seen the smoke that lingered from the bombers' attack. The smoke filled the valley, compressed and held there under the valley's walls.

Too much chatter on the radio, because combat time was closing in on them. Shouts from the more senior fliers for

222

concentration on the briefing detail. And the shouts ignored, and all the pilots talking, and the rockets going, and the machine guns. Rockets and machine guns blasting the damaged homes of the village. Rockets and machine guns hammering at the cave mouths in the shallow slopes of the lower valley walls.

Sergei felt the tremors of rifle fire beating on the titanium-armoured hull of the fuselage. Bullshit against the plate defences of the helicopter. A machine gun had started up. Green tracer rounds shafting their light across the valley. A fucking target, something to bite at that was not a stone built house, or the black hole of a cave, or the green emptiness of tree foliage.

There was a moment when the attention of three pilots was diverted to a cave entrance, the source of the green tracer.

There was a moment when the far side of the valley was not covered by another bird.

There was a moment when a flame streak shone brilliantly against the far side grey valley wall . . . when the shout of the observer in the high-above Antonov bounced into the pilots' headsets . . . when a missile homed onto the hot metal of the engine exhaust of the helicopter piloted by young Sergei . . . There was a moment before the blast of the high explosive detonated above and behind the cockpit canopy.

The big bird fluttered down. Not a direct fall, but an indecisive stagger towards the rocks below. All the rifles were aimed at the helicopter. Smudges formed on the cockpit glass as the bullets were deflected away. The tapping of drum sticks on the armour of the fuselage. The rending of metal when they struck the upper body work above the armour.

The houses swept up to meet his fall, and the river bed, and a rope bridge. Sergei felt the wrenching impact of his landing and the jarring of his spine, and the heaving on his harness, and the helicopter came down nose first. He did not know whether his gunner would have survived. Rifle fire loud on the superstructure around him. Through the canopy he saw the helicopters swerving as disturbed wasps in pursuit of a target . . . Fuck them, screw them, they were the living, he was the dead. A rain of gunfire spattering on the fuselage and canopy glass . . . Trapped like a fucking rat, and fire followed a crash . . . He unfastened his harness. He heaved open the cockpit door. Around him was the steady clamour of the rifle fire, of machine guns, rockets. He had no memory of taking his pistol from the holster beside his knee, but it was in his hand as he dropped from the door to the ground. There were the wretched dry stone walls of a house a dozen metres away. He ran to it. Anything to escape the bullet patter on the helicopter. He ran low and clumsy in his flying suit. He reached an open doorway, sobbing, shouting his fear into the gaping doorway. Behind him the helicopter caught fire, was bloated with flame and exploding ammunition. He threw himself into the darkened room. His face brushed against the hard dry dirt of the floor, and dry dirt was on his tongue. His elbows and knees and forehead scraped the dry dirt. He saw his life as fast flash, framed pictures. Pictures of the street in Kiev in which lived his mother and his father. Pictures of the girl that it was planned he should marry, her face, her breasts, her laughing. Pictures of the briefing room at Jalalabad, of the anger of Medev when the question of anti-missile flares was raised. Pictures of the hurtling movement of the cockpit dials in the second after the missile strike. He was sobbing because he was afraid, he was afraid because he knew that he would die. His fingers groped forward and caught against material, pushed on and fell against the hardness of flesh that was tight against bone. He looked up. He knelt against the leg of an old woman. The light seemed to grow around him. He stared into the face above that was a myriad of age lines, into the bright eyes that were precious stones. She screamed, a high-pitched, clear scream. He heard the battering of the

224

helicopters above, and the gunfire and the explosions. The helicopters were out of reach. He was below, he was dead. And an old woman's scream betrayed him.

It was the women and the girls who came in answer to the scream. Sergei heard their answering calls, he heard the murder of the gunfire above him, fired by the living. He heard the slither of the first footfall to reach the doorway. A shadow fell into the room, and then another. Hands reaching out to him, dragging at his flying suit, tearing at him, wheeling him to his feet, skipping him across the dirt floor. Nails on the skin of his face, scratching at the cheek flesh beside the flaps of his flying helmet. A fist between his legs, from behind and catching at his genitals, and slavering breathing close to his nose. When he opened his eyes he was outside the house and cocooned amongst a bundle of robes and dresses and blankets and head scarves. The hand still on his genitals and the pain took his breath away. Crying his quiet terror, Sergei was hustled from the house. He fell, half was pushed, half stumbled, into the sewer ditch that ran beside the path between the houses. The stench was in his lungs, the slime dripped on his face. He could hear the helicopters, he could not know whether the brother pilots could see him. The face of a grandmother was in front of him, a gap-tooth mouth. The face of a girl, spitting in his eye. The hand at his genitals squeezed, pulled, squeezed, turned. Hands at the zips of his flying suit, and then a knife tearing at the thin material. All the time the pistol that he had carried was in his fist, forgotten in his terror. It fell from his hand. The cotton fine hope that might have sustained him was snapped. Soaring towards his face was a rock held between raw brown fingers, into his face, onto his forehead. He felt the pain, he smelled the warm dribble of his blood and choked. A stone cracked into the back of his skull.

Sergei, on his knees now, saw a woman in the crowd around him, a woman staring at him wide-eyed and in shock,

225

and apart from those who clawed and beat him and hung to his genitals. A lovely, pretty woman. A grey white blouse and a full long skirt. Her mouth was open, as if to scream when she could not.

A knife skewered his hamstring. He collapsed. He would never stand again. The life of the young flier was battered out by pounding stones and flashing knives on the path beside the open sewer.

The helicopters left behind them the cloud of black fuel smoke from Sergei's Mi-24.

After the helicopters had gone the Sukhois returned and the fires in the village were given urgent new life with the blasting of high explosive bombs and the scattering billows of white phosphorous.

And after the bombers had made their last deafening assault the valley was quiet, except for the distant drone of the Antonov spotter.

'We have five who are dead, seven who are injured,' Ahmad Khan said.

'And you have one helicopter,' Barney said.

'They must come again, this evening, after what we have done to them . . .'

'After what they have done to you.'

'One man, three women, one child dead, that is little enough to us. A rocket went into a cave, that was some, others came out from hiding when they heard a Soviet was alive in the village, they would have walked through walls to find him. The bombers will come again this evening.'

They had walked to the rope bridge in the centre of the village. The ropes were torn but holding. Either side of the bridge were crushed homes, crazily bent roofing, rubble piles, all the debris of war.

'Where would you wish to be?' Ahmad Khan said abruptly.

'I want to be in the village. Where I can move after I have fired, where I am not trapped as I was in the cave. I want the heavy machine guns, one on each side of the valley . . .' Barney paused, gazed into Ahmad Khan's face. '. . . Are you better with me than without me? The one helicopter, was that worth what happened to the village?'

'When you have cleared the valley of helicopter flights then I will tell you what has been worthwhile.'

Ahmad Khan walked away from Barney. A group of men had waited for him. They were out in the open, in the view of the circling Antonov. They knelt in prayer.

Barney watched, then turned and beckoned to Schumack and the boy, and led the way into the village.

'They killed him with their hands and with rocks.' She spat the words at him.

Mia Fiori standing, her hands on her hips, her legs wide apart and sturdy, and the disgust twisting at her mouth.

Barney was sitting against the wall of a stone house with the Redeye launcher across his lap.

'They wouldn't even kill a goat the way they killed that man.'

Barney saw the livid anger on her cheeks.

'You come here with your conceit . . . you're no better than a primitive. If you are a part of this people's war then you are a savage. They stoned him to death . . . Christ, he looked at me, he looked to me to save him.'

'He flew a helicopter gunship', Barney said.

'You know where he is now?'

'I don't need to know where he is now.'

'He's where their rubbish is, he's in with their filth. You know what their rubbish is. It's afterbirth, it's shit, it's where the maggots and the disease are. Don't you have a code, doesn't a pretty little European soldier have a code for his prisoner? Don't you get him a drink, and make him comfort-

227

able, and see that he's fed? Don't you protect him from animals? Christ, he was *your* prisoner. You brought him down. Where were *you*, you bastard, when the women pulled the balls off him? They didn't cut them, they pulled them off him. You shot him down, you were responsible. And where were you? A mile away on your stomach in a cave. You make me sick.'

Barney stood up. He took Mia by the shoulders. She did not pull away. Her anger was done.

'They'll come back this afternoon,' Barney said. 'Go back to the caves.'

He let her go. She turned from him, and ran, sobbing, away.

Schumack had watched and listened.

'Stupid bitch . . . where does she think she is?'

'Piss off,' Barney said.

17

Brilliant colours cascading from the late afternoon skies.

A display of dancing, falling lights as if it was a gala, not the battlefield at Atinam.

From the mouths of the caves the fighters watched the flares, from deeper in the recesses the women and the children saw the blues and greens and reds, floating down from the helicopters.

Barney and Schumack had taken a place in a squat stone-built granary built against the cliff to the west of the valley. Barney did not know where Ahmad Khan had positioned himself, but Schumack would know. Schumack had taken it upon himself to be the co-ordinator for the firing of the Redeyes. When Barney wanted the covering fire of the DShKs then Schumack would pass the message. Schumack, veteran of Khe Sanh and Desert One, had found a new officer to care for.

They watched the flares climb to a fire zenith before subsiding.

'Not with those bastards, you can't fire,' Schumack hissed.

'They had to learn something . . .' Barney said.

Around the village from the caves there was the flimsy rattle of automatic rifle fire, answered and dominated by the ripple of the heavy machine guns of the Mi-24s, and their rockets.

'With the flares we're screwed, they'll shaft the village to nothing.'

'What's the pattern of the flares?'

They lay on their backs in the doorway of the granary. Each had covered his body and face with a blanket, leaving free only the eyes. They lay still and close to each other in the small doorway. At Maxie Schumack's side was his rifle, at Barney's side was the loaded launcher.

'You can't fire into the flares, it'll go rogue and destruct.'

'There's a pattern,' Barney said.

Three, four kilometres from the village, the helicopters seemed to queue in their pairs for the run in onto Atinam. They came in fast and low. Barney wondered at the miracle that there was anything remaining in the village to burn, but new fires had started.

'Do you see the pattern?'

'I just see the bastard flares . . .'

'They're firing from Very pistols out of the fuselage doors. They fire a kilometre short of the village, and they fire over the village. Look for the pattern, damn you.'

'All I see is a couple of hookers with their panties down watching rainbow colours.'

Machine gun shells blasted into a building across the path, the wrench sound of a falling roof, the dust crumble of dry masonry.

'Maxie, don't you see . . .'

'I see the mother helicopters.'

'Shut up and listen.' Barney yelling. 'Take one bird, put all the fire onto the fuselage hatch . . . don't let the bugger put his nose out, blast him if he does. He's not firing behind, he's firing forwards and upwards. Look at him . . . He has to lean out on his strap, he has to fire the flare forward or it's gone and dropping too far behind . . .'

Barney's voice died, obliterated by the roar of a helicopter overhead.

'You don't have to fire, not each time they come.' A caution from Schumack. 'Live to fight another day, that crap.'

230

'They've found something new, they reckon they're the whiskers. Hit them now and they'll be on their knees.'

'You have to stand up out there, you can't do it off your gut.'

'I know how to fire.'

'Please yourself, hero man, it's your ass.'

'Not the next pair, the pair after that. Every gun in the village on the right flying bird, the one that flies on the right of the pair.'

'You have to stand out there and face them, you have to be in the open. It's what the mothers want of you. What they're here for, to drag you into the open. Don't you see that?'

'They'll be on their knees, Maxie.'

Schumack was gone. Sprinting from the doorway, jumping the open ditch, falling into the doorway opposite. Cocking his ear, then running for the corner. Hesitating on the corner, then gone.

For what, Barney?

To kill a helicopter, that's for what.

What sort of idiot reason is that?

The only reason . . . because the helicopter is above and smashing a village, pulping it.

Where does stripping a helicopter for MOD's scientists fit into the game?

Fits nowhere, a square block in a round hole.

He saw the huddle of Schumack half around the corner of a building across the path and beyond the drain. Ready for the dash, waiting his time. All right for Schumack. He went where there was fighting, he bought one-way tickets. Anywhere that Sam's backside was kicked was good enough fighting ground for Sergeant Schumack. Lucky sod. You're an arrogant bugger, Crispin. Had to be. Had to be an arrogant bugger to stand out in the open and fire the Redeye at the hot metal engine exhaust of an Mi-24 battle cruiser.

231

Barney felt the warm air panting in his throat, he felt the cold draught in his stomach. His grandfather would have felt the same shiver, the same tremble, the same cold. God, he was scared . . .

Schumack dived down beside him.

'It's the next one that comes, all the fire on the fuselage hatch, like you want it.'

Barney pulled himself to his feet. Weak at the knees, unsteady in the hands. He stamped his foot to put a discipline in his body. He held the launcher across his chest. He felt the tug of the claw at the sleeve of his shirt. Schumack was pointing away down the path, across the fields, across the orchards of mulberry and walnut trees. He saw the two helicopters approaching. He saw the flame spits of the machine guns. He saw the glory of the flare colours. He read the soundless words at Schumack's mouth.

'Good luck, hero man.'

He stood alone in the centre of the path. He raised the Redeye launcher to his shoulder, felt the weight bite down onto the bone. His thumb nudged against, engaged, the battery coolant switch. He heard the low whine of the launcher. He saw the opened door of the fuselage, he saw what he fancied was the figure of the man who would fire the protecting flare to decoy a missile. Ragged rifle fire from the village, perhaps twenty rifles on automatic. Then the steady hammer thud of the two DShK machine guns. Barney saw the tracer reaching for the fuselage.

They had seen him, the pilot and the gunner.

The big forward gun wavered towards him as he stood his ground, buffeted, shaken by the explosions around him. They had seen him too late.

Through the open sight his aim caught the dark hole of the engine exhaust. Three seconds and the whine of the launcher had become a scream at his ears.

Barney fired.

A different flare of light in the sky, a streak light, clean and pure against grey stone and grey valley walls. A purging angel light sweeping up and away from the distant slow descent of the Very flares in their many colours.

No flare had been fired from the right side of the helicopter.

The missile winged at the helicopter seven hundred feet above in a blur of white brilliance.

'Go, you . . .' Barney's scream was cut short by the detonation.

In the moments between the time that the pilot would have seen the lone man with the launcher and the time he could have reacted at the controls of the Mi-24, the missile struck. The helicopter was turning away, but the altitude of the valley determined that its movement would be lethargic in the thinned-out atmosphere. Too slow to hide the exhaust vent from the shrieking speed of the missile. Schumack was heaving at the trouser cloth around his ankles, trying to drag Barney back into the darkness of the granary, and Barney was riveted to the helicopter and the impact point. The final lurch on the helicopter's flight path had confused the missile electronics sufficiently for the hit to be against the tinted glass of the pilot's canopy. He heard the shouting, the squealed excitement of the *mujahidin* who were invisible to him, scattered in the warren of the village. He saw in his mind the gaping hole of the cockpit canopy, and the glass shivers that had slashed and speared the pilot. Perhaps it was because the pilot's hands had locked the control stick in a particular position, but the helicopter seemed to slide down in a gentle arc towards the river bed on the far north side of Atinam. It came down as if the pilot was determined that the landing should be smooth. He saw in his mind a glazed stare on a young pilot's face. He saw a body stripped naked and bloodied and lying on the rubbish heap of the village, where the dogs came, where the vulture birds came.

233

They wriggled out through the back window of the granary a few tight seconds before the building crashed under a rain cloud of rocket fire.

As they ran, weaving, hugging the stone walls, Barney heard the scrape metal crash of the helicopter's landing, heard the spinning whistle of the rotors that the pilot could not stop.

Barney unclipped the empty launch tube, discarded it behind him, let it roll to a drain. Schumack led. Schumack had plotted the ground, chosen the next refuge.

'Another hundred feet and he'd have beaten you,' Schumack shouted. 'That was good luck for you, hero man. I'm not pissing on your ego, but you were lucky . . .'

As he was dragged along, Barney wondered why he had been chosen to be lucky, how it was decided that he deserved luck.

There were loudspeakers rigged in Eight Nine Two's Operations Room.

Those who listened to the helicopter assault on the village of Atinam received little indication of the pilots' excitement as they flew up the valley towards their target, of their nerves as they came over the ground fire, of their elation as they surged up to safety. The communication with the operations room was linked through the laconic and short-worded Captain of Frontal Aviation circling high above the valley in the Antonov Colt, a swimmer treading water. The listeners were Major Pyotr Medev, the Frontal Aviation commander of the Jalalabad base, the Colonel of Intelligence, Rostov and two signal technicians.

The loudspeakers were crudely tuned. The voice of the Captain in the Antonov was magnified and coarse, but his words were clear. Each man in the room heard each word the Captain spoke.

There was no shout, there was no cry of alarm. It was a factual, drab report that carried from the speakers to their ears.

'XJ SUNRAY reports hit . . . XJ SUNRAY radio distort . . . XJ SUNRAY radio break up . . . XJ SUNRAY losing height, speed . . . XJ ROGER clear of target . . . XJ KILO, XJ LIMA engaging missile launch position . . . XJ SUNRAY down . . . repeat XJ SUNRAY down . . .'

The moment when a hammer seemed to strike Medev. The moment when the breath wheezed from the throat of the Frontal Aviation commander. The moment of the fist belting into the palm of the hand of the Colonel of Intelligence. The moment when Rostov squared his back against the plywood wall as if to hide himself. The moment that two technicians stared at the floor's linoleum.

Medev had the microphone in his hand. He gripped it, white-fingered. Almost a strangle hand at his throat as he spoke.

'Confirm XJ SUNRAY down.'

'. . . XJ SUNRAY down, confirmed, visual sighting . . . XJ SUNRAY down one hundred metres north from village perimeter, down into river bed . . .'

'Is XJ SUNRAY destroyed on landing?'

'Negative . . . no fire, no disintegration on landing . . .'

'What is the state of ground fire?'

'. . . pilots report slackening of ground fire, no longer engaged by tracer from machine guns . . .'

'He's out-thought you, Medev.' The snap of contempt from the Colonel of Intelligence.

'They use the machine guns for a single purpose, then silence them. They are more interested in the protection of the weapons than the protection of the village.' The astonishment of the Frontal Aviation commander.

'Have you learned nothing? The machine guns are important to them, and the missile. The village is irrelevant. The destruction of our helicopter is important to them.' Still the sneer of the Colonel of Intelligence.

'Then the village will be destroyed.' Bridling anger from the Frontal Aviation commander.

'Who gives a shit about the village? The attack was on one man armed with a missile launcher. Two air strikes, two helicopter strikes, in one day. And we lost two helicopters for it, for one man. Don't talk about destroying a fucking village.'

'Would you be quiet, gentlemen,' Medev said softly.

There was something of steel in Medev's voice, something of diamond in his eyes. Still the pale skin clench of his fist on the microphone.

'What is the possibility of rescue?' Medev asked of the microphone.

'XJ KILO, XJ LIMA report ground movement in the area of the village closest to XJ SUNRAY's position . . . They are making frequent use of flares on speed passes over XJ SUNRAY . . . they report that it is not now possible to locate the heavy machine guns . . .'

'Repeat, what is the possibility of rescue?' An icy shiver in Medev's voice.

'. . . I am instructed by the pilots to relay that they will attempt a rescue which will involve XJ ROGER landing beside XJ SUNRAY . . . the pilots wish you to authorise a rescue . . .'

'It has to be a landing?'

'. . . XJ ROGER reports he believes that the pilot of XJ SUNRAY would have been injured in the missile detonation . . . XJ ROGER believes he has seen movement in the cockpit, he cannot be certain . . .'

'Repeat, it has to be a landing?

'. . . confirmed . . .'

'Repeat, the heavy machine guns have not been located?'

'. . . confirmed . . .'

'Repeat, it is believed the pilot of xj SUNRAY may be injured, the condition of the gunner is not known?'

'. . . confirmed . . .'

Medev looked to no man in the room for approval. The skin trembled at his cheeks. He was gazing at the map on the wall, at the chinagraph symbols marking the location of area Delta and the village of Atinam.

A clear instruction from Medev.

'Without hazarding the safety of any other helicopter, xj SUNRAY is to be destroyed on the ground by rocket fire. That is immediate, that is an order. Following the destruction of xj SUNRAY the mission is completed.'

Medev stared out of the window of the operations room, out towards the east, away towards the setting of the after-noon sun. He turned back, looked now into the face of the Colonel of Intelligence and saw the dropped eyes and the twisted head. He turned again, faced the Frontal Aviation commander, he thought the man might cry.

He heard the voice of the Captain in the Antonov spotter, a distant sabotaged voice.

'. . . the pilot of xj ROGER requests to be patched through to you direct . . .'

'Refused.'

He put down the microphone. His hand was numb. He massaged his fingers to regain their feeling.

He saw in his mind the pilot, Alexei. He reached out to grip the edge of the table in front of him. He saw in his mind the young face of the pilot who had taken the helicopter xj SUNRAY from the Jalalabad base that afternoon.

After darkness, Barney went to the wreckage of the gunship.

There were no battery-powered torches in the village, the light was from tallow fat and cloth-tipped staves, and by old hurricane oil lamps.

Ahmad Khan had given Barney an hour to work on the

237

helicopter. After an hour his own men would come to strip the fallen bird of all that might be useful to them. Barney had brought the Polaroid camera from his back pack with a clasp of a dozen flash bulbs. Two men from the village and Gul Bahdur carried the flare staves. Schumack held the rusty lamp.

There was something blasphemous about what he was doing, Barney thought, as he climbed inside the twisted airframe of the helicopter. He was like a man who disturbs a freshly filled grave, as he crawled into the flickering shadow of the pilot's cockpit. Three times he photographed the cockpit controls, then another photograph of the radio equipment built in beside the pilot's legs. A stink of aviation fuel, it was extraordinary there had been no fire, and those buggers better keep back with the staves . . . The boffins would go ape when this lot reached the Farnborough research laboratories. What he took from the cockpit, he first photographed. A circular radar display panel, a flying manual that was bullet ripped, a radio communications pamphlet, a flying map from under the cellophane cover on the pilot's knee. There was a stiffness about the pilot's body, because of the night cold, awkward to shift in the cramped bent cockpit. He remembered the instructions he had given to the boy, way back, outside Peshawar, when he had trained the thirteen men who had died . . .

Underneath the gunner's seat, behind armoured doors, is the fixed pod containing stabilised optics for target acquisition and tracking. Beside that is the radio command guidance antenna. Above the gunner's seat is the low speed air data sensor.

. . . He'd had a bloody nerve, talking that gibberish to them.

He could go down past the pilot's boots to the gunner's cockpit, half buried and compacted. Harder to work there. He had had no comprehension of what he asked the tribesmen when he relayed Farnborough's requests. No way the poor buggers could have coped with the electronic intricacies in darkness, in lamplight, in a ruined airframe.

Meticulously he removed, broke away, unscrewed, prised clear the pieces of equipment, handed them with their trails of multi-coloured wiring to Schumack who passed them on to the boy.

He had been at the north end of the village when the helicopter had swooped to attack its downed comrade. Schumack had been beside him and as they lay together Schumack had passed him, without comment, the single-eye spy glass that was tethered to his neck. He had focused on the pilot, he had seen his head tilt upwards at the first ranging bursts. The bastard had known. The bastard had understood that death came at the hands of his own messmates. Barney knew why, Schumack knew why. It was a dimension of war that Barney Crispin had not previously known. Hadn't known it because he had not walked in the battle lull to the rubbish heap of the village and seen the stripped naked body of a previous pilot, a previous casualty. Something terrifying, when a friend found it kinder to strafe his own man rather than let him fall alive into the hands of the allies of Barney Crispin.

Barney came out of the helicopter, climbed onto the upper fuselage to take a last photograph of the rotor mounting.

There were a dozen photographs, there was the ID card of a dead pilot, there were five pages of technical notes, there was a blanket filled with equipment. He saw the waiting men who would strip clear the main armament machine gun, and the rockets, who would siphon off the remaining fuel. It was what he had been sent to do. He took the corners of the blanket, knotted them together. He supposed he ought to have felt a degree of satisfaction. He had fulfilled his mission.

Schumack went with him, the boy behind. They went over the rough and loose stones back to the village. A great blackness around them in the absence of the moon.

'Will you quit?' Schumack asked.

'I've done what I was sent to do.'

'So you'll walk out.'

'I have what I came here for.'

'You have four more of the Redeyes.'

'They go out with me,' Barney said.

'I could use the Redeyes.'

'They're going with me.' Barney felt Schumack's arm brush against his. He could not see him, only sense him, smell him, hear him, and picture the war-torn face at his shoulder.

'I couldn't have your boots?'

Barney smiled, couldn't help himself. 'There are two sets of flying boots up there, if you're in luck one'll be a ten.'

'Your ass is still together, it's the right time for you to quit. If I didn't care what was happening I'd probably walk out myself.'

'Maxie, I am a soldier, I was sent here for a specific purpose, I don't have to listen to that shit.'

'When are you going?'

'When Maggie's loaded, soonest after that . . .'

The claw of Schumack's hand caught at the loose shirt material on Barney's arm. He said urgently, 'Quit fast, hero man, walk out like you're in a hurry, this'll be a bad place tomorrow for someone who doesn't care.'

Barney shrugged him off. He let Schumack walk on alone back towards the village. He heard a shrill scream in the night, a scream of pain that was muffled by a closed door. He let Gul Bahdur catch up with him, and whispered his instructions for the loading of the mule with the parts of the Mi-24 and the three spare Redeye tubes. He heard the scream again. He knew what he would find, and he was drawn to the source of the cry. He was a soldier, he was a professional, a regular in the Special Air Service, he was going home because he had done what he was sent to do, going home to face the whole orchestra. He came to the house. There were holes

240

in the roof tin, and from the holes came the light flickers, and the pain scream was mingled with a lower growl of moaning.

He could not have guessed the extent of what he would find. He opened the door. In the light of the hurricane lamp he saw a mediaeval slaughterhouse. It was a carnage place.

Mia Fiori was the only woman. Her bared hair and her long skirt and her bloodied blouse all identified her to Barney immediately. He thought there were five, six men in the room, splayed out on the floor on the carpets and the blankets. As he came through the door Barney saw the man who screamed. His leg was severed at the join of the right ankle. He screamed because Mia Fiori dabbed at the meat red soft stump with a cloth, and he struggled against the strength of four men who pinioned him, and he screamed because he had spat from his mouth the piece of wood that should have acted as a gag. There was a man who moaned and who was snow pale at his cheeks and whose scalp was pierced by a dark pencil hole wound. There was a man who cried, a little whimper cry, and whose arms were folded across his stomach because that way he held in place the cloths that were laid over the opened wound of his belly, and that heaved and tossed in the surges of his agony. Barney saw two more men with stomach wounds, and one of them had not yet been reached by Mia Fiori and his intestines still protruded from the gash amongst the dark hair of his belly. Barney saw a man whose arm hung loose, useless, fastened to his elbow with a muscle thread. Barney was a soldier, he was a professional, but he had never before seen what he saw in Mia Fiori's casualty station. Ahmad Khan watched the nurse at her work, expressionless, impassive. The one who wore the red waistcoat stood at his side, and beside him was the man who would walk with a limp if he moved. They watched the one woman in the room as she worked, as she cried silently and without an attempt to hide the tears dribbling on her cheeks, as she reached out without looking behind her for

241

more cloths to be given her, as she tossed aside bloodied rags. The sounds of the screams were a bell singing in Barney's mind.

'You have what you came to collect, you are going now?' Ahmad Khan spoke across the room, over the bodies of the fallen fighters. The man who wore the red waistcoat spat noisily onto the floor, the man who walked with a limp stared in open contempt into Barney's face.

Barney spoke stiffly. 'I have the pieces that I came for. It is better I should go in darkness.'

'A price has been paid for your success.'

'There are four helicopters in the valley,' Barney said. 'Four more than before I came.'

'I did not hear myself complain.'

He was dismissed by Ahmad Khan, the schoolteacher turned away from him.

The girl stood, eased herself fluently onto the soles of her feet. Her face blazed at Barney, the tears streamed on her face.

'You came to see what you had achieved?'

Barney's face was tight. 'I have three morphine syringes, I came to leave them for you, and a few other things . . .' He had swung his pack off his shoulders, he was groping in the depths of the pack.

'What would a spy want with morphine?' She flung the words back at him.

'I have three syringes. If you want them, you can have them.'

'And you are going now, so you can be safe away from here tomorrow. You know what happens tomorrow?'

'I have done what I came to do.' He had spoken the words before he had thought out their meaning.

Mia Fiori stepped across the man whose arm was all but severed from his elbow. She caught at the fullness of Barney's shirt. 'All this is yours, you brought it to this village . . . and

242

in the morning when you are gone, they will come back with their helicopters. You are a great hero, Barney Crispin, you are a brave fighting man. Christ, I admire your courage. If you were what I thought you were . . .'

'Do you want the morphine?'

'If you were what I thought you were, you could never leave this place, not when the helicopters will come back in the morning.'

Barney put the syringes in her hand. She turned away from him. She knelt beside the man with the intestines bulging from his stomach. He saw the gentle, narrow outline of her shoulders. He turned and went out of the house.

Schumack stood in the darkness beside the closed door.

'You're on your way?'

'No,' Barney said.

'Listen, hero man. You've had luck you don't know about . . . You caught the buggers when they were soft, when they were slobby. It's their turn to learn smart. You're snuffed when they get smart. Staying behind to fire four Redeyes, that's immoral for a young guy. You're not a Maxie Schumack, an old shitehawk. There's more to you than giving a helping hand to these mothers.'

'Perhaps there isn't.'

'That's pathetic . . . What are you doing with that junk?'

'The boy's going to take it back,' Barney said.

'With the mule?' Schumack asked, a shrewd concern in his voice.

'The boy's going back with Maggie . . .'

'You've one loaded, you've three to carry. You won't go far carrying three tubes.'

'I stay until I have fired all the missiles.'

'You'll need me watching your back, you goddam fool.'

'If that's what you want, then it's your pleasure to watch it,' Barney said.

243

The boy caught up with Barney. He had slipped his arm into the crook of Barney's elbow. There was no argument, there was no disputing Barney's decision. They talked of how long it would take the boy to cross the mountains and reach the Pakistan frontier, three days. How long it would then take him to reach Chitral, perhaps another day. He remembered the name of the man he must meet in Chitral, Howard Rossiter. He remembered where he should ask for him, the Dreamland Hotel. And afterwards the boy was to go back to Peshawar. After Chitral and the Dreamland the part of the boy was finished. Barney could not see his face, could not read his expression as he talked of Gul Bahdur going back to the refugee camps. He asked when the first snow would fall on the high passes over which the boy must travel to reach Pakistan by the northern route, two weeks, perhaps, three weeks, not more before the first snow. There was no wheedling in the boy's voice, no sense of resentment that he was being sent from the valley with the equipment from the helicopter. The boy would go before dawn.

Barney would remain in the valley with four Redeye missiles, and with Maxie Schumack to watch his bum.

'I'm hungry,' Maxie Schumack said.

It was twenty-three hours since Barney had last eaten.

Outside the door of the mess Rostov caught his Major. Rostov had been running all the way from Maintenance Workshops beside the helicopter parking revetments. He had run to catch Medev before he entered the public forum of the mess.

Because he had run, he was panting and able only to blurt out his statement.

'I have just been at the workshops . . . we have to fix a baffle o the helicopters, a baffle that will reduce the hot air content when it is released from the engine vent . . . they say in the workshops that the designers of the Mi-24 ignored the threat of missile attack, not like the Americans and the British and the French, that's what they say . . . at the moment the exhaust protrudes by less than 300 millimetres from the fuselage, the air is hot, the metal around it is hot, and we are taking the hits . . . we have to suppress the quality of the hot air, in the workshops they have been talking about making a baffle for the hot air . . . the senior sergeant in the workshops says that the American and British and French helicopters all have their engine's exhausts set at the rear and the top of the fuselage, we have ours at the side where everyone can see it. To fire at a Western helicopter you have a quarter of a chance less with Redeye than you have with our bird . . . In the workshops they are designing an extension to the exhaust vent, a metre long, but you have to get clearance from the top . . . There would be two effects. When the air emerges from the vent it will have travelled a greater distance through the baffle vent and will therefore have cooled more, that's one effect. The second effect, the Redeye explodes on contact, the warhead is only a kilo of HE, if the explosion is one metre from the fuselage side as against being right up to it, then the damage is proportionally much less . . . that is the idea in the workshops . . . what do you think of their idea?'

'You know what I did this afternoon?'

'I know, Major.'

'I would do anything not to repeat what I did.'

Rostov's face was composed now, the jelly shake was controlled. 'What do you think, Major?'

'You want to fly with chimney stacks on the vents. It is an excellent idea . . . I have one regret.'

'Which is?'

'My regret is that before we thought of this I have lost four helicopters.'

'In the workshops they said that no one had been there to ask their opinion.' A rare candour from Rostov.

Medev went into the mess. The orderly came to his elbow, and offered the familiar brandy. Medev stood with his back to the stove. Some of the pilots were sitting, some stood. There was an atmosphere of hatred and misery in the mess. Every pilot stared at Medev. In front of him was the long table laid for dinner. Two candles burned on the table, floating shadows across two places set with knives and forks and spoons and glasses. Their hostility beat at Medev. He bit at his lip, jutted out his chin. Their misery circled him. He drained his glass, he felt the wash of the brandy in his throat. He stared them out, each in turn, young face to young face. Which one had the courage to answer him? Which of them? Did they think it was easier for him because he had not been high over the grounded XJ SUNRAY? Did they think it was easier to have been distanced by one hundred kilometres from area Delta than to have been there as a witness? Young face to young face.

Onto the young face of the pilot, Vladdy.

Eyes meeting, eyes challenging.

'You are a murderer, Major Medev.' Said quietly, said with a soft emphasis.

A collective gasp in the mess, a little murmur of movement.

'If you didn't hear me, I'll say it again, you are a murderer, Major Medev.'

'Come here and say that.'

Vladdy pushed himself up from his chair, laid his magazine down where he had sat, walked to Medev. His face was a few inches from that of his commanding officer.

'I said you were a murderer, Major . . .'

Medev hit him, hard and with the clenched fist, onto the side of the jaw. The pilot reeled away, half fell, staggered, held his balance. His skin was livid where Medev had struck him.

'Do you want the MilPol?' Rostov at Medev's side.

'I'll not have any fucking Military Police in my mess,' Medev hissed.

As if a signal had been given, the pilots started to move towards the door. They affected a casualness, they did not look at Medev, they shuffled towards the door.

'Get to your places at the table,' Medev shouted. 'Sit in your fucking places . . .'

His voice was a pistol shot. His order was a whip crack. One pilot hesitated, they all stopped.

One pilot turned, they all turned.

One sat, they all sat. Vladdy went to his place at the table, eased into his chair. One of the candles burned beside Vladdy's place.

Medev stood at the end of the table.

'Would you let one man destroy you, destroy Eight Nine Two? One man alone . . . You are here to fight a war, you are not conscripted troopers, you are élite trained pilots, you have been entrusted by the leadership of our nation with a task. We are helicopter pilots, not High Command strategists, not Foreign Ministry strategists. We fly helicopters, and we will continue to do that, to go where we are sent. I make one point, gentlemen, hear me carefully . . . If a pony breaks a leg it is destroyed, it is kinder, it lessens the certainty of pain . . . If one of you is down and cannot be reached, cannot be rescued, then I will order you destroyed, because it is kinder, because it lessens the certainty of pain . . . If any of you are so ignorant of the conditions in Afghanistan that you do not understand the certainty of pain should you be downed and alive and abandoned, then you should go in the morning to Intelligence and consult with them and they will willingly tell you what is the fate of Soviet military who are captured by the bandits. Questions?'

There were none. They ate the meal. By midnight most of the men around the table were drunk in a fraud of forgetfulness.

247

They had eaten hunks of two-day-old *nan*, they had drunk green tea that was thin and sweet, they had chewed the half cooked flesh of a goat that had been decapitated by a bomb splinter. The boy was not invited to eat with the dozen men who took their food with Ahmad Khan, but he sat behind Barney and Maxie Schumack and unobtrusively whispered a translation. They talked of their fighting, of their heroism under fire, they boasted of the helicopters that had been hit with rifle bullets. They did not talk of the Redeye, nor of the half of the village of Atinam that had been destroyed. Nor was it discussed that Ahmad Khan and the men who formed his permanent fighting cadre would move on south down the valley in the morning. Barney had eaten fast, as fast as any of them, tearing the bread, swilling the tea, gnawing at the goat bone he had taken from the pot. Redeye could not make Barney Crispin a part of these men . . . That night the villagers of Atinam slept where they could find a secure roof, where they were out of the mountain winds. Barney's building had survived, after a fashion, survived enough to be slept in.

There was no fire, but as if from a previous ritual Barney and Maxie Schumack laid out their blankets on either side of the dead embers.

He heard the girl cough.

He thought of her face and her eyes and her hands.

Across the heap of charred wood Maxie Schumack watched, balefully. He heard the girl cough again. He sat up.

'She'll eat you, eat you and spit you bloody out,' Schumack said.

Barney rose to his feet, looked down for a moment at Maxie Schumack, then went to the closed inner door. He paused by the door.

'Give her one from me,' Schumack called.

Barney went through the door, closed it behind him. A blackness in the room. He bent his body, stretched an arm in front of himself, had his hand low and close to the dirt floor of the room as an antenna.

She caught his wrist. A gentle pressure to pull him down to her side. Her voice was a whisper, her breath was a ripple on his face.

'Why did you come?'

'To talk.'

'Why with me?'

'I wanted to talk with you.'

'You have your man friend, you have your boy friend, you have your guerrilla friend . . . why with me?'

'I want to talk with you because you are not the man and the boy and the guerrilla.'

Barney heard the narrow brittle laugh. 'Do you want to fuck me?'

'No . . . no . . . I don't.'

'Why not? Because I slept with him, out there?'

'Because I killed two pilots today . . .'

'You want to cry against my shoulder, and cry to their mothers that there was nothing personal?'

'I wanted to talk to you, to someone . . .' Barney said simply.

'While you are crying, tell me what you achieved for the village today. There are seven hundred people who live in this village. They have malnutrition, they have measles, they have tuberculosis, the women and the children are in shock from the bombing . . . But you do not want to talk about that. And you do not want to talk about the men I have tried to keep alive tonight.'

'I wanted to talk to you.'

'Because you have no one else to speak to?'

Her fingers were loose now on his wrist, relaxed, twined gently on him.

'No one.'

'Why should I be the one person you can talk to?'

'Because you don't have to be here.'

'Why are you here?'

'I thought it was helping.'

'And now, what do you think now?'

'When I saw the helicopters killed then I thought I was helping. When I saw what had happened to the village then I didn't know.'

'I was told that you have collected the instruments from the helicopter you killed this afternoon, with that you could go back . . .'

'You have no medicine here, because you have no medicine *you* could go back.'

'And that would be abandoning these people.'

'Running away,' Barney said.

'Showing them our fear.'

'Telling them of the emptiness of our promises.'

'What do you want of me tonight?' Her voice was close in Barney's ear.

'To sleep beside you, to sleep against your warmth, I want that.'

'And in the morning?'

'In the morning we go south down the valley.'

'And what happens to the village?'

'I know what happens to the village,' Barney said.

Barney started to sit up, started to crook his legs under him so that he could stand. Her grip tightened on his wrist. She urged him back, down, beside her. He felt the glow heat of her body through the muslin cotton of her blouse, he felt the shape of her legs against his thighs. He lay on the bend of her arm and all the time she held his wrist.

He slept a dreamless sleep, a dead sleep.

Ahmad Khan and the man who wore the red waistcoat and the man with the limp from the damaged leg worked together. They lifted the wounded who had been treated by the nurse so that their bodies formed a close large mass together in the centre of the room, and as they carried them they whispered to them of the Garden of God, and the glory of the *jihad*. They made their promises of victory, far away but certain victory, and they told of how the names of the martyrs would be remembered and handed down from the old fighters to the young. They were sad moist eyes that gazed up at Ahmad Khan and the man in the red waistcoat and the man with the limp, calm patient eyes as they were gently lifted.

When the work was done, Ahmad Khan knelt and took the cheeks of each man's face in his hands and lifted it to kiss the cheeks.

He took from his belt two RG-42 high explosive fragmentation grenades, and he put them in the hands of the man who had screamed when Mia Fiori had cleaned the stump wound of his leg, and in the hands of the man whose intestines had sagged through his belly wall, and with care he looped the forefingers of their right hands through the metal ring attached to the firing detonator. He was last out of the door, after the man who wore the red waistcoat and the man who limped. He closed the heavy wooden door after him, and he leaned against the stone wall and waited for the twin explosions.

18

Gul Bahdur left the village before dawn.

Maxie Schumack had wakened Barney. He had found him curled against the body of the nurse. He had shaken Barney's shoulder roughly as if embarrassed to find him sleeping beside the woman. She had been awake, he was sure of that, but she had kept her eyes shut. Maxie Schumack had noted that the woman was dressed, that Barney was dressed. Strange man . . . He could understand a man needing a woman after what Barney had done the previous day. Two helicopters downed, and opting to stay and fight, that deserved a screw. Maxie Schumack had been screwing since he was a kid, started with a daughter of the big black woman upstairs, bony little animal the week before the Greyhound ride to Bragg. Didn't get much of it now, not many that liked the sight of the claw. But he thought he remembered what it was like, certainly wasn't like what Mia Fiori had done to him. And Barney was dressed, and the woman was dressed.

Barney walked with Gul Bahdur and the mule, Maggie, out from the north end of the village, past the rubbish heap, past the wreckage of the helicopter. He had written a pencil message to Rossiter. The bundle was loaded on the mule's back. They walked in the darkness of two, three hundred yards together.

'And when you have given it to Mr Rossiter, then you go back to Peshawar.'

'And you?'

'I am coming when I have finished the missiles . . . Gul

Bahdur, without you nothing would have been possible.'

'Thank you, Barney. May fortune ride with you.'

'And with you, Gul Bahdur. We showed them in this valley.'

The boy reached up, caught his arm around Barney's neck and kissed him on the cheek. And then he was gone with the clatter of the mule's hooves on the path into the half-light before morning.

An hour later, the village was alive and on the move.

The armed men of Atinam and the women and the children who were their families gathered together their goat and sheep flocks, marshalled them with the help of the yelping dogs, heaved onto their backs the bundles of their possessions and started out for the ravine side valleys.

'You can't protect them, hero man,' Maxie Schumack said to Barney. 'If you're staying, you stay with us. It's your problem if you hadn't thought that out. You can't protect the camp followers, not even with your sacred Redeye.'

As they went, Ahmad Khan and his fighting force began the trek away from the village and down the valley to the south. Barney and Schumack went with them. One of the missiles was now loaded to the launcher and carried on his shoulder, another was strapped to the top of his pack, his AK rifle was slung on his other shoulder. Schumack had roped the other two missile tubes to his back. There had been eight, there were now four. Barney knew that Schumack's arm was hurting because he had learned the signs of the bitten lip, the quiet curse, the wringing movement of the arm as if the pain was surplus water and could be flicked off. He had not spoken to Mia Fiori before they had left the village. She had gone when he had come back to the building after his short walk with Gul Bahdur. She would have been with the women and the children and their few men. Schumack had watched him come into the large room and go to the inner door and look inside, and had seen the disappointment and held his peace.

253

A sense of failure crept into Barney as they left the village. He would miss the cheekiness and company of the boy and doubted if he would ever see him again. He would miss the cool, worn beauty of the woman and doubted if he would ever meet her again, but the Redeye was his master. There was work still to be completed away from the homes and fields and orchards of Atinam. Barney was trained in the detailed techniques of counter-subversion. Much of the tasking of the Special Air Service was against the hard core guerrilla – Malaysia, Radfan, Muscat, South Armagh – now he played the part of the guerrilla. He appreciated the reasoning that took Ahmad Khan away from the village, could understand why the village must be left to its fate. He had killed four helicopters, he hoped he would kill four more helicopters, yet he felt a sense of failure and incompleteness as he walked away from Atinam.

The column moved in a straggling line along the west edge of the valley wall, keeping in the shadow of the cliff face.

There was high, tumbling cloud behind them, wrapping the peaks of the mountains. Schumack said, a grunt from the side of his mouth, that it would rain, and that if it rained then the first snow would not be long behind. Barney felt the itching of the sores on the flanks of his body and under the hair of his head. The boy was gone, and the woman was gone, and . . . shit, if it rained he had no poncho.

The senior sergeant in Maintenance Workshops had procured lengths of aluminium tubing that were designed as central heating ducts for the new prefabricated barracks occupied by the 201st Motor Rifle Division. It had cost him a bitter argument with an NCO of Pioneers.

The other NCOs who worked on the Mi-24s were regular, but the men under their direction were conscripts, shipped out for limited service, and next to useless the senior sergeant

254

reckoned. As he watched them work, as he heard the hammering of the flanges and screw holes, and the hiss of the welding rods, and the cracks of the rivet guns, the senior sergeant pondered on this new disease that afflicted Eight Nine Two. From the eight that he serviced, four helicopters were gone. There had never been a casualty rate like it. Two replacements had come, but two revetments empty for the world to see and the conscripts to chatter about. He had not seen a portable ground-to-air missile fired, he could barely imagine it even as he scraped his mind for the image. When the Mi-24 was flown over the ground contours, that was danger for so heavy a bird. When the Mi-24 was lifted to the ceiling of its altimeter that too was dangerous. Danger also when the helicopters flew in the 'bathtub', low in the valleys with the bandits in the hills above them. Danger was not rare, not infrequent . . . but four pilots lost, that was something more . . . He knew all the pilots. The senior sergeant prided himself that any of the fliers could come to his shack beside the revetments and talk with him, and share a bottle of beer and talk performance and manoeuvrability. He knew all the pilots, they were the age of his son, he believed he was their friend. The previous day he had watched them out of Jalalabad. Twice he had watched them out, twice he had watched them in. Twice there had been the short-fall.

Usually he was lenient with a conscript who worked bleary-eyed after an evening's hash chewing. Not that morning when they fitted metre lengths of central heating duct tubing to the engine exhaust vents. One conscript, flabbergasted and sullen, he put on an immediate charge, sent to the Guard Room cells.

The work clattered around him. He fussed over every detail. The senior sergeant had only the vaguest of impressions of a homing missile and a stricken helicopter. Impossible for him to comprehend the vulnerability of the big armour plated birds to a portable ground-to-air missile. And it was said in the NCO's mess that only one man fired the missile. One man only . . .

The flicker skim of lightning above the valley's walls. A thunder clap over the valley. The sun gone. The cloud streaming south to overtake the *mujahidin* column. Echoing blasts of thunder. The flashing of lightning. A shadow over all the valley, as far as the men in the column could see ahead of them. A desolate place of rock and boulder and gully and tree and abandoned field.

Ahmad Khan walked at Barney's side. The man who had been a schoolteacher carried only his automatic rifle. His stride was fluent, beside the heavier steps of Barney who was weighed down by the launcher and the spare missile tube.

Barney broke their silence.

'How long have you been in the valley?'

'I came when they took my father to the Pul-i-Charki prison three years ago . . . he died there.'

'How long will you stay?'

'Until it is finished. I will go when the Soviets will go.'

'They have a hundred thousand men, they have the tanks and the bombers and the helicopters. How can you make them go?'

'By our faith, our faith in Islam.'

'There comes a time when, if you have not won, then you have been defeated.'

'They have not won. Perhaps it is they who are defeated.'

'Your people are starving, they can't work the fields, they can't draw in the harvests. That will defeat you.'

'We have the food of Islam. It is nothing to you, it is nothing to the Soviets. To us it is everything. It is a holy war, the *jihad* sustains us.'

256

'The Soviets have the towns and the cities, and the main roads of your country. How can they be beaten?'

'We will win, perhaps long after you have gone. After you have forgotten any adventure you enjoyed in our country, we will win.'

'How will you know when you have started to win?

'I will know we have started to win when I no longer have to look into the sky for their helicopters.'

'I brought only eight missiles . . .'

'Do not give yourself too much importance, Englishman,' Ahmad Khan said. 'We will win with you, we will win without you. You are a butterfly that crosses our path, you are with us and you are not with us. We will be here long after you have left us . . . We will have forgotten you.'

'If I have overstayed my welcome . . .'

'When you have fired the last of your missiles, the day after that you will have overstayed your welcome.'

Ahmad Khan loped away, light-footed, to the front of the column.

'There is concern in Kabul at the level of your casualties . . .'

'And so there ought to be, sir.'

'Don't interrupt me, Major Medev . . .' The rasping reprimand from the Frontal Aviation commander. '. . . In Kabul they are confused by the markings on the missile tube they were sent. American made, but with Israeli and Iranian markings overpainted, yet the missile came from Pakistan and it seems it is fired by a Caucasian white, a European or an American. The evaluation in Kabul is that the missile was intended to be used by the Afghan bandits, but is now operated by this mercenary. Kabul believes the missile was introduced to bring down an Mi-24 for equipment stripping. It would be a prize of exceptional value. Last evening's helicopter did not catch fire, it could be presumed that the opportunity to strip the helicopter has been taken and that

257

the purpose of the mercenary's mission has been satisfied.'

'That he has no more reason to be in the valley?'

'It is presumption . . . as I said, in Kabul there is concern at your casualties. Four helicopters in one week . . .'

'Four pilots in one week,' Medev said grimly.

'The casualties in area Delta have emasculated our patrol programme. I cannot permit a situation where day after day area Delta takes priority over all other flying. Your present strength is . . .?'

'Six, six helicopters.'

'Coming in from Kandahar is a full strength squadron, *sixteen* gunships.'

'I want area Delta.'

'And the new squadron?'

'Where you like, everywhere else, any other valley.'

'Is your squadron, what remains of it, capable of maintaining a presence over area Delta?'

A hoarse snap in Medev's voice. 'Very capable, sir.'

'Are you capable yourself, Major Medev?'

If it had not been the Frontal Aviation commander, his direct superior, Medev thought he would have kicked the shit out of him.

'I am capable.'

'I have heard of something close to mutiny in your mess.'

'It's a lie . . .'

'Careful, Major.'

'I put it to you, we have business in that valley.'

'Revenge is a dangerous business for expensively trained pilots, for expensive helicopters. Tomorrow morning a paratroop regiment will be lifted to the northern end of the valley, to Atinam . . .'

'For what?'

'To punish a village where two helicopters have been destroyed.' A cut of sarcasm from the Frontal Aviation

258

commander. 'There is a wider war, Medev, than your personal war of pride.'

They told him that their names were Amanda and Katie.

He told them that his name was Howard Rossiter, that his friends called him Ross.

He shouldn't, of course, have struck up a conversation in a public place, least of all in the shop where he purchased his groceries. They were ahead of him as he waited to pay for three tins and a loaf and toothpaste and a throwaway razor. They were young enough to have been his daughters. Pretty little things, with tanned faces, and streaky hair hanging on their shoulders. English girls roughing it in northern Pakistan. At home he would have called them 'hippies', and if he had been with his own children when he saw them he would have issued a critical analysis of the younger generation's lack of standards and discipline. But Howard Rossiter was in Chitral and lonely.

He wasn't doing too well himself on standards and discipline. There was stubble on his face and his hair was too long and uncombed. His trousers had lost their creases. His shoes were grubby. They had a nice way with them, Rossiter thought. He liked the way they pecked in the purse for coins for their two loaves, he liked the long flowing skirts and the peeping painted toe nails. He liked the scarves that were slung around their shoulders. He liked the blouses they wore, and the pimples on the bulges that told him what they didn't wear . . . Steady on, Rossiter.

They would have looked over him, they would have wondered where this cuckoo had fallen from. Bit past it for the youngster's trail, wasn't he? Bit past the hash hippy trail to Kathmandu. He'd said 'good afternoon' in his best Whitehall clip and with a smile on his face, and they'd collapsed in giggles. But they waited on the rutted pavement for him to pay his money and follow out after them.

259

Curiosity, he supposed.

They were Amanda and Katie.

He was Howard Rossiter and his friends called him Ross.

They were at the end of six months that had seen them through Nepal and Kashmir and now illegally into Pakistan.

Ross was doing some research, that's what he called it.

'You're very young to be here.'

'We've finished school,' said Amanda.

'Done your "A" Levels?'

'Christ, not that sort of school,' said Katie.

Rossiter knew the accent. He knew the sort of girl. Sometimes an official of his level at FCO was hauled out at a weekend to take a brief down to the home of a Deputy Under Secretary, down to the countryside of Hampshire or Sussex or Gloucestershire. They all had daughters who drawled that accent.

'Where are you staying?

'Tenting at the moment.'

'In this weather?'

'Have you a better idea?'

For the next ten minutes Howard Rossiter of Foreign and Commonwealth Office chatted up two eighteen-year-olds. But then everything about his behaviour would have shocked those of his employers who had previously held up his name as a watchword in reliability.

'I might see you about,' Rossiter said.

'If you wanted a smoke.'

'If you ever get lonely.'

'If I want a smoke and if I'm feeling lonely,' Rossiter said.

'What are you researching, Ross,' Amanda asked.

'Bits and pieces.'

They'd go like bloody rattlesnakes, the pair of them. Any good looking girl from the privileged classes went like a rattlesnake in Rossiter's mind. That was the bloody trouble,

260

it was all in the bloody mind. Except for the nurse in Peshawar . . . that hadn't been in the mind, that had been on his lap on his bed until Barney Crispin had made a famous entrance. He hadn't thought of Barney for half a day . . . Shadows falling, time for the Night Manager to come on duty at the Dreamland. Time to think of Captain Crispin.

'Christ, he's probably a spy,' Katie said, and they all laughed.

'I'll see you about,' Rossiter said.

'You look as though you could do with a smoke.'

'You look lonely enough.'

'Perhaps another time . . .' and he hurried on his way.

One thing to think about it, another to do it. Thinking about it, lovely little tits, sweet little backsides, would see him through a couple of days, waiting on word of Barney. Shadows falling on the streets of Chitral. The lights of Toyota jeeps cutting the gloom. A little rain and the clouds promising more. He bumped into a tribesman, an old man in white floppy trousers and an embroidered waistcoat, with spectacles perched on his nose. He tried to make an apology. The old man stared at him as if the Englishness in Rossiter's voice fitted no other part of him. He'd screwed himself, hadn't he? He'd chucked up the pension and the Pay As You Earn taxed salary. And all for Barney Crispin who was away behind the lines with a Redeye launcher. Try telling Pearl and the kids and the neighbours and Personnel at FCO.

He wondered what a smoke would be like. He wondered how Amanda and Katie would cope with his loneliness.

There was no message for him at the Dreamland Hotel.

The black car and the chauffeur were enough to cause a ripple of curtain lace in Larchwood Avenue. There hadn't been a death and there wasn't about to be a wedding at the Rossiters that any of the neighbours knew of. The street lights were on, they threw enough light for the watchers to

261

see the Brigadier head from his car for the front wicket gate of No. 97. The Brigadier wore a three-piece pin stripe, and below his pressed trouser turn-ups, his black shoes were brilliantly polished. He was looking at the front door for a light, and so did not see the dog mess in his path. There was a glimmer of light in the depths beyond the frosted glass. There was an overgrown flower-bed on one side of the path, and on the other a square of unmown grass bright with dandelions . . . and the woodwork needed a spruce of paint. He rang the bell, heard the chime, and wondered what Rossiter earned in a year.

The door opened and a teenage boy confronted the Brigadier. The boy's hair was short and spiked up like a dandy brush. The boy looked him up and down.

'Who are you?'

'Fotheringay, Brigadier Fotheringay . . .' He smiled sweetly. 'Is your mother at home, Mrs Rossiter?'

'Mum . . . there's a man here,' the boy shouted to the back of the hall, and then ducked into the front room and closed the door. He stood alone. He looked down at his feet. Bugger, and the dog mess had smeared the carpet and up the heel of his shoe.

He was back outside, wiping the sole and heel on the grass when he saw she had come to the door.

'Yes.'

'Mrs Rossiter?'

'I'm Mrs Rossiter.'

He didn't really know what he had expected to find when he had made the decision to drive down to see her. She was a small, tired-looking woman, wearing carpet slippers and an apron. She was carrying rubber gloves. Her hair was grey streaked. The Brigadier surprised himself: he felt a moment of sympathy for this woman.

'Can I come back in?'

They stood in the hall together. She invited him no

further. She looked at him as suspiciously as if he had come to check the television licence.

'It's about your husband, Mrs Rossiter.'

'What's he done?'

'I am sure you know your husband has been away on assignment for Foreign and Commonwealth . . . He's gone missing, Mrs Rossiter,' the Brigadier blurted it out. 'We don't know where he is.'

'How should I know where he is?'

'I wondered if you'd had any postcards,' the Brigadier said lamely.

'From him, when did we ever have postcards?'

'If you'd had any communication with him, if he'd given any indication of his thinking . . .'

'Be a fine time for him to start.' And then: 'Is Ross all right?'

'I've no reason to think he isn't . . . He's gone missing, I can tell you in strictest confidence, Mrs Rossiter, that he's gone missing in rather odd circumstances. That is to say in flagrant disregard of the most clear instruction to return home.'

'Ross has gone missing . . .?'

He saw she was crumbling, he saw the wobble in her throat, and the biting at her lip. He was a fool to have come.

'But you've heard nothing from him?'

'We never hear, not when he's away . . . He'd never talk to us about his work, not even when he's at home, never has. He's all right, you're sure . . .?'

The Brigadier smiled emptily. 'I'm sure he's all right, I'm sure there's nothing for you to worry about. There'll be an explanation. As soon as I have word, you'll be told. That's a promise.' He was backing for the door. 'I'm very sorry to have troubled you.'

He let himself out. He heard her sob through the frosted glass, and made his way circumspectly back to his car.

Rossiter was the Brigadier's man, and the Brigadier knew nothing of him. He'd have bet his best horse that Rossiter would have obeyed every bloody instruction given him. Either Rossiter was dead or he would have lost the horse that he loved.

The boy had been walking for a day, he would walk through most of the night. Without the mules he could not have attempted the forced march into the high passes and plateaus that would lead him between the villages of Weigal to the south and Kamdesh to the north.

Ascent, and descent, climb and fall, valley and cliff face. Now that the sun had slipped away and the light had faded there was only the occasional grey glimmer of the path in front of him when the cloud broke to make a window for the moon. Instinct and memory kept him on the path.

Hours after the darkness had come there was a confirmation for Gul Bahdur that he had taken the correct track, the one that would steer him between the outposts of habitation in this wilderness. A caravan of men and mules and horses and munitions came towards him. Eerie ghost voices at first, and the scrape of hooves, and no faces and no beasts to marry with the sounds until he was upon them. Gul Bahdur was given bread to chew and some dried fruit, and he spoke of the destruction of four helicopters, and he said that aerial patrols were scarce in the valley ahead and that when the helicopters came it was in squadron force.

He heard the caravan straining, creaking, away from him into the darkness. He felt a man. He believed he had passed a test of initiation into adulthood. He carried the news of a battle, the news of four downed helicopters. There was a light flurry of snow. His blanket was tight on his shoulders, his body sheltered from the winds hard against the flank of the mule.

264

Maxie Schumack shook Barney's shoulder.

It was light. He had slept through the dawn.

Rain fell, fine and cloying. Barney shivered. His covering blanket gleamed from the sheen of droplets. His stomach growled in hunger. As soon as he was awake, he had seen Schumack bending over him, had assimilated the rock gully in which he had slept, then the pain itches of the lice scabs were alive on his flesh. His stomach growling, and a different noise, a new sound.

'I would have let you sleep, but you ought to see the show,' Schumack said.

The helicopters flew high over the valley in convoy.

'Mi-8s, Hips we used to call them, can carry up to thirty men each.'

He saw the gunships, escorts on the flanks.

'Only one place that lot's going.'

He saw the cascade of flares falling in regular descent from the Mi-24s.

'Babies are learning.'

'Only one place?' Barney asked quietly.

The convoy was at maximum speed, Barney estimated its ceiling was 3000 feet above him. The Redeye launcher had been under his blanket while he slept, but it was damp now, smeared and wet. He wiped it with his sleeve but made no effort to arm it.

'Give me your glass.'

Schumack dug in his shirt front for the spy glass.

'As you say, the babies are learning . . . they've got baffle tubes on the engine vents . . . I'll have to be closer, every time bloody closer, more of a bastard . . .'

'Can you take one?'

'What'll happen to the village?'

Schumack screwed his face. 'They'll dynamite it, they'll burn it.'

'What about the people?'

265

Schumack shrugged. 'How smart have they been? If they're up high, if they stay in the caves, if they've reached the side valleys, then they won't see much and they won't feel much. Depends what the Soviets want out of it, what sort of lesson they're reckoning to teach . . . They can be mean bastards when they've the mind for it.'

'Your answer is, I can take another one.'

'You're thinking of the lady . . .'

Barney's glance flashed angrily at Schumack.

'. . . That's crap, Barney. She's made her bed, she can lie on it. What do you want? Do you want us to stand around and try to fight for villages when they're going to put troops in . . .?'

He broke off. Above the helicopter convoy, above the cloud cover, reverberated the sounds of jet aircraft engines.

'Guerrilla warfare, Barney Crispin, you're supposed to know what that's about. That's about ducking and weaving, and running for a better day. You think the 'Cong pissed about when we were coming in force? They ran, they went for the cracks in the walls. That's the way it happens. And you having a fancy fanny in there doesn't change anything. Got it, hero man?'

'Why don't you piss off, Maxie.'

'You didn't even screw her, did you?'

'I can take a helicopter on my own.'

'Better you're not on your own, Barney.' A soft kindness from Schumack. 'And a broad isn't worth us getting scratchy. Listen here, hero man, if you start getting emotional about fighting, personal, then you're in deep shit, you and all the bag carriers you've collected.'

'If you could get me two RPGs on the east side . . .'

'And you'll climb on the west side?'

'Right.'

'And take them on the way back?'

'Right.'

266

'Don't get scratchy with me, hero man, and don't put a bit of fanny in the way of whatever you want to do here, whatever that is . . . because I'm going to be beside you, and if you're crapping about because of a fanny then I'm going to get scalped with you.'

They were both smiling. Schumack had crowbarred his way into Barney's life. He was a stray dog that had come to a kitchen door, and no way would the beggar be turned aside.

'Just get me two RPGs on the east side.'

They had been in the morning to the village of Atinam escorting the troop-carrying birds, they had returned to Jalalabad. In the late afternoon, still spewing their flares, and wearing their fresh painted engine vent baffles, they had come back to Atinam to collect the big Mi-8s.

Behind them now, as they flew south in the valley, was a village where two companies of Airborne troops had done a job of work. A violent, bloody job of work. They had been landed beside the village on the valley's floor, also on the roof of the valley. They had secured the side valleys and the waterfall ravines, they had cleared those caves that were close to the village. A violent, bloody job.

By the end of the day the cloud levels had fallen. The helicopter convoy flew beneath the cloud ceiling on full power. The flares were brilliant on that early evening. Any light would show up on that early evening, any flash of flame.

They had not been attacked. They had not taken ground fire either at the village or on the way there or on the way back. They were escorting butchers back from a long day's work. There was little for the gunship pilots to feel proud of.

The *Reaktivniy Protivotankovyi Granatomet*, the RPG-7, is the smallest and most widely used anti-tank launcher utilised by the Soviet armed forces and their satellite allies. Through capture from overwhelmed Soviet and Afghan

Army units, this weapon has become standard equipment in the arsenals of the *mujahidin*.

When fired, the RPG-7 emits a fierce flash signalling the rocket's ignition.

On that evening, in the shadow of the valley, in the gloom of the rain clouds, the flash would be white light, easily seen. Glimpsed cursorily through the curved distortion in the wings of the Mi-24's cockpit bulb, the ignition of an RPG-7 could give the appearance of the malfunctioned firing of a Redeye missile.

Schumack had talked with Ahmad Khan.

Ahmad Khan now talked with the man who wore the red waistcoat and the man who limped when he walked.

'You are our leader, and we tell you as we have the right to tell you, that you give this unbeliever too much,' said the man with the red waistcoat.

'It is as if you have given to him the decision of your tactics, when you strike, how you strike,' said the man who limped when he walked.

'He is a poison in your mind.'

'The one place in the valley where we were assured of food and some safety was the village of Atinam and, because of the unbeliever, Atinam is destroyed.'

'You should never have offered him your hospitality.'

'He should have been food for the eagles.'

'He has not stayed to help us.'

'He has stayed to fornicate with the woman.'

'He will destroy you as he destroyed Atinam,' said the man with the red waistcoat.

'He will destroy us all,' said the man who limped when he walked.

Ahmad Khan had not spoken during the denunciation of Barney Crispin. Now he waved his hand irritably for quiet. He spoke abruptly.

'You will fire the launchers. He said that before he came

268

there were no helicopters killed in my valley. You will fire the launchers on my command. Where I had killed none, he has killed four helicopters in my valley.'

There was no further argument. To have disputed further would have caused the man who wore the red waistcoat and the man who limped when he walked to trek out of the valley to search for a new commander.

On that evening, and where the valley was a little less than eight hundred metres in width, the two RPG-7s were sited on the east side. On the west side, hidden on a rock bluff, was Barney Crispin.

Barney thought of the woman. He thought of the bombers that he had heard overhead above the cloud cover. He thought of the troop carriers that he had seen ferrying the combat troops to an undefended target.

He saw the approach of the returning convoy and their flares. They came above the centre of the valley. They came level in height with the rock where Barney waited. The Redeye launcher rested on his shoulder.

Schumack crouched at his side.

Two spurts of light from the east side of the valley. Almost simultaneous. Two sheets of flame from the east side of the valley floor. Two explosions trailing the picture.

Barney saw the tracer fly from the gunships, heard the snarl as the engine power increased, as the birds manoeuvred, as the Mi-24s bucked away from the east side firing positions. Redeye on his shoulder. Over the open sight and onto the helicopter that flew wide to the west side of the valley before turning to flail the flash fire positions with the big nose-cone machine gun.

Battery coolant on. Hearing the first whine of the contact.

How would the baffle tube work against the Redeye? Didn't bloody know. He did know that the girl had stayed behind at Atinam with the women and the children and the

269

old men, and Barney Crispin was alive and fighting on another day.

The howl in his ear of the infra-red contact. Point blank for Redeye. The squeeze on the launcher trigger.

First flash, second flash . . .

Barney and Schumack lit up, bonfire kids, illuminated by the second stage ignition.

Barney should have been running. He watched the light ball plunge out across the valley. He was captivated by the light power he had created. Schumack was pulling, yelling at him.

One brilliant explosion.

The tension burst from Barney's body. They tumbled together down the valley wall and away from the exposed rock bluff. Schumack sobbed in a cry of pain as his stump arm cracked down onto rock. Sliding and stumbling together.

They found a gully, a damp crevice where a little of the rain water had collected, where they could cover their heads with their blankets, where they could merge into the feature-less valley walls.

'Did I kill it?'

'It's still up.' Dead words from Maxie Schumack, a cold message.

'But the explosion?' Barney shouted.

'It's still up.'

The helicopters did not stay to hunt down the fire posi-tion. The gunships were on escort. There was a cursory strafing of the area from which the Redeye had been launched. They had wavered towards the first trap, they would not be baited a second time.

When they reached the floor of the valley Ahmad Khan waited for them.

He took Barney to the east side. Barney had seen the stone face of the young schoolteacher, set and expression-less. He knew what he was to see.

270

In death he could recognise the two men who had fired the RPG-7s. Through the nightmare death of a helicopter's machine gun bullets, Barney could remember their features.

'I had a hit,' Barney said bleakly.

'I see no helicopter.'

Ahmad Khan walked away, left Barney to look down on the bodies. Barney saw the man who wore the red waistcoat and his shirt was red also, and his thighs and the skin of his face. And the leg of the man who limped when he walked was two metres from his body, and the brain was splashed further. Barney took a launch tube from Schumack's back and reloaded the Redeye.

The pilot, Vladdy, brought the helicopter gunship back to Jalalabad and the blazing apron lights, and the waiting ambulances, and the fire tenders. One of the twin turbo shafts had been damaged. There was an oil leak. Hard, slow flying on one functioning engine, but the pilot brought it back.

Medev was on the apron. When Vladdy climbed down from the cockpit, when the rescue services had driven away, when the maintenance crews began to scramble up around the shattered baffle tube, Medev took the pilot in his arms. He held the shaking young man against his chest, hugged him, squeezed him, poured out against him his gratitude that the big bird had not been lost.

'It is the end of his luck,' Medev whispered.

'We got it back, that's all . . .' the pilot said dully. 'It'll be days before it's operational again.'

'Not important, he fired and he failed. He has all night to think on that. He fired and he failed to destroy you. The first failure is the hardest . . . What now does he have to look to?'

'Will we go back to the valley?'

'Of course.'

'For what?'

271

'To kill him,' Medev said. 'To kill him now that he is at the end of his luck.'

The pilot broke clear and walked fast away. Once he turned to Medev who followed him.

'You fly with us . . .' the pilot shouted at Major Pyotr Medev. '. . . Now that he is at the end of his luck, you fly with us, and see what it is like when the missile is fired. Just the one time you come with us to know what it is like to live because of luck.'

19

Two long days slipped by, two long nights.

The weather had closed over the valley. Rain and snow flurries, a cloud ceiling down onto the river bed and the orchard trees.

No helicopters were seen. Only once there had been the distant sounds of an Antonov. High beyond the clouds.

A caravan came through the valley under cover of that cloud.

They were Jamiat men and wary of crossing Hizbi territory. There were formal greetings and respect was shown to Ahmad Khan by the leaders of the caravan. They took tea together and shared food, and perhaps some of the munitions carried on the backs of the horses and mules had been pilfered. The cloud cover saw this caravan through, not the power of the Redeye launcher that was never more than a yard from Barney's hand day or night. The talk told the Jamiat men of the destruction of the helicopters in the valley and sometimes these travellers hovered close to the Englishman and the American and stared at them. Ahmad Khan made no attempt to bring Barney and Schumack close to the evening gathering when two goats were slaughtered and cooked across open fires. A mullah who went with the Jamiat men once came aggressively forward to divert the attention of a group of the younger men of the caravan who had ranged themselves close to Barney and were pointing to the weapon as if it were a thing of magic.

A wall, slowly built, was erected to shut out the *kafirs*, the

273

unbelievers, and Barney knew that he was the cause of the barrier, not Schumack.

'Maxie, what happened at the village?'

'I don't know,' Schumack looked away. 'No one told me.'

Barney had thought this a large caravan. Schumack told him another was expected, larger in man power and supplies and heading for the Panjshir. Perhaps that would be the last caravan to come through before the snow blocked the passes.

Summer had fled the valley. The winds clipped the trees of their foliage.

Barney brooded, became an entity of his own.

Schumack was always with him on those two days and nights. He should have sent Schumack away, should have kicked him away as a man will kick at a stray dog. Barney was a lone man. He took his food outside the main group of fighting men, the same food and drink that was cooked in the same pots and bowls but eaten apart from them. Barney slept apart from them with only Schumack for company, huddled under the thinning valley trees. The first night and the first day after the burial of the men killed by the helicopter he had not noticed the wall that crept up around him. By the second day he had been certain of it. They had come to a deserted village, close to the crash site of the first helicopter that Barney had brought down in the valley. That was an age ago, a summer ago. There were close to a hundred men in Ahmad Khan's group. There was no wood near the village, and they reached it after dark and too late to go down with axes and chop at the orchard trees for firewood. A miserable wet and cold evening. There was no hot food and the men found in one house a wooden chair that they broke up for a fire that would heat their green sweet tea. Schumack brought the food to Barney in another house away from the building in which the mass of men had collected. While they ate bread and dried fruit, Schumack talked of Vietnam. He talked without emotion of what he called Sam's balls-up. Of medivacs, of

274

free fire zones, of the 'Cong coming in human waves onto the wire and the Claymores, of the far-from-home screams of his conscripts, of the base camp coke and heroin pushers, of the clap caught by the East Coast officers. Sam's foul-up . . . Barney knew the pattern. Later it would be Sam's foul-up when the Ambassador was butchered in Kabul. Later when he wanted to sleep, it would be Sam's foul-up at Desert One.

Barney waved his hand at Schumack, cut him off in full flow.

His mouth was filled with the coarse grained bread. He could not remember how many days before he had stripped off his shirt and his socks and washed his body.

'I haven't asked you, you haven't told me, why I'm shut out.'

'The helicopter didn't come down.'

Annoyed, Barney shook his head. 'You can't bring every bloody one down.'

'You didn't tell them that. You were all full of shit and wind. You were like Sam, you promised and you didn't deliver.'

'I brought four down.'

'With the hairies you're as good as your last, your last didn't come down. When you're a cocky bastard then you have to deliver.'

'I had a hit. I'm certain of it.'

'Don't cry over it, hero man. They took a hit too, they lost two men.'

'They also lost a village, I didn't see them weeping in their bloody cups then . . .'

'You don't learn, Barney. The RPG is special to them, it's the best thing they have when they fight the tanks and the APCs. They get right up close with the RPGs, they don't piss from a distance. They'll blow a culvert in the road, they'll stop the convoy, and they'll get in to forty, fifty metres before they fire. Takes some bottle to do that . . . You know what

275

they used to do before they had the RPGs? They used to get on top of the tanks and shove cow's shit over the drivers' vision slits then put mines under the tracks, takes some cool to do that . . . The RPGs are special, and the two men on them were special to Ahmad Khan.'

'How special?'

'Very special . . .' The old lined face close to Barney. The old white combed quiff of hair. The old claw on the stump gesturing in front of Barney. 'One was the husband of Ahmad Khan's sister, one was his uncle.'

Barney nodded his head, his eyes were screwed tight as if he resisted a pain. 'Thank you.'

'He gave you his best, he gave you what was special to him. Seen his way, you broke a faith.'

'Why does he let me stay in the valley?'

'Because you have three more missiles, because he has another caravan to see through . . .'

'It's my neck as well, it's not just his uncle's neck, and his wife's bloody brother's neck,' Barney flared.

Again the jab of the claw close to Barney's face.

'You've come late, Barney, you and old Redeye that's damned near a museum piece. You've come late and you're going early. Got it?'

'Got it.'

'What did you want? Did you think you were the second coming?'

'Got it.'

'They need a hundred Redeyes from Sam, they need a thousand tubes. All they get is crap from Sam about what heroes they are, crap about the nobility of fighting for the Free World . . . and they get Barney Crispin out of the clouds with one launcher and eight tubes.'

'Got it,' Barney said quietly.

'You asked . . .'

'Why don't you go back to your friends?'

276

'Because you're dead without me.' Barney's two hands fastened onto Schumack's one good hand. Held it.

'Thank you.'

Barney stood at the window of the room.

He held back the sacking that had taken the place of glass when the house had been occupied.

He saw the scudding movement of broken cloud that obscured and then presented the stars. The same stars that his grandfather would have seen before combat. The same stars that had shone down and winked on all the cavalcades of the invading armies. The men caught in the Third Afghan War would have noted those stars, and the men of the Second Afghan War, and the men of the First Afghan War would have seen the stars on the night before they went to be slaughtered in the passes on the road to Jalalabad. And the men who followed Genghis Khan and who followed Tamerlane and who followed the great Alexander. All the invaders, all of the armies of foreigners, would have seen those stars on the night before they made war in the uplands and the lowlands of Afghanistan. He felt a sense of time, gaping and incredible. He wondered if a pilot, the flier of an Mi-24, stood outside the sleeping quarters now at the Jalalabad base and stared up at the time space above him.

'Can't you sleep?'

'It's stopped raining, the cloud's breaking.'

'So they can be back,' Schumack said.

'They can fly tomorrow.'

'So they can fly tomorrow, so what?'

'Then there'll be one less of the bastards.'

'And what does that do?'

'You have to believe in victories of a sort, otherwise there's no point,' Barney said.

'That's officers' crap. There'll be a shitehawk in Jalalabad who thinks when he gets your arse that he's won a victory.

277

He's won nothing, and when you hit another helicopter then you've won nothing. Me, I'm not an officer man, not a hero man, I wouldn't know a victory if I saw one . . .'

'Go back to sleep.'

'You going to get yourself a flier tomorrow?'

Barney let the sacking fall back. The stars were gone from his view. He couldn't see Schumack in the darkness.

'I don't know.'

'You need to get one, hero man; or you've overstayed.'

Barney sank down onto the floor. He was shivering. The cold gripped his body. His hand brushed against the launch tube of the Redeye. He held the tube.

'Maxie . . .' an urgent whisper from Barney. '. . . If you were the squadron commander in Jalalabad, would you come back? After the losses, would you come back here?'

'Myself, I'd go somewhere else where I can keep my arse tight, I'm not an officer. Your man at Jalalabad, he's an officer. He'll come back every day, every day until he's had you.'

Barney lay hunched on his side, knees drawn up to his chest, the blanket wrapped over his body.

'You're a hell of a comfort, Maxie.'

'If it's comfort you want, hero man, then get on your feet and start walking.'

'Christ . . . go to sleep, damn you.'

They had eaten their first food of the day, they had scattered and dispersed among the rocks as precaution against aerial attack, they had seen the glimpses of blue sky between the breaking clouds, they had their weapons armed and ready.

They saw the women and the three old men and the children walking south along the track beside the river bed.

Barney was with Schumack and sitting a hundred feet above the valley's floor on the east wall. When she was a full

278

mile away he recognised Mia Fiori, with the women and the old men and the children.

The group walked slowly along the open space in the centre of the valley. It was as if they believed that no danger could threaten them any more. She carried a small child tight against her waist and her breast, she held the hand of another child that walked beside her. Half a dozen women, three men with grey white beards and stooping gait with ancient Lee Enfield rifles slung at their shoulders, and a gaggle of children. Once as she walked the sun flickered on her and the blouse she wore was lit, and her hair shone, but it was a long way off from Barney and the vision of an instant only.

Schumack said nothing. He sat cross-legged beside Barney.

One woman limped, another helped a matriarch, two were burdened by knotted bundles that rested awkwardly on their upper backs, and there was Mia Fiori. She walked at the front and the children trailed around her, and the women were behind her, and the old men hung at their heels like dogs. She walked straight, she walked tall-backed, she walked as though the ground was smoothed in front of her. She walked as if she were dreaming. Barney could not see her face, could not see it when she was close to the emptied stone houses where he and the *mujahidin* had spent the night, because the head of the child that she carried obscured her face. He wanted to reach out, to push aside the head and the face of the child so that he could see her.

In front of Mia Fiori and the children and the women and the old men, where before there had been only the desolation of boulders and scrub bushes, there was now movement. The men appeared from their hiding place and stood and waited for the column to come closer. Hard men, fighting men, and they stood and waited for the women and the children and the old men. Barney's hand left the Redeye launcher, left it with care alongside Schumack. He rose to his feet. He ran away

279

from Maxie Schumack down the slope to the valley's floor. He ran through the scrub bushes where the thorns grappled against his trousers, he ran over the rock boulders and the stones to the path. He ran towards her, past the fighting men who stood and waited close to the DShK machine guns and the mortars and the RPGs.

She seemed not to see him.

She seemed to gaze only ahead of her.

He was running with the hunger ache in his stomach and with the lice sores on his body and with the cloy of damp in his boots and with the dirt on his cheeks.

He reached her and his arms fell around her neck and he gathered her against him, and the child that she carried gurgled against the beard on his face, and the child whose hand she held was pressed close to his leg. He saw the tears in her red swelled eyes, he saw the river run of the tears through the mud on her face. He kissed her eyes, he kissed her tears. The children went on past him with the women and the old men. Barney clung to Mia Fiori and to the one child she carried and to the child that hugged his leg.

He kissed her forehead, he kissed her cheek.

She looked up at Barney into his eyes. She had woken from a dream. She looked into his eyes and the weakness took her, and he held her against him as she cried, and the child she carried chortled happily between them.

In a whispered small voice, she told him:

'After you had gone, after we had left the village and tried to climb into the side valleys and find caves to hide in, they came in the helicopters. The village had been bombed again, and then the helicopters machine gunned the village and the side walls. Then bigger helicopters came and they landed the soldiers at each end of the village, and also on the roof of the valley. Those on the roof of the valley moved down, quite slowly so that they would not miss a hiding place, and those at the bottom of the valley covered them with machine guns.

They could not find all the caves, they found enough of the caves. We had gone further than most, I don't know why, but we were further and outside the cordon that they had set. We lay in a cave with the children pressed against us because they tried to cry in their fear of the explosions and the shooting, and we buried their crying under our bodies. Into the caves where they found people they threw grenade bombs . . . Barney, the people were screaming, perhaps we did not have to bury the children that were with us against our bodies, their crying could not have been heard above the screaming when they were throwing the bombs into the caves. They took some men they had captured down to the village, and they took them to the mosque building and put them inside and they set fire to the mosque. They had a gun aimed at the door and when the men tried to run from the fire they shot them with the gun, and all the time they fired at the windows of the mosque. Nobody came out of the mosque, only the screaming came out . . . After that they burned all the grain stores of the village, the people cannot live in the village in the winter without the food store, they burned all their food for the winter. In the afternoon they left. When they had finished, the helicopters came again for them and lifted them away . . . I am not strong, Barney, not strong enough for what we saw. There were wounded people there, and I had nothing to give them, nothing, nothing. I had come here to help these people, and I could not. I had nothing to offer them. I was as frightened as these people. I was crying with these people. They have scattered now, those that are alive, they have gone high into the mountains, but there is snow in the mountains. Barney, where was your bastard missile?'

A whispered, small voice that died on the valley's floor.

He took onto his own shoulder the child that she had carried. He took the hand of the child she had led.

281

'I have to have a plan, I have to have your help with a plan.'

'Three days ago I saw your plan and I buried two men because of your plan.'

Barney Crispin and Ahmad Khan were standing beside the old sewer ditch of the deserted village.

'I have to have the help so that the fire positions are co-ordinated.'

'You want the help so that other men cover your life with their lives.'

'That's bloody rubbish.'

'Always you demand a diversion fire that puts at risk my men, my friends. Always my brothers must stand as a shield for you so that you can fire and you can escape. Find your own plan.'

'If you want to kill the helicopters, if you want to clear the valley, you have to help me with a plan.'

Ahmad Khan stiffened, tight veins at his throat. 'I have to do nothing.'

'Don't you want the valley cleared of them?'

'I have a valley to defend, I do not have just one man to defend. I see more than one man. I see the time before you were with us, I see the time after you have left us . . . You ask my brothers to give their lives to keep safe your plaything that you will not even let us hold . . .'

'Because you don't bloody know how to use it.'

The spittle of Barney's anger fell on Ahmad Khan's nose and cheeks and was wiped away with the sleeve of his jacket.

'You may stay with us until the missiles are fired, but I will give no man's life to protect you. You will take your chance as we take our chance, we in the sight of Allah, and you wherever you can find chance.'

Ahmad Khan walked away. Schumack came to Barney's side. His head was shaking, his mouth was squeezed wide and together in sadness. 'They're proud, and you piss on that pride with your Redeye. One day you'll learn, hero man.'

'What do I do?'

'You stay a mile from them, always south of them so the birds come over you, and you hope that if the poor bastards are zapped that you'll get one launch away.'

'Where'll you be?'

'Where I always am. Stop playing like you're God to these people. They've got Allah, they don't need you.'

'If I take three more helicopters . . .'

'They'll have forgotten you before you've time to fart . . . You're not doing it for them anyway. It's private and personal to you, whatever you're doing. Everyone can see that.'

Away from them, sitting in the shelter of a compound wall was Mia. She was more than a hundred yards from them. She squatted on her haunches and had found a blanket that was over her shoulders. She was with a group of children. She was absorbed and attentive to them. Barney could smell the scent breath of her mouth that he had kissed, and the salt taint of her tears. He saw her in the darkness of a cave covering the body of a child as the rockets and grenades and machine gun fire burst over the valley. He watched her. He slung the Redeye launcher onto his shoulder.

'Don't come with me, Maxie . . . watch her for me, please.'

He strode away, going south down the valley, measuring out a mile.

He found himself a shallow cut between two granite grey rocks, and settled under his blanket, and waited. And his ears strained in the quiet of the valley for the sounds of the helicopters' coming, as the clouds rose and fragmented.

One woman had broken cover.

Under the suffocation of the memory of the attack on Atinam, one woman had run from a crevice hiding place as the first helicopter pair powered overhead.

She stood up, and ran.

Some men rose to their knees to clutch at her dress and pull her down, and failed to halt her stumbled, hysterical flight. The helicopters thundered above them tilting to starboard and port side alternately. The flares of rainbow colours shimmered in their slow fall in the valley. On the sighting of the running woman, and as the men near to her betrayed their positions, one helicopter came down low, spitting machine gun fire, and the three big bird comrades climbed for altitude and the broken cloud ceiling and the observation platform.

The *mujahidin* cannot lie on their faces in the dirt and between the stones while the tracer and the rockets are falling amongst them. Fear is infectious, fear is a disease, and a man who has a rifle or a DShK wheeled machine gun will try to fire back. And as each man fired up at the helicopters so he handed the aerial marksmen the location of his position.

The fighters were chopped down, slashed down between the stones of the river bed, beneath the scrub bushes where the leaf cover was already withered, around the compound walls of the deserted village. Meat for the helicopters' gunners, drink for the helicopters' rocket pods and 12.7mm four-barrelled machine guns.

Barney had no way of knowing where Mia hid, no way of knowing whether Maxie was with her.

He saw from the distance of a mile the red light of streaming tracer sinking from the camouflaged helicopters, and the flash light of their rockets, and the puff smoke of their ground strike. The woman that he thought he loved was beneath the tracer and the flash light and the puff smoke . . .

Barney watched.

He saw her face. He saw tears on her face, blood on her body. From a mile away, from safety, he saw the tracer and the rockets.

He crawled to his feet and the blanket dropped from his body.

284

He stood. The flares drifted in the skies above the valley. Three helicopters circled and manoeuvred high above the valley's cliffs.

The launcher rested on his shoulder. He aimed without hope for the strafing low-flying helicopter. Flares falling . . . Red, green, blue, yellow, technicolour flares. He engaged the battery coolant switch . . . the hum in his ear. The helicopter was at least a thousand metres away, port side on. A flare floated between Barney and the target helicopter. The woman that he loved was under the tracer and the rockets.

Barney fired.

The flash, the signal, the give away. The light careering from his hiding place.

The Redeye sped from Barney, homed low towards the helicopter, towards the flare. The flare had fallen to the ground and the helicopter was banking and losing the port side profile.

A missile gone rogue.

It flailed away from the target line. It swept up and then curved, then fell, then swung again towards the upper skies. Bright, brilliant light cavorting over the valley. Useless light trailing a mindless warhead. For twelve slow seconds the light behind the warhead swooped and dived and rose again from the valley's floor, then the final inbuilt command of the missile's brain, then the self-destruct explosion echoed between the valley's walls.

Barney lay under a lip of rock.

For half a dozen minutes the stone work was fractured and wrecked by the shrapnel slivers from the rockets, by rock fragments from the machine guns. His leg was bleeding, the side of his chest dribbled blood.

The vengeance fury of the helicopters was turned on a lip of rock. Barney lay on his stomach, he cuddled the ground as if the ground was a woman's body. He could not believe that

285

the short roof of rock would withstand the battering, he could not believe that the squealing ricochets would not find him. On his stomach, and his mouth was filled with rock dust and his ears were deadened by the explosions.

Long after the helicopters had gone, his hands were still pressed tight against the sides of his head.

Schumack found him, lifted him up, supported him, dusted him down.

'She wasn't hurt,' Schumack said. 'Shit knows what sun shone on her.'

Drinks on Medev's bill in the mess.

Medev with his tie loosened and his shirt button undone. Medev playing the father with his young pilots. Singing too, songs from the old Ukraine, and the old Frontal Aviation anthem. A cossack dance from Vladdy, legs raking out and arms akimbo on his chest, and the other pilots and Medev clapping to a frenzy. Drinks on Medev for his pilots. Lifting the roof of the prefabricated mess, showing the fliers of the new squadron that Medev's men had come through their ordeal. A pilot had tried to take the tablecloth off the end of the dining table, had smashed every plate and broken every glass, and spilled food and wine and vodka on the carpet. The men of the new squadron had watched and had not joined, had not been invited to join.

The Frontal Aviation commander was framed in the doorway.

And Medev had forgotten the bridge-building invitation, and was straightening his tie, buttoning his collar, shouting for quiet, and the commander was waving with his arm that ceremony was out of the window, down the bottle.

'Today it all worked . . .' Medev's voice was slurred and proud. 'We hit a concentration of them, out in the open. They broke cover, ran like fucking rabbits, hit them like fucking rabbits in cut corn. The missile was fired, fired once, went rogue. The flares decoyed it, up and down and sideways and back into its own arse. We went in hard after the firing position, plastered it . . . that was Vladdy . . . Vladdy, I am pleased to introduce you to the Frontal Aviation commander . . . they plastered the place, nothing that's bigger than a mouse's arse could have lived through it . . . right, Vladdy?'

'Right, Major.'

'You said you would bring me his head,' the Frontal Aviation commander remarked easily.

'With what was put down on him he won't have a fucking head,' Medev chirped. 'Brandy, you'll take some brandy with us . . .?'

The orderly brought brandy. Medev and the Frontal Aviation commander chinked glasses. The party erupted back to life.

Medev had promised the head of the man who fired the Redeye . . . But Vladdy was an experienced pilot. He had not seen the man, only the location of the firing flash. But Vladdy had seen the ground into which he fired. He would have known. A pilot knew the damage capabilities of his firepower. If the pilot, Vladdy, said that no man could have survived the blasting of the machine gun shells into the rocks and the rockets, then so be it. He would have liked the body, he would have liked to have kicked the bastard's balls, dead balls or live balls, kicked them with a full-swung boot. He would have liked to have seen the face of the man, and known the man who had challenged him for area Delta.

The Frontal Aviation commander downed his glass, he looked at Medev, a half smile on his face. 'Why do you think he fired into a field of flares and at helicopters with baffles fitted, and when he had no covering fire? Why do you think he did that?'

'We'll have to go and ask him,' Medev shrieked in his laughter. 'If there's anything left to ask . . .'

287

The drink flowing, vodka, brandy, beer, enough drink for them to bath in.

'Where's that arsehole Rostov?'

'Why doesn't Rostov share with us?'

'In his sack and playing, that's where the arsehole will be.'

No more sport to be gained from singing and dancing and drinking. The pilots needed new sport. The Frontal Aviation commander smiled indulgently, remembered his own youth. Rostov, Medev knew, would be in his bed, Rostov was not one to participate in a mess night carousal. Carousing was for fliers. Rostov was not a flier.

'Let's get the anus.'

'Rostov shouldn't be left short of an invitation.'

For a moment Medev pondered whether then and there he should put a brake on them. But Rostov didn't fly in area Delta, Rostov hadn't flown against the missile . . . screw Rostov. Medev saw them surge out through the doorway.

They were men at war, his pilots, and they were the cream and they were the power, they and the big birds that they flew. If they weren't hard, if they weren't right bastards then they would never have flown into the valley to find the missile, to destroy the man who fired the Redeye. Down the corridor he heard the shrill shouts of complaint, and Medev stayed silent.

Shit. He was wearing turquoise pyjamas, soft material and creaseless, and he was shaking like a piece of bloody jelly.

The pilots held Rostov up, and they poured beer from a bottle down his throat and he was gagging on the drink and slurping it from his mouth and down the front of his pyjama jacket. And the poor bastard was too frightened to struggle. And the pilots were fit, muscled and strong and Rostov was flabby and weak. And the pilots tore the pyjama jacket from Rostov and ripped the buttons away, and they were shouting and howling and below the rolls of Rostov's waist they were

288

tugging at the cord of his trousers. Rostov was trembling, and whimpering, and his hands were together and tight against his privates. And the pyjamas went to the stove, and the flames soared, and there was the stink of the synthetic fibre blazing. And the pilots pushed Rostov down to his hands and knees, naked, and they rode him in turn like a donkey around the dining table of the mess.

The fliers of the new squadron sidled away to their sleeping quarters. Without warning, the Frontal Aviation commander spun on his heel and walked out.

Rostov was no longer a game. Rostov was in the far corner of the mess, huddled on the ground, weeping. Rostov was alone, crying to the floor.

Medev loved his pilots, and they were animals. The Redeye missile had made animals of them, he said that to himself.

Medev walked uncertainly across the carpet, skirted the table. He lifted Rostov to his feet. He hated a grown man to cry. He took Rostov out of the mess, back to his quarters. For Medev's pilots the party would continue until the first light of the new day.

On the mattress on the kitchen floor of the bungalow, Rossiter snorted and sighed and squealed through his hoarse and quaking throat.

It was rank, rich, bad pleasure. Cheeky little bitches, both of them. Cheeky was an understatement. Bloody outrageous. Parents should have been ashamed of them. It was what came of sending them to schools that didn't rate examinations. Rossiter was naked and dosed with sweet clinging hashish smoke, and Amanda without clothes against his back, and Katie without clothes against his belly. Christ knew where they'd learned it. Tongues and teeth and finger nails, and his skin was alive and his mouth was dry, and he ached down there like someone had punched him. What happens to

289

you, Howard boy, when you loiter with intent outside the open front of a Chitral grocery store. Fingers in his crotch, fingers in his backside, heaven knows what they learned at that school. Amanda holding another smoke to his mouth, couldn't hold it himself, hands couldn't hold steady after what they'd done to him, and Katie's fingers at him again so he was going to burst, so he was going to go mad, mad and insane, insane and delirious. He didn't know what they wanted of him, didn't know how they could find him an entertainment, and hadn't the energy to push the question.

At around the time he was enjoying his third smoke and mildly remonstrating with Katie that she couldn't expect him to respond again and again. Gul Bahdur walked heavily, limping, to the desk of the Dreamland Hotel on Chitral's Shahi Bazaar. Slung across the boy's back, awkward from its angular contents, was a filled sack of coarse cloth material.

20

There was a narrow glow of sunshine at the dawn, an intermittent light because the winds blew hard in the valley and pushed the clouds across the face of the rising sun. A pit had been dug in the darkness hours. The bodies had been laid in it of seven men and two women and a child who was laid on a woman's breast before the blankets were wrapped around the corpses. It was said that more than one hundred thousand people had died in the prisons and the valleys and the deserts and the mountains of Afghanistan since the invasion of the Soviet armed forces in December 1979. Ten more here for the records. The grave was filled and topped by a cairn of stones. The words spoken by Ahmad Khan to the mourners carried briskly, ferried by the wind, to where Barney stood, a sing-song of defiance. Mia Fiori was with the mourners. She had come from Atinam with the women who had died, she had carried the child who was buried. Schumack stood with the mourners, indistinguishable as a foreigner amongst these people, head bent, shoulders swathed in a blanket, his billowing trousers snatched at by the winds.

Barney leaned against a tree trunk, away from the mourners, away from the burial. As he watched, his face was blank of expression. He had not spoken to Ahmad Khan since Schumack had found him under the rock lip, bleeding and trembling. They had seen each other, eyed each, but they had not exchanged words. Barney had wasted the bloody missile. The missile was as precious as his arm. He had wasted the missile because there had been no plan. If there had been a

291

plan he need not have thrown his decoy into the skies, into the flares. The safety of Mia Fiori had taken precedence, even over the life of a pilot and a gunner and an Mi-24 helicopter . . . The bitterness he felt at the waste of the missile was a pattern in his mind. Again and again he saw the track of the rogue missile . . .

The cairn was built, and Schumack joined him under the tree. A caravan was coming through the valley within the next three, four days. More than a hundred mules and horses. Enough ammunition and mortar shells and RPG rounds to hold back a Soviet divisional attack into the Panjshir once the mountain passes were snow closed. Ahmad Khan wouldn't come to tell him, but Schumack would: the caravan had to be protected. Barney nodded ruefully. Would there be a plan? A quick shallow grin from Barney. He squeezed Maxie Schumack's shoulder, because this man had helped him when he had limped back from his shattered hiding place to the open rock ground where the *mujahidin* had been caught by the gunships.

After Schumack had gone, ambling away, the girl came and sat beside Barney. She was pale, the bones of her cheeks seemed to have risen in her face. She was tight and hunched inside her blanket. She rested against Barney's shoulder staring out across the valley. He had slept the previous night with Mia Fiori lying on one side of him and the Redeye launcher on the other. She knew, and all of the camp knew, that he had fired the missile to win her safety.

Her hand now lay under Barney's hand.

'When will you go?'

'When the caravan is through, while the passes can still be crossed.'

'Will you take me with you?'

'I will,' Barney said.

'There is nothing more for me here.'

292

'Perhaps there was never anything for either of us.'

'When you go back to your home what awaits you there?' her head tilting up to him, her eyes questioning, her small lips opened.

'It's a bit of a disaster, when I get home.'

'You were sent here?'

'I came myself, as you came yourself, we are the same. When I get home I will have to answer for that.'

'What will your answer be?'

'That I thought it right to come.'

'Yesterday I told you to kill a helicopter . . . Was it wrong to ask that?'

'From what you had seen at Atinam it was right to ask me to kill a helicopter. You had also seen the death of a pilot, but you had forgotten that.'

'I had forgotten.' Her head swung away, to gaze out over the lightening valley. '. . . When you go home, to whom do you go?'

'To nobody.'

'There is a someone, there must be a someone.'

'No. There is nobody.'

'I have nobody, when I go to Paris there is nobody.'

Barney took her hand, lifted it to his lips, kissed the knuckles of her fingers.

'We will go home together, so that we shall each have someone.'

Barney stood up, his teeth were clenched shut. He slung Redeye onto his shoulder. He was remembering the way she had bathed the slashes and nicks and cuts in his side and legs. He felt again the finger touch of her hands.

'As soon as the caravan has cleared the valley I will take you.'

A light rain was falling. Rain in the valley, snow on the high ground.

She called after him.

'When you leave this valley, will you look down on it for a last time?'

'No,' said Barney.

Even the piercing hangover failed to deter the light step of Pyotr Medev as he left the office of the Frontal Aviation commander. While the launcher was loose in area Delta there was no possibility of his being permitted to take the monthly trip to Kabul for the de-briefing at the High Command's Taj Beg palace. He had taken coffee with his commander, black and mercifully thick, and he had been given his clearance. He would be a celebrity at the Taj Beg, he was told. He was the man who had fought off their most serious threat. It didn't bear thinking about if the helicopters could not fly at will in the mountain countryside to which the tanks and the APCs were denied access. His experiences would be picked and sifted. He would tell them about the flares and the emergency baffles.

And he would see the wife of that fool, the agronomist of Kandahar . . . And he would buy a present in the bazaar for his wife. One more week in Jalalabad and he would be flying the long haul, to the transport base of Frontal Aviation south of Moscow in the belly of the big Antonov 22. A week's packing up and winding down in Jalalabad and then a freedom bird home. Shit . . . and the woman at home had better be in a happier humour when he came through the front door. Her last letter was all whining about shortages, the child's cold, about him not writing regularly . . . nothing sweet, nothing feminine. But he was damned if the thought of her would take anything from the anticipated delight in the agronomist's wife in Kabul.

In his operations room he read the forecast for the 24 hours ahead. Rain in the valleys in area Delta, snow on the high ground. Let it rain, let it snow. Let the rain fall and snow flake down on the body of that bastard foreigner. He was only

294

sorry he had never seen the body and never had the chance to kick the arse off it.

They had stayed on the mattress the whole day through.

He couldn't believe they could sleep so long. Both stark naked, the blankets all over the place, and sweet clean satisfied sleeping breathing. A bloody eye opener for Howard Rossiter were Katie and Amanda. In the middle of the day he had first extricated himself from where he had slept between them. He'd made them some tea, felt bloody ridiculous standing beside the cooker while the kettle boiled and him wearing only a drying-up cloth knotted around his waist. No tea wanted . . . He'd gone back to the mattress, crawled over Katie, snuggled up to Amanda.

That had been the day, unique in the life of Howard Rossiter.

The room was darkening again. The way they'd slept through the day frightened the hell out of him. God alone knew what energy they'd have stored up for the evening's work. He lit a cigarette and flicked the dead match into the emptied soup tin on the floor near their heads. The cigarette didn't taste much, not after the night-time smokes, nothing to get his throat onto. When the cigarette was finished, he stubbed it out in the tin, and climbed again over Katie, saw her eyes twinkle and open, saw her mouth curl in a giggle. Bloody idiot he was. And bloody marvellous it had been. He muttered that he had to go out, saw the eyes close, saw the mouth settle. There was a law against this sort of thing at home, and for all he knew probably a law against it in Chitral. Probably get him castrated in public, if he only knew.

He closed the kitchen door quietly behind him. He went to the side of the bungalow, looked into the kitchen, saw the debris of clothes on the floor, saw the girls sitting up on the mattress, saw their heads jumping in mime laughter.

295

He hurried away for his nightly rendezvous at the Dream-land Hotel.

Outside the dull-lit façade of the hotel, Rossiter hesi-tated. The night and day that he had spent on the mattress, with Katie and Amanda, were now just a taste in his mouth and a weariness in his gut. The training had taken over. He raked the street around him, he found no tail.

He heard his name called. Rossiter swung round. He jack-knifed straight. A slight persistent voice. He twisted towards the source of the sound. Shadow beside a parked lorry. His name again. He waited for a movement, for a figure to emerge from the shadow. He walked forward. No movement in the shadow. He was sweating. He felt the thin light of the street lamp fade from his face. He walked into the darkness.

'Hello, Mr Rossiter . . .'

'Who is it?' A stiff, quavering voice from Rossiter.

'It is Gul Bahdur.'

Christ, the boy who had come to the Peshawar bungalow with the bandage on his head and trapped Barney into the lunacy of the long walk into Afghanistan.

'Is Barney here?'

'No, Mr Rossiter.'

'Is he hurt? Is he all right?'

'I saw him four days ago, he was not hurt then.'

'Where did you see him?'

'Three days west of the border, in the north of Laghman, in a village called Atinam.'

The boy lifted from the ground a dark sacking bundle, held it between them. 'Barney said to bring this to you.'

'Oh, my God . . .'

'It is the parts of an Mi-24, the parts that you wanted, Mr Rossiter.'

'He actually shot one down?'

296

'Four, he shot down four. He fired four missiles, from the fourth only could he take the pieces you wanted.'

A hiss of shock from Rossiter. 'And why is he not with you?'

'He wants to kill four more helicopters. He wants to clear the valley where he is of helicopters.'

Rossiter was dazed, his hand took the weight of the sacking bundle. He reached to feel the concealed angular pieces.

'Clear a valley?'

'Drive out the helicopters, that is what Barney is doing,' the boy said. 'There are photographs as well, and notes that Barney made about the helicopter, and he wrote a letter for you.'

Rossiter grasped the folded paper that the boy had taken from the inside of his waistcoat. He hadn't his reading glasses with him, and it was too dark anyway to make out anything written on the torn edged paper. This was where it ended, what it had all been about, in the shadow on a pavement at the side of the Dreamland Hotel and holding a bag of a Hind's electronics. He was jolted, struck back from the thought of how crazy it all was.

'Will he make it out?'

'It is snowing in the passes.'

'Does he know the route?'

'Perhaps he will have a guide, perhaps not.'

'How long does he mean to stay there?'

'He is with the Resistance and he has pledged to clear their valley of helicopters.'

He had been screwing through the night, taking his pleasure, gasping his happiness on his back. He thought of Barney. He saw the determination in his face. He saw the deep distant eyes. Barney was out there, fighting a war. He thought he might vomit up his food and the hashish and the sweat tastes of the girls. Out there, out beyond the mountains, out beyond the borders of all sanity. Barney fighting a war with gunship helicopters while Howard Rossiter screwed himself towards senility.

He took the bundle in both hands and slung it over his shoulder, and put the letter in his top pocket. He led the way back to the bungalow. Gul Bahdur told him, as they walked, of the smoke that had crawled from a cave, of the tethered mule and of stone-filled clothes beside a river bed, and of the light streak across a valley, and of the destruction of the helicopters. The boy told him of the bombers' run on the village, and of the helicopter strikes that had followed . . . Rossiter said nothing, nothing for him to say, a world beyond his comprehension . . . Gul Bahdur told him about an American called Maxie Schumack who had one hand and one claw. He told him about a nurse from Europe who worked without medicine in the village. He seemed hardly to hear the boy. The bundle concerned him. If there was anything to be saved from the awfulness of the boy's stories then that salvation lay in the bundle. How to shift it, how to get it away from Chitral, those were the new, furious preoccupations of Howard Rossiter. If he failed to get it away then he had destroyed himself, and broken Barney Crispin. The boy was telling him of a guerrilla leader called Ahmad Khan, and of a Soviet pilot whose testicles had been ripped from his body. Rossiter no longer listened.

Rossiter stopped at the gate to the bungalow. He gripped Gul Bahdur's shoulders, placed him beside the gate, and went on alone up the driveway.

He paused at the window.

The girls were sitting up on the mattress, smoking. He saw his teethmarks, a double weal, in Amanda's shoulder. He felt a growing outrage. He saw what he thought was an incarnation of the Devil. He saw Katie teasing the nipple of her friend.

The tears thundered in Rossiter's eyes. He pounded open the kitchen door. The room ahead of him was a moistured blur. He swept into the room. His feet were close to the mattress.

'Go away . . .' he screamed.

He turned his back on them, could not look down into their faces.

'Go away, you little bitches . . .'

He heard behind him the scurry of their movement.

'Away . . .'

He heard the sounds of their dressing, the whispering of their clothes, the clatter of their sandals, the sweeping up of their belongings.

'Away, out, out, out . . .' Rossiter shrieked.

He heard the crash of the kitchen door heaved open. He heard their feet sliding on the mud and gravel of the driveway. Then he turned, and saw the mattress and the brief powder blue pants discarded on the linoleum. He picked up the pants and pocketed them.

Rossiter went back to the gateway to collect Gul Bahdur. The boy said nothing of the two phantom shapes that had run past him, loud in their laughter.

Later, when he had examined the contents of the sacking cloth bundle, when he had stared into the clear quality of the Polaroid photographs, when he had glanced over the notes describing the Mi-24 cockpit interior, he left the boy in the bungalow and set off again for the Dreamland.

At the hotel he found a telephone. He waited twenty minutes for the connection to the Night Duty Officer at the High Commission in Islamabad. He asked for a message to be passed as a matter of urgency to Mr Davies. It was past office hours, the caller would appreciate, Mr Davies had gone home.

'*Just do it*,' Rossiter said. When he was outside again, it was raining. He tucked his neck down into his chest. If it was raining in Chitral, then snow would be falling on the high mountain passes over the border.

He wiped the rain droplets from his nose and started to run, a slow shambling run back to the bungalow.

Barney and Schumack were a thousand yards ahead of the column. He walked with the loaded launcher across his shoulder and with the last of the missile tubes strapped to his back pack, and with the AK-47 assault rifle hanging at his side.

There was now a plan, negotiated by Schumack. The column was moving south and Barney would be ahead and clear of the column, and if the helicopters surprised them, flew north up the valley, they would pass over Barney on the attack run, and he would have the chance to fire on the engine exhausts. The two DShK machine guns wobbled on the wheels inside the column, one in the centre and one in the rear. If the helicopters came, then the DShK fire would draw their attention. That was the extent of the plan. Mia was away behind him, with the children and the one woman who had come with her from Atinam.

The column was moving to a place near the centre of the valley where a side valley came down from the west and where a side valley rose up to the east. It was a place where the main trail from the Pakistan border crossed the valley on the route to the liberated zones of the Panjshir. The big caravan of munitions would come down the side valley from the east and the men would rest their animals in the valley before climbing again to the west. In one day, or in two days, or in three days the caravan would arrive. The men who would come with the caravan were not of Ahmad Khan's allegiance. But the code of *Pushtunwalah* ruled in the valleys and the mountains, the hospitality to a traveller, the sharing of bread and meat. The code dictated that Ahmad Khan would fight to his last man, to his last round of ammunition, to ensure the caravan a safe crossing of his valley. For the caravan's sake Ahmad Khan allowed Barney Crispin to walk with his column.

300

Barney was aware of Schumack's exhaustion. He didn't suggest the American should carry the spare missile. Usually when they walked together Barney was a yard or two ahead, sometimes now he had to stop to allow himself to be caught. The claw was hurting Schumack. He seemed to wring the claw more frequently and to pinch at the flesh above the strapping as if that squeezed a poison out of his arm. Deepening age lines at the eyes and a slower step and a wheezing breath.

'Why don't you come out with me, when I go with her?'

'I'm not running.'

'It's not running away, not to come out of this place.'

'I've done my running, did it for Sam. We ran out of 'Nam, holding our arses and running like we were scared. We ran in Kabul all the way down to the airport to load "Spike" Dubs' body on the transport because we'd screwed saving him. We ran out of Desert One before we'd even started. You ever run away, hero man? It's dirty as shit. Doesn't count that some mother with tabs on his shoulder, gold on his cuffs, tells you it's not running, that it's strategic withdrawal or tactical abort. I'm not running any more, and thank Christ, Sam can't tell me to run any more . . .'

'Your gut's in trouble, hell only knows what insects you've got crawling around inside you.'

'If I come out where do I go? Back to Sam? They had us run out of 'Nam after we'd filled 55,000 bags, takes some counting when you're running, fifty-five thousand stiffs and, nine years later, they've just got round to remembering the fifty-five thousand who couldn't run when they gave the shout. Back in Sam, they treat them like crap, those who ran when they were told. Treat them like they're some sort of mother disgrace. You ever been in Sam, Barney? . . . It's diseased. It's all queers and pervs and hippies and weirdos. It's rotten like my gut, it's got rotten with running.'

'Do you have no one to go back to?'

'No one.' A whistle of breath between Schumack's teeth. 'I'm past running to go looking for someone . . .'

Barney turned, still walking, to look at Schumack. He saw the strain and the tiredness. He saw a man who stamped his feet onto the rock path to keep up his speed. He saw the pallor of the stubbled cheeks and the dark eye caves.

'Will the helicopters come for the caravan?'

'Sure the Antonov'll find them. That mother always finds them. When the Antonov recce finds them, then we'll have the helicopters come . . . Specially after you've missed twice.' A dry laugh from Schumack.

Barney could not remember how many days ago he had come to the valley, but there had been flowers between the rocks then, the pink of the wild roses and the mauve blue of the violets. Now he saw no flowers. He saw the grey green brown of the rocks and the scrub bushes and the trees that were losing their foliage.

'Let me take you out when I go.'

'Did I ever tell you about Kabul?'

'You will,' Barney said lightly.

'You're not *my* fucking officer. Don't you piss on me . . . We are the most powerful nation on earth, that's what Washington calls us, and the Ambassador is the representative of the most powerful nation on earth, got it Captain Crispin? . . . In Kabul we had less clout than a black used to have in Baton Rouge. Three shites had the Ambassador in a hotel room, and the Soviets were running the "rescue" show, some fucking rescue. The Soviets wouldn't let us up the stairs to the landing where our Ambassador was held, they wouldn't talk to us, wouldn't let us talk to them. They shut every fucking door on us. We were shouting stall and play for time and delay, and the Soviets were arming up the attack squad, machine guns and rockets and automatic rifles. We wanted to play the old softly softly, they were going to storm before it was even decent. We were the most powerful nation

302

on earth and we couldn't shift those mothers, those crap Ivans ignored us, they pissed on us. I don't know whether they shot our Ambassador themselves, or whether the Afghans did, or whether the gooks who'd taken him did. He was pretty dead by the time they let us get to him, damn near dead. I'll give you a long word you didn't know I had. I hate impotence, I hate fannying about, if that's easier for you. So, no, I'm not going.'

'I understand.'

'I didn't ask your opinion, hero man, I was telling you.'

'I understand what you're saying, but there has to be somewhere better for you than here.'

There was no reply. Barney heard only the stamp of Schumack's boots and the rasp of the breath in his throat.

The British High Commission in Islamabad is run on rigid and compartmentalised tracks.

To the Night Security Officer who had taken Rossiter's call, Davies the spook was Mr Davies with the rank of Second Secretary and member of Consular and Visas. No way that a Night Security Officer, with 22 years service in the Black Watch behind him and a Regimental Sergeant Major's stripes thrown in, was going to shift himself after office hours by telephoning a Second Secretary. Not for him to know who was the High Commission's spook in residence. And the message for Mr Davies was incomprehensible.

The message paper was folded, left in Davies' pigeon hole, and since the spook did not come to the High Commission until late the following afternoon, that message had already gathered a fine film of dust.

'Package to collect 3550 lands of dreams 7156, Miss Howard.'

That was the message.

Enough to make the spook weep. All right, yes, security men had a tail on him in Islamabad. All right, yes, there was a

303

tap on his telephone . . . But this was so ghastly melodramatic. He'd known as soon as he met Rossiter that the man was
lacking a scintilla of style.

From his map of Pakistan he traced out the co-ordination
of 35 50 North 71 56 East. His finger nail converged on the
place name of Chitral. Bloody Howard Rossiter up on the
bloody border. He took from a shelf a well worn 'Pakistan – a
Travel Survival Kit', too right, everything was survival in
Pakistan. Under 'Accommodation and places to eat in Chitral', he found a one line reference to the Dreamland Hotel on
Shahi Bazaar. Not very sophisticated Mister Howard bloody
Rossiter, and a piece of luck that the lumbering fool on night
duty at the High Commission hadn't put the message over his
home telephone. He wouldn't have reckoned that the crack-
ing of this code would have taken Pakistan Security five
minutes more than it had taken him.

Not that the spook could make the trip up country, not
with the tail that had been on him since Rossiter and his
Action Man had disappeared. The new fellow in Information
would enjoy a drive out of town. He could take the High
Commission land-rover.

The spook had heard the rumour from the Americans,
where else, that in one valley in Laghman province helicopters had been shot down. They dropped their silver about
and they heard the most . . . He looked at his map. Laghman
province and Chitral were not adjacent, but not a million
miles.

'Alexander? . . . Davies here . . . I need a spot of help, I
wonder if you could pop up before you shut your shop for the
night . . . it'll keep till I see you . . . Cheers.'

It would be a job for the Diplomatic Bag. And after he'd
bagged the package then he'd have to find a way of shipping
the bloody undesirables out, new passport, overland into
India, and all the rest of the paraphernalia . . .

Bugger London, bugger them for messing his patch.

He strode away down the corridors of the Taj Beg, out into the autumn light, past the sentries in their spick-span uniforms that never saw the shit filth of combat, past the fat arse staff officers who knew fuck-all of the war in the mountains, past the MilPol jeep with the lolling shites who rounded up the fighting men when they were on a Twenty Four in Kabul and looking for hash or tail, past all the cretin apparatus that thought the war was winnable.

Go where my pilots go, pigs. The silent shout from Medev. See how you fucking like it. Fly between the tight arse valley walls and see if you're so sure. Fly through the ground fire cones of shells and smell your shit-heavy pants when you've landed.

From the de-briefing staff pigs, Medev reckoned he had received the barest of understanding on the problems of flying helicopters inside a confined valley space and against a ground-to-air missile marksman. He had lost four helicopters . . . He had lost eight crewmen . . . His pilots were not novices, he was told, they were expected to have assimilated the training received in Warsaw Pact exercises where they flew over simulated Redeye and Stinger and Blowpipe battlefields. But where were the flares he'd requested a clear week earlier? Why weren't the flares sent from Be-gram or Central Equipment Depot? Why did he have to use distress flares . . .? Because no bastard would get off his arse. None of the pigs were impressed by the engine exhaust baffles. The bandits had won a victory, he was told, the losses were insupportable. But the bastard was dead, Medev had shouted back at his interrogators, the bastard was chopped . . .

Medev was not a celebrity, he was a commander who had taken fierce casualties.

Still seething, he boarded the shuttle bus between the Taj Beg headquarters and the secure accommodation provided for Staffers and visiting field men. There was an armed guard beside the driver, half awake and half asleep, and half dead he'd be if he were on his feet in area Delta.

He wore his best dress uniform. He wore medal ribbons on his chest. He wore his cap jauntily. He wore a polished leather pistol holster on a polished leather belt.

The bus dropped him by the entry to the old city's bazaar.

He waited on the pavement after the bus had gone for a group of his countrymen to form. He would not go into that bastard warren bazaar on his own. There were some off-duty soldiers. He saw the red flash of the Mechanized Infantry, the Army's donkeys. Two out of half a dozen were armed. Little more than boys, any of them, about eighteen years old. They led the way into the first of the narrow bazaar streets, and Medev followed a few metres behind. There were three civilians behind him, a hundred metres behind. He felt safe.

The anger sidled away from him as he walked the bazaar street, threaded his way through the people and the smells and the indifference. In her last letter his wife had sent him a list of items she wanted him to bring back. What did the silly cow think he was going to do? Hire a lorry and drive over the Oxus river bridge at Termez, and take a north west left turn for Tashkent and Orenburg and Kuybyshev and Ryazan and Moscow, two and a half thousand klicks . . . chests, carpets, cotton materials, a refrigerator . . . did she think the squadron commander of Eight Nine Two had a line in looting on the side? Silly cow . . . he had stopped beside a stall. It would be a quick purchase. He looked down at three lapis lazuli brooches. He thought he should spend the same on his wife as he had spent the month before on the agronomist's wife. He loved the deep clear blue of the stone, the blue of the early morning skies through the tinted canopy of the helicopter cockpit. He pointed to one brooch. He looked up and saw the backs of the soldiers of Mechanized Infantry merging with the cloaks and blankets and turbans and caps from Nuristan. He heard the price, he reached for his wallet. He looked back down the street and glimpsed the raincoat of one of the civilians. Just once he did not haggle over the purchase price. He paid what he was asked. He could not have explained to himself the sudden edge and suspicion he felt in the pressing bazaar street, with the crowds flowing close around him, with the buildings lowering above him with the flaked paint and the hanging washing. He slapped down the Afghani notes.

He heard a single shot. He grasped his pistol from its holster. He was wild-eyed, turning, spinning.

He saw the soldiers from Mechanized Infantry close huddled to each other, and the space growing around them, and the fallen shape beside their black walking-out boots. He saw the terror in their faces.

He started to run.

He ran away from the soldiers and past the three civilians, frozen on their feet. Only when he was clear of the bazaar and out in the main wide street did he stop running. He realized then that he had dropped the brooch of lapis lazuli.

He returned his pistol to the holster. His head was shaking, slowly, sadly. Pyotr Medev walked away from the bazaar. He felt no shame that he had run, just the soaring pleasure that he lived and that another had been chosen.

In the half an hour that he took to reach the Mikroyan residential complex his hand never left the opened flap of his holster.

His knees had steadied now, the tight fear in his belly was behind him.

He was saluted by the sentries at the main checkpoint barrier of the complex that was the home of the majority of Soviet citizens working in the Kabul government ministries and on the Fraternal Air programme. A different world behind these perimeter wire-topped walls. A world of women gossiping about home in faraway Kiev or Gorki or Volgograd or Saratov, of brightly dressed and blond haired children falling from slides and climbing into swing seats . . .

A world where his shirt would be slid from his chest, his trousers from his thighs. A world of warmth, and a bottle of beer, and a sausage sandwich, and the sweet taste of a woman. And the waking in the arms, against the body of a woman in the second floor flat of the Mikroyan residential complex.

Medev smiled at the children who ran past him. He backed away to allow a girl with a bag full of shopping from the Commissariat to go up the stairs of the building ahead of him. Second floor, he could have sleep-walked to that door.

As he pressed the bell button, he was grinning to himself.

He had never seen the man who stood in the door.

A thin, gaunt, tanned man. An unclipped beard, bleached sparse hair on the crown of his head, a yellow athlete's vest, a pair of baggy fawn trousers gathered at the waist by a thin belt.

The grin fled from the face of Major Pyotr Medev.

The man in the doorway looked at him, waited on him.

Medev felt the chill damp under the peak of his cap. He saw the agronomist's wife at the back of the small hallway. He saw the unbuttoned fall of her blouse. He saw the shrug of her shoulders. He saw the brooch of blue stone pinned to the breast of her blouse.

The bastard was home from his ditch in Kandahar.

'I'm sorry, stupid of me, I must have come to the wrong door.' Medev ducked his head, the gesture of casual apology. The door was closed in his face. He turned swiftly away and went down the tile steps of the staircase.

'When is Major Medev back?'

'He only went this morning . . .'

'I know when he went, when is he back?'

'We received a message from Kabul Movements that he was trying to get on a flight back this evening, but we heard

308

later there was no available flight. Normally he stays overnight, I don't know why he wanted to come back.'

'Goddamit, Rostov,' bellowed the Frontal Aviation commander. 'Cut out all the background crap and just tell me
when he is due here.'

'Tomorrow afternoon, sir, fourteen hundred . . .'

'Reconnaissance reports a considerable column moving
through area Delta. Intelligence believe this column will
have reached your Major's valley by tomorrow morning.'

'What do you want me to do, sir?'

'Attack it . . . what else, serve it with tea?'

'Can this not wait for Major Medev's return?'

'It cannot wait. There will be another Antonov flight at
first light. The decision will then be made on the tasking of
Eight Nine Two . . . I am assuming Major Medev would not
wish another squadron to fly into area Delta . . .'

'Major Medev would prefer that the pilots familiar with
area Delta should continue to fly there.'

'Your pilots should be ready to fly as soon as the report is
evaluated.'

Rostov made his way out of the offices. Shit, the squadron
to fly and Medev in Kabul. Medev had told him of the
agronomist's wife and her flat in the Mikroyan, told him
when they were drunk together. And the message had come
through that Medev had tried to get back that evening. Must
be her period, or the clap . . . and Medev would be foul-
tempered if he was back and found the squadron airborne.

Rostov went to the mess to find Vladdy. Only a few days
ago he would have been looking for Nikolai, or Viktor, or
Alexei, or Sergei. But Nikolai and Viktor and Alexei and
Sergei had all gone back to the Motherland, in the bodybags.
And after what the bastard Vladdy had done to him in the
mess, done to his pyjamas, to his dignity, he didn't mind
hoping that if there had to be another bodybag it would be
Vladdy's.

21

Medev had gone to his billet angry and drunk. He blamed it on the return of the agronomist from Kandahar. He had been unable to sleep. He had heard every shout from the sergeant of the perimeter guard as he livened up his sentries. Three times he had heard the rattle of automatic fire, and an accompanying thud of detonating hand grenades as the war came closer to the centre of the capital city.

He cut himself when he shaved because he had brought a new razor to Kabul and the water in the basin tap was cold.

He tried to telephone the Jalalabad base. He was told there were no lines. He shouted that it was a matter of operational necessity for him to speak to the base. He was told that he should make the call on a tactical military exchange if it were a matter of operational necessity. From the billet it was not possible to make the connection, later perhaps.

He took the half hourly shuttle bus to the airfield.

At the airfield he had four hours to wait.

It was his hope that there might be a helicopter or an aircraft seat for an early lift to Jalalabad. The Sukhois were taking off for the first of the day's bombing runs against the Panjshir. Helicopters were warming their engines for the start of operations against the bandits dug into the mountain range to the south of the capital. He saw a file of men, clutching their civilian suitcases, walking to the steps set against the fuselage of an Aeroflot four-engined Ilyushin Il-76. Going home, lucky bastards. He saw another Ilyushin,

310

a turbo-prop and smaller, taxiing across the concrete waste-
land towards a knot of parked ambulances away in the far
distance, so that the loading of the casualties would not
attract attention. Most of the wounded went to Dushanbe, in
Tajikstan. If you lasted through the field hospitals in Afghanistan then you'd last through anything. If you lasted through
Casualty Reception at Dunshanbe, then you'd been visited
by a miracle and you deserved a goddam medal, that's what
Medev's pilots said. He saw a General jump down from a
small Mi-2 transport helicopter, a swaggering little man with
a webbing holster at his waist and a lanyard round his neck,
and the camouflage tunic of the Airborne, and a scurrying
aide at his heels. Come to tell them at the Taj Beg that the
war's won? Go and tell the poor bastards who are waiting for
a lift to Dushanbe that the war's won, they'd be happy to
know that. Tell them it's all been worthwhile. Tell them
there's nothing personal in their being flown out of a quiet
airfield corner so they won't be seen by all the others, the
whole and the healthy who've still got it coming.

He had been allocated a seat at 13.00 hours.

The corporal on the Movements desk didn't give a fuck
for a major in a hurry if that major had no priority order to
travel. What couldn't wait until a 14.00 landing at Jalalabad?

One bastard . . .

Hey, wait a minute, Pyotr Medev, that one bastard's
dead. Vladdy said that one bastard was dead.

The caravan had come into the valley in the last hours of
darkness.

They would rest under the trees and the scrub bushes,
amongst the rocks, until the middle of the day. They would
be gone by the early afternoon. The pack animals were taken
to the river bed where the rains had made a small stream of
clear water. The mules and horses would not be unloaded
while they drank and while they scavenged for fodder. There

311

were more than three hundred men accompanying the caravan, and not a woman amongst them. For some the uniform of the *mujahidin* was the traditional Tajik tribal costume, the flowing trousers, the tented shirts, the loose wound turbans. For some it was the dress of Nuristan, tighter grey blue trousers, puttee-bound shins, closer shirts, the rolled rim of the cap of the district. For some it was the dress of the modern fighter, courtesy of the Soviet Union and the Afghan Army, khaki trousers, heavy serge military tunics, woollen jumpers issued to the enemy for winter service, the close skull-fitting helmets taken from the slaughtered drivers of ambushed APCs.

A sharp bright morning with the dawn frost winkled away by the sunlight.

Barney was a mile down the valley from the main body of men and caravan animals, and their fires, and Ahmad Khan and his lieutenants who took tea with the travellers. Where the valley side was steepest he had climbed five hundred feet to find for himself an eagle perch, a harrier's roost. The sound of radios carried from the valley's floor, popular songs from the Kabul government station, exhortations from the clandestine Resistance transmitter. He saw the movement of toy figures leading the horses and mules to a small river pool.

The launcher was on the rock beside him. Schumack was with Barney.

Down in the valley was Mia Fiori. Twice he had taken Schumack's spy glass and magnified the valley floor, but he could not find her. He had left her early in the morning, before the sun came. He had not seen her face when he had slipped from underneath the blanket that had covered them. She had been sleeping. He had bent low over her, and kissed her, kissed her between the eye and the ear. All through the night, Barney had held her close against his chest, held her tight in his sleep. In the middle of the night when the men who had come with the caravan had slept, and the men of Ahmad Khan had slept, and the pack animals were quiet, when the frost settled on their blanket, she had wriggled against him and pulled the tails of her blouse from her skirt waist and flicked her fingers amongst the buttons of her blouse and pulled it open, and Barney had felt the heat of her breasts and the warmth of her skin against the coarse cloth of his shirt. He had lain with her in his arms, sheltering her, and with her body warm against his, and they had slept. In the morning, when he had woken, he had groped in the darkness to where Schumack had slept and found the man awake and sitting hunched against the cold, and they had gone to their eyrie above the valley.

He might die that morning. And if he died on the eagle's eyrie, on the valley walls, then he wouldn't have the memory of her face with him, not her face of that morning.

'You have to take the first one that comes.'

Barney shook away the picture of yesterday's girl and looked at Schumack.

'The first is the most dangerous.'

For answer, Schumack gestured with his claw away down the valley to the south. Barney heard the soft sounds of an aircraft engine.

'If they come and they get in amongst that lot then all your crap game's wasted. The only reason for you to be here is to take out the first one.'

'Then we'll be smashed,' Barney said.

'There's a war going on here, hero man. You're not playing ball in the park.'

There was the growing whine of the Antonov reconnaissance aircraft.

'What's down there, that's what's needed . . .' Schumack was matter of fact. 'If they don't have what's on the mule packs and the horse packs, then they're stuffed and screwed. You couldn't sit up here and watch that. You couldn't watch

313

it happen while you're waiting for a safe shot. Christ, I couldn't . . . you couldn't.'

'The first one.'

'It's the way it is. There's no running from here, Captain Crispin, there's no fart face with gold scramble on his arm telling you to run . . .'

'Why did they light the fires?' Barney said bitterly.

'Because they don't care about dying . . . sounds crap and it's true. They're not afraid, like we are. If they cared about dying, do you think they'd still be going? We're soldiers. They're peasants, they're crap ignorant, and they don't care. Clever bastards like us, we care about getting zapped. We say, time to move out, time to run. They're not smart, and that's why they're staying the course. No smart arse takes on a hundred thousand Soviets and the gunships and the Sukhois, that's not for clever bastards . . . Got the message, Captain?'

'Loud and clear.'

He saw the Antonov bank into a turn. He heard the cough splutter as its engine throttled back.

Schumack grabbed at Barney's hand.

'I hope you make it with the woman,' Schumack whispered. 'Truly I hope you do.'

'We'll take the first bastard that comes,' Barney said.

Alexander Hawthorne, First Secretary of the Information Section, had driven through the night to reach Chitral.

Rossiter had hated the hanging around, the waiting within sight of the Dreamland Hotel. He hurried forward as soon as he saw the Corps Diplomatique plates on the land-rover and had intercepted the First Secretary as he still sat at the driving wheel. He must have seemed a scarecrow, and the diplomat had gawped at him. The heavy sacking bundle was handed over, a whisper of explanation that there was a letter enclosed, and Rossiter was gone. He had faded from Hawthorne's sight within a few moments, vanished into the daytime crowds of the Shahi Bazaar.

Hawthorne untied the bundle on the passenger seat behind him. Christ Almighty. Davies hadn't told him what he would be collecting, only that it was important to HMG. Bloody aircraft parts, the little bastard. Transporting aircraft parts across Pakistan, that was espionage in Alexander Hawthorne's book. Christ, the spook had a nerve . . .

The jumble of numeral patterns spilled onto the telex in Century House, the home of the Secret Intelligence Service that was the paymaster of Davies, the spook. A computer translated them into letters and words in a matter of seconds. One copy to the Assistant Secretary, Near East Desk. One copy for file. One copy for the immediate attention of the Director General. One copy to be couriered to the Ministry of Defence, eyes only to Brigadier Fotheringay.

'It will bloody well not happen again,' the Assistant Secretary bellowed at the astonished young man just down from Jesus, Cambridge. 'Never again will I have those army louts lumbering all over our parish, using us as bloody errand boys.'

'But we've the electronics of a Hind coming in, sir. Isn't that rather special?'

'Wrong. We've *not* got the electronics of a Hind coming in. MOD's got it . . . and that's insufferable.'

He'd soon learn, the innocent little pest, because if he didn't he'd have his arse kicked right down the stairs of Century House and half way across the bloody Thames.

Take off at noon.

Rostov had made a feeble attempt to delay the mission

315

into area Delta. He had been overruled by the Frontal Aviation commander. His caution had been sneered at by the pilots.

Take off at noon. They would be coming back as Major Medev landed from Kabul. The Frontal Aviation commander had insisted that there was no reason for a delay. Through Vladdy, the senior pilot, the fliers made it known that they wanted to get into the valley and get some damage done to the bastard caravan sitting on its arse there.

Rostov gave the pre-flight briefing. There had been no apologies for the mess night from the pilots, and no one referred to it.

Met reports were good. High cloud ceiling. Light west south west winds of 10 knots. Minimum of 20 kilometres visibility. Reconnaissance reported the bandit concentration as scattered, but in the open. He gave the map co-ordinates. Vladdy to lead. Two pairs following at 1000 metre intervals. Very flares to be used at all times . . .

'What for?' Vladdy.

'Because that is the procedure laid down by Major Medev for flying over area Delta . . .' the brittle response from Rostov, '. . . and not rescinded.'

'That was when we were up against a missile.'

'You have no confirmation of the kill.'

'You weren't there, Captain Rostov, you don't know what confirmation I had. If you'd been there, you wouldn't be talking about flares . . . I want to go in fast and low . . . 20, 30 metres. I want to catch them while they're still playing with themselves. I don't want to be stooging and lobbing out flares, telegraphing we're coming . . .'

'The Antonov will have telegraphed your coming.'

'You want to come with us?' Vladdy smirked at him. He heard the laughter of the pilots around him. He saw Rostov's blush.

'I shall be in Operations, with the Frontal Aviation commander.'

Rostov hated the arrogant bastards. Someone had to be on the ground, in support of them. His head was down as he hurried through the rest of the briefing. He gave the radio frequencies over which the pilots could talk to the Antonov above. He gave the fuel loads and the weapon loads that would be carried. Without looking into their faces he wished the pilots good luck and good hunting.

He hated every last one of them.

The Brigadier had waited for an hour outside the office of the Foreign Secretary.

The Foreign Secretary was in conference, had been all morning. There would be a short break in his appointments at eleven o'clock.

The Personal Private Secretary brought the Brigadier a cup of coffee and a plate of biscuits.

There was a rising murmur of voices approaching the door of the Foreign Secretary's secretary's office, the door opening, a stenographer flashing a high skirt at the Ambassador of a Gulf state as she made way for his exit, aides tripping out in his wake. The PPS went forward to catch the ear of his master and gestured back through the open door to the Brigadier. He was waved forward, into the sanctum. He waited for the door to close behind him.

'The news from Pakistan is extraordinarily good, Foreign Secretary.'

'You mean, we've got our man out?'

'On tomorrow morning's Tristar out of Rawalpindi, in the Diplomatic Bag, will be the major parts of the electronics equipment of the Hind Mi-24E gunship helicopter. That is the extraordinarily good news. It's going to require a big bag, a really large one. In addition we have cockpit photographs, notes written by our man, and also the pilot's manuals.'

317

'What about the man?'

'As to that, Foreign Secretary, there is something I would like to say. My department would wish to put on record our very great appreciation of the freedom you have given us in this exercise. If I might be so bold, very few of your predecessors would have permitted an operation such as this. In the Intelligence field we have scored splendidly.'

'Brigadier, kindly come to heel and tell me about the man.'

'He's delivered, sir. He's broken every rule in the book but he's delivered. You could say he's saved his neck, and that of his controller. It's been a first class coup.'

'Will you give me an answer to a simple question. What has happened to the man?'

'He's a peculiar fellow, that's the least I can say about him. He's taken up residence in a valley in Laghman province. Our last reliable information reported he'd shot down four helicopters.'

'Four?'

'It is apparently his intention to use up all the missiles he travelled with. That'll go against him but, by delivering, Captain Crispin has gone a long way to saving his neck.'

'If I believed that Captain Crispin were more at risk from you than from the Soviet armed forces, I'd . . . I'd bust you right out of the army. No, by God, I wouldn't. I'd bust you to Lance Corporal and then I'd stamp on you, fingers, throat and all.'

The Brigadier smiled a cold little smile. 'It was fortunate that on this one occasion your fantasies and our requirements were able to coincide.'

'You don't give a damn about our man,' the Foreign Secretary's voice rose to an angry snarl. 'You don't give a damn whether he comes out or not.'

'Quite wrong, Foreign Secretary. If he doesn't come out I care hugely. I care that if he doesn't come out, he's dead and not captured. If you can get these wild notions of scooping the pot from the Americans out of your head, you should also care he's not captured. If he's captured, it's not just his neck on the block, I fancy it's yours as well.'

'Get out, please. Get out this instant.'

'Good day, Foreign Secretary.'

The Brigadier walked smartly from the room.

He had tried to reach the Jalalabad base again by telephone, but had been unsuccessful. Medev succumbed to more coffee and some sandwiches of lettuce and tomato, and to conversation with a Mechanised Infantry major. Worse than the coffee and the sandwich was the tedium of the major's war stories from Mazar-i-Sharif. The coffee he could take, and the sandwiches when he poured salt into them, but the war stories of another of the converts to ultimate victory wounded him.

'I tell you, Major Medev – that's your name, yes? – we have these shit pushers on the run. If we hold the pressure on them for this winter, then it's my belief they'll start to disintegrate. They're just bandits you know, extortionists. From what I've seen we've brought great benefits to this country through Soviet generosity. We've brought schools, roads, education and literacy, and now I think we have a military stability that we can build on to go forward for the final elimination of these gangs . . .'

'Have you seen action here?'

'Not actual action. At Mazar-i-Sharif I was with Sixteen Motor Division headquarters. I expect I'll see action when I'm at Jalalabad. I often say that Afghanistan is an incredible opportunity for the younger Soviet officer to learn the realities of war, a very useful training ground. But you would know that better than I, Major Medev. You must have learned considerably about combat flying in the months you've served here. You'll be richer . . .'

'We have all learned something.'

Medev stood up.

He dropped his coffee beaker into a rubbish bin and walked away.

He looked at the wall clock. He lit another cigarette. He wanted only to be back in Jalalabad. He looked back at the major of Mechanised Infantry. Go walk in area Delta, you bastard, and you'll find out everything you ever wanted to know.

Barney at peace. Barney waiting and staring down to the southern bend of the valley.

Schumack leaned his shoulder against Barney's back, silent and brooding away the hours.

Beneath them were the distant sounds of the caravan making ready its departure up the side valley to the west.

Thoughts of the woman that he loved, thoughts of Maxie Schumack who was his companion in arms. Thoughts of the woman that he had found on a battlefield, thoughts of an old fighter who would never again turn his back. The woman who slept with the blood-warm breasts against his shirt, the man who sat with the automatic rifle beside him to protect his back. All that he valued now breathed and lived in this valley, the woman who was a mile away, Schumack who was beside him.

The prospect of death no longer frightened him. Barney Crispin was at peace.

The Antonov was still patrolling wide circles over the valley. He rarely bothered to look up at it. The launcher was beside him under his blanket. He smelt his own body and wondered how the woman could have slept against him. He ran his fingers through the tangle of his hair. He rubbed at the caked mud on his beard. He felt the lice scabs on his chest.

He looked across the valley. He saw the grey rock face

and the fissure lines in the opposite cliff and the tiny flutter movement of a hawk, and the summit peaks and the snow slopes. He saw the scar of the river bed beneath him, and the green of unused fields, the scrub of lost land, and the caravan forming columns.

Schumack took his arm and stabbed with his claw to the south.

One helicopter. Seen but not yet heard.

'The first one,' Schumack said.

The helicopter scudded over the valley floor. Coming fast, coming at more than a hundred kilometres an hour. Hugging the ribbon track of the river bed. A camouflaged shadow skimming towards Barney.

'Two pairs coming after, same height, same sort of speed.'

Barney was on his feet. He faced away from the helicopters, back up towards the north of the valley for the rear hemisphere firing.

'You've got the mother.'

'How have I got it?'

Schumack had his spy glass to his eye. He pressed against Barney's side.

'The mothers aren't using flares.'

'No flares?'

'Don't argue with the mothers, they've fired no flares.'

He could not comprehend why there were no flares.

It would be a down shot, down through the rotors, it would be a five hundred metres shot, it would be a shot against which the baffles of the engine exhaust would be helpless.

'Battery coolant, switch it.' Schumack's calm nasal instruction.

He heard the first whine of the engagement of the battery coolant. The freezing of the argon gas around the missile's seeker of infra-red optics. He heard the whine and his mind was blank except for the words he had read far back in the manual . . . IR seeker optics and sensor element plus head-coil and cryostat cooling element mounted inside a sealed atmosphere of dry hydrogen . . . He heard the thrust of the helicopter engines . . . Seeker operates on conical scan reticle principle . . . Barney swung to face the valley wall opposite him . . . Bugger the seeker optics and sensor element . . . The hammer din of the rotors in his ears . . . Screw the conical scan reticle principle . . . Steady on his feet, and the launcher was steady on his shoulder. One hand tight on the grip stock, one hand steadying the launcher sight.

'Coming now . . .' Schumack shouting in Barney's ear, and his ear was flooded with the noises of the helicopter engines and the first crisp crackle of the machine gun fire.

He saw the helicopter.

The whine from the launcher cried in his ear. The sight found the engine exhaust, found the baffle. The whine piercing his ear, shrieking for action. He aimed high, he aimed ahead.

He fired.

It was the seventh Redeye missile he had fired in the valley. Still there was no anticipating the first burn flash, and the missile drawling out of the tube, the smoke wreath, then the brilliant explosion. The hot gale wind whipped over Barney as he ducked his head. The heat stung his eyes, seemed to singe at the beard on his jaws and cheeks. And the light was gone, careering away from him, winging for the helicopter.

He could not move.

He heard the voice of Schumack howling close to him. He watched the scrubbed pure light home on the dirt dull camouflage of the gunship.

A crashing impact.

It was the perfect shot. It was the shot down through the spinning circle of the rotor blades. A rotor blade slicing at the

322

tube of the missile and splintering in the fraction of a moment before the warhead detonated. It was the damage to the rotor blade that killed the helicopter, not the spread of the warhead's shrapnel around the baffle.

Barney surrendered to Schumack. They went down the cliff together in a small avalanche of stones and dirt dust.

Once Barney looked up, he saw the helicopter had risen, had struggled for altitude away from the valley floor. He saw the shuddering motion of the bird, as if a rotor blade was fractured. That was death, a broken rotor blade was the death of a helicopter. He plunged on down the valley's wall, onto the more gradual slope below, on towards the gaping mouth of the cave. He heard Schumack behind him. He carried the launcher with the spent tube in his hand, he had the last tube strapped to his back pack. He sprinted for the mouth of the cave. He heard the machine gun fire thrash closer to him. He heard the devil roar of the helicopter behind him. He saw the rock gouged in front of him. He dived for the cave mouth, fell rolling and tumbling into it.

On his stomach, panting great gulps of air, Barney saw the stricken helicopter come down. The big bird coming to rest. A gull flopping to a refuse tip. Across a quarter of a mile he heard the metal scrape tear as the undercarriage tore across the stone boulders.

A helicopter swarmed above him and past the entrance to the cave, and all of his vision was clouded by the dust storm of machine gun shells, and his ears sang with the whistle cry of the ricochets from the rocket splinters.

God . . . Oh God . . . where was Schumack . . .? Barney had run, and Barney had saved himself . . . where was Schumack?

The storm film cleared, and the valley appeared, and the rock rubble in front of him, and the rims of the cave mouth beside him, and he saw Schumack.

He saw the blood soaking the ripped trouser leg.

323

He saw Schumack using his rifle as a support stick, and saw the pain lined on his face.

He saw the helicopter's tracer reach down towards him and gather him into red streaks and lift him and throw him and destroy him.

He saw the death of the man for whom he had not waited.

Barney lay on his face and cried his tears into the stones at the mouth of the cave.

The pilot, Vladdy, ran from the helicopter. He ran as an automaton, because the terror of being fire-trapped over-whelmed him. If he had calculated his best hope, his one hope, he would have stayed beside the helicopter. But his mind was turned by fear. He ran towards the side of the valley.

He ran until he saw the movement in the rocks in front of him, the glimpse of a ducking turbaned head, the flash of a rifle muzzle, the flicker of a shadow between boulders.

He froze still.

He lifted his head, he filled his lungs, he screamed to the helicopters above. He screamed for their help, and his voice choked in terror. The single shots pecked close to him, around him.

The pilot, Vladdy, saw the helicopter approaching him. A brother flew alongside with the spits of fire pouring from the nose canopy machine gun. There was tracer rising towards the helicopters, the heavy green tracer of the DShKs . . . Vladdy knew those bastards . . . Who flies steady when the big tracer of the DShKs is coming up? . . . Please . . . please . . . you bastards, my brothers, fly steady. The gunner of the approaching helicopter had worked his way back through the pilot's cockpit, into the fuselage hold, ripped open the fuse-lage hatch. A thin rope ladder snaked down from the hatch, it brushed against the rock surface, it jumped towards Vladdy. Crying his thanks, he reached for the rope of the ladder. Close enough for him to see the heavy machine gun fire striking the belly of the helicopter and the canopies and the fuselage. Fly steady, you bastard, please . . . please . . . He grabbed for the rope. He caught it with his fingers, fastened on the light steel of the ladder's rungs, stumbled over a boulder and lost his hold. He was running after the rope ladder, groping behind it. He caught it again, snatched his raw fingers onto the steel rung. He felt the wrench in his arm sockets as he was lifted above the rocks, as his feet cannoned off a boulder. He swung wildly, desperately arching for a foothold, but he could not hold his grip.

Vladdy fell fifteen swinging feet into the rock-strewn ground.

Two helicopters made a run at him, fast and with their machine guns firing. They stripped the life from him as he lay oblivious of the pain from a broken shoulder, and cried for their help.

When they had killed the pilot, Vladdy, the helicopters strafed his big bird with rockets. The gunner had been told never to leave a downed helicopter, to wait for rescue. He died inside his nose canopy.

The helicopters rose, flinging their last vengeance at the caves in the valley walls, at the scattered caravan, and flew back to Jalalabad.

Major Medev landed at two o'clock.

As he came down the wheeled steps from the aircraft, Rostov was waiting for him. Medev saw the red rimmed eyes, heard the shocked quaver of the Captain's voice.

Medev followed Rostov's gesture. He looked across to the helicopter revetments. He saw the ground crew scrambling over four helicopters. He saw four.

For a moment Medev seemed to stumble, but he caught himself, and it was the briefest indiscretion. He looked Rostov in the eye.

'Tell me what happened . . .' Medev said calmly.

325

In the afternoon, after the sun had dipped behind a rain cloud and the valley lay in shadow, long after the caravan had disappeared up the side valley in the west, Barney walked from his cave.

He walked across the open ground in the middle of the valley carrying the body of Maxie Schumack. He had loaded the last of the missiles and tied the launcher to his back pack. On one shoulder was slung his own rifle, on the other was the American's Kalashnikov. Barney's forearms were out in front of him and made a cradle for Schumack's body.

He walked past the body of the pilot, and past the helicopter. He walked through an orchard where the trees' leaf cover had been stripped to the ground. He skirted an old 500 kg bomb crater.

He walked to where Ahmad Khan stood, his men in a half crescent around him.

He said nothing. He laid the body on the ground close to Ahmad Khan's feet, and put the rifle beside it. He knelt and kissed the white cheeks of Maxie Schumack. He wiped a blood stain from his hand onto his trousers.

Mia stood alone, apart from the men.

Barney took her hand lightly in his own. He saw the dribble of tears in the dust on her face.

'We will go in the morning. We have to go before the snow closes the passes,' he said.

22

While it was still dark, in the quiet of his quarters, Pyotr
Medev dressed.

For once he ignored the brief elasticated pants and the
cotton vest that were habitual to him. He pulled over his body
the combination thermal wool garment favoured by the pilots
when winter is coming, when they fly high in the mountains.
He selected a pair of heavy knit socks. In place of a starched
shirt, he took from a drawer the sweat top that carried on the
chest the crest of Eight Nine Two. He left on the hanger in the
wardrobe his uniform tunic top and the matching trousers
with the blue piping on the seam line, he struggled into his
one-piece flying suit and pulled the zipper from waist to neck.
From another drawer he lifted his flying cap. From the
bottom of the wardrobe he picked out his soft leather flying
boots, ponderous but lightweight, and dust covered. He blew
the dust from his boots, sat on his unmade bed to draw them
onto his feet. He felt a warmth and a sense of comfort now
that he was dressed for flying. He looked around his room, it
did not concern him that he might not see the room again.
The room had been his home for a year. A small bare room
with little of ornament and less of decoration. An anonymous
room, and easy for a new man to slip into the bed of a flier
who had no need of it because a bodybag was taking him
home.

Before he left the room he reached out to the bedside
table and took from it the leather-cased photograph of his
wife. He took her photograph from behind the glass and held
it near to the light and close to his face, and saw the slight

smile on the lips and the careworn eyes and the blonde hair that had been prepared for the photographer. From the bedside table he took, also, the cellophane folder that contained his military identity card. He placed the photograph of his wife into the folder, covering the card.

He went to the door, he switched off the light, he closed the door quietly behind him. He walked away down the corridor.

The memories of the previous evening swam over him as he walked the bright strip-light length of the corridor.

Start at the beginning, start with Rostov, quivering in jelly nerves, telling the story of the loss of the pilot's, Vladdy's, helicopter.

Move on from the beginning to the grounding of the squadron, what remained of it, on the express and personal order of the Frontal Aviation commander.

Continue the road, listening to the report of the Antonov's spotter who said that a large caravan had moved immediately after the airborne attack from the valley and high into the mountains to the west.

Finish at the end, finish with the scathing anger of the Frontal Aviation commander and Pyotr Medev face to face across the desk of the commander's office.

'. . . The squadron is grounded because it has proved unable to carry out the duties assigned to it, because it has repeatedly provided false information on the capabilities of the enemy . . . I will not stand aside and see young pilots butchered for a piece of rock that means little to the strategy of our operations. The caravan will be interdicted from Kabul when it is further down the line, out of our responsibility. For fuck's sake, Medev, don't you understand anything, your squadron has been slaughtered, it's barely operational . . . I'll tell you what I'm going to do, I am relieving you of your command and I don't give a shit whether you like it or you don't like it. At the end of the week you're going home.

Get out of this office, Medev, before you say things that will have a permanent effect on your record, on your career . . . The valley is not worth the loss of another helicopter, certainly not worth the loss of another pilot . . .'

Seven doors down, on the left side of the corridor, was the room of Captain Rostov. Medev went inside without the courtesy of a preliminary knock. He switched on the light. Rostov was sitting up in bed, blinking at the ceiling light. He wore florid red and orange and blue pyjamas. Without speaking, Medev went to the wardrobe, rifled out of it a winter anorak with synthetic fur lining and a roll neck sweater, and the severely polished boots, and thick socks and wet weather trouser overalls. He threw the clothes and the boots onto Rostov's bed, across his legs. He thought that if Rostov had protested he would have hit him, bloodied his mouth. He saw the tin of talcum beside Rostov's basin, and the bottle of after-shave lotion, and the canister of underarm deodorant spray.

'Five minutes, in the operations room . . .' Medev said.

Medev went out of the sleeping quarters building, into the small hours' darkness. He saw the bright perimeter lights. He saw a cruising jeep of MilPol. He saw the tanks, nose down, behind their bulldozed earthworks. He saw the helicopters in their revetments with the gaping spaces between them.

'What area do you want?' The question from the corporal in the Meteorological section.

'The north of Laghman province, area Delta.'

He scribbled down into his notebook the information he was given. Wind speeds were strong, temperature was dropping, forecast of rain showers in the valleys and snow falls on the mountains.

He went to the operations room. Rostov stood there, awkward and comical in his overall trousers and anorak, he wore a fur hat on his head, he was wiping the condensation from his spectacles. Medev ignored him.

329

'XJ LIMA, what state?' He asked the question of the night operations clerk.

'Fuelled and armed.'

Medev gestured with his head for Rostov to follow. Medev walked ahead dissuading conversation. Twice Rostov had managed to reach his shoulder, twice he had seen the bleak face of the Major, and had dropped back. They went to the munitions depot. Medev shook some life into a sleeping man, half spinning him from his chair.

'I want distress flares and a Very launcher pistol.'

'They come in tens, the flares, packs of ten.'

'Ten packs.'

They carried the flares between them, and the Very pistol, to the helicopter revetments. The courage to ask came slowly to Rostov. It came finally.

'Where are we going?' A timid voice.

'To find him.' A cold and grudging reply.

'But the squadron's grounded . . .'

'Then I am disobeying the order, and regretfully you will be a party to that disobedience.'

'What am I to do, I'm not a flier . . .' Fear in Rostov, but the greater fear was of challenging his major.

'You'll fire the flares.'

'Then there is no one for the machine gun.'

'The rockets will be sufficient.'

Rostov thought he saw a madness in Medev's eyes. He did not possess the courage to refuse and walk away.

Medev looked up at the gunship, XJ LIMA. He saw the bruises in the paintwork from previous ground fire hits. He saw the smears on the cockpit canopy where bullets had been deflected. He hunted one man. He was sorry he had to take Rostov, but without flares the combat was unequal. It should have been Medev alone against this one man, but Rostov did not outweigh the balance, Rostov equalled the scales. He saw in his mind the vague outline shape of a man who carried a missile launcher on his shoulder, the vague outline shape from a magnified photograph.

It was his only thought as he opened the cockpit hatch of the helicopter XJ LIMA.

They shook Barney's hand with a limp correctness, as if they had seen such a gesture of formality on an old American film and regarded it as the proper usage of manners. He walked down the line of the *mujahidin* of Ahmad Khan and took each hand that was outstretched and murmured a word of farewell. Behind the men were piled their baggage pieces that they would soon load on their backs and carry away. He would go north and east towards the passes, they would go south down the length of the valley. By the time that the snows came to the valley's floor, they would have moved to the villages at the mouth of the valley where they could survive the winter. The destruction of five helicopters in their valley had won for Barney no display of overt affection. He wondered if, when they came back to the valley in the spring and they found the helicopter wreckage that had been snow-covered and was now revealed again, whether then they would remember him.

He came to where Ahmad Khan stood, a little distanced from the line of his men. Close to Ahmad Khan was the cairn of stones that marked the resting place of Maxie Schumack . . . New Yorker far from home, veteran of Khe Sanh and Kabul and Desert One and buried where there's no running from, thanks for the memory, kiddo, thanks for the memory of the humble grave of a mighty man . . . Barney shook the hand of Ahmad Khan.

The mocking sweet smile of Ahmad Khan. 'Did you achieve in our valley what you came to achieve? Or are you like all the foreigners that have come to Afghanistan? Perhaps you have stamped your foot on rock. Perhaps you have left no imprint.'

Barney looked into the cavern-brown eyes of the school-teacher. He saw what he believed was a nobility. He saw the clear gaze of the eyes, he saw their certainty.

'I have learned something that is my own. Perhaps that is my achievement . . . Goodbye, Ahmad Khan.'

'Goodbye, Barney Crispin.'

He walked away from Ahmad Khan, away from Maxie Schumack's grave, away from the line of men.

When he reached Mia Fiori he took her hand.

They went together, away along the dirt path in the slow growing light of the morning. The rifle hung from Barney's shoulder and the Redeye launcher with the last of the missile tubes rested beside his neck. As they walked Mia Fiori twice looked back, turned her head to stare behind her into the depths of the valley.

Barney never looked back, he had said in his arrogance that he would never look back on the valley where he had killed five helicopters.

He set a fierce hard speed up the water gullies of the side valley. It was as if his sole goal was to be clear of the valley and the memories of the valley. She did not complain, she did not ask him to be allowed to rest or to drink from the water that he carried. They climbed towards the snow peaks at the side of the valley, they scrambled on the rocks and the smooth stones where the first ice sheen had formed. When he heard her breath behind him, sagging, panting, he took her hand tight in his own and dragged her after him. In his mind were the instructions that Ahmad Khan had given him for the route to the passes that would take him to Pakistan.

He never looked back. When they had reached the roof of the valley, when they had flopped gasping for the rare air, he did not turn to look back and down into the valley, to search for one last time to find the wreckage specks of the helicopters he had killed.

332

'Did you find nothing there that you valued?'

For answer he reached to her and took her head in his hands and kissed the wetness of the rain and snow spray from her lips, and buried his head against her, and held her head and kissed her again.

'Did you find nothing else that you valued?'

He stood up, he took her hand tight in his own. He saw ahead of him the scape of the plateau stretching eastwards between the mountain summits. He felt the winds buffet against him, felt her stagger against the blast force of the wind. He held her hand, he led her forward onto the plateau where snow patches had formed, away from the valley.

Rossiter awoke. He rubbed at his face, cleared the sleep haze from his eyes. He looked at the mattress across the floor from him. The boy had not come back in the night. It was the second night since he had found the boy gone. He had given the little bugger food and water, even some rupees, and that was the thanks. The creature had scarpered when Rossiter had taken the bundle down to the Dreamland. Left nothing of an explanation. In your pocket and dependent one moment, gone the next and leaving you to whistle for a reason. The boy had been allowed to edge too close to Barney Crispin, that was Howard Rossiter's opinion, that's what made him so bloody cocky. Only a bed of bloody nails for your pains when these people were allowed to edge too close.

He had little to look forward to. Another day alone in the bungalow. At dusk he would go into Chitral for his shopping and the contact with the Night Manager of the Dreamland. It was raining against the windows above his mattress.

He wondered when Barney Crispin would come, if he would come . . . He felt a greater sense of despair than he had known before. A piss wet day waited for him, and not even the wretched boy to talk with. And he must wait. That

333

was the fate of Howard Rossiter and his kind, to sit with their hands under their arses and to wait.

He flew due north. He climbed to clear the mountains ahead of him. With his tanks fully loaded he possessed a flying range of 475 kilometres. He would not waste fuel by skirting the direct route to area Delta and flying the winding river beds. The calculations he made on his knee told him that he would have an hour over the valley, an hour to find his one man.

The wind came from the north, came into the teeth of the helicopter's flight path. One hand hard on the stick to hold the big bird stable, with his wrist wrenched as the power of the gusts caught at the airframe and beat on the bulk of the cockpit canopy and the machine gun bubble. Rostov would be sick, sick as a pig dog in the big hold behind the pilot's cockpit. He'd be strapped down in a webbing seat, puking his guts and shouting that he didn't volunteer to come, and no bastard hearing him. With his free hand Medev traced clear pencil lines on the map, directed himself to the place where the contour lines ran in tandem rails, where the valley was overstamped 'area Delta'.

The static burst in his ears, then the distort call of the radio.

'. . . XJ LIMA come in. XJ LIMA come in. XJ LIMA come in . . .'

A quiet mirthless smile on Medev's face.

'XJ LIMA.'

'. . . Medev, this is the Frontal Aviation commander, Jalalabad base. You have disobeyed an instruction. You are in violation of orders. You are to return to your base immediately . . .'

Stupid fart. He'd have the Political Officer standing behind him with his book and pencil ready, ready for the Court Martial evidence. Now the shit was spinning he'd have

334

brought in the Political Officer, and put out the signals orderlies and the clerks. Wouldn't want them to hear the Frontal Aviation commander given two fingers over the radio set.

'You know my destination, you know the range of the helicopter. From that you will know when I am returning.'

A hollow chuckle in Medev's mouth. His fingers slipped down, flicked off the radio switch.

One man, one man only had dragged him to this flagrant breach of orders. High above the mountain peaks, sometimes blinded in cloud, sometimes seeing the snake river lines beneath him, he gave up the logical and consequential thoughts that on any other day and in any other place would have dominated him. Alone in the cockpit of the big bird, alone behind the wind-beaten canopy, he never doubted that he would find the one man, the one man only.

It was a bare landscape. A landscape of small rock and broken gravel and stunted weed. No trees and no scrub bushes had survived the age old ferocity of the wind, and no great rocks here.

They went fast onto the plateau.

Because there was no cover, Barney pushed their pace. She was strong, Mia Fiori. He was not a man who willingly praised others. He would shout her praises, because he loved her, because she was strong, because she did not fight the pace he set.

He saw no hiding place on the plateau. He had no way of knowing at what altitude they walked. He knew they would be close to the altitude ceiling of the Mi-24, he had no way of knowing whether this plateau was above or below the helicopter's ceiling. It was hard to breathe on the plateau, the breathing was like the punching of a sponge. He struggled to win the flow of air down into his lungs. He wondered how Mia

Fiori could manage. He was a shield for her body against the wind.

It was the ceiling of the world, the roof of the hemisphere. Around the plateau were the great mountains, the chimney stacks of the roof. The Hindu Kush and the Karakorams and the Himalayas were the mountain ranges to the west and the north and the east.

He thought that he had never loved a woman before in the way that he loved Mia Fiori.

The winds struck him, staggered him as he dropped his shoulder to take the charge of the gale winds. There had been girls at home, girls in the back of his car, girls on their parents' sofa, girls to escort to the Regiment's cocktail parties, girls to take to the Aqua Club under the Qurm Heights in Oman. There had never been a woman who was widowed, a woman who took her holiday in the mountain ranges of Afghanistan, a woman who could climb without protest and rest up the side gullies of a battlefield valley. There had never been a woman like Mia Fiori.

All the time that they walked he held tight on her hand, and she was close behind his back, and the horizon for her eyes would be his back pack and his slung rifle and the Redeye missile launcher low on his shoulder.

They could follow the path. The path was tramped with hoof and sandal prints. Piebald with snow, the path was clear for them to see, curving into the emptiness of the plateau.

Barney shouted at the wind gusts.

'I love you, Mia Fiori.'

The answering shout, fleeing away from his ears on the wind, a smaller voice.

'I love you, Barney Crispin.'

'There has to be something for us, beyond this path.'

'There will be something.' Fierce and vibrant and sure.

Barney's head was ducked onto his chest, his chin hugged his throat, the winds whipped his cap and his hair strands.

'Before I came here I had nothing.'

'I, too, I had nothing.'

'Together we will make something, together we will never be alone.'

'After the place we have been, I think it is a crime to be happy . . .'

'Only for ourselves have we achieved anything.'

'If we have made ourselves happy is that sufficient achievement?'

'Mia Fiori, I love you, and I am happy, and I do not know the answer.'

He felt the strong grip of her fingers in his. He felt the brush of her leg against him as his stride faltered in the face of the gale gusts. He felt the wet in his boots and the dirt in the crevices of his body and the lice scabs on the flanks of his chest.

On across the plateau. On away from the valley. He was true to his promise, never to look back, never to turn and look back at the roofs of the far walls of the valley.

He flew up the valley fast and low. A speed of a hundred kilometres, an altitude of fifty metres. He flew the pattern of a coil, a coil of wire that has been released and is now spread out, so that the view of the baffles on the engine exhaust vents would always be minimised. The pattern was wasteful on fuel. He had saved the tanks while coming over the mountains, flying the direct route, now he turned the coin and was extravagant with his fuel. Over the radio he talked softly, calmly to Rostov. A pattern of flying was established, a pattern also of firing the Very flares from the fuselage hatch. He had Rostov in the hatchway secured by a hold strap to his waist. On each circle of the coil he saw the newest of the flares that Rostov had fired, falling prettily into a grey morning sky. He saw the deserted villages, he saw the wreckage of three helicopters. He came to Atinam where the bomb craters

337

were clearly formed in the flat stepped fields, where the devastation of the houses was complete, where there was the wreckage of two more helicopters. He had passed over the place where the pilot, Vladdy, lay broken in the rocks, he had passed over the place where the jackals hid before returning to feast on the body of the gunner who was trapped in the seat of the machine gun canopy.

The man would know, the man would understand. Medev believed that if his man, his one man only, was in the valley, that he would stand and present himself and fire. When one helicopter came, one helicopter alone, to search out the valley then the man would know. He would understand that this was the challenge of single-handed combat. Medev had come without the support of the Antonov reconnaissance aircraft and without the gunships flying behind him. Pyotr Medev believed that if the man were on the valley floor or on the valley walls that he would stand and take his chance and back his skill against the helicopter and the flares.

He was sick in disappointment as he cruised in a loop over Atinam.

Where was the bastard? Come out, you bastard . . .

He saw the rubbish heap where the body of the pilot, Alexei, had been discarded. He saw the scar marks where the rockets had taken the helicopter of the pilot, Sergei, close to the river trickle . . . come out, you bastard . . . he heard in his headset the plea of Rostov that enough was enough, that the search was unsuccessful . . . He climbed to three hundred metres.

When he went back, south down the valley, he abandoned the circle coil pattern. He flew straight, over the river line with Rostov blasting the flares forward and above, and all the time he nudged the stick right and left so that the helicopter's motion was that of a pitching boat in a cross swell. The flares guarded his upper hemisphere, the regular fast tilt of the undercarriage would prevent a clear sight of the engine exhaust vents needed by a missile marksman.

Come out, you bastard.

Not a shot was fired at him. He gazed until his eyes ached down into the shadow gullies and the ravines and the deserted villages and the autumn orchards. He saw a single shepherd who sat proud on a rock beneath him near to a grazing herd. He saw dogs that ran wild. He came to the southern end of the valley.

Rostov yelled into Medev's headset.

'You've done enough, Major . . . You don't have to do any more . . .'

'Keep the flares going.'

He banked the helicopter, he turned north again. He pulled the stick back to the warmth of his groin, flew the helicopter up and up and up towards the roof of the valley.

'He is too much of a coward to show himself.'

'The man who has killed five pilots, five helicopters, he is not a coward.'

The winds bundled against them, the helicopter sagged in the thin air, dropped and fell, yawed back to its station. As if a sledgehammer beat against the walls and canopy of his cockpit.

'They'll flay us when we get back.'

'If you don't keep the flares going, you won't get back . . . From where did he kill Viktor? From the top of the valley . . . keep the flares going.'

And Rostov had sunk back to silence. A flare of brilliant green arched up forward of his vision. He was above the valley and he nudged the helicopter away from the chisel cut below and took a course on the east side of the valley and a kilometre from the cliff edge. Again he flew north. With his left hand he hung to the stick, feeling the pull strength of the winds, with his right hand he made the pencil calculations of speed and minutes and fuel capacity and range from the north end of the valley back to the music at Jalalabad. It was a chance. At this altitude, in this gale wind, the engines gulped the fuel. He had not flown that morning from the base at Jalalabad to ignore any chance. He flew one hundred metres over the bare, weather-savaged ground that bordered the valley's cliff walls.

Another flare burst in a cascade of yellow light ahead of him. So tired, his eyes. So tired, the wrist that held the flying stick. Another flare, and another . . . and the fuel gauge needle sliding on the dial, and the ache in his eyes and the pain in his wrist.

Rostov saw them, Rostov made the sighting.

A shrill voice in Medev's ear.

'Starboard, out there, two of them . . .'

The helicopter swung right, banked, hovered. In front of Medev was a wide plateau reaching to a mountain break. His gaze swept the smoothed flat surface. A rain squall, snow flurry, splashed on the screen of his canopy. He snapped down with his finger onto the wiper switch. The arm passed over the screen, cleaned it. He saw them. He saw the outline of the missile. They were in the open, past low cloud, short of low cloud. He had wanted a battle, and they were without cover. He flew the helicopter forward, low down over the floor of the plateau.

'Listen very carefully to me, Rostov, no flares until I say, nothing until I say . . .'

He estimated they were a little more than 3500 metres ahead of him, and they had no place to hide from his rockets, not while they were short of the low cloud belt that was ahead of them, across their path.

Only the sounds of the wind and the strike of their footfall on the stones and the pounding of their breathing.

He felt the grip of her fingers tighten. He felt the nails of her fingers cut into his hand. She stopped, he pulled. She had stopped, she would not move.

'We can't rest, we can't stop . . .'

340

Again Barney pulled at her. His eyes were watering from the wind's cold. He saw ahead of him a tooth gap in the mountains, the end of the plateau.

As if she were anchored she took the force of his pull. He turned to her. Her arm was outstretched and pointing back along their trail. There was despair, there was an agony. He followed her arm, he wiped his eyes.

For Barney there was a first instinctive moment for preservation. His head spun, fast, the full cycle. He saw the expanse of the plateau, he saw the shallow fall of the sides of the plateau. There was nowhere to run. He had no cover. It was a knife thrust in his side. There was no place of safety from the helicopter. The wind purged his back, stumbled him a yard forward and into Mia Fiori . . . He had thought he had achieved something, he had achieved nothing . . . He had achieved a place on a killing ground of open plateau, without cover, without the possibility of defence.

The helicopter hovered a kilometre from Barney and Mia Fiori. It was low and he could see the dust arc under its belly. It had no need to advance and to be hazarded. He saw the dim shape of the rocket pods under the stub wings. Mia Fiori clung to him.

'What are you going to do?'

'He is different to all of the others. He knows I can do nothing.'

'You have to do something.'

'To fire I must see the engine exhaust vents, I can't see them.'

'Then we are going to die here, you have to do something . . .'

What was the point of a gesture?

But taking the Redeye into Afghanistan had been a gesture . . . killing the helicopters in the valley had been a gesture . . . and the support of Howard Rossiter had been a gesture . . . and the journey of Gul Bahdur who had walked

341

back with the launcher to Peshawar after thirteen men had died, that had been a gesture.

He prised Mia Fiori from his arm. He set the Redeye on his shoulder. He aimed a little above the helicopter. He waited for the flash spurts of the rockets. He saw the helicopter hovering above the dirt cloud. It was only a bastard gesture.

Why doesn't he fire his rockets, why doesn't he finish it?

He engaged the battery coolant. A low whine in his ear. Just the low whine because there was no target.

Barney fired the Redeye.

The last firing of eight Redeyes. No longer fire and forget. No longer the running stampede in the moment after the second flash flame of ignition. Nowhere to run, nothing to forget. For a fraction of time the missile seemed to run true to its aim, then it careered away to the left, a joking ball of brilliance that climbed and then fell and then curved in a death throe, that died on the hard stone scree of the plateau.

He dropped the launcher and the empty missile tube to the ground. He pressed Mia Fiori down to her knees. His rifle was at his shoulder . . . another gesture.

He saw the light spits as the first rockets were fired.

Nowhere to run to, nowhere to turn to.

The howl of the rockets hitting the ground around him. He stooped to cover Mia Fiori. He felt the scream of pain in his shoulder. He was tossed and moving and falling. He fell on his side, on his wound. He felt the blood wet on his hand when his fingers reached for his shoulder.

He heard the thunder of the rocket strike close to him.

She crouched now above him, she threw her blanket away from her shoulders. She wrenched for the buttons of her blouse. She was crying, croaking her tears. She heaved her blouse over her head.

She stood. She waved the blouse high above her. A grey white blouse, a grey white surrender flag.

342

He had been as far inside the hold of the helicopter as the strap clipped to his waist would permit. Rostov had knelt against the armoured bulkhead behind the pilot's cockpit from the moment he had seen the man standing with the missile launcher at his shoulder.

'What happened?' Rostov called plaintively into the face microphone of his helmet.

'While you were shitting yourself?' The dry quiet reply in Rostov's ears. 'He fired, he had no target, the missile destroyed itself.'

'Why did he fire?'

'To show he was not what you called him, not a coward.'

'I heard the rockets.'

'He is wounded, I think. I don't think he is dead. A woman is with him, she has surrendered for them.'

Excitement surging in Rostov. 'Well done, Major, well done . . . a prisoner, that's a triumph . . .'

'Perhaps, Captain Rostov.'

The pain was an open river in his shoulder. With his head bent he could see the rent hole in the blanket where the rocket shrapnel had passed, he could see the torn thread of his shirt, and the pink mush flesh of the wound.

The dust was in his eyes, the spurting grit was in his face and in the wound at his shoulder. Fifty yards from Barney the helicopter landed. Beside his face were Mia Fiori's sandals and bare ankles and skirt hem. He saw the bareness of her back, goosed by the wind, he saw her hair blowing on her shoulders, he saw the blouse high above her head and outstretched by the gale gusts. He lay on his rifle, he had no chance to manoeuvre, to aim it. In front of Barney the roar of the rotors sagged in a spent force. He saw the mightiness of the big bird, saw its power and weight and grandeur. Protruding from the fuselage hatch was a white owl face with pebble spectacles, rimmed by a flying helmet, and in front of the face

343

was an aimed Very pistol. His mind clouded and was confused because the helicopter carried no forward machine gunner, the gun compartment was empty. The helicopter sat squat on its wheels. The cockpit hatch opened, swung away, broke the lines of camouflage painting. He saw the pilot pull off his helmet and then appear in the hatch, and jump down and land loosely and easily on the ground. He carried no weapon.

A stocky blond man, with sharp military cut hair and a browned face, walking with the confidence that no threat existed. Barney saw the markings on the shoulder flags of the flying suit, saw the man's ranking.

The pilot walked briskly to Barney and the girl and when he had reached them he bent down and picked up the girl's blanket and smacked it with his hand to clear it of dust, and without speaking he held it up and then wrapped it over the shoulders of Mia Fiori, covering her. He smiled, a curt small and sad smile at her. He knelt beside Barney. He took Barney's right hand. Right hand on right hand. He gazed into Barney's face, as if by the meeting of their eyes he might find an answer.

'Pyotr Medev . . .' The pilot pointed to his chest.

'Barney Crispin.'

'One . . .?' He struggled for the simple word in English.

They had no language. They met on the roof of the world, they could not speak to each other. It was a strong face that Barney stared into, made weak only by the lack of the common language.

'I was alone, I was one man.' Barney raised a single finger.

It seemed the answer Pyotr Medev had expected. He looked from Barney's face to Barney's wound, his face was caught in a grimace, something of sympathy.

The pilot stood and then walked quickly back to the helicopter, and all the time the owl face with the Very pistol covered Barney and Mia Fiori. The pilot climbed to his hatch and reached inside.

The pilot, Pyotr Medev, returned carrying a brown cloth field dressing and a roll of bandages. He gave them into the hands of Mia Fiori.

Again he held Barney's hand, a terrible glimpse of anguish on his face. Barney peered back into the torment of the eyes. He thought he understood. Barney's hand was dropped, fell back to the ground. The Major nodded to Mia Fiori as if his control was regained. He went to the discarded Redeye launcher. Again the sad smile. He picked it up.

He carried the Redeye launcher under his arm as he walked back to the gunship.

When the helicopter took off Mia Fiori covered Barney and his wound with her body, saving him from the dirt storm.

A hundred feet above them the helicopter's nose dipped as if in salute and Barney struggled to his feet, stood like a soldier and waved a farewell.

Later, when it was gone, when it was no longer a throbbing speck going west over the plateau, she started to dress Barney's wound.

Later, when the ringing of the helicopter's engines was no longer in their ears, she supported him as they went, snail pace, towards the mountain break to the east, towards a blowing blizzard of snow.

All the pilots of Pyotr Medev's squadron had gathered to watch their Major land at the Jalalabad base. They had distanced themselves from the Frontal Aviation commander and the Political Officer who was at his side, and the MilPol jeep with the idling engine. To give an estimated landing time he had broken his radio silence just the once. All the pilots were there, hushed since the first sighting of the Mi-24, coming high and fast and silhouetted against the mountains that were across the Kabul river. The pilots watched as the helicopter was brought down surely, carefully, without bravado and exhibition. The engines were cut. They saw Rostov at the fuselage hatch, hesitating, unwilling to take the responsibility of being the first to drop his boots onto the concrete apron.

Medev climbed down from the pilot's cockpit hatch. He carried something in his hand, a piece of brown painted equipment, he climbed with the heaviness of a man gripped by exhaustion. He looked around him. He looked into the face of the Frontal Aviation commander.

He walked to the Frontal Aviation commander, handed him the launcher and optical sight of the Redeye missile system. He bobbed his head in respect. He walked past the commander, and the Political Officer, and the pilots of his squadron, walked towards the prefabricated block, which housed his quarters and his bed.

Two days after he was wounded, in a storm flurry of snow, they heard the cry of his name.

A sharp clear desperate voice calling to them.

On the beaten path, shadows in the driven snow, were Gul Bahdur and the mule that Barney had called Maggie.

When the boy found them they were sitting, they were frozen cold and wrapped together for warmth.

23

It was a routine meeting of North Atlantic Treaty Organisation countries at Foreign Minister level, and hosted by the West Germans in one of those Wagnerian castles in Bavaria. Fake history, the Foreign Secretary thought it.

Because the Director of the Central Intelligence Agency was attending, the Foreign Secretary had added to his entourage the name of Brigadier Henry Fotheringay MBE DSO, who would travel with a well-filled briefcase.

They had gathered in mid afternoon and gone immediately into full session, politicians and advisers, all present bar the Italians, fogbound at Ciampino. They had broken for drinks, and then repaired to the theatre for the lights out classroom session of the Director. As the Director droned on, a young man with cropped hair and large spectacles stabbed with a pointer at the projected maps and statistics in rhythm with the speech. The Foreign Secretary wondered whether they had rehearsed the act on the aircraft over.

At the end of the Director's presentation, the representatives of some of the minor NATO powers actually applauded. The Director flushed with pleasure.

The Foreign Secretary recalled the bitter exchange at the American Embassy in London, months ago, but remembered as if it had been the previous day. He recalled also the visit of the Brigadier to his office in Whitehall six days before, where their earlier acrimony had been glossed over, where the Brigadier had made the introductions. He hadn't had long, he was to leave in a few minutes for Questions in the House, but he would not quickly forget those that he had met that afternoon. A young man who carried his right arm in a sling and whose face was gaunt and thinned-out and white where a beard had recently been shaved, and who quietly told a story of the combat between a missile-launcher and a helicopter squadron, and of the warfare for a valley, and of a Soviet flier who he said was too proud for the barbarity of revenge. The young woman who held the hand of the young man, and who had said shyly that she was pleased to meet him, and nothing else. The older man, Major Rossiter, who was going to get a Colonel's pension, by heavens, and whose contribution had been to drink three whiskies in twelve minutes, and who had the glint in his eye of someone who has recently discovered religion or sin or something. He remembered the notes and photographs of the Hind attack-helicopter that the Brigadier had brought with him, and that he had pored over before his rushed, running late, drive to the Commons.

They met after dinner. The Director came at the invitation of the Foreign Secretary to an ante-room off the main salon, with a coffee in his hand.

The Brigadier stood, the Foreign Secretary stayed seated, as the Director pulled a chair close to them.

'What can I do for you, gentlemen?'

'When we met in the spring . . .' the Foreign Secretary said. The Director raised his eyebrows momentarily. '. . . You gave me to understand that certain actions inside Afghanistan by British nationals had caused you to abort a mission to recover the working parts, the classified working parts, of a Soviet Hind class helicopter.'

'I most certainly did.'

The Foreign Secretary said affably, 'We took it to heart that we'd got in your way.'

'Oh, yes, Foreign Secretary? What about the man with a Redeye missile? I hear he was killed. That's what my people in Peshawar say.'

'I suppose we don't have your expertise, Director. It's hard for us to learn not to meddle. It's probably a lesson we need to learn.'

'I'll tell you frankly, Minister, we don't sit around. That Hind in Afghanistan was back in the spring, we're fall now ... I'll tell you something else. Don't get me wrong, what I'm telling you is in the knowledge that there's nothing you can do at this stage to stop us...' The smile of the Director glowed in the Foreign Secretary's eye. '...You were after some bits and pieces, we're going to have the whole thing, all of Hind. We've bought a Syrian pilot, Tel Aviv as the middleman. We're going to have a Hind D flown out of the Bekaa valley into our marine base at Beirut...You'll get all you need, when we've evaluated, you'll be first on the list. I'm glad you've learned that lesson.'

The Brigadier said, 'I've told the Foreign Secretary, Director, you win a few and you lose a lot.'

'That's right...if you'll excuse me, gentlemen, I've a meeting.'

The Director stood. He was smiling now, coolly, pleasantly.

'You're a busy man,' the Foreign Secretary said. 'But if you've the time, this might make some reading to drop you off to sleep.'

The Foreign Secretary reached out his hand. From the Brigadier's briefcase came an OHMS stamped buff envelope, bulky, bulging.

They were both laughing, the Foreign Secretary and the Brigadier, as the Director walked snappily away, the envelope under his arm.

There was a handshake.

'There's a bar down in the dungeons. That's where I'll be if you want me,' the Brigadier said.

The Foreign Secretary went to his bed. Before he slept,

he thought of the Director, scavenging the contents of the envelope, the photographs, the diagrams, the transcripts. But when he closed his eyes, he thought he saw the ruins of a far away mountain village, and the pale, hurting eyes of the young soldier . . . which haunted him into a troubled sleep.